A MATTER OF TRUST

WINNIE GRIGGS

WILD HEARt
BOOKS

To my wonderful writer friends who helped me with their time, encouragement and critiques when I was first getting my start in this business. Some of them are still around—Connie Cox, Catherine Mann and Joanne Rock. And some have passed on into the next life—K. Sue Morgan and Jean Walton.

CHAPTER 1

"The preacher's cat is an elegant cat."

"The preacher's cat is a frightened cat."

"The preacher's cat is a gregarious cat."

"Gregarious." Toby drew the word out as he stretched the band on his slingshot. "What does that mean, Ma?"

Lucy Ames smiled down at the boy walking beside her. *The Preacher's Cat* was a favorite game of Toby's. He collected new words like other six year olds collected rocks and bugs.

"It means to be sociable, to want to be part of a group of other folk rather than off by yourself all the time." Lucy pointed to the floppy-eared dog capering along beside them. "For example, Jasper here is very gregarious, but Mustard, for all his skills as a mouser, isn't."

"Oh."

Lucy watched him mentally file away her definition. Her sweet,

1

curious, intelligent little boy, so precious to her. Now that her mother was gone, he was all she had in her life that truly mattered.

Her smile faltered at that reminder, and she pressed a hand lightly against her bodice, comforted by the feel of her mother's locket, cool against her skin. Then she hitched her shoulder, shifting the weight of the basket she carried. It was a beautiful day, tranquil here in the dappled shade of the woods, and they had an afternoon of picnicking and berry picking ahead of them. Time to concentrate on her blessings, not her losses.

She stepped over a knobby root and paused while Toby and Jasper studied a large beetle lumbering up the side of a hickory tree. There was no need to hurry, no sense of urgency. After all, the walk was as much a part of the outing as the destination. They'd been strolling along this leaf-carpeted trail through the woods for about thirty minutes, and the creek crossing was just past the bit of heavy brush up ahead. Some of the choicest blackberries in the county grew there.

Once they'd picked enough for Lucy to make a cobbler or two, Toby's favorite treat, they'd eat the picnic lunch she'd packed. Afterwards, they could wiggle their toes in the creek, or look for cloud pictures, or—

A noisy commotion from somewhere up ahead caught her attention. At the same time, Toby reached for her hand. "Ma," he whispered. "What's that?"

"I'm not sure." Lucy gave his hand a comforting squeeze as she tried to interpret the sounds. Was that a horse's high-pitched whinny? The confusing sounds seemed to come from the clearing at the creek crossing, just beyond that bit of brush.

Putting a finger to her lips, Lucy reached into her skirt pocket, drawing courage from the feel of the pistol and two bullets hidden there. Ever since a rabid dog attacked the Conners boy in these woods a year ago, she'd made sure she could defend herself and Toby when they went out, even if they were only going berry picking.

She motioned for Toby to take hold of Jasper and stay put.

After silently praying and loading the gun, she eased over to where she could see past the brush to what was causing all the fuss.

Merciful heavens! Roy and Vern Jefferson were beating the tar out of a man she'd never seen before.

She cringed at the viciousness of the no-holds-barred fight. Even though he was outnumbered, the fast moving stranger fought back with amazing agility. Then Vern picked up a fist-sized rock and hit the stranger on the head.

Lucy swallowed her cry of protest and scooted back to Toby.

This wasn't her fight. She had no idea what it was about. For all she knew, the stranger could be as rotten as the Jeffersons. And there was Toby to consider. If she got involved and it turned against her, she'd be putting him in danger, too. The smart thing would be to keep hidden until the Jeffersons left, and then do what she could to help their victim.

But heaven help that stranger. Those brutes enjoyed hurting others. They weren't likely to let up until he lay unconscious. Or worse.

She couldn't just sit here and do nothing. Surely, with her gun and a bit of bluster, she could run them off. They might be meaner than a sack of rattlers, but they were cowards who'd run at the first hint they'd lost the upper hand.

Dear Father, please give me the courage to do what is needed here.

"Keep a tight hold on Jasper and stay here," she whispered to Toby. "Stay very quiet, and don't dare show yourself until I tell you it's clear. No matter what. Do you understand?"

Looking at her with wide, frightened eyes, he nodded.

"Don't worry." She tousled his hair again. "I'll be all right."

As Lucy moved away, her smile vanished. Inching forward, she took another peek into the clearing. The stranger lay on the ground, belly down and unmoving. Roy and Vern stood nearby, rifling through his saddlebags.

Now *that* changed matters considerably. Lucy slipped further back into the cover of the brush. She might intervene to save a life, but not property. No, she'd wait until they took whatever they wanted and left. Thank goodness she wouldn't have to—

Lucy stiffened as the stranger stirred and pushed himself up. She watched, open-mouthed, as he launched into Roy.

Some of Lucy's sympathy evaporated as she silently fumed at his recklessness. Why couldn't the fool just play possum until they rode off? Surely nothing in that saddlebag was worth dying for.

The injured stranger's bravado proved no match for the bullies. Vern grabbed him from behind, pinning his arms. Roy, with a vengeful smile, punched the stranger in the gut. Then he pulled his fist back for another blow.

She didn't dare wait longer. Offering up a silent prayer, and ignoring the nervous churning in her stomach, Lucy stepped into the open, pistol leveled.

"Roy! Vern! That's enough. Let him go."

The heads of both brothers snapped around to face her.

After the first tense seconds, Roy relaxed and his smile stitched shivers up her spine. "My, my, Lucy girl, you gave us quite a start. Now, you just put that gun down and run along. This fancy-pants stranger here is gonna help stake us for a little trip down to San Francisco. Ain't ya?"

Roy punctuated his words with a savage kick to his victim's leg before turning back to Lucy with a leer. "Course, if you want to wait around, we'd be glad to take you along."

Despite her revulsion, Lucy kept her tone firm, relieved to see her hands hold steady. "I'm dead serious, Roy. You two just ride on out of here. I won't let you keep beating this man. Daddy taught me to use this thing, and you know how good he was."

Roy sneered. "Yeah, but you ain't your daddy. I don't think you have the stomach fer it." He took a swaggering step forward.

Lucy shot one of her precious bullets, nicking the toe of his boot. She quickly steadied her aim, ready to fire again.

Speaking quickly, so Toby would know she was all right, Lucy narrowed her eyes. "I don't have to kill you, Roy. The next one's aimed right at your kneecap. That'll drop you in your tracks and won't cost me a minute's sleep. Now, let him go and move on."

Dear Lord, please don't let him call my hand.

Roy's hands fisted with white-knuckled intensity as he eyed her venomously. Lucy knew if he had the means, he'd kill her without a bit of hesitation, and likely enjoy doing it.

Finally, he motioned to his brother. "Let him go."

As Vern complied, the stranger fell to all fours.

Though her attention focused on Roy, from the corner of her eye Lucy saw the stranger lurch to his feet again. Didn't this misguided fool know when to stay down?

Impossibly, he plowed headfirst into Vern. Only as he dropped it did she see the gun Vern held. She swallowed hard, realizing that the stranger had likely saved them both.

Still staggering, the injured man made a clumsy dive and came up holding the weapon. Backing to a nearby tree, he lifted the gun with both hands. "You heard the lady—get going. Now, before I decide she's too generous. And leave my things."

Lucy cast a quick glance around, surprised by the sound of the stranger's voice. Its clipped tones lacked the familiar drawl of the locals. He obviously wasn't from these parts.

What could have brought him to such an out of the way spot?

~

*R*eed Wilder knew he couldn't stay on his feet much longer. But he sure wasn't about to leave a woman to handle these two wharf rats alone, not as long as he drew a conscious breath.

The larger of the bullies yanked the stolen wallet and pocket watch from his shirt, throwing them down in disgust. The thug then reached for his own pistol lying nearby. Glad for an excuse to get some of his own back, Reed fired. He watched with vicious satisfaction as a burst of dust and rock stung the beefy hand.

With an oath, the frustrated thief backed away and mounted his horse empty-handed. He turned his glare, not on Reed, but on the woman. "I'll not be forgetting this," he growled.

She lifted her chin. "Oh, I think it best that you *don't* forget," she shot back. "You said you were headed for San Francisco, and I think that's a real good idea. 'Cause I'll be helping this man press charges against you. Sheriff Morton will finally have the excuse he's been after to lock you up if you ever show your faces in Far Enough again."

With another oath, the hull-scum of a highwayman turned his horse and rode off, his partner right behind him.

Free at last to give in to his injured body's demands, Reed slid to the ground. His back, already lacerated from hurtful contact with the rocky ground and berry brambles during the fight, suffered further agony against the rough tree bark.

He'd put his whole mission in jeopardy with his carelessness. All those years behind a desk had dulled his reflexes. He couldn't even stand under his own power right now.

Good thing his father couldn't see him. It would just confirm his already strong suspicions that Reed lacked the command, the call to adventure, that was the Wilder family's hallmark.

"It's all right, they're gone." The soothing words came from his rescuer, now kneeling by his side. He tightened his hold on the gun as she tried to pry it from him.

"Might come back," he explained. Blast, even talking hurt. But he had to be ready, had to protect her from another possible assault. His lack of vigilance had already cost too much.

The woman, however, didn't seem to understand the danger. "Not those two cowards," came her foolishly confident reply. "If it'll put your mind at ease, though, we'll set a watch." She glanced over her shoulder. "Toby!"

A small boy, accompanied by a yipping dog, shot out of the brush and wrapped his arms around her hips as she stood. She spoke reassuringly to the child, then pointed in the direction the thieves had taken. It was hard to hear, to think straight, with the buzzing in his ears.

Reed groaned when the boy drew himself up and brandished a slingshot as if it were a fearsome weapon. Hang it all, he'd been saved by a pair of artless innocents.

Ignoring the boy for now, Reed concentrated on the woman.

He blinked.

His eyes must be playing tricks on him. Surely this slip of a girl wasn't the gritty warrior-woman who'd faced down those two bottom feeders? Why, his rescuer looked more of a sprite than an Amazon.

Frowning, Reed studied her again, trying to reconcile her appearance with her earlier actions. Willowy slim and not an inch over five foot two, she had a nice heart-shaped face, crowned by a mass of light brown hair pulled back into a demure bun. Her face was graced with a pert, tip-tilted nose and lips that were full and perhaps a bit too large.

When she turned to Reed, he felt as if the breath had been knocked out of him again. Those eyes! Large and luminous, they were a tawny color, dusted with flecks of gold. Filled with an I'm-here-to-help-you reassurance, they focused fully on his face, and he could lose himself in their depths.

He'd traveled halfway across the country, from Delaware to Texas, on this quest. He was out to confront a conscienceless tramp and force her to return the Wilder family heirloom she'd stolen. More important, he intended to claim her illegitimate son as a newly-discovered Wilder heir.

But *this* woman, this sweet Samaritan, with her contradictions of diminutive size and a lion's heart, of innocent expression and seductive eyes, could almost distract him from his meticulously planned undertaking.

Almost.

His rescuer dropped to her knees again and put a comforting hand on his arm. "Now," she said, her voice a mix of command and concern, "put the gun down and let me see how badly you're hurt."

At least the buzzing had diminished enough for him to under-

7

stand her. Reed released the gun, but not because she asked him to. The effort to hold it had just become too much.

He tried to reassure her. "Thanks, but I'm better now." He grimaced at the sound of his voice, slurred like a drunken sailor's. What sort of impression was he making on her? "I'll rest a minute, then I think I can get back on my horse and make it to town."

"Don't be ridiculous!" She gave him a stern, schoolmarm look. "Your lip's cut, you've one eye swollen shut, and that gash near your temple's bleeding buckets. I saw you get hit with that rock. Why, I'd be surprised if you can even stand."

"I said I'll manage." To prove his point, Reed tried to push himself up, but his head started spinning, and he fell back.

No! He could *not* afford to lose his wits now. There was too much to do. He had to find the boy—his brother's illegitimate son. And he had to confront the unsavory woman behind all this, that sordid schemer named Lucy Ames.

Daylight dimmed and then the blackness engulfed him.

CHAPTER 2

*A*larmed, it took Lucy a second to determine the stranger was still alive. "Toby, fetch the things we left behind in the woods, please." Then, spying the dog's excited attempts to lick the man's face, she nudged him away. "And take Jasper with you."

She shifted closer to the unconscious man. "Now, let's have a look." Taking his face in her hands, she grimaced sympathetically. Every visible inch of his long, lean frame appeared bruised or bloodied. His clothes, damp and muddy, were plastered to him.

She smiled approval as Toby hurried up with the trappings of their abandoned outing, and then sent him to scoop some water into the berry pail.

Lucy pillowed the picnic quilt under the stranger's head, wondering what sort of man she was ministering to. He'd faced his attackers with an almost reckless willingness to push the limits of his endurance. Then again, his grit *had* saved her from that blunder with Vern, probably saved her life. Foolhardy, stubborn, *and* heroic. Not an altogether bad combination.

Ignoring the dirt, she moved his fair brown hair aside and probed behind his left ear. Yep, just as expected, an egg-sized lump.

"No sir, Mister," she said to her unconscious patient, "I don't think you'll make it into town today."

But he couldn't stay out here. His injuries required tending, possibly even some stitching. And the wet, dirty clothes had to come off, the sooner the better.

Besides, she wasn't as sure about the Jeffersons not returning as she'd led him to believe.

"Is he gonna die, like Grandma Bea did?"

Lucy took the pail from Toby. "Of course not," she said with as much assurance as she could muster. Her mother's passing last month had been Toby's first experience with mortality. From his expression, she could tell he was remembering, worrying.

She needed to find something else to occupy his mind. A quick look around provided a solution. Roy and Vern had tossed the stranger's things haphazardly as they rifled through his belongings. She hoped the papers he carried weren't important, because those that hadn't landed in the creek lay on the muddy bank. "Toby, why don't you gather up this man's things and put them back in his saddlebags."

Toby stuck the slingshot in his back pocket and set to work. Satisfied, Lucy turned back to her patient.

"Time to wake up," she coaxed, sprinkling water on his face.

He stirred and opened his eyes. They were nice eyes, a soft gray-blue color.

"Mister, I need to get you to my house. It's about two miles straight through those trees. Do you think, if I help, you can mount up on that horse of yours?"

His pain-fogged eyes slowly registered the fact that he'd passed out. Grim-faced, he nodded as he struggled to sit up. "I think I can manage that much." He immediately started shivering.

Lucy knew the wet clothes were part of the problem, but he was likely suffering from reaction to his injuries as well. Quickly she took the quilt and placed it on his shoulders. He drew it closer with not quite steady hands.

"Ready?" she asked, bracing herself. "Take it slow and easy now. Lean on me, and I'll try to help you stand."

Slowly, they rose. With both admiration and exasperation, Lucy realized he'd braced his back against the tree, trying to spare her some of his weight.

Yep, definitely bullheaded, though in a noble sort of way.

Finally they were upright. He was taller than she'd realized, more than a head taller than her. But then again, *most* men were taller than her. And he was heavier than he looked, too. That lean build of his must be mostly muscle.

Glancing down as she gave him time to recover, Lucy drew in a sharp breath. "Toby! Toby, get over here."

The stranger tensed and looked around warily. "What is it? Have they come back?" His grip tightened on her shoulder as he tried to place his body in front of hers.

"No, no, hold still will you." Lucy attempted to steady the stranger with her shoulder, while she pointed down with fingers that trembled a bit. "There, Toby, a daddy long legs, crawling on my boot. Get it off! Please, get it off!"

Toby dispatched the spider, and Lucy's panic subsided.

Unable to meet the stranger's gaze, she watched from the corner of her eye as he stared at her in disbelief.

He gave a sudden bark of laughter, a gasping, gurgling sound. "Sorry." His boyish, repentant grin invited her to smile back. "It's just, the thought of you getting hysterical over a spider, after standing up to those brutes, was too much. Forgive me."

Lucy grinned, feeling sheepish. "I guess it *is* a bit funny at that." She shivered melodramatically. "But I can't stand spiders. They make my insides feel all jangly and unraveled."

She staggered as he sagged against her. It took all she had to keep him upright. He recovered in a few seconds, but it was enough of a reminder to focus on the business at hand.

Once she'd steadied him, Lucy turned to Toby. "See if you can lead the horse over here, please."

The stranger, grim faced, gave her shoulder a light squeeze.

"No, wait." Before she could question him, he whistled, a surprisingly piercing sound given his condition.

Across the clearing, the horse raised its head. Then, docile as a pet dog, the animal approached. As soon as the horse was close enough, the injured man pushed away from the tree and grabbed hold of the saddle.

Have mercy! The back of his shirt was shredded and bloody. Why had he put himself through that additional agony against the tree?

"Wait," she cautioned, putting a hand on his shoulder, careful to avoid his injuries. "Let me help you."

He didn't turn around. "And how do you propose you do that—lift me bodily into the saddle?"

She recoiled from the raw anger in his voice. Then, realizing it was self-directed, felt a twinge of sympathy. It mustn't be easy for a never-give-up fighter such as him to feel so helpless.

Visibly gathering his strength, he placed a foot in the stirrup and pulled himself into the saddle. The effort left him white and thin-lipped, but somehow he kept his seat.

Eyeing him closely, Lucy thought he seemed in danger of tumbling off at any moment. "Do you think you can stay up there on your own?"

"I'll manage." The curt words and stony expression were those of a man determined to push himself.

Lucy certainly hoped he was right. Taking a deep breath, she placed a hand firmly on his leg. Maybe, if she supplied a little extra support, he could keep his seat as far as her house. "Toby, you lead the horse, and I'll walk alongside."

They hadn't taken more than a couple of steps before he slumped lower in the saddle, seeming on the verge of losing consciousness. This would never work.

Time for a change in strategy. "Mister, make room, I'm coming up there with you."

The man frowned. "That's not necessary, I—"

"No arguing. You're never going to stay up there without a little help. Now make room, 'cause one way or the other, I'm coming up."

Clenching his jaw, and exerting what seemed like a great deal of effort, he slid back behind the saddle.

Instructing Toby to keep the horse still, Lucy placed her foot in the stirrup, grabbed hold of the saddle, and heaved herself up.

And came right back down.

Mounting wasn't going to be easy. Eyeing the saddle as if it had issued her a dare she couldn't ignore, Lucy grabbed and tried again.

After three woefully inadequate attempts, she finally decided she needed a bit of a boost.

She scanned the area and finally spied what she needed. "Mister, hold on, we're going to make a short trip."

Then she turned to Toby and waved toward her goal. "Will you lead the horse over to that boulder please?"

With a nod, the boy did as she asked.

Heaving herself up onto the horse from the boulder proved much easier and this time she made it on her first try. Her feeling of triumph faded almost immediately, though, as she realized what the next step would be.

Taking a deep breath, she looked over her shoulder. "Now put your arms around me," she said as matter-of-factly as she could.

He complied, but gingerly, maintaining a small distance. Definitely a gentleman.

She placed one hand protectively over the man's hands where they met around her and, grabbing the saddle horn with her other, she nodded to Toby. "Lead us home."

The boy rubbed the horse's nose again for a few minutes, whispering as he did so, then he took the reins. When he moved away, the horse followed placidly, at a pace slow enough to not overrun his short legs.

Then she glanced back over her shoulder. "Don't be afraid to use me for support. I'll never get you back up here if you fall."

"I'll keep that in mind." His tone was dry, as if she'd said something utterly ridiculous.

They rode along in silence for a while, the only sound being his labored breathing and the soft plop of the horse's hooves against the ground. Twice he slumped against her and immediately jerked himself up again.

"Listen to me."

Lucy started at the terse words. She'd thought the stranger beyond conversation. "I'm listening."

"If those two come back before we reach your house, take the boy and find cover. Don't worry about me."

"Don't be ridic—"

"Will you just do as I say?" He growled the words, and Lucy heard the effort it cost him to speak. "I'm in no shape to protect you, and they'll be ready this time. Now, I haven't the strength to argue. Give me your word, or so help me I'll drop off this horse right here, and you can go on without me."

A stubborn hero indeed. "All right, I promise. But there's no need to get so worked up. I'm sure the Jefferson brothers are miles away by now."

He responded with a doubting grunt, then lapsed into silence. A moment later he slumped against her once more—this time didn't pull away.

Alarmed that he might have passed out, Lucy tried to twist her head around to see him. "Mister, are you okay?"

"Just need to rest a minute." The words were mumbled, barely intelligible.

She patted his hands as she faced forward again. "Take whatever time you need."

Then there was nothing left to do except try to keep the two of them in the saddle, and wonder about this man with his arms around her. He shifted again and leaned more heavily against her. It was all Lucy could do to keep herself upright. How disquieting this was, with his arms wrapped around her and his head slumped against hers.

She could still remember how he was back there at the creek—the determination in his voice, the concern for her and Toby in his actions, the air of command that surrounded him.

The man seemed so determined, so disciplined, so honorable. Just like a storybook hero.

Lucy felt her face warm. Goodness, what was she thinking? Now wasn't the time for her to turn fanciful, mooning over some stranger like a schoolgirl, regardless of how intriguing he seemed.

This stranger's well-being depended on her, and she'd best get her mind back on the business at hand.

&

*R*eed roused from his near-stupor to discover they'd stopped.

"Mister," he heard his female rescuer say, "do you think you can sit on your own for a few minutes? We've made it to my house, and I'm going to have to get down first so I can help you."

He leaned back, releasing her and removing his weight from her back.

"Just a few more minutes and we'll have you in the house where you can rest a bit." She turned to smile at him as if he were a child needing reassurance.

Reed felt strangely bereft when she slipped out of the saddle. He'd felt every step Ranger took on that interminable ride. The pain in his chest and the pounding in his head had protested each jolting movement.

But the comforting feel of having his arms around her, the soft warmth of her back at his chest, had kept him from giving in to the waves of nausea and unconsciousness threatening to drown him. Her encouragement and praise, spoken so sweetly over her shoulder, had given him incentive to dig deeper into his resources. He didn't want to let her down.

A gentle pressure on his legs drew his attention back to her, and he tried to focus on her words.

"Your turn now. Just take it slow and easy, whenever you're ready. I'll help as much as I can."

Reed dragged his leg over the saddle and tried to ease himself off the horse. His traitorous control failed him, though, and he hit the ground hard, his left leg buckling in agony. The jolt doubled him over, and only the woman's quick action spared him the indignity of collapsing on the ground at her feet.

She allowed him time to recover, patiently standing with her hands at his waist, his arms on her shoulders. They stood facing each other, with him bent over and panting in her face. Reed's frustration at his own helplessness rose.

She shifted slightly, flashing him an encouraging smile before looking over her shoulder. "Toby, fetch Grandma Bea's walking stick please."

When the boy returned, Reed took the cane in his left hand and eased some of his weight from his uncomplaining rescuer. She insisted, though, that he keep one arm around her shoulder and he didn't argue. Truth be told, he needed that added support if he ever hoped to make it inside.

Sliding an arm around his waist, she took a deep breath. "Ready?"

"Let's go," he said in clipped tones. He must sound surly, but thunderation, he didn't like this helplessness! He was supposed to be the one who took care of everyone else, not the other way around. Besides, if he didn't get inside soon, he'd pass out right here in her front yard.

With a nod, she inched around so they both faced the clapboard farmhouse. It was only then that Reed noticed the almost total isolation of the home she'd brought him to. There was no sign of a town, or even another neighbor, anywhere close by.

Tightening his jaw, he cleared his thoughts of everything but the stretch of ground between himself and the front door. He willed his legs to move, determined to make it inside without collapsing. His angel of mercy let him set the pace, merely guiding and supporting his progress across the uneven ground.

His grip on the cane turned white-knuckled with the effort to climb the porch steps, but at last they were behind him.

Then, focusing all his efforts on putting one foot in front of the other, he noted only sounds—the groan of door hinges, the creak of floorboards, his own labored breathing.

They finally entered a small bed chamber, and she helped him ease down onto the mattress. He flopped down, unable to stifle a groan as his lacerated back took his weight. Blast, he couldn't even sit upright without her support.

While he struggled to get his breathing back under control, the boy delivered water and cloths, and the woman promptly sent him off again to fetch her medicine box. She wet one of the rags, squeezing most of the water out and turned back to him. "I'll go as easy as I can."

"I can wash my own face." Reed struggled to sit up. "You've already done enough."

"Undoubtedly." She reached over to help him. "But you can't see your injuries as well as I can."

Reed nodded with gritted teeth, knowing she was right. His pride would just have to bear with the blows. Once up, he leaned a shoulder against the headboard, determined to retain what dignity he could.

The boy returned, carrying what must be her medicine box.

"Why don't you take our guest's horse into the barn and give him some oats and water," she told the boy. "I'll see about unsaddling him after I get through here."

Reed clenched his jaw. This was all his own fault. If he hadn't let his guard down, hadn't allowed those cowardly thugs to ambush him and then beat him to a bloody pulp, he wouldn't be sitting here, helpless as a newborn.

He blinked as she took his face in her hands. Though her hands were callused, her touch felt feather light. She smelled nice—the fresh clean scent of sunshine and flowers. And her arresting eyes, even when narrowed in concentration, looked like burnished brass.

Then he frowned and gave his head a mental shake. Where had

those thoughts come from? He normally wasn't much for poeticisms.

Reed closed his eyes, and surrendered himself to her ministrations, strangely at peace for the moment. It had been such a very long time since anyone fussed over him this way. He found himself sorry when she paused.

But she wasn't finished. She moved her ministrations from the area below his eye on to the cut on his lip and then the gash on his forehead, gently washing away the dirt and caked blood.

"I declare, mister, you're going to look as pieced together and colorful as a brand new quilt for a while." Her voice was as warm as the rag was cool.

Opening his eyes, he watched her rinse and wring out the rag. She really was an extraordinary woman, a fighter and a healer. Like a diminutive Athena, the mythological symbol of both warfare and womanly wisdom.

He owed her a great deal. Perhaps, once he'd dealt with the thief and trollop he'd come to Texas to confront, he'd come back and find a way to repay this homespun Good Samaritan.

Remembering the boy, he frowned. Was there a husband? Fool question—of course there'd be a man in her life.

But where *was* the man?

Could she be widowed? Not that he'd wish for such a thing. But he hadn't seen much to indicate a man's presence in this place.

He'd find a tactful way to ask her later. Right now it was too hard to think clearly.

She took his chin again, interrupting his disjointed thoughts. "I think I've cleaned the cuts well enough, and the bleeding's stopped. I'll need to apply some dressing to that gash on your forehead, though."

Her brow furrowed as she brushed a lock of hair from his temple. Reed wanted to lean into her touch and his fingers itched to smooth the worry lines from her face.

"That lump behind your ear is a bit worrisome," she mused. "Too bad Doc Lawton's out of town."

She opened a jar of foul-smelling salve. Slathering it on a bandage, she applied it to the cut on his head.

Reed bit back an exclamation. It stung as if she'd applied pure salt. Seconds later, though, it began to feel soothingly cool and numbing.

Nodding in satisfaction, his would-be nurse wiped her hands on a clean rag. "Now, let's get your shirt off so I can get a look at your chest and back." Her expression and tone were matter-of-fact. But Reed noted her gaze didn't quite meet his and there was hint of red rising in her cheeks.

He reached for the top button on his shirt, trying to match her all-business demeanor, wanting to make things as easy for her as possible. But his hands refused to perform their function properly and his movements were clumsy at best.

She finally brushed his hands aside with a *tsk* and quickly performed the task for him with a laudably impersonal air.

Perhaps he'd been mistaken about her earlier embarrassment.

Once she'd finished, Reed extended his arm so she could ease the shirt off.

As she peeled the shirt away it was all he could do to bite back a groan. Blood and mud had glued the fabric to his back, and he felt each and every cut and gouge reopen with a vengeance.

She drew in a sharp breath. "Mister, this looks awful!"

"I'm sorry to put you through all this, ma'am," he said as steadily as he could manage. "If you'll allow me to rest here a while, I should be able to move on and leave you to get on with your life."

Her expression conveyed just how little credence she put in his claim, but she didn't argue. "I think I'd best tend to this first, then you can rest as long as you like."

She cleaned his back with the same soothing strokes she'd applied to his face, and then applied that blistering salve. Reed clenched his jaw, determined to bear her ministrations without further movement or sound. He wouldn't repay her kindness by causing her further distress.

At last she was done. "How does that feel Mr...." She paused a moment, then continued in a wry tone, "I don't even know your name."

That buzzing sound was back, making it harder to concentrate. Reed struggled to stay upright. "It's Reed Wilder. And it feels just fine, thank you ma'am."

"I know—you'll manage."

Her words and dry tone caught Reed by surprise. As a rule, people took him very seriously. Yet he found her tendency to poke gentle fun at him appealing. In spite of his deepening disorientation, his lips twitched in response. "Exactly."

She rewarded his smile with one that took his breath away. It wasn't a smile of sympathy or impersonal politeness, but one of shared understanding and appreciation.

~

*L*ucy's spirit stirred as if awakening from a deep sleep. It had been such a long time since she'd met someone she could share a bit of playful teasing with.

She placed a hand behind his shoulder. "Well, Mr. Wilder, let me help you get more comfortable." His face had acquired a gray tinge to it, and he seemed less steady now than a moment ago.

As soon as he lay down, she moved to the foot of the bed and sat. "Now, let's get shed of your boots, shall we?"

He protested, of course, but Lucy ignored him. She took his feet on her lap and tugged off his boots and socks.

"There, that should feel better." She dusted off her skirts as she stood. "I suppose I should introduce myself..." She stopped, realizing he'd either passed out or fallen asleep.

She couldn't help but notice that Mr. Wilder was a fine figure of a man. Not a burly farmer, but neither was he spindly. Easy to see how he'd been able to hold his own for a time against the Jeffersons.

She wondered if he was married, and felt a flicker of envy for the woman who would be his wife.

Shocked by her emotional reaction, Lucy averted her eyes and got to the business of settling him in.

She slid his bulk around, removing the soiled bedcover from under him and tossing it on the floor with the quilt and his muddy shirt.

Careful not to jar him more than necessary, she tucked a fresh coverlet around her patient. She couldn't resist the temptation to brush that wavy lock of hair from his forehead once more.

Then, gathering up the laundry items, Lucy left the room.

She met Toby as he staggered in the front door, struggling under the weight of a bulky saddlebag and bedroll.

"I took care of the horse," the boy said. "Unsaddled him and rubbed him down best I could and gave him some of Moses' oats."

Shaking her head, Lucy took part of the burden from him, "You didn't have to do all of that. I told you I'd unsaddle the horse."

"I know, but I wanted to help. It weren't any trouble, honest."

"*Wasn't* any trouble," she corrected, tousling his hair. "Thanks. I declare you're just growing up too fast for me."

Toby grinned and hefted the bedroll to his other shoulder. "His other things are on the porch. Where should I put this?"

Lucy remembered seeing the belongings scattered across the clearing. "In the bedroom with him. I'll take care of all this."

It went against the grain for her to go through someone else's things without permission, but she knew it would be best if she sorted out the wet items and set them aside to dry.

She dropped the soiled linens and clothing on the kitchen floor and then, with a twinge of conscience, emptied the saddlebags on the table.

CHAPTER 3

A pistol slid out first. Well that, along with the one the Jeffersons had left behind, would be put away somewhere out of sight and out of Toby's reach.

She didn't take chances when it came to her boy.

Next she picked up a sheet of paper, apparently the only one Toby had retrieved. It was a mess, smudged with dirt, and damp enough to make the ink run. Oh well, she'd let it dry and the stranger could decide for himself whether to keep it or not.

She shook her head at the state of his clothing and placed it all by the back door, ready to add to her laundry tub in the morning. His ammunition she set aside with the gun. The rest of the items seemed to have been spared major damage, only needing a wipe here and there.

Deciding a good airing wouldn't hurt any of it, including the saddlebag, Lucy set everything out on the back porch.

She and Toby took turns looking in on Mr. Wilder that afternoon and on into the evening. After completing the supper chores, Toby volunteered to sit with their guest. His voice held the eagerness of a youngster hoping to avoid being sent to bed.

Lucy smiled. "Thanks, but it's your bedtime, young man. I can keep an eye on Mr. Wilder while I tend to my sewing."

She gave him a small pat on the backside. "Now scoot and get into your nightshirt. I'll fix you up a bed in the parlor."

"So, any special requests?" she asked later as Toby climbed onto the cot. She always sang him a song as she tucked him in.

He requested *Rock of Ages*, and Lucy pulled the covers up under his chin. Most nights, by the time she finished her song, Toby was droopy-eyed, if not asleep. But not tonight.

Admonishing him to settle down, Lucy went to her own room where she changed into her nightclothes, took down her hair, and pulled on a wrapper. Then she padded back into the kitchen.

It was a long, airy room, stretching the entire length of the house. The far side, facing the back of the house, contained the kitchen proper. The Ames women had also chosen to situate their small dining table here.

The other end, which had formerly been the dining area, had been transformed to a sewing room. A dressform, a sturdy worktable and a couple of comfortable chairs were situated there, along with shelves for fabric, notions, and pattern books.

She and her mother had spent many a companionable hour here —her mother working on mending and quilting, she fashioning the dresses that she exchanged for credit at the mercantile.

Lucy removed the frock hanging on the dressform and picked up her sewing basket. She peeked into the parlor as she passed, relieved to find Toby had finally drifted off to sleep.

Then she headed down the hall toward Toby's bed chamber, which was now serving as the infirmary.

Settling in the rocker by Mr. Wilder's bedside, Lucy spread the dress on her lap and threaded her needle. She just needed to add the buttons and this one would be finished.

Instead of plying her needle, though, she found herself studying her slumbering guest.

His dark, wavy hair hid most of the bandage on his forehead. His face was long and lean, like the rest of him, with a dimple notching his chin. Though his lips were distorted by the cuts and swelling, they had a bold fullness that appealed to her. That pronounced brow lent character to his face without detracting from the overall boyishness of his appearance.

His eyes were closed now, but she remembered the smoky, blue-gray color. It put her in mind of weathered cypress. When he was angry they had a piercing quality to them. Nothing boyish about those eyes.

One of his hands had escaped the covers, and she reached across to tuck it back under. With long, square-tipped fingers and neatly manicured nails, they weren't as rough and callused as a laborer's would be, but they weren't soft either. In fact they felt quite strong and masculine.

He moved suddenly, grimacing in his sleep, and Lucy guiltily tucked his hand back under the sheet. She had no right to take such liberties.

Then she frowned as he rolled over and kicked off his covers. If he kept this up he'd aggravate his injuries, or worse.

Thirty minutes later, Lucy had her hands full. Despite her efforts to soothe him, Mr. Wilder continued to toss fitfully in his sleep. She began to fear he would actually harm himself further.

Wanting to help but unsure what to do, she finally tried what worked when Toby was sick or hurting. She took his hand again and sang to him, drawing on a lullaby her mother had crooned to her years ago.

Her song faltered then resumed as his hand closed around hers in a reflexive gesture. Though he remained unconscious, Lucy felt a sudden sense of connection, of shared purpose.

After only a few moments, the singing seemed to help. Mr. Wilder stilled and some of the lines on his face smoothed. Whenever she paused to rest her voice, however, he grew restless again.

Inching the rocker closer to the bed, Lucy settled herself in for a long night.

~

*R*eed pried his eyes open. He tried to get his bearings, to figure out why his head was pounding like an over-stressed ship's engine, to orient himself in his night-shrouded room. A moment later he realized he wasn't in his own home. But his memories were coming back with all the sharpness of sludge.

He'd been traveling, he remembered that much. Yes—headed for some backwater town in Texas named Far Enough, to confront a thief and find a missing nephew. How far had he gotten?

It all came back to him in a rush. The ambush, his feisty little rescuer, and the in-and-out of consciousness trip to her place. He shifted and then settled back with a groan—apparently he still had some healing to do. A glance toward the window revealed the faintest glimmer of dawn's approach. Almost morning then. But of what day?

The sound of soft breathing drew his gaze to the bedside.

His rescuer slept in a rocker, her head pillowed in her arms on the edge of his bed.

Had she sat with him through the night, watching over him as he slept?

Tenderness washed over him. She looked so sweet and pretty, with her hair down and in disarray around her.

He tried to reach out and touch a stray tendril, to see if it felt as soft and silky as it looked, but his muscles wouldn't cooperate.

Blast! His head still pounded.

Things got better when he closed his eyes.

His thoughts drifted, and snatches of a recent conversation he'd had with his father came back to him.

"You're twenty-eight years old," his father had said. "Don't you think it's time you got your head out of those ledgers and put some thought into starting a family of your own?"

Perhaps his father had been right.

The vision of a heart-shaped face graced with tawny eyes floated through his mind, along with a half-memory of sweetly sung lullabies.

He relaxed. Maybe a few more minutes of rest would help.

~

*L*ucy lifted her head with a start.

Was that the rooster crowing already?

Grimacing as she worked the kinks out of her neck, she stood and looked down at Mr. Wilder. He slept easier now. His color was good and his breathing no longer labored. He would hurt like the dickens when he woke up. Otherwise, he should recover just fine.

She tucked the covers around him more securely and then watched him a moment, wondering again where he was from and where he might be headed.

Well, whatever his destination, she hoped he wasn't in a hurry to get there, because he certainly wouldn't be up to traveling *anywhere* for a few days yet.

Not that she minded the idea of having him around a little longer. She wasn't happy for the circumstances that had brought him to her home, of course, but having him here would give her and Toby a bit of a distraction from their isolated life.

She gathered up her sewing things and headed for the kitchen.

After stoking the stove and setting a kettle of water to boil, Lucy stepped out on the back porch. She leaned against the rail, taking a deep breath of fresh air, and watched the sun rise. This morning everything seemed fresh and new and full of promise.

She'd finished work on the dress last night, which meant she could go to town soon and get the supplies she needed. That also meant she could get sugar for the cobbler Toby'd been hinting about. It would be nice to be able to set a proper table when their guest was able to take meals with them.

But she wouldn't be able to do any of this until she was certain her patient could be left on his own for the time it would take to get to town and back.

Lucy lifted the saddlebag from the rail and headed inside, her steps light. She'd repack it now, before she got dressed. That way she could put it in the room with Mr. Wilder, right where he could see it when he woke.

Placing each item carefully inside the roomy bag, Lucy savored the masculine feel and scent of his things. She picked up his shaving kit, and recalled a till-now-forgotten memory of a time she'd watched her mother shave her father.

I wonder what it would feel like to shave Mr. Wilder?

Smiling at her own whimsy, Lucy put the kit in the bag and reached for the last item, the rumpled sheet of paper. It was dry now, but woefully smeared. She gave it only a passing glance, not wishing to invade Mr. Wilder's privacy.

Then she paused.

Was that her name?

Lucy took a closer look, no longer quite as concerned about the stranger's privacy. Yes, that was definitely the word "Lucy," though she couldn't read the other words around it.

She tried to decipher more, but the few words and phrases still legible were too disconnected to mean anything.

The heavily inked letterhead, though, was still discernible.

The Charles Dobbs Detective Agency, Baker's Cove, Delaware.

Without glancing down, Lucy pulled a chair from the table and plopped down.

Was Mr. Wilder a detective?

So what was he doing here and why was her name in his report?

∾

The next time he woke, Reed felt more alert, better able to cope. A glance toward the window indicated it was near midday. He was alone now and he wondered if his memory of the woman asleep by his bed was only a dream.

He remembered her touch as she'd tended to him, and he

27

smiled. Something in him responded to her sweet ministrations with a pull that still surprised him.

And he didn't even know her real name. For now she would just be his Athena.

"Morning, Mr. Wilder."

Reed looked around to see a boy standing in the doorway, studying him with the unabashed curiosity of a child.

"So it seems. It's Toby, isn't it?" Reed tried to sit up but found it a struggle.

"Yes sir." The boy grinned as he moved closer to assist, obviously pleased that Reed had remembered his name.

"Well, Toby, it seems I owe you a big thank you. If I remember right, you stood guard over me with your slingshot."

"Yes sir." Toby's chest puffed out. "I've been practicing and I'm getting pretty good at hitting a target."

With the boy's help, Reed managed to prop himself up against the headboard. "Thanks again," he said when he regained his breath. It was hard on his pride to realize he couldn't even sit up without help.

"Are you feeling all right, mister?"

"I'll live, though I imagine you've seen squashed bugs that looked healthier."

Toby's grin indicated he agreed with Reed's unflattering assessment. "Don't you worry none. Ma will see that you get well. She's good at making things better." His expression was earnest now. "She sat up with you last night, you know. I heard her singing."

"Did she now?" So perhaps he hadn't dreamed her earlier appearance at his bedside. "And what of your father?"

The boy shrugged. "My father died a long time ago. It's just me and Ma here."

Reed felt a guilty relief that she was unattached. His earlier thoughts of spending time getting to know her took firmer hold. Yes, as soon as he completed his mission, he'd take a few weeks for himself. And he'd spend it showing the lovely Athena how grateful he was for her rescue and hospitality.

Then Toby took a tentative step toward the door. "Excuse me, but Ma said I was to get her as soon as you woke up."

"I thought I heard voices."

Reed turned to discover Athena standing in the doorway.

She gave him a polite smile before turning her gaze to the boy. "I thought I told you to fetch me when he woke up. Now get on to the kitchen and wash up. Lunch'll be ready in a bit."

Despite her words, her tone and expression made it obvious she wasn't angry. He watched them exchange easy smiles as Toby scooted off to do as she asked.

Reed still found it hard to credit that this petite female, who looked about as threatening as a frisky pup, had single-handedly rescued him, transported him here and tended his injuries.

He felt that strange awareness again, but steeled himself against it. He wouldn't repay her kindness by scaring her with unwanted forwardness.

Besides, he had business to see to, and that had to come first. Later there would be time for him to examine where this unexpected attraction might lead. He could wait.

She moved to his bedside. "I hope Toby hasn't talked your ear off. I'm afraid we don't get many visitors out here and he's curious by nature."

Reed smiled. "Answering his questions is a small price to pay for the debt I owe you."

She waved away his gratitude. "I'm afraid we didn't do much more than provide a bed and shelter for the night. Your own constitution did the rest. And you seem to have made a good start toward recovery, considering the way you looked yesterday."

He raised an eyebrow. "Come now, ma'am, you did a great deal more than that. If you hadn't intervened I'd probably be dead now. Not to mention what you went through to get me here."

Reed paused for the merest second, his unaccustomed dependency still rankling. "Toby tells me you sat up with me last night. It seems I'm doubly lucky you're the one who happened along. Not everyone would take a stranger into their home, especially one who looked as disreputable as I must have yesterday. You have my sincere gratitude."

"Well, you're quite welcome." She seemed uncomfortable with his words.

"I understand from your son that the two of you live here alone. I apologize for adding to your burdens this way."

She stiffened, her expression turning guarded.

Reed mentally kicked himself when he realized how threatening that must have sounded. She was a woman, alone except for a small boy, and she knew nothing about him.

Before he could come up with the words to reassure her, she gave him a reserved smile. "Please don't concern yourself with that. We just need to work on getting you back on your feet."

She smoothed his covers as she spoke, her movements efficient and unhurried, her gaze not quite meeting his.

He hated that he'd put that wariness in her expression.

She straightened. "There now. If you'll excuse me, I'll go dish up your lunch." She stepped away from him. "There's a chamber pot under the bed." A faint blush tinted her cheeks but her tone never wavered. "And there's fresh water in the washbasin along with clean cloths if you've a mind to make use of either while I'm gone. I'll send Toby back to help you."

"That's not—"

He halted mid-sentence when she raised a hand.

"I know." Her tone was long-suffering "You can manage without my help. But humor me. I imagine I could get you back in bed if you fell or passed out. However, I don't really relish finding out. Now, I thought you'd be more comfortable with Toby's help than mine, but if not, I'll stay."

Reed snapped his mouth shut. Was she laughing at him?

He gave a curt nod. "Very well, send the boy. Where are my clothes, by the way?"

Her understanding smile mollified him somewhat. "The Jeffersons made a mess of your things. I went ahead and added your clothes to my wash this morning. They'll be ready for you later today."

She paused and then lifted her chin, as if about to deliver unpleasant news. "You'll find the rest of your things in that corner of the room, with a few exceptions. I've put your gun and ammunition away for safekeeping."

Reed nodded, surprised but not concerned. It was quite sensible of her to take such precautions.

"The other thing missing is the sheaf of papers you had. I'm afraid it got tossed about with the rest of your things."

She squared her shoulders and took a deep breath. "Most of it ended up in the creek. Toby did retrieve one page, but it's badly smeared. I hope it wasn't anything important."

Why did she seem so worried? Surely she didn't think he'd blame her? Losing the detective's report was inconvenient, but not a major problem. He'd memorized the pertinent facts, and the detective agency kept a spare copy on file if he should need it later.

At least it hadn't fallen into some local's hands.

He smiled hoping to alleviate her concern. "A pity, but don't worry, it's not irreplaceable."

Some of her stiffness eased and she moved away. "I'll close the door behind me and send Toby in. Send him for me if you need help."

And with that she was gone.

Reed threw off the covers and sat up straighter, then paused as the room spun nauseatingly.

Blast! He couldn't win a fight with a kitten at the moment.

He'd better be more careful or he'd land in a heap on the floor. The last thing he needed was to have to ask his hostess for help if he fell. He was in no mood for an *I told you so*.

He supposed there was nothing for it but to delay his confrontation with the disreputable Miss Ames. No matter how much he wanted to find the boy for his father's sake, he couldn't face her like this, wouldn't give her such an advantage. No, he'd wait until he could stand squarely on his feet again.

When planning this trip, Reed had figured he'd need a week at most to settle matters once he reached Far Enough. So he'd allowed for two. As usual, his ability to plan for contingencies would stand him in good stead.

Even with this delay, he should be able to complete matters in the available time. He'd make it back to Bakers Cove a good three weeks before his sister's wedding and two weeks before the Claymore deal was set to close. An acceptable cushion.

Reed's gaze wandered to the corner Athena had indicated earlier. As promised, there were all of his things, neatly stacked on a wooden chair. Even his boots were there, cleaner than when he'd pulled them on—was it only yesterday? In addition to her other talents, it seemed the lady was a conscientious housekeeper.

And he'd let her get away again without learning her name.

~

*L*ucy rubbed a hand across her tired eyes as she stepped into the kitchen. The smudged document had worried at her ever since she'd read it. Having a detective interested in her, especially one who'd come such a distance, seemed ominous.

Then again, she didn't know for sure she was the Lucy mentioned in his report. It was a common name.

It could have nothing to do with her at all.

She raised her hand to the locket hidden under her bodice.

Oh Mother, I miss having you to talk to. What would you tell me to do? Confront him? Wait and see what happens next?

What was he doing here? Her instincts told her he was honorable, but she wasn't sure she trusted her instincts any more. Because she found herself liking this man without knowing very much about him. And that was a dangerous thing.

Lucy moved to the stove and ladled up a bowl of broth. She would just confront him, admit she'd seen the name Lucy on the paper and ask him outright if it had anything to do with her.

As she poured up a cup of tea, though, she paused. What if the truth, whatever it turned out to be, made it awkward, even impossible, to have him in her home? In his current condition, she couldn't just throw him out.

Perhaps she should wait a day or so, until his condition improved. But could she live with the uncertainty that long?

And could she keep her name from him that long?

Squaring her shoulders and picking up the tray, Lucy decided she'd have to take it one step at a time.

~

*B*y the time his hostess returned to his room with the promised meal, Reed was comfortably settled again.

She set the tray on a bedside table and smiled his way. "If you'll allow me?" She added another pillow behind him, helping him sit up straighter, then ladled some broth and held the spoon to his face expectantly.

Reed frowned. What did she think she was doing? He wasn't so helpless that he couldn't feed himself.

He opened his mouth, ready to set her straight. Then, catching the expression on her face, he paused. She no doubt expected him to protest, and was ready with one of her dry observations on his stubbornness.

Well, he wouldn't give her the satisfaction.

Mulishly, Reed opened his mouth to accept the bite she offered. There, that should set her back.

Instead of chagrin, he saw what looked suspiciously like an amused twinkle in her eye. Drawing on his dignity, Reed picked up the biscuit and took a bite. Then winced. He'd opened his mouth too wide and nearly reopened the cut on his lip.

Seeing her wince in sympathy, he let go of his umbrage and smiled guiltily. "Looks like I'll be taking smaller bites for a while. Too bad, this meal deserves to be eaten with gusto. My compliments to the cook, Miss...."

"Thank you, but seeing as you haven't eaten for at least a day and a half, I'll set that compliment down more to your hunger than my cooking skills."

Reed swallowed the bite before answering. Had she missed his bid for her name? "You're being too modest, but I don't want to argue. From your comments I assume that my run-in happened yesterday, that I've only lost the one day."

She nodded, raising another bite to his lips. "Uh-huh. Did you have an appointment you were trying to keep? Is there someone I should contact?" She spooned up more of the broth. "There's a telegraph office in town if you need me to send word somewhere."

"Thank you, but no. I'll be back on my feet before you know it. No point worrying anyone unnecessarily." He hastily changed the topic. "I take it you know the men who attacked me."

She grimaced as she fed him a bite. "They're Roy and Vern Jefferson, local boys, but not anyone we're proud of. I'm afraid you'd have to look long and hard to find a meaner pair. I suppose they were out to rob you, not that they need much of a reason to get ugly."

Reed still felt guilty for having involved her in his troubles. "I'm sure they're not thinking very kindly of you right now. Have you reported this to the Sheriff?"

"No, but if you're worried about them coming back and making trouble, don't. They'll be long gone by now. They said something about heading for San Francisco."

He frowned. "Still, I don't want you to get in trouble on my account. That's an ugly pair for *anyone* to have to face."

She picked up the cup of tea. "They're also a couple of yellow-bellied cowards."

She didn't seem to be taking this seriously enough. "Cowards make the most dangerous enemies. I'd feel better if I thought you had some sort of protection out here, Miss...."

Again he let his voice trail off in question.

"Now, you might as well quit worrying over what you can't change. Drink this up. It's a special brew my mother swears by for helping a body heal. Then I want to have a look at the injuries to your head and back before you settle down."

She'd missed his request for her name again.

Well, he'd just have to quit being so subtle. He'd ask her straight out, right after he drank her "special" tea.

Determined to prove he wasn't entirely helpless, Reed raised his right hand and closed his fingers over hers on the handle of the cup as it reached his lips. An immediate tingling, a sort of shivery energy, passed from her fingertips to his own.

Reed inhaled the subtle scent of roses that clung to her, felt the rough yet vulnerable touch of her callused hands even as he watched her expression change from pleasant, polite interest to startled awareness. Her quickly inhaled breath drew him even deeper into the moment.

The taste of the tea was lost amid so much sensation. He could not have said if it was bitter or sweet, hot or cold.

Reed fought the urge to toss aside the cup and pull her closer to kiss those lips that parted in sweet surprise.

If she gave him even the smallest bit of encouragement, he'd be lost.

CHAPTER 4

*L*ucy watched the play of emotions across his face and the darkening of his eyes—it both drew her and confused her. Unnerved by the onslaught of sensations she'd never felt before, she glanced into his storm-gray eyes and found herself caught fast, unable to look away.

The teacup trembled—was it due to his lack of control or her own? Lucy had never experienced such intense *awareness* of another person before. She wasn't sure if she felt more relief or disappointment when he finally released her hand.

Lucy forced herself to look away as she set down the cup and moved the tray aside, taking time to pull herself together. What had just happened? How could a man she barely knew affect her this way?

She had to remember that letter, remember that Mr. Wilder could well prove to be an adversary.

Taking a deep breath, Lucy turned back to her patient. "Well, let's have a look at your injuries, shall we?" She hoped the briskness of her tone hid the confusing mix of emotions that tumbled through her.

He nodded, and she felt his gaze boring into her. Desperate to replace the crackling tension in the room with a tamer, more businesslike air, she firmly cupped his chin in her hand. The contact elicited that tingling sensation again, but this time she ignored it. "There doesn't seem to be any infection in these cuts. Let's just check the one under the bandage."

She removed the bandage from his forehead and washed away the residue left by the salve and blood. "It looks better today. How's it feel?"

"Sore."

"I imagine so." His staring was beginning to rattle her. "I think we'll leave the dressing off and see how it does on its own."

Mr. Wilder leaned against the headboard with a nod of acceptance. "You're the doctor."

"I wish I were. Mother was so much better at this."

"Was?"

She turned away, ostensibly to set down the washrag. "Mother died a few weeks ago."

"I'm sorry."

Hearing the hint of empathy in his voice, Lucy turned back and touched the bedcovers near his hand. "Thank you."

Then she returned to her polite briskness. She must keep control of the conversation, to avoid having him ask for her name again. "Now, if you'll lean forward, I'll take a look at your back."

As he complied, Lucy heard him bite back a groan. He must be in a great deal of pain, but the man was not a complainer. There was that touch of hero again.

"What's the verdict?" he asked when she finished her examination.

"Everything's healing cleanly. You're a lucky man." Then she smiled an apology, realizing what she'd said. "All things considered, that is."

His lips twitched. "A somewhat unique perspective, but I find I agree."

Lucy moved across the room and fetched his saddlebag. "I'll set this right here," she said, hanging it over the sturdy headboard.

"That way it'll be in easy reach if you should want any of your things."

Then she reached for the tray, ready to make her escape. "Now, get some rest while I check on Toby."

"Thank you, Ma'am. But I've been meaning to ask—"

"I have a request," Lucy interjected quickly, afraid of what his next words might be. "Would you mind if I left you on your own for a bit. I need to go to town to pick up a few supplies, but I shouldn't be gone more than an hour or so."

She allowed her brow to wrinkle in concern. "I can put it off another few days if you feel I need to stay nearby." Lucy knew instinctively that such solicitousness would annoy him enough to make him forget his question.

Mr. Wilder's expression held a hint of irritation, but he kept his tone polite. "Please, don't put it off on my account. Take as long as you need. I'll be fine."

She nodded. "Good. I have a few things to take care of first, but Toby or I will check in on you before we go." She crossed to the door. "I'll leave this open. Just call out if you need anything." And she slipped away before he could ask his question again.

~

*R*eed shifted, trying to find a more comfortable position as he watched her go. His reaction to her was unsettling. It wasn't the first time a woman had caught his eye, of course. But he'd never felt such a strong, immediate attraction before.

When she'd looked at him over the rim of that cup, her eyes all wide and wary, he'd almost grabbed hold of her, almost gave in to the temptation to pull her close enough to kiss those rose petal lips, just to see if she tasted as sweet as he imagined.

Most likely it was his weakened state that had made him so susceptible to these unaccustomed emotions. But whatever the reason, Athena had definitely gotten under his skin. He was almost willing to forgive the Jeffersons their assault, just because it had brought her to him.

He couldn't really afford such distractions right now though. He had business to settle, a devious kidnapper to track down and confront.

❧

"*L*ook, we're almost there!"

Lucy obediently glanced down the road, and sure enough, the first buildings at the edge of town were visible. Toby did a little skip step, nearly overturning the wagon he pulled behind him. Jasper, picking up on Toby's mood, bounded ahead and then back, his long ears streaming behind him like banners.

Lucy smiled at them, not allowing her concern to show. She went to town rarely, maybe once or twice a month for supplies. Her mother's funeral two weeks ago had been the one and only time Toby accompanied her. Until today. She didn't have a choice any more; she couldn't leave him home alone. Her mother's death had changed her life in so many unexpected ways.

Remembering the funeral, Lucy's hands fisted at her sides. They'd come, all those "friends" who'd never bothered to visit her mother after they moved to the Jeeter place. Hypocrites! She'd wanted to shout, to rail at them for their ghoulish interest in her and Toby's grief, for the hurt their aloofness inflicted on Beatrice while she lived.

But of course she hadn't.

These same people would no doubt purse their lips and question her motives for taking Mr. Wilder in. The way they'd whispered and pointed after that night with Lowell in the woods. Good intentions and the truth didn't seem to matter, only appearances.

Of course, with Lowell everyone had known how innocent it all was. With Mr. Wilder...

Lucy shivered, remembering the feel of his hand closing over hers. Odd how this stranger could elicit such reactions from her. There was something about him...

Stiffening her posture, Lucy put those thoughts aside. There were other matters to face right now.

Like how this trip to town would affect Toby. She loved him fiercely and would protect him with her own life if necessary. She knew she couldn't shield him from the unpleasant realities of life forever. But he was still much too young to face the rude stares and snubs of their neighbors.

As they approached the town, Lucy took Toby's hand and raised her chin a notch, avoiding a direct snubbing by the simple expedient of not allowing anyone to catch her eye.

She smiled when she spied Jed and Tom Emerson seated outside the mercantile. The brothers, twins, could have been any age from fifty to eighty, and had looked just as they did today for as long as Lucy remembered. They appeared identical, from their sparse gray hair and observant brown eyes, to their spare frames and long limbs. They even wore matching blue shirts and faded overalls. In fact, the only sure way to tell them apart was from their positions. Jed always sat on the left and Tom on the right. They spent most of their time on that bench, a site ideally suited to view the activity on this one main street through town. The brothers were notorious gossips and a better source of news than any newspaper might have been. Tom ferreted out the news, and Jed reported it.

She paused and smiled in greeting. "Good day Mr. Jed, Mr. Tom. Anything happening today?"

Jasper bounded onto the sidewalk and sniffed at the brothers' boots. Absently, Tom reached down and scratched the dog behind the ears, letting his brother do the talking. The Emersons always greeted her with a smile, even during the height of the scandal six years ago. Of course, their avid curiosity about anything and everything accounted for some part of their friendliness. Nevertheless, it was nice to have at least two welcoming faces to greet her on her trips to town.

Jed launched into a report without further prompting. He always led off with the least important tidbits and worked up to the more interesting items. "Doc Lawton got back from Lewisville yesterday, and he's sporting a beauty of a poison ivy rash. Anna Carson had a baby girl last night. She and Joe plan to name her Katy Rose. And Ida Jefferson finally kicked those good-for-nothing boys of hers out. She up and sold her place, too. Moved in with her sister, so there's no place for them boys to come back to, even if they tried."

So, Miss Ida kicked Roy and Vern out. That must be part of what caused them to act so brazen yesterday. Lucy hoped Far Enough had seen the last of them.

After she commented appropriately on Jed's news, Tom went into action. "I see you brought Toby with you today?"

Lucy drew the boy up beside her. "Toby, you remember Mr. Jed and Mr. Tom. You met them at Grandma Bea's funeral."

Toby looked with delight from one identical face to the other. The Emersons, in turn, studied Toby with equal eagerness. Lucy knew his appearance in town would be included in the next snippet of news the brothers passed on.

"How do you do, sirs," Toby said with formal politeness as he stepped forward.

Tom nodded. "Fine, fine. Helping your ma with the shopping today, are you?"

Toby's chest puffed out slightly. "Yes sir. I'm pulling the wagon for her."

Jed flashed him a conspiratorial wink. "Good boy. Maybe it'll earn you a piece of penny candy."

Lucy hid a smile. The Emersons had a well-known fondness for sweets. They lusted for penny candy as passionately as any six year old.

"Do you know if Sheriff Morton's somewhere about this afternoon?" she asked, affecting a casual tone.

Tom shot her a probing look. "He rode out 'bout thirty minutes ago. You not having trouble out at your place, I hope."

"No, nothing like that. I just wanted to speak to him a minute. It can wait until next time I come around." If she even hinted that she had a visitor, it would be all over town in no time flat. She didn't need any additional notoriety attached to her name.

It seemed Mr. Wilder would be in her charge for another day or so. That meant more work and more disruption to her daily routine. So why did she feel more pleasure than annoyance?

Stifling the urge to grin, Lucy took firmer hold of Toby's hand. "Lowell doing much business today?"

"Fair amount. Mrs. Hopkins and Connie Sue are in there now."

The urge to smile fled as her stomach knotted.

Eleanor Hopkins, the mayor's wife, was one of the leading citizens of Far Enough. Before Lucy's fall from grace, her mother and Mrs. Hopkins had been best of friends. The woman had made numerous visits to Beatrice's bedside during the early days after the accident. Her unbending disapproval of Lucy's "sin," however, became increasingly obvious and finally drove a wedge between the two older women. The same distancing eventually occurred with all of her mother's friends. Lucy had never overcome her guilt for triggering this situation.

Connie Sue Morton, on the other hand, was several years younger than Lucy. Her father, Sheriff Morton, was a widower, and Connie Sue took her role as Sheriff's daughter seriously. When the Mortons first moved to Far Enough, the townsfolk were both amused and touched by the gawky thirteen year old's earnest efforts to get involved in community work.

Lucy had very little direct contact with the girl since returning from New Orleans. She suspected that the Sheriff and the community at large made sure to keep Connie Sue isolated from such an undesirable as herself.

At the funeral, Connie Sue had approached Lucy, took her hand, and offered what seemed sincere condolences and sympathy. But Lucy, hurting and angry, hadn't reacted well. She regretted her churlishness now, but wasn't quite sure how to make amends.

Squaring her shoulders, Lucy prepared herself for the reception she knew awaited her inside. She took her leave of the Emersons, then paused as Jasper tried to follow them. "I think it best if we let Jasper stay out here," she told Toby.

Toby looked ready to protest, but Jed came to the rescue. "Don't worry son, we'll keep an eye on your dog."

Lucy flashed them a grateful smile. Then, taking a deep breath, she stepped through the door with Toby close to her side.

All conversation ceased the moment the two of them entered. Mrs. Hopkins glanced pointedly from Toby to Lowell, as if looking for, and finding, similarities. Lucy, keeping firm hold of Toby's hand, walked toward the end of the counter farthest from the ladies. As she passed by the women, Mrs. Hopkins drew herself up as if afraid of physical contact. Connie Sue smiled a tentative greeting. Lucy returned her smile and continued on.

Lowell acknowledged Lucy with a short nod, then went back to serving his other customers.

Lucy glanced at Toby, then relaxed. His eyes scanned the shelves and counters, and he wore an expression of awed delight. Remembering this was his first visit to the mercantile, she looked around and tried to see their surroundings through his eyes.

To their right lay the grocery section, stocked with a wide variety of canned goods, jars of jams and jellies and relishes, bins of flour and sugar, packages of teas and coffee and crackers, rounds of ripe cheese. The dry goods section took up the other side of the store. It contained neatly arranged bolts of fabrics and trims, trays of buttons and needles, skeins of yarn, and even a rack of ready-mades. The hardware section came next, items such as hammers and nails, hoes and bushel baskets, paint and whitewash. Beneath the store's long counter stood glass cases containing everything from penny candy to cigars to jewelry. And behind that, on the back wall, Lucy saw several small pelts displayed alongside brightly painted wooden toys and ladies' gloves.

She watched Toby close his eyes and take a big sniff, and, with a smile, followed suit. In the tantalizing mix that she inhaled, she could identify lamp oil, coffee, molasses, tobacco, and vinegar.

Opening her eyes, Lucy caught Mrs. Hopkins staring at her disdainfully, and her pleasure dissolved. She breathed a sigh of relief as the mayor's wife turned to leave.

A few minutes later Connie Sue completed her purchases also, but rather than leave, she turned in Lucy and Toby's direction.

Lucy watched her give Toby a smile and then take a deep breath before meeting her gaze. "Hello, Lucy. I want to say again how sorry I am about your mother's passing."

"Thank you." Even to herself, Lucy's words sounded stiff, and she tried to soften them with a smile. She was still suspicious of Connie Sue's sudden interest. The girl had a well-known penchant for taking up causes, championing the helpless and needy. Lucy had no desire to be the focus of such attention.

Connie Sue, apparently encouraged by Lucy's smile, pressed on. "We could use someone with your beautiful voice in the church choir, especially now that the Stantons have moved away. I thought maybe you'd consider rejoining us. I would be glad to fetch you and Toby in our buggy next Sunday."

Lucy knew what Connie Sue was trying to do. If she and Toby showed up as guests of the Sheriff's daughter, it would be difficult for the congregation to reject her. Though touched by this consideration, Lucy felt no temptation to accept the offer. True, no one would throw her out. But the icy stares, the whispers, and the unkind cuts would be unbearable. She wouldn't put herself through that again, much less Toby. Besides, she preferred to fight her own battles rather than hide behind someone else's skirts.

Lucy drew her shoulders back. "Thanks for the offer. But when I decide the time is right to return to church, Toby and I will provide our own transportation."

Connie Sue's cheeks reddened. "Yes, well, I hope we'll be seeing you there soon then."

Lucy immediately regretted her rudeness, and smiled an apology. "I'm sorry, Connie Sue, it really was kind of you to offer. I just don't think I'm ready yet. Please, give my best to your father when you see him."

Connie Sue relaxed and smiled. "Of course. Just remember, the offer stands, any time you care to take advantage of it." Then, with a wave to Lowell, she left.

Lowell rounded on Lucy. "For goodness sake, Luce, did you have to be so rude? Connie Sue's a sweet girl and it's not as if you have a lot of friends in this town."

Lucy refused to give ground. "I won't be taken on as someone's charity case." She pushed the brown paper wrapped parcel she'd been carrying across the counter. "Now, I've finished the last order you placed. You can take a look while I do my shopping."

The two of them had formed a working arrangement some years back. Lowell supplied the materials and specifications, and she produced dresses, about two a month, that he sold through the mercantile. In return, he provided her with credit to purchase the staples she needed from his store.

The arrangement included an agreement that no one discover she worked for him. The ladies of Far Enough would never buy the product of a 'fallen' woman. Besides, Lowell's wife Anne was still alive at the time they'd struck their bargain, and she wouldn't have reacted well to the arrangement, however businesslike it might be. Instead, Lowell advertised the dresses as made by a seamstress from one of the premier dress shops in New Orleans. And since Lucy had indeed worked in such an establishment at one time it was a true statement.

Today, however, Lowell didn't even glance at her handiwork. Instead he studied her. "We need to talk about the Jeeter place," he said abruptly.

Lucy tensed, needles of alarm prickling her skin. The Jeeter place belonged to Lowell's father. The settlement made when Beatrice Ames sold her own home to Mr. Crowder six years ago stipulated that she would have lifetime use of it. But her mother was gone now.

Lucy tried not to let Lowell see her worry. "What about it?"

Wearing an I've-finally-got-you look, Lowell leaned back. "Now that your mother's passed on, the place reverts back to my father. I believe it's time you started paying the rent."

Her eyes narrowed. "Your father told me at the funeral that Toby and I were welcome to stay on for as long as we needed to."

He shrugged. "Father's getting on in years and tends to be overly sentimental. He's turned over most of the family's business matters to me now. Of course, you and Toby can stay on just as he said, but only if you're willing to pay the rent."

A flash of anger mixed with panic swirled through Lucy. She couldn't believe he meant to throw her out. Not Lowell. They'd been through too much together.

Why would he put her through this?

CHAPTER 5

" *L* owell Crowder, you know very well it's not a matter of being willing. I have no money, other than what you pay me for these dresses."

Lowell spread his hands, his smile sly. "Of course, if we got married, you wouldn't have to worry about rent payments, or anything of the sort. I could see that you and Toby lived in style and comfort."

Lucy thinned her lips in irritation. She should have anticipated this. Lowell had pressed her to marry him since shortly after Anne died. His motives were laudable, even if misguided. He wanted to make her respectable again. Oh, that's not how he put it, but Lucy knew him too well to be fooled.

She adamantly refused to consider his offer, abhorring the idea of being on the receiving end of such a sacrifice. But he remained steadfast in his support of her, albeit clandestinely. Without the employment he offered, she could never have provided for herself, much less Toby and her mother.

Lucy knew the assumption some in the community made as to how she paid her bills at the mercantile. It couldn't be easy for Lowell to live with that, though the townsfolk seemed more tolerant of a man in these situations. Just one more bit of unfairness surrounding her whole situation.

"There must be some other way we can work this out."

He gripped the counter and leaned toward her with a clenched jaw. "Is marriage to me really so repugnant to you?"

When she remained silent he threw up his hands. "Of all the stubborn, pig-headed—" He took a deep breath. "All right. You want to earn your rent another way, so be it. I think three dresses a month, one a fancy gown, ought to about cover it."

"Three dresses!" Lucy's heart sank. "If I do that much to pay rent, what do I do about the supplies I need?"

A shrug indicated that wasn't his problem. "Anything you can do in addition to those three can still be applied toward credit here at the store. Besides, you've one less mouth to feed now. Maybe one dress a month will cover it."

Lucy felt slapped in the face by this unfeeling reference to her mother's death, and struggled to keep her expression neutral. He was just angry, not really cruel.

As if reading her thoughts, Lowell's expression softened and he rubbed the back of his neck. "Aw Luce, why don't you just go ahead and marry me? There's no point making this so difficult. I'd provide a good life for you and Toby."

She sighed. "I know you would. We've been through all of this before. You don't really love me, and I don't love you. That's not the kind of marriage I want."

He reached across and took one of her hands. "How do you know I don't love you? Besides Luce, I hate to sound unfeeling, but your chances of a better offer are pretty slim."

Lucy flinched and drew her hand back. Lowell pressed harder. "Is it fair to deny Toby this chance for a real family life, just because you're too stubborn to let someone help you?"

She wavered. He'd found her weak spot. Besides, it seemed more and more, the struggle just to survive took everything she had. She wasn't sure she had the energy to continue fighting him. Especially alone.

Her hand reached for her locket. *I do miss you, Momma.*

Then she stiffened her spine. She wasn't ready to give in just yet. "Very well. Three dresses a month it is."

Lowell tried again. "And if it's too much for even you?"

She met his gaze with head high, forcing herself to say the words without flinching. "If, by the end of the month I haven't met your price, we'll talk about a wedding."

It wasn't much of a commitment, but Lowell's self-satisfied smile indicated he thought he'd won a victory of sorts.

Lucy already regretted her words. For some reason, Mr. Wilder's image came to mind and she resolutely pushed it away. "While you look over the two dresses I brought in this morning, I'll collect the items I need to purchase today."

She did a quick mental revision of her shopping list. With a guest in the house, especially one trying to rebuild his strength, she couldn't pass on the staples. The whitewash and nails would have to be left for another time, though. And no question now of getting fabric for a new dress. She'd make over one of her mother's instead. But she *would* get cloth to make Toby a shirt. He grew so fast these days.

She glanced at the copper-headed boy gazing longingly at the jars of candy on the counter. Surely she could spare one of her precious pennies of credit for a peppermint stick. It might be the last time she could splurge on such a treat for a good while to come.

~

*R*eed shifted position for the fifth time in as many minutes. He'd dozed off after Athena left the house, but now he was wide awake and bored. He wished she would return to keep him company. She was an intelligent woman and he enjoyed conversing with her. Not to mention watching her, and listening to her voice, and—

Shaking his head, Reed grinned wryly. He'd been reduced to

adolescent daydreaming. Better find something to occupy his mind before he began composing maudlin love sonnets.

And he knew just the thing. Reed pushed himself up to a semi-reclining position, grimacing when he bumped a tender spot on his back. Then, ignoring the painful protesting of the muscles in his torso, he lifted the saddlebag from the headboard.

He sat there gasping as if he'd just run uphill. Right now it seemed a good thing Athena *wasn't* around. He sure as thunder didn't enjoy having her see him in such an unflattering light.

Gritting his teeth, Reed unfastened the buckle of his bag and rummaged inside. Finally, with a grunt of satisfaction, he withdrew a small leather-bound journal and a pencil. Since the report from the detective agency had been destroyed, he'd make notes from memory to remind himself of the pertinent facts.

He had to hand it to Dobbs, the unassuming detective was very thorough. He'd been hired to track down a slippery bit of baggage who'd stolen a Wilder family heirloom from the widow of Reed's older brother, Jonathan. When the detective discovered the thief of the ruby ring was also mother to an illegitimate son, he'd explored a bit further. And what he'd learned made recovering the family heirloom a secondary concern. Because Dobbs' information linked the boy to Jon. Not definitively, but there was enough evidence to warrant closer scrutiny.

The possibility that this unsavory woman could be raising Jon's son had upped the stakes considerably. Reed could no longer leave it in the hands of a detective, no matter how trustworthy. But he couldn't tell his father of the new developments. It would be unbelievably cruel to raise the old salt's hopes that his favored older son had left an heir behind if those hopes later proved false. So Reed had set out on his own, letting his father believe he was merely after the ring.

Focusing his thoughts, Reed wrote without pause for several minutes. Then he leaned back and reviewed what he'd written.

1. Lucy Ames left Far Enough seven years ago in the midst of a scan-

dal. She'd been found in a compromising position with a married man, one Lowell Crowder.

2. During the six months previous to Jon's death, Lucy Ames had lived in the same boarding house as Jon.

3. Lucy Ames' boarding house fees had been partially paid for by Jon.

4. Lucy Ames had an illegitimate son, born near the time of Jon's death.

5. After Jon's death, Lucy Ames was handed the Wilder heirloom ring from an accident survivor with the intent that she deliver it to Iris, Jon's widow. Iris never received it.

6. Lucy Ames claimed friendship for Iris and promised to keep in touch when she left New Orleans to return to her home in Texas. Iris never heard from her again.

Not a very flattering picture of this woman.

Iris' reaction when she'd learned of the thievery had been one of disbelief. "Lucy was a very dear friend, like a sister to me. After Johnny died, she stood by me, nursing and comforting me when all I wanted was to curl up and die myself. I couldn't have made it without her."

Then Iris had looked at Reed's father, her expression a mixture of confusion and pain. "Poor, dear Lucy. She must have been desperate to do such a thing. No wonder she didn't keep in touch after she returned home as she'd promised."

Reed wondered now what Iris would think if she knew about the boy. Sweet, vulnerable Iris. If news of her friend's betrayal could cause such pain, how would she react if he brought home proof of Jon's infidelity? He hated to see her hurt again.

If the child turned out to be Jon's son, though, he'd bring him back home to Delaware with him, regardless. As Jonathan's heir, the boy should be raised among the Wilders and afforded all the advantages of wealth and education that were due him.

Of course, Miss Ames might prove difficult on this point. She *was* the boy's mother, after all. He'd just have to be firm. If she'd been good to the boy, he'd offer her a generous stipend for her trouble.

Then again, once she learned that the man she'd known as Johnny Carlson, working class riverboat captain, was actually Jonathan Wilder, oldest son of a wealthy businessman, she might turn greedy. Reed clenched his jaw. If the opportunistic Miss Ames attempted blackmail or extortion she would live to regret it. He had no compunction whatsoever with using all the power and influence behind the Wilder name to achieve his goal.

Reed pictured himself carrying the newly discovered heir home. His father would be overjoyed to find Jon had left a son behind, even one born out of wedlock. And Reed would be the one to deliver not only the news but also the boy himself. He'd finally be able to pull off a feat his father would be proud of, and in as dramatic a fashion as any Wilder could desire.

Reed shifted position again, and with a frown reread the notes. Something bothered him, some hole in the list of facts or something that didn't quite fit with the rest, but he couldn't put his finger on just what. Like a pebble in his boot, it was a niggling irritation he couldn't ignore.

Well, worrying over it wouldn't resolve anything. The answer would come to him eventually.

Reed cocked his head to one side. He thought he'd heard voices. There, he definitely heard a door opening. Athena and Toby must be back from their trip to town.

He put his writing materials away, a smile of anticipation on his lips.

~

*I*ris walked down the hall of the Wilder family home and stepped into the upstairs sunroom. The three daughters of the house, Lisa, Bella, and Julia were already gathered there and she paused in the doorway. "Lisa, your dress is gorgeous, and you look absolutely fabulous in it."

Lisa adjusted a ruffle and smiled over her shoulder. "Do you truly think so? Do you think Steve will like it?"

Lisa's older sisters laughed. Bella winked slyly. "Steve will most definitely like it. Why, I'll be surprised if he can concentrate on the ceremony once he gets a look at you in this."

Lisa preened in front of the mirror. The soon-to-be-bride was having the final fitting of her wedding gown, and Julia, Bella, and Iris had gathered to provide an admiring audience.

Iris felt both grateful and lucky to be included. After they'd discovered her just three months ago, the Wilders had accepted her, made her feel like one of them, a sister rather than an outsider. It was still a dream come true to find herself part of such a large, loving family. Why had Johnny run away from them? Even when Reed and Captain Wilder tried to explain it to her, it didn't make sense.

"I'm jealous," Julia sighed. "Reed was horridly stingy when I was planning my wedding. My dress wasn't half as fine as this one."

Lisa hurried to defend Reed's actions. "Oh but you know he was only looking out for all of us. There just wasn't much to go around in those days."

Julia wasn't appeased. "Still, it was my wedding, after all. There were those who would have loaned us the money. If he had an ounce of the romantic in him he would have found a way."

Bella gave an unladylike snort. "Oh Julia, this is Reed we're talking about. I don't believe there's a romantic bone in his body."

"He did what he thought best at the time," Lisa insisted. "And you had a very nice wedding as I remember."

Julia placed a fist on her hip. "Nice! What bride wants nice? It should have been spectacular, a major social event."

"Yes, but—"

"Really, Lisa," Bella interrupted, "you don't need to defend Reed to us all the time. We love him too. It's just that he seems so exasperatingly fusty sometimes, even for a big brother."

"Amen." Julia's hand fluttered and then dropped. "Why, I can't believe he just took off like he did the other day. I declare, I don't know what to make of it. It's so spontaneous, so absolutely unlike Reed."

Bella, checking her appearance in the mirror, tucked a stray lock of hair in place. "Has anyone heard from him since he left?"

"No. But I know where he went."

Three pairs of eyes turned to Lisa in surprise.

"Well don't just stand there looking smug. Tell us," Bella said at last, exasperated by her sister's coyness.

Lisa smiled triumphantly. "He's gone to Texas, of all places. Can you imagine Reed in a frontier setting?"

"Texas!" Julia pulled her sister over to the settee. "How do you know? And how could you have held out on us like this?"

"I went to his office the day before he set out, and heard him telling his secretary where he would be. And I wasn't holding out, I just haven't had an opportunity to tell you before now."

Julia wrinkled her nose. "Whatever in the world would he be going to Texas for? That's so far away."

Bella obviously relished the mystery of the situation. "My guess is that there's a girl involved in this somehow."

"Oh Bella, really." Julia tapped her arm affectionately. "Can you honestly see Reed chasing after a girl?"

"There's a first time for everything," Bella answered airily. Then she turned back to Lisa. "But are you sure it was Texas?"

"Positive. I remember because it was such a strange name, Far Enough, Texas. It got me wondering how a town could get such a name." She grinned. "Picture this, a settler passing through the wilderness, dragging his family with him. Suddenly, his wife calls a halt saying 'This is far enough, you'll not drag me another step.' Isn't it absurd?" Her giggles drew grins from her companions.

Iris's, however, was a bit forced.

A few minutes later, she excused herself and headed to her room. She no longer smiled, and her head ached.

Reed had gone to Far Enough. That could only mean one thing. Captain Wilder must have sent him to track down Lucy Ames to find the ring. She should have known he wouldn't let the matter drop.

Everything would change now. The new peace and happiness she'd found here with the Wilders would be ruined.

Reaching her room, Iris threw herself on the bed. *I should never have come here, should never have let myself succumb to the lure of being part of a loving family.*

Iris pressed a hand to her throbbing head. She had to think, had to decide what to do. She could either face them with the truth, or run. She could no longer just hold her breath and hope for the best.

She'd grown to care so much about the Wilders. Why hadn't she told them about the boy right from the first? How could she explain the situation to them at this late date? The fact that she'd fallen in love only complicated the matter further.

CHAPTER 6

Once Lucy had finally settled Toby down, she returned to the sewing room. After their return from town, while Toby practiced his penmanship, she'd finished the most pressing of the mending tasks, clearing the way for her to concentrate on the sewing projects Lowell had demanded as rent payment.

She pulled out one of the bolts of fabric and then paused. Her hand inched up to pull the locket from the bodice of her dress. Ever since her mother's funeral, feelings of not just loneliness, but restlessness and discontent had hovered around her. This afternoon, while she'd concentrated on making evenly spaced stitches, her thoughts had organized themselves, had coalesced into a decision of sorts. She was tired of this small, stifling prison of a life the community of Far Enough had relegated her to. It was time for her to do something about it.

What that something would be she wasn't yet sure, but some action on her part was definitely called for. Of course, she'd wait until Mr. Wilder was recovered and on his way before taking any drastic steps. That should give her time to come up with an acceptable plan.

At this reminder of her bedridden houseguest, Lucy decided to take a quick look in on him. She slipped into his room, and stood next to his bed, resisting the urge to tuck the covers more snugly under his chin, to touch his face. No point in waking the man, he needed his rest.

She'd somehow managed to keep from revealing her name this afternoon, but it hadn't been easy. The thing was, the better acquainted she became with Mr. Wilder, the more she was drawn to him. She still remembered how, weak and in terrible pain, he'd tried to step in front of her there in the clearing when he thought the Jeffersons had returned. He was so nice, treating her like a real lady, though not in a stiff or formal way. Seeing his ready smile and willingness to banter, it was easy to forget that he was likely still in a great deal of pain.

Even when he was grumpy or up on his high horse over some offer she made to help, she found him endearing. Hopefully, he was over the worst of his ordeal. Perhaps that would improve his prickly disposition a bit.

In a few days he should be well enough to travel, at least as far as town. Lucy crossed her arms tight against her chest, no longer inclined to smile. It was for the best. He had to leave sooner or later, and it would be better if he left before she got too used to having him around.

Of course, once he made it to town, he'd learn who she was. Not just her name, she'd give him that before he left. But he'd hear all the stories about her, learn of her sullied reputation. After that, she'd rather not see him again. It would be much nicer to have these memories to hold to, rather than a disdainful, hurtful dismissal.

Lucy squared her shoulders, trying to shake her sudden gloom. Maybe a good night's rest would help her see matters more clearly. But she had work to take care of before she could seek the comfort of her own bed.

With a last look at the slumbering patient, she retreated, leaving his door open a crack. Satisfied that she would hear him if he should call out, Lucy returned to the sewing room. With a critical eye, she studied the pattern and specifications attached to the bolt of fabric Lowell had provided.

Her brow furrowed. What in the world did Lowell want with such a gown? He couldn't possibly think someone in Far Enough would buy it. Why, she couldn't even imagine someone in Silverton having a use for such an elegant creation. It was the sort of thing found in Madame Robicheaux's establishment in New Orleans. The sort of gown one wore to the opera or to a grand ball. No, Lowell had a purpose other than making a sale. He intended to make it as difficult as possible for her to fulfill the order.

Lucy closed her eyes and groaned. Had she really agreed to discuss marriage with Lowell if she couldn't meet the rent payment? What had she been thinking? Because if this *was* the ultimate answer, she should have married Lowell when he'd first asked. To give in now would be saying she'd put herself and her family through four years of hardship for nothing more than stubborn pride. And she wasn't ready to admit that, couldn't live with such a burden on her conscience.

Recalling her earlier decision to make some changes in her life, Lucy dragged a hand across her tired eyes. In the meantime, she *would* get the requisite dresses finished. Having an extra person in the house to care for, especially someone as distracting as Mr. Wilder, would make it more difficult. But she could do it, she *must* do it. The alternative was too unpalatable to contemplate.

Lucy spread the fabric and reached for her scissors. It was going to be a long night.

∿

*T*he next morning, Reed opened his eyes to find Toby hovering nearby once again.

"Good morning, sir. How're you feeling?"

"A little better today, thanks."

"I'll let Ma know you're up so she can get your breakfast ready." And, with a quick grin, Toby left.

Reed sat up a bit straighter and ran a hand through his hair, wishing he had time to do more to make himself presentable. Five minutes later, Athena tapped on the door, tray in hand. "Good morning Mr. Wilder. I trust you passed a more comfortable night last night."

"Yes, thank you. And whatever you're carrying there smells delicious." Reed watched her cross the room, admiring the effortless grace of her movements.

She set the tray down, then reached over to adjust the pillow behind him. "It's just soup and biscuits," she said. "I made the broth richer this time and left some chunks of carrots and potatoes in. I thought perhaps your appetite would be heartier today."

Trying to focus on something other than her nearness, Reed inhaled the aromas wafting over from the tray of food, and his mouth curved in an appreciative grin. "Regardless, it smells wonderful."

Smiling, she sat in the rocker. "I believe you're up to feeding yourself today. Why don't I just hold your bowl here where it's in easy reach and let you set your own pace?"

"Yes, ma'am."

She raised an eyebrow in response to his meek tone.

"Don't look so surprised," Reed explained. "I've decided to wait to exert my independence until I have the strength to back it up. You obviously have the upper hand at the moment and my battered pride couldn't survive another defeat."

"Quite sensible of you," she answered with mock-primness. Reed liked her quick wit and dry sense of humor. No coy miss, his Athena.

They sat in comfortable silence while he ate his breakfast. He tried once to ask her name, but she overset a cup just then, and in the process of cleaning up the mess, the question was lost. Not that he minded. He'd thought of her as Athena for so long that it now seemed the only possible name for her.

Then, as he reached for the last bit of biscuit, another thought intruded. "This is Sunday isn't it?"

She nodded. "It is."

"Then, and pardon me if this is too personal, but I hope you won't let my presence keep you from attending church service, if it's your habit to do so. I can take care of myself while you're away, just as I did yesterday."

"It's kind of you to offer, but not necessary. We have our own service here at home on Sunday mornings. Just some readings from the Bible, shared prayers, and singing." Only the briefest of pauses preceded her next words. "You're welcome to join us. We can hold our prayer service in here today, rather than the parlor."

"I wouldn't want to put you to any additional trouble."

She waved off his concern. "It's no problem and we'd be pleased to have someone share our service. All we'd need to bring, besides ourselves, would be the Bible. We can do without the piano for one Sunday."

Reed agreed to her offer, and not just for his own spiritual edification. He'd gotten the impression she had avoided him yesterday. No doubt their little encounter over the teacup had made her wary. He wanted to get back in her good graces.

His hands clenched on the covers as he watched her move in an extra chair. It went against the grain for him to let a lady perform such tasks while he sat back. He knew he had to conserve his strength, give his body time to heal, if he wanted to be of use to her or anyone else anytime soon. But this whole invalid business was worse than the beating itself. At least that had been over quickly. This seemed to be dragging on forever.

Toby entered the room, carrying a large, well-used Bible. The boy handed the book to his mother and took a seat.

She moved to the bedside, hugging the Bible to her chest. "As I said, our Sunday service is very informal. We normally begin by reading a passage from the Bible. Then we each speak as to its meaning to us personally. Afterwards, we share a prayer and have a time of quiet meditation. Then we end with hymns."

Understanding her diffidence, Reed smiled reassuringly. "I appreciate your allowing me to participate."

She extended the Bible. "As our guest, I would be pleased to have you select and read our passage this morning. It would give us a chance to hear a fresh voice and perspective."

Then, as if afraid she presumed too much, she added, "But if you don't feel up to it, I'll be glad to do it myself."

Reed pondered a moment and then held his hand to take the Bible. "I'd be honored, ma'am."

As she took her seat, he turned to the passage he wanted and began to read. *"But he, willing to justify himself, said unto Jesus, 'And who is my neighbor?' And Jesus answering said, 'A certain man went down from Jerusalem to Jericho, and fell among thieves, which stripped him of his raiment, and wounded him, and departed, leaving him half dead....'"*

Reed read the entire parable and then closed the Bible.

Athena rose to take it from him. "Thank you, Mr. Wilder. That was well done." She returned to her seat and bowed her head as if in prayer. Then she smiled at Toby. "Would you go first?"

Toby nodded, apparently not discomfited at being asked to provide his thoughts to the adults. "Well, the story of the Good Samaritan teaches that a person isn't good or bad because of how he looks or where he comes from, but because of how he follows God's teachings. You know, like 'Love thy neighbor.' One way to see how much somebody *really* believes is to watch how they treat others, especially if they think nobody's looking."

She smiled her approval. "Very good, Toby. Now, I'll go next, if I may."

She shifted in her chair, taking a moment to gather her thoughts. "What you said is very true and I'd like to add to it a little. This parable also teaches that we should treat everyone with love and compassion, regardless of who or what they are. That we are to allow God's love to shine through us. When someone needs help, we shouldn't concern ourselves with how helping him will hurt or help us personally, but rather with meeting that person's need. It is, in fact, a purer act if it's done without fanfare or acclaim. That is the true spirit of love. Everything else is false and self-serving."

Reed, turning her words over in his mind, realized she wasn't parroting some sermon she'd heard. From what he'd observed, she actually lived her life that way. He was living proof of it.

Focusing back on his companions, Reed saw their expectant expressions. It appeared they were waiting for him to speak. Reed considered passing, then changed his mind. These two had openly shared their thoughts and beliefs with him. It would be an insult to shrug it off or be less than sincere.

All right, he could do this. Choosing his words with care, Reed tried to express his feelings without giving away too much of himself. "As you've probably already guessed, I picked this passage because of what happened the other day. Those events forced me to view the parable and its lessons from a different perspective than the one I've had in the past. Always before, when I've considered these verses, I've identified with the Samaritan, and looked for what truths I could learn from his actions and motives. But having been placed in the position of the victim, I see that there are other lessons to be learned. Such as the folly of pride, and the need to accept help with humility and honest gratitude. It's also taught me that anyone, regardless of their size or circumstances, can be a hero, a Samaritan if you will."

When he'd finished, he glanced up to find Athena studying him. Reed found the approving smile that teased her lips a sweet reward for his effort.

"Thank you for sharing your thoughts with us, Mr. Wilder. If you'll allow me, I'll close our discussion with a prayer."

She then bowed her head and closed her eyes. "We thank You Father, that You have blessed us with another day. Thank You for the continued physical healing of our guest, Mr. Wilder. Thank You for the spiritual strength and renewal we have gained through the reading of Your word this morning, and for the new insights into its promise and message. Thank You for the bounteous harvest we continue to reap from our garden, and for all the many blessings You provide to meet our physical needs. Forgive us where we have fallen short of Your will. Guide us constantly to follow in Your teachings and to find joy in the simple gifts of daily life. Amen."

She and Toby remained seated with their heads bowed and eyes closed. Reed recalled her mentioning they spent some time in quiet meditation, and assumed that was what they were doing. Studying the two bowed heads, alike in demeanor and spirit if not in looks, Reed reflected on their idea of a Sunday service, so different from what he was accustomed to.

After about five minutes, Athena raised her head and opened her eyes. She seemed disconcerted to discover him watching her, and again he was held by her oh-so-expressive eyes. Only when Toby stirred a moment later, and she turned in the boy's direction, did he feel able to take a normal breath again.

"Well, Toby," she said, "I'm afraid we'll have to sing without the piano this morning. That is, if you're up to a few hymns, Mr. Wilder. If you're tired we can leave you to rest."

"No, please, don't hold back on my account."

"In that case, is there a favorite hymn you'd like us to start with?"

"Do you know *Amazing Grace*?"

"One of my favorites." She hummed a few introductory notes, then led them in the singing.

From the first note, Reed was enchanted. Not only did she have a pleasant singing voice, but it seemed infused with a sweet reverence and expressiveness that couldn't help but touch a responsive chord in her listeners.

They sang all four verses and then three more hymns before she called a halt. "I think that's enough for now. Mr. Wilder, I thank you for taking part in our service this morning, but we don't want to wear you out. Would you like me to help you settle back down so you can rest?"

Regretfully passing on the chance to have her touch him again, Reed shook his head. "If you don't mind, I think I'd prefer to sit up a while longer. Do you have any reading material I might borrow?"

"Of course. My mother was a schoolteacher and kept a

respectable library. What do your tastes run to? We have a smattering of just about everything. If you prefer academic reading, there are texts on astronomy, philosophy, geography, history, and ancient civilizations. On the other hand, if you prefer classic literature, there are volumes of poetry, essays, Shakespeare and the like. I can even offer a few less-than-classical novels if you're in the mood for something lighter."

"I think I'll have a go at the philosophy text."

With a nod she left the room and returned a few moments later. "Here you are." She handed him the book and then moved back to the door.

"We take our day of rest seriously," she said, pausing in the doorway, "but there are certain chores that have to get done, such as feeding the animals and cooking the meals. So if you'll excuse me, I'll get started on our lunch."

~

*A*s Lucy worked in the kitchen, she hummed to herself. Having Mr. Wilder participate in their Sunday morning service had enriched it considerably for her. He'd gone right to the passage he wanted, with little fumbling or back and forth searching, so he was no stranger to the Bible. He read with confidence, his inflection sure, and he sang with an unapologetic gusto. He had a nice voice, strong, rich and warm, and hearing it sent pleasurable vibrations thrumming through her.

She'd never met anyone like him before. In addition to being stubborn and heroic, Mr. Wilder was intelligent and God-fearing. He could laugh at himself but she'd guess he didn't do it often, and he had a strong streak of mule-headedness. Not exactly a fairy tale Prince Charming, but she'd always found perfection a bit boring.

She didn't find Mr. Wilder boring at all.

Lucy's humming faltered as less whimsical thoughts intruded. There was still the matter of that slip of paper with the name Lucy on it, and her need to confront him about it. Wondering what it all meant was tying her in knots.

Thirty minutes later, Lucy checked on her houseguest to find him dozing over the book. Before she could slip out again, he opened one eye.

"Don't leave on my account." He sat up straighter. "I'm not really sleeping, just resting."

Lucy took a step farther into the room, ready to let him convince her to stay. "Sorry if I disturbed you. I just wanted to see if you needed anything. Looks like that book didn't provide much in the way of entertainment."

He grimaced good-naturedly. "I'm afraid this text didn't hold much that I hadn't already read or learned on my own. I could use a bit of company, though."

She hesitated, torn between her desire to spend more time with him and her fear of that very desire.

"Just a bit of conversation to pass the time," he coaxed, looking forlorn.

"Very well." A few minutes of conversation seemed a harmless enough indulgence. "Let me fetch a bit of mending, and we can talk while I sew." She returned a moment later with the picnic quilt.

"Thanks." Mr. Wilder laid the book aside and shifted his weight, further exposing his broad shoulders and bandaged chest. Lucy resolutely kept her eyes focused on her mending.

She could feel him studying her work. "Is that the blanket you had with you that day in the woods?"

"Uh-huh."

He frowned. "I suppose I'm responsible for that tear you're trying to mend."

She gave him a quick, reassuring smile. "Don't let it bother you. It's already old and worn, and this isn't the first time it's needed mending. I made this quilt years ago, when I was first learning the craft. We used it for picnics when I was little and it took quite a bit of abuse."

Her words only seemed to make him gloomier. "So it's a family heirloom."

Lucy laughed. "Mr. Wilder, it's a quilt, and it was meant to be used. Quilts have their own special beauty, but they are first and foremost functional. According to my mother, it would be heresy to let the appearance of one of them come ahead of the comfort it was meant to give."

A slight smile tugged at his lips. "I think I would have liked your mother."

Lucy returned his smile. "And she would have liked you as well." Then, recollecting herself, she returned her gaze to the work on her lap.

"So, tell me about this place," he asked, as if aware she was ready to turn the subject. "It's a farm of some sort, isn't it?"

"I suppose you could say that." Lucy wrinkled her nose with an apologetic smile. "The only livestock we own is a cow, a mule, and some chickens. There's the vegetable garden, of course, but it's just big enough to meet our needs. Oh, and there's a half dozen peach trees that are doing exceptionally well this year."

He raised an eyebrow. "You take care of the whole place on your own?"

Lucy shrugged. "As I said, it's a small place. And Toby's getting to an age now where he can really help."

"I take it we're not in the town of Far Enough proper?"

She shook her head. "No, we're about two miles southwest, well off the beaten path. The only folks who make it out this way are peddlers and travelers looking for a drink of water or directions."

This time his raised eyebrow suggested sympathy. "Sounds lonely."

Endlessly, achingly so. But pity isn't what I want from you. "Toby and I have each other." She strove for a serene tone. "The chores keep us busy, so there's little time for socializing. And we do go to town once or twice a month for supplies." Then, taking advantage of the opening he'd provided, she turned the tables on him. "You're not from around these parts are you?"

"No, I'm from back east. Delaware to be exact."

"And what brings you so far from home?"

He shifted again, as if suddenly uncomfortable. "Just doing some field research. I'm afraid I'm not at liberty to go into the details."

"Of course. Forgive my prying." Well that bit of fishing had gotten her nothing, other than the feeling that Mr. Wilder had something to hide.

"Please, don't apologize." He flashed one of his boyish grins. "Besides, I'd rather talk about you."

I'll just bet you would, Detective Wilder. Lucy smiled as she stood. "I'm afraid my life wouldn't make for very interesting discussion. Besides, it's time for me to get back to the kitchen and check on our lunch. I'll send Toby in to keep you company if you like."

∾

*B*y the next morning, Reed was thoroughly fed up with his invalid status. Today Athena would see him as something other than her patient. He threw off the covers and sat up.

The room spun for a moment, then righted itself. He'd have to remember to move slower. But he *would* get up and get dressed today.

No sign of Toby this morning. Good. Better on his dignity if there were no witnesses to his fumbling efforts.

Reed carefully slid his legs over the edge of the bed. Holding on to the headboard and then the bedside table, he stood and made his morning ablutions. So far so good.

He spotted a cane leaning next to the bed and vaguely remembered having used it to get into the house. Taking hold of it, he took a deep breath and started across the room. Pleased to have made it to the chair without stumbling, he plucked a change of clothes from the neatly piled stack of his belongings. After throwing it over his shoulder, he made his way back to the bed.

It was a small room, thank goodness, with bare pine floors that felt cool to his equally bare feet. Hobbling past the dresser, Reed spared a smile. The top of it was cluttered with a collection of little boy treasures—curiously shaped rocks, brightly colored feathers, a snatch of shed snakeskin, a now empty wasp nest.

Reaching the bed at last, Reed plopped down, shaky but pleased with himself. That hadn't been so bad.

He dressed slowly, his injuries protesting every stretch and bend. By the time he'd fastened the last button, Reed decided he could dispense with the belt and boots for now. After limping to the door, he moved into the hallway. Keeping a hand to the wall, Reed steadfastly ignored his body's protest. He'd rather endure the aches and pains than spend another day in bed.

It was time to go find Athena.

CHAPTER 7

$\mathcal{R}$eed paused to orient himself at the corner of the hall. He now faced the screened-door entryway of the house, and to his left, an open doorway led into a parlor. The sounds of activity and the aroma of cooking came from a room further along.

He limped past the parlor to a wide, doorless entrance. Reed leaned against the frame, studying the surprisingly large room. To his left was some sort of workroom. But it was the area to his right that claimed his attention.

It held the kitchen, along with a small dining area. Athena stood with her back to him, busy at the stove and humming a pleasant tune. What a wonderful picture she made. It evoked images of hearth and home and simple pleasures.

Reed watched appreciatively as she bent to check the fire and then stood on tiptoe to place a pan of biscuits in the oven. Something inside him was drawn to the sweet, homespun picture she made. How would she respond if he slipped up behind her and put his arms around her waist?

A week ago, such a thought would never have crossed his mind. But something was happening to him, something unexpected. Perhaps it was because he was away from his family, away from the demands of Wilder Enterprises. Athena didn't know him, didn't expect him to be strong, to make difficult decisions or to fit some assigned role. She offered him shelter and friendship, looked for nothing in return. It was liberating. Here, for a while at least, he could just be himself. Whoever that was.

What did she think of him? There were times when he could believe she felt the same tug of attraction between them that beset him. Yet yesterday she'd seemed standoffish. Perhaps it was only her natural caution. After all, they'd met less than three days ago, and he'd been unconscious a good part of that time.

"Mr. Wilder!" She looked up, blowing a stray hair out of her flushed face. One hand pointed a cook spoon his way and the other fisted on her hip. "You shouldn't be up and about on your own so soon." Her voice scolded, but her smile welcomed him.

Reed smiled back. "I'm feeling better this morning, and I decided to spare you the trouble of bringing my meal to me." He swayed as he pushed away from the wall, spoiling the hale and hearty image he'd hoped to project.

"Here, let me help you to the table." She hurried to his side, *tsking* in concern, and placed an arm around his waist. Reed's mood brightened. His weakness did have this one positive aspect.

"You should have stayed put, or at least asked for help if you wanted to get up," she said, continuing her gentle scolding. "It won't aid your recovery any if you over-exert yourself."

Reed frowned at this reminder of how she viewed him. "I'm afraid I'm not very good at handling forced inactivity." He tried to soften his words as he sat. "Mother used to say she was glad I was such a healthy sort because I was a terrible patient."

Athena bustled back to the stove. "My sympathy to your mother. Now, you timed your entrance well. I was trying to decide whether to fix you another bowl of soup or something more solid."

He turned in his chair so he could face her while he talked. "Whatever you're preparing for yourself and Toby will be fine with me, if there's enough to go around. The smells alone are enough to make me feel stronger."

"Fine. Eggs, potatoes and biscuits it is." She cracked a few more eggs and added them to the sizzling skillet.

Reed watched her, fascinated by the mix of domesticity and femininity she projected in this setting. He hadn't taken a meal in the warm informality of a kitchen since he was a youngster who'd sneak down to steal a snack from cook. "Where's Toby?"

Athena kept her back to him as she cooked. "He's doing the milking and no doubt checking on that horse of yours one more time. He's looked in on him three times already this morning."

"Toby seems like a fine boy."

She smiled at him over her shoulder. "He is that. Toby's special. Intelligent, sensitive, and, of course, as capable of mischief as any other six year old." Then her smile turned self-deprecating. "Of course, I may be just the tiniest bit prejudiced on the subject."

Her tone had warmed. Praise for Toby seemed to soften her mood. Reed smiled back at her. "I've seen nothing so far to indicate you're wrong."

She scraped the skillet with practiced efficiency, and a slight melancholy tinged her voice when she continued. "He hasn't been around other children, just mother and me. Mother began giving Toby lessons almost as soon as he could talk. I know he misses the time he spent with her."

"Thank you for taking care of my things, and for the use of this cane," Reed said, attempting to change the mood. "Let me say again how grateful I am for all you've done for me. I'll have a hard time repaying the debt I owe you."

She shook her head, casting another quick glance over her shoulder. "Nonsense. This had nothing to do with you. I would've done the same for anyone in such a situation."

Reed's lips twitched at the asperity of her tone. "Well, that certainly put me in my place."

Athena flashed him an abashed grin. "My apologies. As I said before, we don't get many visitors out here and my company manners are a bit rusty."

"Apology accepted."

Toby burst through the back door, carrying a full pail. "Here's the milk. Sorry I took so long, but I just took a quick look in on Ranger and—" He came to a full stop as he noticed Reed, the pail threatening to spill as it knocked against his overall-clad legs. "Oh, hello, Mr. Wilder."

"Hello Toby. And how is Ranger?"

The boy grinned self-consciously. "Just fine. He's a beauty, sir. I've never seen a horse so fine before."

Reed accepted Toby's praise on Ranger's behalf with a nod. "Glad you approve."

"I fed Ranger along with the other animals this morning." Toby rinsed his hands at the sink. "A full portion of oats. Then I turned him out in the barnyard to get some exercise. Poor Moses is sure put to shame."

"Thanks Toby. I'm sure Ranger appreciates the attention as much as I do. And just who is Moses?"

"Our mule."

Reed's lips twitched. His proud horse would be affronted if he knew he'd been compared to a mule, even favorably so. "Maybe you'd like to ride Ranger later, sort of as a thank you."

Toby's head came around with a snap, and he smiled as if he couldn't quite believe his luck. "Oh, yes sir, could I?"

"As long as your ma agrees, I don't see why not." But, as Reed looked Athena's way, he realized he didn't have her support.

Toby's gaze followed Reed's, his heart in his eyes. "Can I, Ma? I promise to be careful and do what Mr. Wilder tells me."

She shot Reed a disgruntled look before turning to Toby with a placating smile. "I don't know, Toby. Mr. Wilder's horse is different from what you're used to with Moses."

Before Toby could voice the disappointed protest visible on his face, Reed intervened. "Don't worry, ma'am, Ranger's well trained. I'll be leading him, and I promise to watch closely. Toby will be completely safe."

"That's very kind of you," she said, not sounding at all grateful, "but you really should take it easy today."

Reed paused. Why was she so hesitant to let Toby ride Ranger? After a moment's reflection, though, he decided it came from her having to raise the boy without a man's balancing influence. Not her fault, but it wasn't the best upbringing for the boy.

Keeping his voice friendly but firm, he countered. "I won't take him out until I'm back up to strength, you have my word." She'd thank him later. A boy shouldn't be coddled so much.

She still seemed unconvinced, but, as she looked from Reed to Toby's yearning expression, she gave tentative approval. "Very well, but only when I think you're ready."

Even that stricture couldn't suppress Toby's enthusiasm. "Thanks, Ma." Then he turned his face-splitting smile back to Reed. "I'll bet Ranger can really go fast, when you let him."

Reed returned Toby's grin. "He's fast, all right, especially when he goes full out. We'll keep it nice and easy, though, at least the first time."

Toby's face beamed as he took his seat.

Athena placed the plates on the table, each loaded with the promised eggs, potatoes and biscuits. There was also jam and butter to spread on the biscuits. She placed a glass of milk in front of Toby and then turned to Reed. "Coffee or milk?"

"Coffee, please, right from the pot. No cream or sugar."

She poured up two cups and carried them to the table.

After she said the blessing, Reed picked up his fork and addressed Toby. "Thank you for giving up your room to me the last few nights. I hope you found a comfortable place to sleep."

"Yes sir," the boy answered with a quick nod. "Ma fixed up a place for me in the parlor." Then Toby asked a question of his own. "Ma says you come from Delaware. Is that very far?"

"Quite a piece. I passed through more than a half dozen states to get here."

Toby's eyes grew round. "Gosh. You must be after something really important to travel such a long way."

Reed shifted in his chair, but Athena came to his rescue before he could frame an answer. "Now, Toby, you shouldn't ask such personal questions." Then she changed the subject. "After breakfast, perhaps you can take Mr. Wilder into the parlor and play him a game of checkers. If he's up to it, that is."

"Yes, ma'am." Toby turned eagerly to Reed. "Do you want to, Mr. Wilder? Do you like checkers?"

"Sounds like a good way to pass the time." He raised his fork, pointing it at Toby as if in warning. "It's been a while since I've played, but I was good, if I do say so myself. I used to trounce my older brothers severely when I was a boy."

Toby flashed a grin, undaunted by Reed's challenge.

Later, Toby carried his plate to the counter and began pumping water into the sink, but his mother waved him away.

"I'll take care of the dishes. You go on and set up the checkers, and I'll help Mr. Wilder into the parlor."

"Thanks Ma." Toby ran to do as she bid, not needing to be told twice.

Reed leaned back in his chair. "That was delicious, ma'am. I hope I'm not being too much of a burden for you and Toby."

She shrugged as she worked the handle of the pump. "No point in worrying about something you can't change. You're welcome to stay until you can get your strength back."

Reed frowned as he reached for the walking stick. Was she hinting she'd be glad to see him move on? "I appreciate your hospitality. I feel guilty leaving you to do the cleaning up by yourself."

Athena's gaze speared him with all her lady-of-the-house authority. "And just how much help do you figure you could be to me in your condition? I don't need you working yourself into a relapse."

She certainly didn't mince words, and his show of initiative this morning hadn't done much to convince her he was capable of taking care of himself. "Yes, ma'am." Reed gave a short nod, resisting the temptation to salute.

"Here, put your other arm on my shoulder." Her tone was more mother-henish than conciliatory.

Affronted, Reed drew himself up. "That's not necessary."

She gave him another of her exasperated looks. "Then do it just to humor me."

Unwilling to lock horns with her, Reed complied. They crossed the room in stiff silence. As they entered the hall, he relaxed and settled his arms more comfortably on her shoulder. He inhaled the faint scent of flowers from her hair and decided that really, this *was* better than holding on to the wall.

She cut him a questioning look, as if sensing his change in mood, but said nothing until they entered the parlor and he eased himself down on the sofa. "Now, you two enjoy your game." With a quick smile for Toby, she left them.

Thirty minutes later, Reed looked up from the checkerboard to see his hostess step back into the parlor. He tried to rise, but she forestalled him. "Don't stand, please. I just wanted to see how you were doing. Toby isn't wearing you out, I hope."

Reed mentally gritted his teeth. This mollycoddling was getting tiresome. He controlled his irritation, though, and flashed Toby a companionable grin. "Not at all. I find a good challenge invigorating, and Toby's quite a checker player. I barely managed to win the first game and he's giving me a run for my money this go round."

Toby beamed at the implied compliment, and she smiled fondly at the boy before turning back to Reed. "I've taken the liberty of drawing a nice hot bath for you. I thought your injuries might benefit from a soothing soak. I've added a few herbs to the water that ought to help speed the healing process for those raw spots on your back."

She gave him an abashed smile, as if uncomfortable with so personal a topic. "I'll be out in the garden for a while, so you won't need to hurry on my account. There's a kettle of water heating on the stove you can use to warm it up if need be. And Toby can help you remove your bandages and lend whatever other assistance you might need. I think we can safely dispense with the bandages from here on out."

"Thank you, ma'am, that sounds wonderful." And it did. A

basin and washrag were no substitute for a real, honest to goodness bath.

She nodded. "You're welcome. And, Toby, don't worry about the rest of your chores for now. You stay close to the house in case Mr. Wilder should need some help."

Blast! Did she *enjoy* rubbing his nose in his invalid status?

After she'd gone, Reed, with Toby's eager assistance, fetched his pack and returned to the kitchen. A wooden screen stood near the stove, and behind it a bathtub filled with pungently scented water. The tub was brass, set on rollers for mobility, and surprisingly roomy. An unexpected luxury in this simple farm house. But Reed, stepping out of the last of his clothes and then taking a bar of soap from his bag, blessed the incongruity.

He took his time, letting the warm, herb-steeped waters ease the stiffness and soreness from him. It wasn't until the water began to cool that he stirred himself enough to wash. By the time he'd dried and redressed, he felt amazingly refreshed.

When he walked out from behind the screen, Toby jumped up from the table. "You take a seat here, Mr. Wilder, and I'll take care of emptying the tub for you."

"How about we tackle it together," Reed suggested with a smile. The boy was certainly no slacker.

Toby looked doubtful. "It won't take me but a few minutes sir, and Ma says you need to rest so you can get better."

Now she had Toby treating him like a helpless invalid! Reed managed a smile. "True. But it'll go faster with two of us, and I promise to take it easy."

The boy tilted his head to one side with a considering look. "Well, all right. But only if you use Grandma Bea's cane, and if you promise to stop if you get to feeling shaky."

"I promise," Reed agreed solemnly.

They each grabbed a bucket and ladled water out. Once they had it down to a manageable level, they rolled the tub outside and tipped it over the side of the porch. When they were done, Reed was winded and very aware of the bruises on his abdomen.

A couple of yips drew his attention to the ground in front of the porch. There, near the bottom step, stood a dog of questionable lineage, keeping a close eye on Toby.

Of course, there'd been a dog with them during the fortuitous rescue operation. This dog, shorthaired and soulful-eyed, didn't stand much taller than Toby's knees. He was a muddy brown color, with two splashes of tan, one across his nose and one on his right front leg. The tip of his tail looked as if it had been dipped in tar. The mutt's most noticeable feature, however, was a pair of the longest ears Reed had ever seen on a dog, literally dragging the ground when he stood.

With a raised eyebrow, Reed nodded toward the dog. "Who've we got here?"

"That's my dog, Jasper. Don't worry, he won't hurt you, he's just saying hello."

Reed sat down on the top step and scratched the dog behind the ears. "Seems mighty friendly."

Toby hunkered down next to them. "Jasper's the best dog there ever was, real gregarious too."

Reed smiled at the boy's use of such an unexpected adjective. But Toby continued in a proud tone. "Don't let him fool you, though. He's a good watchdog. Nobody gets near this house without Jasper barking up a storm. Only reason he didn't bark at you is cause he could tell we were friends."

"Smart dog." Reed gave the dog's ears another scratch and then pulled his hand back to rest on his leg as he studied the area behind the house. Over to his left stood the small grove of peach trees Toby's mother had mentioned before, and straight ahead the vegetable garden bloomed with the lushness of late spring.

The rustic Athena, as tidy as ever in her starched white apron, reached the end of a row of beans just then, spotted them and gave a wave before she turned down the next row.

To the far right he saw the barn and barnyard. There stood Ranger, sharing space with the mule Moses, and a milk cow.

"Watch this," Toby said, recapturing Reed's attention. He held a stick and, after waving it in front of Jasper for a second, tossed it as far as he could.

Jasper, obviously familiar with the game, bounded after the stick, ears flapping like bird wings, and returned in no time to deposit it at Toby's feet.

As Reed applauded their efforts, an old washstand up on the porch caught his eye. He ran a hand over his chin thoughtfully.

"Would you mind fetching some water for that basin over there while I get my shaving things? I need to get rid of this stubble before it turns into a full grown beard."

Toby shot up. "Sure thing, Mr. Wilder. Can I watch?"

"Don't see why not," Reed answered with a smile. He rose, with the aid of the cane, and decided he felt quite a bit stronger. The bath and fresh air had done him good.

Heading inside to fetch his things, Reed wondered how long Toby had been without a father. It wouldn't hurt for the boy to get a little avuncular attention. It seemed a small enough thing to do to repay the hospitality he'd been shown in this household.

Stepping outside, Reed gave Toby a man-to-man smile. "Give me a minute to set up, and I'll show you how this is done."

Finding a nail strategically located on the wall above the basin, Reed hung his shaving mirror and got his first look at his face since leaving Silverton.

He frowned. *This* was the image Athena had been viewing for the past few days? No wonder she kept treating him like a helpless invalid. Cuts and bruises distorted his features, giving him a villainous look, and the four days growth of beard added an element of slovenliness. He didn't consider himself handsome, but he prided himself on maintaining a neat, orderly appearance.

After shedding his shirt, Reed threw a towel over his shoulder and proceeded to demonstrate the fine art of shaving to an enthralled Toby.

Athena came up to the porch as he rinsed off. Reed swiped his face dry and turned to greet her. "My thanks for the tub of water this morning, ma'am. It was just what the doctor ordered."

"You're quite welcome." She set her produce-filled basket on a crate by the door, and then pushed the straw hat back off of her head. A fine sheen of sweat covered her flushed face. Reed's hand itched to brush the stray tendrils from her forehead.

She took a good look at him as she pulled the door open, and smiled in obvious appreciation. "It does seem to have done you some good, at that." Then she propped the door open with her foot, picked up the basket and went inside.

Battling the urge to give in to a cocky grin, Reed gathered his things and followed her into the kitchen, Toby at his heels.

He watched her set the heavy basket on the table and felt a stab of guilt at his inability to help with the manual labor. High time he got off his backside and started earning his keep.

She paused, arching her back and rolling her neck to relieve her tired muscles.

Reed cleared his suddenly dry throat. "I know my presence must be a burden to you, ma'am. Perhaps there are some chores you could set me to, to help me feel I was paying my way a bit."

There was that mother-to-wayward-child look again. "That's kind of you, Mr. Wilder, just not very sensible. You may feel stronger, but you're far from recovered, and it wouldn't take much to set you back again."

He set his jaw, refusing to take no for an answer. She *would* see him as something other than a patient. "Surely there's some task that doesn't require a lot of brute strength that I can help with."

She studied him as if to judge his sincerity, and then nodded. "Very well. I'm planning to make a cobbler with these peaches. You can peel and slice them for me, while I tend to a few other things." The look she sent him held a hint of challenge, as if she expected him to back down from the chore.

While it wasn't exactly what he'd had in mind, Reed smiled and asked for a knife.

～

*L*ucy returned to the kitchen to find Mr. Wilder and Toby talking comfortably, the bowl of neatly peeled and sliced peaches between them, and each munching on a juicy slice.

They both looked up at her, identical guilty expressions on their faces, and it was all Lucy could do not to smile. It was rather endearing to see Mr. Wilder in this hand-in-the-cookie-jar light. He seemed to be genuinely enjoying Toby's company—she could forgive him a lot for that. "Well gentlemen, did you leave enough to make a decent sized cobbler?" she asked as severely as she could.

"We only took a couple of slices. Honest, Ma." Toby glanced from Lucy to Mr. Wilder and then back. "And it was my idea. I told Mr. Wilder you wouldn't mind. You don't mind, do you?"

Lucy relented from her teasing and smiled forgiveness. "Well, as long as it was only a couple of slices, I guess we can consider it payment for a job well done."

Toby flashed their guest a relieved smile. "See, Mr. Wilder, I told you she wouldn't mind."

"That you did. I guess you know your ma pretty well."

Mr. Wilder's share-a-smile-with-me grin did funny things to Lucy's insides. Telling herself she just wasn't used to such attention, she turned back to Toby. "The water in the trough is low. Why don't you fill it for me while I get started on lunch."

"Yes, ma'am."

Once he'd gone, she smiled at Mr. Wilder and reached for the bowl of peaches, trying to shake off the sudden feeling of awkwardness in his presence. "Thanks for taking care of these." She placed the bowl on the counter, then turned back to her guest.

An idea had been taking shape in her mind ever since he'd made his offer to help. "Toby seems to have taken a shine to you," she said casually.

Mr. Wilder leaned back with a smile. "The feeling is mutual. He's a fine boy and he's got a good head on his shoulders."

She wiped an invisible spot on the counter. "Do you have much experience with children?"

His brow furrowed at the change in subject. "Well, I've three younger sisters that I helped raise, but they're grown now. The youngest will be getting married soon. And I have a niece and two nephews that I see often enough. Other than that, I can't say my experience is very great."

Lucy watched him closely as she worked up to her request. "I've been thinking over what you said about wanting to help, and I thought of something you might do for Toby and me, if you're still willing." She paused, wondering if this was really such a good idea after all.

He leaned forward with an eager smile. "Just name it."

"You seem to be an educated man. You've demonstrated you know how to read, and I assume you can write as well." When he nodded, she took a deep breath and plunged in. "Mother used to work with Toby on his lessons, teaching him to read and write and do sums. I don't have as much time to spend with him, I'm afraid, what with trying to keep this place running. Would you be willing to spend some time while you're here working with him that way? Just for an hour or so a day. It would mean a lot to Toby, and would help me to concentrate on some other things I need to do around here."

Mr. Wilder never even hesitated. "Say no more, I'd be delighted to work with Toby. Just give me a general idea of what he's been working on."

Lucy felt a mixture of relief and trepidation that he seemed so willing to help. It would be a good experience for Toby and would free up time for her to work on those dresses Lowell demanded. But she would be putting her baby into this stranger's hands for an hour a day. Somehow, though, Mr. Wilder really didn't *feel* like a stranger any more.

She moved away from the sink and motioned for him to follow. "Of course. Come on into the parlor."

Lucy led him to one of the bookshelves and pulled out a well-worn volume. "Mother was teaching him to read from this primer. The place where they left off is marked. They also spent time practicing writing and basic arithmetic." She motioned toward a small desk in the corner of the room. "Toby can print his name and simple sentences fairly well. He can also count past a hundred and they'd done some work with addition and subtraction."

Mr. Wilder took the book from her and thumbed through it. "And what sort of routine did she set for him?"

"Nothing very structured. As I said, she worked with him mostly on reading, writing and arithmetic. But sometimes she'd just take out a book on history or geography and read to him, then they'd spend time discussing it together. Basically, they'd concentrate on whatever subject caught their fancy that day. You can feel free to do the same."

He closed the book and nodded. "Well, this doesn't sound too demanding. I won't promise I can live up to your mother's standards, but I'll do my best."

Mr. Wilder reached past her to replace the book, and his arm brushed her shoulder. The unexpected contact raised tingly goose bumps on her arms.

She could tell he'd noted her reaction, but his expression remained passive. Tucking a stray lock of hair back over her ear, Lucy tried to pretend she'd been just as unaffected. "I'm sure you'll do a fine job. Now, I need to tend to lunch, and I imagine you're ready to rest a bit after the morning of activity."

But he shook his head. "I'm not a bit tired. If you don't mind, I think I'll familiarize myself with your library. Maybe even go outside for a while. I'd like to check on Ranger, and I feel the need for some fresh air."

"Of course," she answered, feigning indifference. "Feel free to wander anywhere you like. Toby can show you around if you wish."

As she headed back toward the kitchen, Lucy found herself sending up a small prayer that Mr. Wilder would wait an extra day or two to take his leave.

For Toby's sake, of course.

But whatever the case, it was nearing the time for her to confront him about that letter she'd found in his bag.

~

*A*fter she'd gone, Reed scanned the titles on the bookshelves, impressed by the variety and quality of the selection. He picked one at random, a book on astronomy, and thumbed through the pages without really seeing them.

He'd be healed enough to ride by tomorrow, if he took it easy. He'd imposed on her hospitality long enough, it was time he moved on. Though she didn't seem to begrudge him anything, he could see she didn't have much to spare in the way of material goods. Besides, he had a mission to carry out, and the sooner he got to it, the better.

He'd deal with Miss Ames quickly; discover what had become of the ring and then find out about the boy and take him back to Delaware if he was indeed Jon's son. Then he'd take care of the Claymore deal and see Lisa married. After that, he'd be free to come back here and see what he could do to repay his lovely rescuer for all she'd done for him.

As he put the astronomy book back on the shelf, a slim, elegant-looking volume caught his eye. Bound in supple leather with intricately tooled design work on the cover and gilt-edged pages, it stood out from its neighbors. Drawing it out, he discovered it was a book of Elizabethan sonnets, and he smiled, wondering if his practical Athena had a hidden, romantic side.

Reed thumbed through the book idly, and was just about to return it to the shelf when it opened to the flyleaf. There was an inscription, penned in a bold, masculine hand: *To my darling Lucy, All my love, Dad.*

Lucy!

Reed stared at the inscription, his smile fading as he absorbed the implications. A withering chill seeped into him, frosting over the still tender growth in his heart.

CHAPTER 8

*R*eed gripped the rail of the barnyard fence, staring at the pastoral scenery without really seeing it. He'd left the house in a blinding rage. The oh so demure lady of the house had been focused on giving Toby a gentle scolding as she stripped him of his soaked clothing, so Reed's hasty exit went unremarked.

Making a fist, Reed pounded the rail once, almost welcoming the pain that shot up his arm. Of *course* his hostess was Lucy Ames. If he hadn't been so distracted by her seeming kindness, he'd have realized it before now. Look at all the clues he'd had. She lived out here on her own, an unacceptable situation for a respectable lady, even for a widow and even in this less civilized part of the country. And there was Toby, exactly the right age and with that distinctive copper-colored hair.

A part of him still rebelled at the thought of his angel of mercy and the woman he'd come to confront being one and the same person. But he savagely squelched that line of thought.

Athena, hah! More like Apate, the mythological being that represented deceit. No doubt she was being so sweetly helpful so she could milk him for a fat reward.

This was a woman who'd stolen a dead man's ring while his

grieving widow lay helpless on her sickbed. Someone who pretended friendship with a trusting young wife, while secretly taking her husband as a lover.

Still, the woman had saved his life. How could he do what he'd come to do when he was so deeply in debt to her?

Well, first things first. He'd deal with his anger and get himself back under control. Patience and logic were the tools he wielded best. Listening to his emotions only clouded his thinking, made him vulnerable and ineffective. He'd learned that ten years ago. Too bad he'd let himself forget that little lesson when he'd arrived here. Like a besotted adolescent, he'd let his attraction for her distract him from his goal. It was time to press on as planned, so he could put this matter, and this woman, behind him.

Reed straightened, trying to decide his next step. She was still unaware of his reason for being in Far Enough, and that gave him an edge, one he meant to take full advantage of.

Wait a minute. Did she suspect something? Is that why she seemed so reluctant to give him her name? It could just be natural caution, or a guilty conscience. Then again...

"Mr. Wilder!" He turned at the hail and found Toby trotting up to him, Stetson in hand. "Ma asked me to bring this to you. Said to tell you to be sure to take it easy out in this heat."

Reed reined in his anger. The boy, at least, was innocent in all this. Then he checked. It had just sunk in that Toby was the target of his search, his probable nephew. "Thanks," he said, taking the hat. "So, are you out of hot water already?"

Toby grinned. "Oh sure. Ma never stays angry long. See, she even gave me a peach slice. Are you going to check on Ranger?"

"Yep. Thought I'd look over your place a bit while I was at it. Care to show me around?"

"Sure! Come on over to the barn and I'll introduce you to Moses and Pansy." Toby moved to the gate, Jasper at his heels.

As he followed the boy, Reed studied him, firmly squelching any emotional reaction. Those only led to trouble—as recent events had quite clearly proven. No, cool-headed analysis and logic were what he needed here.

He could definitely see signs of Jonathan in the boy. His eyes were that distinctive Wilder green and he had that same unruly reddish-brown hair. And there was something about the nose and mouth. The conviction that this was indeed his nephew grew stronger by the minute. Which meant he had to get him out of that immoral schemer's clutches as soon as possible. No matter how much she cared for the boy, such a woman was not fit to raise a Wilder.

Pansy turned out to be the milk cow, a mournful-eyed Jersey. Reed also had a chance to admire the brash rooster and dozen hens whose coop occupied the far corner of the barnyard.

"See that cat over there?" Toby asked, pointing to a lean calico slinking through the barn door. "That's Mustard. She's a good mouser, but she's not very sociable. Spends most of her time in the barn or out in the field behind the garden."

Reed leaned against the fence rail. "It must be a lot of work to take care of such a place. Your ma is lucky to have you to help her."

Toby shrugged, though a touch of pride colored his voice. "I take care of feeding and watering the animals, and I gather up the eggs every morning. And for the past couple of weeks I've been taking care of the milkin' too." Then his expression sobered. "It's been hard on Ma since Grandma Bea died. She doesn't smile as much any more. I wish I'd hurry and grow up so I could help her more."

Reed was touched by the poignancy of that statement. A six-year-old shouldn't have to bear such emotional burdens, no matter how mature he was. "I'm sure you're a big help around here. It's hard when someone you love dies."

With the resilience of youth, Toby nodded and skipped on ahead. "Come on, I'll show you around."

They rounded the corner of the house and Reed stopped to admire a magnificent oak tree that dominated the front yard. The trunk measured at least eighteen feet around and the long sweeping branches fanned out in every direction. A large, irregular log rested against the trunk forming a serviceable bench.

Toby grinned, obviously enjoying Reed's reaction. "What do you think of our tree? Isn't it great?"

"Sure is. I imagine you can see for miles from up there."

Some of Toby's enthusiasm faded. "Ma doesn't like me to climb it. She thinks I might fall and get hurt or something."

Reed felt his jaw tighten again. Here was one more reason to get Toby away from here. The woman was going to stifle the boy's adventurous spirit.

Then Toby grinned conspiratorially. "But I'll tell you a secret, if you promise not to tell her."

Reed, who could guess what the secret involved, nodded and solemnly gave his word that the secret would be safe with him.

Toby's voice lowered a notch. "Once, when Ma was busy in the garden and Grandma Bea was napping, I climbed it. Made it almost to the top too. I felt like the king of the world, and I could almost see town from up there. It was wonderful."

"I'll just bet it was." So, being raised by women hadn't completely softened the boy.

Moving his gaze from the tree, Reed took a look around at the rest of the place. While the yard itself appeared neat and well tended, there were numerous signs of disrepair.

The house, an unpretentious white clapboard structure, could have benefited from a fresh coat of paint. A roofed porch, at least eight feet deep, stretched the full length along the front.

A roomy looking swing hung to the left of the front door. However, it only hung by one chain. The other end dragged the ground forlornly.

A picket fence separated the front yard from the nearby road. The profusion of flowers lining it only partially disguised the fact that it sagged in several places.

Toby didn't allow Reed time for further study. "Hey, if you're up to a walk, there's someplace I'd like to show you."

Smiling, Reed nodded his assent. "Lead on. Just remember, I'm not moving too fast at the moment."

Reed followed him around to the back of the house, past the garden and peach trees, along a path through a small thicket of bushes and weeds, and over a gentle slope. There, on the other side, he found himself at the edge of a very large pond.

Toby spread his arms wide, as if trying to encompass the whole area. "Isn't it great! Ma and I come out here for picnics sometimes. It's my favorite spot in the whole world."

"I can see why," Reed said appreciatively once he'd gotten his breathing back to normal. "A good place to cool off with a swim when the days get too hot."

Toby kicked a stray rock, not meeting Reed's eyes. "I never learned to swim." Then he brightened. "I do wade out there sometimes, though. It's not very deep on this side."

"How about skipping stones, have you ever tried that?"

Toby shook his head but his expression indicated an eagerness to try.

"Here, I'll show you." Reed squatted, wincing at the painful protesting of his abdomen, and searched the ground for the right kind of stones. Finding several he deemed appropriate, he straightened with the aid of the cane, and grinned. "Now watch and let's hope I haven't lost my touch."

Reed's first attempt met with mixed success. The stone skipped, but only once. After a few more attempts, though, he managed to get the number up to a satisfying five skips.

Toby, impressed, clamored for lessons.

Reed explained to him what sort of stones to look for and, after a suitable number were gathered, taught him the proper technique. Fifteen minutes, and countless throws later, an excited Toby watched one of his stones match the 'five skipper' Reed had thrown. "Did you see that, Mr. Wilder? Wasn't that something? Wait till I show Ma."

Toby hunted for more stones, while Reed leaned on his cane, watching. He realized how much he was looking forward to claiming this bright young lad as a Wilder, how rewarding it would be to spend time with him, to teach him about his heritage and introduce him to his grandfather, Reed's own father. And the sooner the better. No telling how much he'd have to undo of the upbringing the boy'd had at the hands of his mother.

Then he paused, remembering her kindness. Remembering the prayer service yesterday. That didn't mean she was innocent by any means, but perhaps she'd changed in the ensuing years since his brother's death.

He decided to try some gentle probing while he had this opportunity, away from Miss Ames' watchful eyes. "Do you remember much about your father, Toby?"

Toby didn't even look up from his search. "No sir, he died before I was even born. But Ma's told me a lot about him. He was a riverboat captain, a real good one, Ma says. Doesn't that sound exciting? He died a hero, too."

"Is that right?" Reed kept his voice carefully neutral.

Toby did look up this time, his expression earnest. "Honest. He saved a bunch of folks when his ship caught fire. He died trying to save the last of 'em. Ma says he was always thinking of others." At least the woman had spoken well of his brother.

Toby lobbed another stone and jumped up. "Hey! Did you see that? It skipped six times! I beat yours."

"So you did."

Before Reed could steer the conversation back toward Toby's father, the boy looked back over his shoulder. "Listen, that's Ma calling. We better head back to the house."

Reed trailed behind, schooling his features as he prepared to face Miss Ames for the first time since learning her identity.

Throughout lunch, he managed to hold up his end of the conversation, though the friendly smile took a bit of effort. He studied his hostess with newly opened eyes, searching for signs of duplicity. She was mighty good with that innocent facade. And he could tell her concerned mother demeanor was no act—she really cared for Toby. No wonder he'd been taken in so completely.

Later, pushing away from the table, Reed smiled at Toby. "I hear you're on your way to becoming a reader. How about doing a little practicing with me."

"Sure!" Toby popped up at once. "Come on, I'll show you where my book is."

Athen—No, Lucy Ames, sent him a grateful smile over the boy's head. "I'll be in my room if you should need anything. Don't let him wear you out."

Reed wondered cynically if she'd put him up to this just so she could steal off for an afternoon nap. No matter, having time alone with Toby fit right in with his own plans. "We'll be fine. You do whatever it is you need to, and don't worry about us."

~

Setting down the scissors, Lucy felt pleased with her progress that afternoon. At this rate, she'd finish the initial construction on the first dress by tomorrow. Unfortunately, the pattern called for some complex beadwork on the bodice, a time-consuming process.

Working in her bedroom rather than the sewing room was a bit restrictive, but she had given her word to Lowell to keep their arrangement secret. Mr. Wilder would likely have paid very little attention to her efforts, but there was no point taking chances.

Humming, she put away her sewing things and headed back to the kitchen. Her thoughts drifted to her current dilemma—how to go about reclaiming control of her life.

You always dreamed of owning a dress shop.

Lucy frowned and raised a hand to her bodice, tracing the outline of her mother's locket. Where had that thought come from? No matter, it was a foolish notion anyway, no one in Far Enough would patronize a store she owned or even worked in.

So go somewhere else, advised the matter-of-fact voice in her head, the one that sounded suspiciously like her mother.

Lucy frowned. Leave Far Enough? She couldn't do that.

What's keeping you here?

She gave that question some thought. Six years ago she'd had a newborn baby and an invalid mother to care for. Both of those responsibilities had kept her tied to this place. But her mother was gone now, and Toby had reached an age where he no longer required her constant attention. Starting up a new business, however, would require money, something she didn't have.

Lucy Jane, look around you. You own livestock and furniture and that piano in the parlor. You have the means. Do you have the courage?

Lucy turned that question over in her mind as she filled the kettle with water and placed it on the stove.

Did she have the courage? Maybe, if she were only gambling with her own future. But she had to think of Toby's future as well.

No, she'd find another way. She resolutely ignored the disappointed silence of that voice in her head. Instead she eavesdropped on the conversation coming from the back porch.

"The preacher's cat is a miserable cat."

"The preacher's cat is a naughty cat."

"The preacher's cat is an ornery cat."

"The preacher's cat is a playful cat."

She smiled. So, Toby had introduced Mr. Wilder to his favorite word game.

Then her smile faded. Mr. Wilder looked much better today. Soon he'd be able to continue on his way. She'd already felt a slight withdrawing from him at lunch. Nothing tangible, just a certain feeling of distance that hadn't been there before. Was he thinking about moving on? She prayed it wouldn't be too hard on Toby when that happened. She steadfastly refused to admit it would have any affect on her at all.

∾

*T*hat evening, as Toby set up the board for a third round of checkers, Reed headed for the kitchen, looking for a drink of water. He wondered what Miss Ames was up to. Supper had been over for quite some time and she had yet to leave the confines of the kitchen.

Turning the corner into the room, the answer to his question brought him up short.

There she was, seated by the stove, brushing out her freshly washed hair. And what hair! The still-damp tendrils were shining in the lamplight, the nondescript brown of the daytime turned to a warm honey color. And it fell in long, shimmery waves all the way down to the small of her back. She'd pulled half of it over her far shoulder, brushing it rhythmically in long, slow strokes. Her eyes were closed and a dreamy expression caressed her face. The side of her neck nearest to him lay exposed, and he found himself staring at that creamy expanse.

Reed stood there for a moment, not moving and not making a sound. He must have made some noise, or perhaps the sheer force of his stare alerted her to his presence. Her gaze swung to his in a sudden, startled movement. A blush stole over her cheeks, her eyes widened, and he heard her quick intake of breath. It was a disturbingly innocent sound.

Had he made a mistake, was this not Lucy Ames after all?

Reed drew on the remnants of his control. Clearing his throat, he tried for a nonchalant tone. "Sorry, didn't mean to disturb you. I just came in here to get a glass of water."

"No, that's quite all right. Please help yourself." Her voice had a breathless quality that did funny things to his insides.

With a supreme effort of will, Reed kept his stride easy and relaxed as he walked to the cupboard, got a glass and filled it at the sink. Despite her blushing appearances, if she was indeed Miss Ames, she was no innocent. The woman was a thief and a Jezebel! He wouldn't be surprised if this little tableau had been staged for his benefit. And he'd fallen for it, reacted like a besotted fool. What in the world had happened to his control, how could he be attracted to such a woman?

Reed stood with his back to her as he drank, his control once more in place. Then he turned, and with a casual "excuse me," left the room. All this with barely a glance in her direction, though he felt her wide-eyed gaze follow his every movement.

~

*A*lone again, Lucy leaned back in her chair and closed her eyes, allowing the tension to drain from her body. She resumed brushing her hair with hands that trembled slightly. How could he overset her with just a look? She'd never felt this way before, and she found it unnerving. For a moment she wondered what it might be like to be kissed by him...

What was she thinking! Did it really take so little to turn her into the woman everyone painted her to be?

Twenty minutes later, Lucy was able to enter the parlor, Toby's bed linens and nightshirt in hand, without a visible trace of nervousness. She found Toby and Mr. Wilder in the middle of a checker game that Toby seemed to be winning.

Mr. Wilder stood as soon as she entered, then looked sternly over at the still seated boy. "A gentleman always stands when a lady enters the room, Toby, and remains standing until she takes her seat. You're not too young to start learning such things."

Toby scrambled to his feet at once.

Lucy's smile froze on her face. How *dare* Mr. Wilder presume to lecture Toby that way? Was he insinuating she wasn't doing a good job of raising him?

"Is anything wrong?"

Lucy took a deep breath and mentally stepped back. Surely Mr. Wilder was only trying to set a good example. Still...

She shook her head. "No, I'm just a little tired. You two go on with your game. But Toby, it's getting late. After this game is over you need to prepare for bed."

"Yes, ma'am."

The match was over in a matter of minutes, with Toby coming out the winner. Lucy suspected Mr. Wilder let Toby win, but if so, he did it with such skill that it wasn't obvious.

As they rose, she handed Toby his things. "There's a basin of warm water in the kitchen for you. I'll have your bed ready by the time you're finished."

Then Lucy reached behind the couch to pull out the folding cot, but Mr. Wilder forestalled her. "Here, let me get that."

It was nice to have a gentleman doing such things for her, even if that stiffness she'd noted earlier seemed more pronounced now. Had their encounter in the kitchen put him off? Had she insulted or offended him without knowing? Or was he just tired from the activity of the day?

In a few minutes the bed was set up in the middle of the room. Then he helped her make it up. Lucy wasn't sure whether she welcomed or regretted Toby's return, but it effectively eased some of the tension she'd felt building up inside her. Time to put some distance between herself and Mr. Wilder.

Placing a hand on Toby's shoulder, Lucy turned to her guest. "Is there anything you require before you retire? You've had a long day for someone in your condition, and you must be tired."

Mr. Wilder took the hint, with only a slight tightening of his jaw. "No, thank you, ma'am, I'll be just fine. I think I'll take a short walk outside before I turn in. Good night to you both and I'll see you in the morning." He took the cane and limped into the hallway.

Toby climbed into bed. "I really do like Mr. Wilder, don't you, Ma?"

Lucy tucked the covers in around him while she carefully worded her reply. "He seems like a very nice man, Toby. And even though he'll be leaving soon, it's nice to have some company while he's here." She wanted to make sure Toby understood Mr. Wilder would be moving on and out of their lives soon.

Toby, however, refused to let go of his optimism. "Well, I hope he decides to stay for a while. He promised to let me ride Ranger tomorrow."

She stifled a sigh. "Just be sure you don't pester him too much. He's a guest, after all, and still recovering from his injuries. Now, let's decide on a song for tonight."

~

*R*eed stood on the front porch, trying to decide what his next move would be. He was here to find the truth about the boy. His gut told him Toby was Jon's son, but he wanted some further, more substantial proof. So far he knew two things for certain. One, the boy bore a strong physical resemblance to the Wilders. And two, the father Miss Ames had described to Toby couldn't be anyone but Jonathan. Good signs that Reed wouldn't be going home empty-handed.

The problem was, much as it galled him to admit it, he still owed Miss Ames a debt. No matter what her motives might have been, she'd saved his life. He needed to repay her somehow, erase his indebtedness. And it would be easier if he took care of that matter before he announced his reason for being here.

Unbidden, he saw her in his mind, combing out her siren's tresses unaware of his presence. Reed didn't try to fool himself; he was attracted to her. It couldn't go anywhere of course. Yet, he hadn't experienced that particular tug with such force in quite some time, and he felt thrown off balance by it.

A few minutes later, as he slipped back into the kitchen, Reed pulled up short. He could hear her singing the soft strains of a hymn.

He stood in the hall, caressed by the sweetness of her voice, and didn't move until the last strains died away.

It was difficult to reconcile this seeming Madonna with the schemer he knew her to be. But perhaps it was worth investing a few days to figure it out.

CHAPTER 9

*T*he next morning, Lucy sat on the back porch, snapping beans and letting her mind drift.

"Mind if I join you? I could use a bit of company."

She started, momentarily breaking the rhythm of her movements. Mr. Wilder stood over her with a cup of coffee in his hand and a smile on his face. She'd been caught daydreaming by the very the subject of her daydream. Returning his smile, she hoped he'd missed her reaction to his arrival. "Not at all."

Lucy scooted over as Mr. Wilder joined her on the step. He stretched his injured leg out and sipped his coffee, watching the movements of her hands as she resumed her work.

After a few moments Lucy relaxed. This morning he seemed his friendly self again. There were no signs of that difference, that tension in him, she'd noted yesterday afternoon. Perhaps it had just been her imagination after all.

They sat without talking, the only sounds being the crisp snap of the beans, the soft plop as she dropped them in the pan, and the moist sounds of his sips from the cup.

Gradually, Lucy felt a subtle tension build in her, a reaction to his closeness and his silence. When she couldn't stand it any longer, she broke the silence. "I want to thank you for your kindness to Toby. He's only had me and Mother in his life till now. I know he enjoys the time you spend with him."

He met her gaze with a wry smile. "No, it's I who should thank you for the excellent care and hospitality you've shown me. I'm well on my way to recovery, thanks to you. In fact, I'm ready for a bit more activity than I've had the past few days."

So, that was what was on his mind. He felt better now and was ready to move on. She'd been expecting this, just not how sharp a reaction she would have. It was a curious thing how quickly Mr. Wilder had fit himself into their small family.

"I imagine you're eager to return to whatever business took you out this way." Lucy was pleased to find her voice sounded matter-of-fact, with no trace of the letdown she felt.

But he shook his head. "No, not at all. Thing is, I just wouldn't feel right leaving before I've found a way to repay the debt I owe you. I'm afraid I don't have much money on me, so I thought of another way to show my gratitude."

"Please, that's not necessary." Lucy shifted in her seat, uncomfortable with such determined gratitude. "To be honest, you've provided a welcome bit of excitement to our routine existence. Consider that repayment enough."

"Come now, that's hardly a fair exchange. I'll admit I'm not up to full strength yet, but I can do light work." He stared at her resolutely. "What I'd like to propose is that I stay on for a while and help out where I can. I couldn't help but notice that you could use the services of a handyman around here."

Then, as she began to protest, "Please, allow me to do this. It would mean a lot to me. I wouldn't feel right about things otherwise. Just give me two weeks to assuage my conscience. If you're uncomfortable having a stranger in the house, I could move my things into the barn."

Lucy wasn't at all sure that his proposal was such a good idea, especially since she felt so tempted to say yes. And what of Toby? He was already forming a strong attachment to their guest.

Extending Mr. Wilder's stay would only make the parting harder on the boy.

She busied herself picking some trash out of the beans while she thought through her next words. Now that he was back on his feet, it was time to give Mr. Wilder the information she'd held back. After that, the question might well be moot.

Lucy squared her shoulders, took a deep breath and turned to face him. "It occurs to me that I never did properly introduce myself to you. My name is Lucy Ames."

She waited, not sure what sort of reaction she'd get. But she couldn't spot even a flicker of surprise or recognition on his face.

"Glad to formally make your acquaintance, Mrs. Ames. Now, please say you'll allow me to do this for you."

Lucy blinked. He hadn't recognized her name. So, maybe she wasn't the Lucy named in his report after all. She still had another disclosure to make, though, one much more difficult to deliver. "It's Miss."

This time he did look surprised. "I beg your pardon?"

Lucy lifted her chin and braced herself for the sting of rejection that was sure to follow. "It's Miss Ames, not Mrs."

"I see." His expression turned thoughtful but not judgmental. "Very well then, Miss Ames, I'm still waiting on your answer."

She frowned. Didn't he understand the implications of what she'd said? Dare she hope he was the kind of man who didn't rush to judge others? Or was it only that he didn't care, or that his sense of obligation was strong enough to overcome his distaste?

Well, as long as she was clearing her conscience, she might as well get it all out. "I have another confession to make."

He raised an eyebrow. "Yes?"

"That page from the report you were carrying, the one Toby managed to rescue for you. I read part of it."

She detected a sudden wariness about him now, and something else, probably irritation at her invasion of his privacy. "It was mostly illegible," she confessed, eager to get it over with. "But I did read the letterhead. I know you work for a detective agency."

He sat there a long moment, just watching her, his expression unreadable. "And does that bother you?" he finally asked.

"Oh no." She was appalled he'd think her so shallow after he'd accepted her own, more severe, social stigma. "I'm sure you conduct yourself with honor. And it's really none of my business anyway. I just wanted you to know that I knew. I hope you'll forgive my prying."

He nodded. "Given all I owe you, I imagine I can forgive so small an infraction." He smiled, but Lucy wasn't fooled. She could tell from his eyes that this last admission bothered him more than the first two.

"Now, back to my offer," he continued. "Since my profession doesn't put you off, can I assume you'll agree to let me repay some part of my debt?"

Mr. Wilder was as stubborn as he was honorable. But she couldn't let herself take advantage of his integrity. "This really isn't necessary, you know," she said, trying to give him a graceful way out.

"Yes, it is." His words were softly spoken, but firm.

And in a sudden flash of insight, she understood that he meant it. He needed to do this, to satisfy his own code of honor. She would not be sparing him by saying no.

"Very well, Mr. Wilder," she said impulsively. "If you're so intent on doing this, I will allow it, but you have to promise to set a reasonable pace. I don't want you reinjuring yourself."

He gave her a smile, tinged with some of that annoyance she'd come to expect whenever she brought up his injuries. Before he could say anything, she added, "And I won't hear of you moving into the barn. You're still favoring that left leg, so it would be best if you didn't try to climb the ladder to the loft. I appreciate your consideration, but it's not necessary. We seldom have visitors, and those who want to think the worse won't let the fact that you sleep in the barn stop them."

He raised an eyebrow, then nodded. "Thank you. I promise to make myself so useful you'll wonder how you ever got along without me."

And that, Lucy thought as she rose and moved into the kitchen, *is exactly what I'm afraid of.*

~

*R*eed watched her go, her pot of beans perched on one hip. He plucked a long blade of still-dewy grass from the ground at his feet as he sorted through his ambivalent feelings.

He'd lain awake for quite some time last night, working through this plan in his mind. It meant he'd be staying here about a week longer than he'd planned, and that was assuming he left with Toby as soon as his two weeks in her service were up. But he could still make this work. It wouldn't give him quite as much time to study the final contract on the Claymore deal when he returned, but he was used to pushing himself.

Besides, he couldn't do less and still feel he'd repaid her. Not that this would clear the debt altogether, but he planned to make some sort of financial arrangement with her after he explained just what he was here for.

Her assumption that he was a detective had startled him, but would account for some of the wariness he'd noted in her earlier, especially given her background. He wound the strand of grass around his finger, weighing pros and cons, and finally decided not to disabuse her of the notion. It would save him from having to explain why he carried a detective's report with him. He didn't think she'd deciphered any other information from that sheet of paper. He himself had only given it a cursory look, and then tossed it away as useless.

Her name, though, had been offered defiantly, as if she expected it to mean something to him. Had she seen more of the report than she'd admitted to? Or was it just concern that news of her notoriety had already reached his ears?

She wasn't trying to hide her sins from him, though, at least not any longer. She admitted her marital status without apology. But she'd braced herself, as if for a blow. He'd momentarily felt some admiration for her bravery and honesty.

Then he remembered who he was dealing with. He whipped the blade of grass from between his fingers, and sliced open a stinging cut in the process. Sourly, he compared Miss Ames' innocent appearance to the innocuous-seeming strand of grass. Both posed hidden dangers for the unwary.

She sure was good in the role of wronged innocent though. And it was galling to realize that he was so gullible, so weak, that he would let himself be attracted to such a woman.

Her brazen admission was consistent with the image he'd had of Lucy Ames, but it was the only piece of the puzzle that was. A petite brunette rather than a leggy blond, spirited rather than clingy and simpering, straightforward and confident rather than coy and flirtatious. No, she was a far cry from what he'd expected. And despite all he knew about her, he still felt that irritatingly strong tug of attraction.

Small comfort to realize that he wasn't the only Wilder who'd been tempted by her. But he was resisting the urge to act on it. How could his stronger, older brother, who'd had a loving wife by his side, have done less? *Blast it all, Jon, I always considered you a man of honor. What did this woman do to you? And will she try to work the same on me?*

He sucked a drop of blood from his finger, tossing the grass aside in disgust. He'd make himself useful around here for the next couple of weeks. He'd tackle every bit of work he could find to do on the place. Then he'd take care of the business he'd come for and get away from here, his newly-found nephew in tow.

❧

"*L*ook, I'm riding him, Ma, I'm riding Ranger!"

Lucy tried not to cringe as Toby lifted one hand from the pommel to wave enthusiastically. Toby and Mr. Wilder had made a very effective pair of petitioners, one looking at her with his heart in his eyes, and the other authoritatively assuring her that there was nothing to worry about. Lucy had finally agreed to the riding lesson, though not without some trepidation. True, Toby was handy with animals, but Ranger looked so *big*, and the boy had never been astride anything more formidable than Moses before. However, Mr. Wilder stayed close to the animal's side and seemed to have things well in hand.

After a few more turns around the yard, Mr. Wilder led Ranger right up to the front porch and Lucy was persuaded to pet the horse's nose.

Toby's expression had a glow about it that Lucy hadn't seen in a long time. "Isn't he just the finest horse you ever did see Ma?" He reached down and patted the horse's neck.

She bit her tongue against the warnings she wanted to give him, and smiled instead. "He is that."

Unaware of Lucy's inner struggle, Toby turned to their guest with an ingenious expression. "How fast can he really go?"

Lucy shot Mr. Wilder a warning look and saw his lips twitch before he answered Toby solemnly. "Practically flies when I let him go full out."

Toby's expression turned hopeful. "Do you think I might be able to take a real, flat-out gallop on him sometime?"

That was too much for Lucy. "Now, Toby," she started to admonish, but Mr. Wilder interrupted.

"I'll tell you what," he said. "If your ma will allow me, I'll get up behind you and take you for a quick run down the road and back."

Toby jumped on this compromise. "Oh Ma, could we, please?"

Lucy's jaw clenched. Mr. Wilder was doing it again, challenging the limits she set for Toby, and she had a feeling he knew it. Perhaps he thought she was overprotective? She tossed her head. Even if she was, it was none of his business.

On the other hand, looking at Toby's eager expression, and knowing deep down that he really would be all right as long as Mr. Wilder rode with him, she couldn't bring herself to refuse. "Oh very well, but just a short ride. Mr. Wilder, I trust you'll be careful. And, Toby, make sure you hold on with both hands, please."

A face-splitting smile rewarded her concession. "Thanks! I'll be careful, promise."

Lucy took the cane as Mr. Wilder climbed up behind Toby and gathered the reins. Then, tossing her a reassuring smile, he turned the horse onto the road. She watched them trot away, looking carefree and liberated. Despite her trepidation, she couldn't help but envy the picture they made.

They turned back just before the road curved out of sight, for which she was grateful. Toby caught sight of her and waved, and she raised her arm in return. A moment later she watched as he looked up to say something to Mr. Wilder, and Mr. Wilder threw back his head and laughed.

Slowly, Lucy lowered her arm and felt her vision blur. Toby deserved more than a few stolen moments of such happiness, such fatherly attention. Had it been arrogant and selfish of her to have denied him what Lowell offered, simply because it would force her to swallow her pride and deny her own dreams?

Toby's cheeks were flushed and his eyes were shining as they rode back into the yard. "Did you see us Ma? Wasn't that something? I've never felt so grand in my whole life."

Lucy nodded, still disturbed by her earlier thoughts. She gave herself a mental shake, pushed away from the post, and smiled. "Absolutely grand. But I think that's enough for now."

Toby raised his voice in protest. "But—"

"Don't argue with your ma, Toby. Let's get Ranger back to the barn and you can help me brush him down."

Lucy watched the two of them move away, not sure whether to be pleased or bothered by Mr. Wilder's continued efforts to take a hand in providing discipline and guidance for Toby.

CHAPTER 10

*R*eed found that things quickly settled into a routine of sorts. The day started with a hearty breakfast, and then they scattered, Miss Ames and Toby to their chores, Reed to his self-assigned tasks. He drove himself, seeking out the toughest, dirtiest jobs he could find. He was determined to do his utmost to pay the debt he owed this woman, to mitigate any advantage she'd have over him when he confronted her about Toby.

Around noon, they gathered again in the kitchen for lunch. Afterwards, Miss Ames disappeared into her room while Reed worked with Toby on his lessons. More often than not, he'd reward Toby's efforts by giving him a riding lesson while Miss Ames prepared supper.

In the evenings, he and Toby played checkers while Miss Ames worked on mending or played a soft tune on the piano. Sometimes, though, Toby would practice his reading or play with Jasper while the two adults chatted or squared off in a game of chess.

Later Reed would soak in one of those herbal baths while he listened to his hostess sing a lullaby to Toby down the hall.

It was this time of day, these quiet, gentle, shared evenings that unsettled Reed the most. Despite his efforts to reason the attraction away, he continued to catch himself watching her with a fondness that was foreign to him. And it was becoming more than a physical attraction. Her intelligence, her seeming courage and compassion, tugged at him as well, whispered that he was mistaken about her character.

Not that he'd let things go any further. Reed reminded himself several times a day just what sort of woman he was dealing with. Knowing she'd not only succeeded in seducing Jon but had stolen the ring only added to his resolve to resist her.

On Thursday morning, Reed thought of an additional way he could help even the scales with the Lady Samaritan. He waited until Toby was otherwise occupied to broach the subject.

"I realize I must be putting a strain on your provisions. I'd like to do something to supplement your larder if I could."

She stiffened, drying her hands on a dishrag as her brows drew down over those lioness eyes of hers. "That's not necessary. I know our meals aren't fancy, but they're filling and nourishing, and we're happy to share with you. You're already doing more than enough to earn your keep."

Reed realized he'd ruffled her feathers, again. He noticed that seemed to happen whenever he intimated she might need help with something. Stretching the noble survivor act a bit too far, in his estimation. After all, a woman who would accept rent money from her married lover and steal from a grieving widow shouldn't be too proud to accept a handout.

But he wasn't supposed to know about her past, so he played along. Spreading his hands, he gave her a placating smile. "I didn't mean to disparage your meals. The food's excellent. I was just thinking, though, that I could add some meat to your table if I had my rifle back."

She stared at him, her face closed, the warmth he'd come to count on from her, missing. Didn't she trust him? And why did the thought that she might not bother him so much?

After a pause, he shrugged. "If the idea makes you uncomfortable, please forget I asked." He moved toward the door. "I plan to work on the front fence today. I'll try to be careful of your roses, but you might end up with a few broken stems." Reed kept his voice light. He knew her caution was reasonable, but still he was disappointed.

"Just a minute." She left the room, returning a few minutes later carrying both his hunting rifle and his pistol. Without saying a word, she handed them over to him.

So why had she changed her mind? What was she up to now? "Thank you. I appreciate the fact that you trust me with these."

"I feel that my trust isn't misplaced." Then, as if regretting the softly uttered words, she squared her shoulders. "Besides, I know that if you wanted to harm me or Toby, you wouldn't need guns to do it. I only ask that you keep them away from Toby. He's been taught to respect firearms, but I'd rather not put temptation in his way."

Before he could do more than nod agreement, Toby charged through the door, skidding to a halt when he saw what Reed held. "Hey, what do you have the guns out for?"

"I'm going hunting. Maybe I can scare up some game for lunch."

Toby's eyes brightened. "Can I come along?"

Reed saw Lucy's look and, mindful of her earlier request, intervened before she could say anything. "Not this time. But I tell you what, I saw a couple of cane poles in the barn. I thought you and I might try to catch a few fish from that pond of yours later."

Toby's disappointed pout turned immediately into a smile. "Great! When can we go?"

As he and Toby made their plans, Reed allowed himself to wonder again why her trust had seemed so important to him. And with a gut-lurching sense of guilt, he realized that he should be building walls, not tearing them down. Because in less than two weeks time, he would betray the very trust she'd just extended, when he made his family's claim on her son.

~

*L*ucy watched the two of them head outside, and sighed. The more she learned of Mr. Wilder, the more difficult it became to keep up her guard. He'd worked so hard these past few days despite his still healing injuries. Then this morning he decided he no longer needed to use the cane, and insisted on moving his sleeping quarters to the barn loft. He said he felt guilty taking over Toby's room, but Lucy suspected it had at least as much to do with his concern for the proprieties.

That he continued to treat her as a lady, despite her admission of not being a widow, warmed her as nothing had in quite some time.

~

*R*eed was less than pleased with the results of his hunt. "I'm afraid I only bagged two rabbits. But I saw signs of deer, and I'll try again tomorrow."

Lucy wiped her hands on her apron and smiled as he plopped his offering in the sink. "You're being too modest. Two rabbits will make a fine meal. No point bringing in more than we can eat."

The afternoon brought a rain shower, postponing the fishing expedition. Reed gave Toby some simple math problems to work through, and then wandered out to the front porch with the idea of taking a look at the broken swing. There he found Lucy, attempting to repair a loose porch rail.

"Here, let me have that." He took the hammer, and squatted beside her on the solidly planked floor. "That's my job now, remember?"

She smiled and straightened, dusting her hands against each other. "Thanks. I wanted to fix that before Toby leaned against it and fell."

As Reed worked, he was acutely aware of her standing behind him. He felt her eyes boring into his back, heard the rustle of her skirts, inhaled the faint spicy scent of cinnamon that clung to her from her earlier baking efforts.

"Do you get to travel a lot?" she asked after a few minutes, her tone wistful.

Reed shrugged. "I generally stay pretty close to home, but I've seen my share of the country." Then he looked up, taking advantage of the opening she'd just handed him. "How about you? Have you ever traveled very far from this place?" He'd give a lot to hear her story from her perspective. Maybe it would help him untangle his feelings about her.

"Once. I spent a nearly year in New Orleans when I was nineteen." Then her lips compressed, as if she wanted to unsay the words.

"New Orleans! Now that's a far sight from this corner of Texas, and in more than distance. What took you down there?"

"A job. But about—"

He cut across her words, pretending to miss her attempt to change the subject. "Must have been quite a job to take you so far away."

He watched as she carefully formed her reply. "It was a chance to work with one of the finest dressmakers in the country. I had ambitions of becoming a designer myself. Besides, I was as interested in the chance to see a part of the world outside Far Enough as I was to accept the job itself."

Reed cocked his head to one side, careful to display only friendly curiosity. How far could he press her? How much would she admit to? "So why did you come back? Was the outside world not what you expected?" Or did she run back home once her lover, her source of "extra income," died and left her carrying his child?

She shook her head. "No, it wasn't that. Mother needed me, so here I am."

He felt a small twinge of conscience at the sadness he saw in her eyes. Then he tamped it down. It could merely signify she missed her old life.

That thought drove his next question. "Is that where you met

Toby's father?" He immediately wished the question back, or at least the unintended harshness of his tone.

She stiffened and flinched, a hot flush of color rising in her cheeks. Her fists clenched at her sides as tension seemed to thrum through her. Then her countenance smoothed into an expression of reserved politeness. "Excuse me. I need to start supper." Her voice held no inflection whatsoever.

Reed took her wrist before she could move away. "I'm sorry. That was unforgivably rude of me. Please don't go just yet."

Her expression didn't soften. "Don't worry, Mr. Wilder. You're not the first to let your curiosity get in the way of your manners. It hardly bothers me at all anymore." She tossed her head back. "Now, if you'll excuse me, I do need to get supper started."

This time he let her go.

~

*L*ucy braced her hands against the kitchen sink, and hung her head. It had been years since anyone slipped past her defenses enough to make her feel her disgrace so keenly. It wasn't just the question he'd asked, but the speculative, calculating look that accompanied it.

It always came back to this vulgar curiosity, fascination almost, about her "wicked indiscretion." No matter how much time passed, no matter how proper and disciplined she tried to be, people wouldn't let her forget her status as a fallen woman. She'd been foolish to forget that herself, to let her emotional guard down, even for a minute. Naive of her to think that Mr. Wilder, a relative stranger, would be less judgmental than the people she grew up with.

She moved one of her hands, laying the palm against the bodice of her dress, trying to draw comfort from the locket, to tap into the feeling of closeness to her mother it had brought her in the past. But today all she felt was her own bitter disappointment. It had just been so nice to have the illusion of a friendship unmarred by her questionable past. Well, she knew better now, and would just have to see that she didn't let her guard down again.

She straightened. Lowell was right, she was foolish to even dream of ever being respectfully courted. Only respectable women with their reputations still intact deserved such consideration.

～

*R*eed pounded the nail viciously. Why in the world did he feel as if he'd just plucked the wings from a butterfly? Lucy Ames was no sweet innocent. She was a thief and an unwed mother.

Problem was, he was having a hard time remembering that. Lately his struggle to maintain a polite, non-antagonistic facade had turned into an effort to remember his righteous anger. What had happened to his ability to be dispassionate, to distance himself from emotions and take a purely businesslike approach to solving problems? He *knew* what kind of woman she was, it was all spelled out there in Dobbs' report.

Well, if he had to entertain emotions, he'd do well to concentrate on the satisfaction he'd get from seeing the look on his father's face when he delivered Toby to him. The family patriarch would view the discovery of this grandson, Jon's son, as a greater achievement than all the work Reed had done to salvage Wilder Enterprises. His father would be proud of him.

And that was worth a whole lot more than the sensibilities of the woman who'd thrown herself at his married brother.

CHAPTER 11

*R*eed was ready to put his fist through a wall. Ever since his graceless prodding yesterday, the formerly warm Miss Ames had been excruciatingly polite, but as distant as the moon. There'd been no small talk, no lingering glances, no smiles that invited his response. She maintained a brisk, impersonal air, interacting with him only when absolutely necessary.

He'd already decided that a businesslike relationship was what he needed to cultivate with Miss Ames, was what would serve him best when the time came to confront her with who he was and why he'd come. So how come he missed her open friendliness so much?

Almost without knowing how, Reed found himself in the garden, watching her pick beans. She wasn't wearing her hat today, and she was flushed from the heat of the sun. Stray tendrils of hair had escaped the confines of her bun and curled at the nape of her neck. As always, she carried herself with a quiet grace and dignity that was a pleasure to watch.

He stood there, inhaling the green earthy scents, listening to her rustling progress along the row, waiting for her to notice him. She, however, seemed to be studiously ignoring his presence.

Finally, he marched forward, irritated that she'd left him to make the first move. He reached for the bucket she carried. "Here, let me hold that for you."

She looked as if she would refuse. Then, with a shrug, handed it over. Snapping another handful of beans from the bushy vine in front of her, she dropped them into the bucket and moved down a step. They worked in silence for several minutes. Reed was at a loss as to what to say to her, and she remained stubbornly silent, offering no help to his dilemma. A bark caught his attention, and he glanced toward the house to see Toby and Jasper playing their toss and fetch game.

Remembering how talk of Toby always softened her attitude, he finally broke the silence.

"Toby's lessons are going well. He's a sharp youngster. You've every right to be proud of him."

Her eyes followed his to the boy and dog. "I don't know what I'd do without him."

Reed felt a stab of guilt at her softly uttered words. Taking the boy away from her was the right thing to do, but he was coming to believe he wouldn't find it as easy as he'd thought earlier. "Don't you have other family?"

She tucked a strand of hair behind her ear. "Oh, distant cousins of my mother's. They live in Virginia and I've never met them. My parents were both only children, like me, and their parents are long gone. What about you? You mentioned sisters the other day. Do you come from a large family?"

Reed accepted her turning the tables on him with good grace. At least she seemed more relaxed, more approachable now.

"Besides my three younger sisters, I had two older brothers."

"Had?" Her question and quick glance were soft with sympathy, as if she already knew what that word indicated.

"They're both dead now, as is my mother. Father's still alive though. In fact, he's still a very active sea captain."

"A sea captain!" She sounded impressed. "I can see why you ended up raising your sisters. If you were as good with them as you are with Toby, they were lucky to have you."

"I'm afraid they didn't quite see it that way." Reed realized from the expression on her face that he'd let some bitterness creep into his voice. But she held her silence, merely raising an eyebrow in unspoken question.

Reed almost changed the subject, but, guilty with the knowledge that he would soon be wresting her son from her, he found himself answering her question.

"The year I turned eighteen, the family business ran into some financial difficulties. My two older brothers were gone by that time and father found it necessary to return to full time duty as a ship's captain. I was never suited for life on board a ship, so I did what I could to salvage the financial end of the business and watch over my sisters."

Her expression turned thoughtful as she paused. "You were young to take on so much responsibility. It must have been difficult."

He shrugged. "Luckily I knew how to read and analyze the books and contracts. It took a lot of digging, a lot of planning, a lot of time, and I made some mistakes, but we pulled through. But I had to put some stringent restrictions on the family's personal spending, even sold off part of our operations along with a number of heirlooms. There were some heated objections from my sisters, and even some from my father. I was viewed as an unfeeling villain for a while. An older son's lot I suppose." Reed said this last lightly, realizing he'd betrayed more of himself than he'd intended.

But she didn't return his smile. "Your sisters were rather young at this time I imagine?"

Reed shifted the bucket to his other hand and rubbed the back of his neck. "Nine, twelve and fourteen."

She moved down the row apiece. "Yes, I can see how they would have rebelled against having their world turned upside down. It must have been hard on someone with your temperament to play the role of taskmaster and keeper of the purse strings."

Reed stopped in his tracks. "My temperament? Actually, handling ledgers and enforcing rules seems to be what I'm best suited for." Just what did she mean by that? Most people assumed those were *exactly* the right roles for him.

"Oh, I didn't mean to imply you wouldn't be good at it," she hastened to reassure him. "After all, you're tenacious and you seem to take your responsibilities quite seriously. I just meant I don't imagine you enjoyed the role."

"And just what would you know about my temperament or the sort of things I enjoy?" Reed didn't try to hide his irritation.

She withdrew from him at once, turning her attention back to the plants. "I'm sorry, I didn't mean to cause offense. I have a bad habit of speaking impulsively. Let's talk of something else, shall we?"

But he wasn't ready to let it go. Moderating his tone, Reed tried again. "I'm not offended. I'd just like to hear what you think you've discerned about me on such short acquaintance."

She looked up, her expression guarded. "No, I was out of line. You're right. I haven't known you very long, after all."

Was she deliberately trying to annoy him? "Come now, it's not like you to be coy. Just tell me what you think you know."

She shot him a sideways look and then sighed, pausing to look at him straight on. "Very well. But remember, you asked."

Reed swatted a deerfly away from his face as he watched her gather her thoughts.

Her brow wrinkled in concentration. "Let's see if I can explain this. I can tell from watching you with Toby that you have patience. You also avoid talking down to him, which shows you have an innate respect for the dignity and capabilities of others. From the way you tried to shrug off my ministrations, it's obvious you're an independent sort, with more than just a touch of male pride. You've made good on your offers to help around here, despite your injuries, so I can tell you believe strongly in paying your own way."

She moved down the row apiece as she continued, "Now then, as far as the physical goes, you have enough strength to master an animal like Ranger. That's not the horse of a timid or weak man.

And, as I've already observed for myself, you know how to handle yourself in a fight."

Reed snorted. "You seem to have a faulty memory. I lost my last fight rather spectacularly, if you'll recall."

She flashed him an *I-know-better-than-that* smile. "The Jeffersons may have had the upper hand in that fight, but they had numbers and surprise on their side, and still they wore enough marks to prove you held your own for a while.

"Now, if I may continue." She raised an eyebrow in mock severity. "I'd say, despite the fact that you seem to drive yourself rather hard, and can't tolerate any signs of self-weakness, you are a man of intelligence, spirit, courage and, when called for, action. You enjoy working with both your mind and your hands. It couldn't have been easy for you to be the one to stay at home and pull the reins in on everyone else. But you did what needed to be done, and it sounds to me like you got very little thanks for the effort."

Reed gave a harsh laugh. "Most people who know me would disagree with your assessment."

She shrugged. "You asked me what I saw in you, and I told you. I may very well be wrong, but I don't think so."

Perversely driven to prove to her just *how* wrong she was, Reed countered in acid tones. "Let me explain something to you. My family takes a great deal of pride in the legends that paint my great-grandfather as a notorious pirate. The Wilders are known for being outrageous and flamboyant, even the women. Take my sisters; one's a writer, one's an artist, and the youngest is getting ready to join her soon-to-be-husband on a world concert tour. It's a given that the Wilders are all spirited, dashing figures. All except for me, that is. I'm considered an atypical Wilder."

Reed spread his hands in a sharp movement to emphasize his words. "And as if that's not bad enough, I didn't even have the grace to be an acceptable sailor. The Wilder men have *always* been seamen. Until me. And do you know why I'm not? Because I get seasick! Literally, green to the gills, emptying my stomach over the sides, legs can't hold me up, sick. Not an admirable quality in a family of sailors. So I handle the family's business matters. I'm afraid the best my family can say about me is that I'm good at dealing with ledgers."

He stopped talking and clenched his jaw. Now why had he said all of that? It was almost as if he'd been goaded into his revelations, even if he couldn't pinpoint what she'd done to make him feel that way. She'd stood there, looking so sure of her assessment, so approving and confident of his character. All at once, it had seemed very important that he prove to her just how wrong she was.

And apparently he'd succeeded. Because now she wouldn't even look at him. For several minutes she just walked down the row, picking beans, her eyes focused on her work. Reed had reached the point of saying something, anything, just to break the silence, when she spoke up. But rather than remarking on what he'd said, she took the conversation off on a tangent.

"My family life wasn't always like what you see today. When I was growing up, we lived in a big white house on a hill at the edge of town. Father was the sheriff. He was a wonderful man, and physically very impressive."

She shot him a dreamy grin. "I wish you could have met him. He stood about six foot three, and was strong and burly. He wasn't a violent man, but he could shoot a gun faster and truer than any other man in these parts. He also won the log splitting contest at the county fair almost every year, if that gives you some idea of his physical strength."

She turned back to her work, methodically dropping beans into the dented metal pail. "But it wasn't just his strength and skill with a gun that impressed folks, he was intelligent and generous too. The neighbors knew if they ever had a need, they could turn to either of my parents and find help."

Why the sudden change of subject? Had his confession made her uncomfortable, or was she trying to reciprocate by giving him a personal insight into her own life?

"Sounds like a father to be proud of," he said when he realized she'd paused.

She nodded. "True, but Daddy wasn't perfect. In fact, he harbored a rather shameful secret. I've seen him face down an angry mob bent on carrying out an injustice, and I've seen him go into a burning building to rescue a trapped child. But he was afraid of snakes." She paused and cocked her head. "Can you imagine? He couldn't get within six feet of one without turning white as a sheet, even useful, harmless ones like king snakes. Sort of the way I am with spiders. But he was a man, and men are supposed to be above that sort of thing."

With a shrug, her hands resumed their movements. "Now, I know snakes wouldn't be much of a problem in a big city like you're likely used to, but here in the country they're unavoidable. Of course, most of them are harmless, but that didn't matter to Daddy. Mother and I loved him anyway. We protected his feelings as best we could. Whenever we saw a snake, one of us would take care of it and not say a word. Of course, folks found out, and he took some good-natured teasing about it. Some even called him a coward.

"Do you think my daddy was a coward Mr. Wilder?" She kept her face averted and there was a touch of vulnerability just below the nonchalance of her tone.

Reed felt a sudden urge to reassure her and placed a hand on her arm. "Of course not. We all posses some weakness. It's what makes us human and keeps us humble. What matters is how we respond to our fallibilities. Your father sounds like a good and decent man."

They reached the end of the last row, and Lucy reached for the bucket, her eyes finally meeting his. To his surprise, he saw no vulnerability there, no gratitude for his understanding. Instead he found himself regarded with a calm, steady gaze that seemed to see straight through to his soul.

"I agree," she said pointedly. "One failing or frailty does not cancel out all the other good qualities we possess. And being afraid of snakes is as inconsequential in the scheme of what makes a man, as being prone to seasickness, don't you agree?"

Without a backward glance, she walked past him toward the house.

Reed, caught off guard by her words, watched her go. How in the world could this slip of a backwoods country girl continue to surprise him? Not that her words were particularly insightful. She had woefully misinterpreted his character, seeing a nobility in him that didn't exist. He certainly wasn't the man she painted him to be. Still, it felt sort of nice to think she saw him that way.

Then he frowned as doubts assailed him. She could have said those things just to flatter him, maybe hoping for a larger reward when he took his leave. He couldn't, wouldn't, let his attraction to the woman make him vulnerable to such manipulation.

At least she was thawing a bit. He could enjoy her company without succumbing to her charms.

Couldn't he?

$\sim$

*A*fter supper, Reed invited Lucy to try out the newly repaired porch swing.

Toby seconded the idea. "Come on, Ma. It works as good as new. Even better, cause now it doesn't squeak like it used to."

With only a little coaxing, Lucy allowed herself to be persuaded. She ruffled Toby's hair as they moved to the porch. "Mr. Wilder's proving to be a lucky find for us, isn't he?"

Reed held the door open for them and returned her smile. "The luck was mine, I believe."

His smile kindled a warm feeling inside her. When he sat beside her and set the swing in motion, Lucy felt a sense of rightness that was both pleasant and faintly unsettling. The man sure knew how to breach her defenses!

For the next thirty minutes, Lucy sat beside him, swinging back and forth in gentle rhythm while they talked comfortably of inconsequential things. Toby and Jasper chased fireflies and sticks, and rolled on the ground in mock battle, providing a pleasant, safe focus for their attention.

Later, when Lucy sent Toby scooting to get ready for bed, she and Reed stood on the porch a minute longer, studying the night sky. She watched him surreptitiously, and again that feeling of rightness stole over her. She was honest enough to recognize part of it as a longing for connection, but there was more to it than that. Finally, she put a name to it.

Family. They felt like a real family tonight.

"I want to thank you for everything you've done for us," she said softly.

Reed looked down with an intensity in his gaze that triggered a warm fluttering inside her.

He laid a hand over hers on the porch rail. "No need for thanks. Right now I'm where I want to be, doing what I want to do."

His words, and the way he said them, brought an unexpected lump to her throat. The touch of his hand on hers only intensified the feelings churning within her. Like the time she found him watching as she dried her hair, she felt breathless, expectant and altogether strange.

Suddenly afraid of those feelings, Lucy strove to recover her composure. He would be leaving soon and it would be foolish and heartbreaking for her to believe otherwise. How could she so quickly forget the resolve she'd made only yesterday?

Lucy slipped her hand away from his, and didn't quite meet his gaze as she spoke. "I'd better get Toby tucked in. Everything's set out for your bath and the kettle of water is on the stove."

He nodded, his expression mirroring some of her own unsettled emotions. "Thanks. If you'll excuse me, I'll fetch my things and get to it."

∼

*T*hirty minutes later, Reed stepped outside, headed for the barn. The spontaneous words he'd uttered there on the porch had taken him by surprise. He was even more surprised to realize he'd meant them.

Turning back to the house before entering the barn, he noticed a light shining from Lucy's window. She'd burned her light late last night as well. He wondered if she was one of those people who liked to read a bit before they settled in for the night. As early as she rose and as hard as she worked, it didn't seem possible she would have trouble getting to sleep at night.

As he climbed the ladder to the barn loft, Reed found himself imagining what she must look like there in her room, sitting up in bed reading her book.

She'd have her hair down around her shoulders, he decided, like the other night when she sat combing it by the stove. Only it would be dry now, falling in long, silky waves. It would smell faintly of flowers like it always did right after she washed it. Snuggling against her neck would be like burying his face in a cloud of flower petals.

He settled down on his makeshift bed but didn't expect to get much sleep. But sometime later he woke abruptly with a feeling that something was wrong. It wasn't until he heard the sound again, though, that he realized what had roused him.

Someone was crying out in pain.

CHAPTER 12

*B*arely pausing to slip his pants on, Reed slid down the ladder and raced to the house. By the time he reached the hall, he knew the cries came from Toby's room. When he got there, he found Lucy bent over a writhing, tearful Toby. She stood massaging his calves and crooning a soft lullaby.

Reed halted beside her, wanting to help but not sure how. "What's wrong?" he asked softly.

Lucy paused her crooning long enough to answer. "Leg cramps."

"Can I help?"

She hesitated only a second. "Take his left leg and rub it. Just like I'm doing with his right."

Reed studied her movements for a moment and then, taking Toby's leg, began to imitate them. He could feel the tight, bunched muscles in the small legs under his fingers, and worked to ease their stiffness. The two adults kept up their efforts for a good ten minutes, working in near-perfect unison. The only sound was Lucy's soft, patient singing, and Toby's sobs, until, finally, the boy began to quiet and relax.

At last Lucy turned to Reed. "If you would stay with him and

121

continue the rubbing, I want to fix a cup of willow bark tea. It'll help him relax and go back to sleep."

"Of course." Reed gave her an encouraging smile and then shifted position as she stepped back. Laying a hand on each of Toby's legs, he continued the rhythmic movements as she left the room.

By the time Lucy returned, Toby looked sleepy. She sent Reed a warm smile for his efforts as she moved to the head of the bed. Placing an arm under the boy's shoulder, she lifted his head and gently coaxed him into drinking the tea.

"There now," she said, laying him down again, "how do you feel?"

Toby managed a weak smile. "Better. I'm sorry I woke you up. I didn't want to, but it just hurt so bad."

Lucy smoothed a lock of hair from his forehead. "Now don't you worry about that. That's what I'm here for. Don't you ever feel bad about calling me when you need me."

"Thanks, Ma." Then he looked across at Reed, and his face took on an uncomfortably embarrassed expression. "I suppose you think I'm just an old cry baby."

Reed, understanding Toby's self-consciousness and seeking to ease it, smiled sympathetically. "Not at all. Sometimes you get in a fix where you just have to let someone else help you out. Look at how I was when I got beat up the other day. Didn't you say your ma sat up with me the whole night?"

Toby thought about that, and his spirits seemed to improve. He snuggled down under the covers and soon fell sound asleep.

Glancing away from the sleeping boy, Lucy signaled for Reed to follow her out into the hall.

"Thank you, Mr. Wilder. It would have taken me much longer to settle him down without your help."

He eased the door closed behind him and raised an inquisitive eyebrow. "Don't you think it's time we used first names? Mr. Wilder seems rather formal under the circumstances."

She looked startled at his suggestion, then gave him a slow, shy smile. "Very well. Thank you for your help, Reed."

Reed took a good look at her for the first time since their little midnight rescue operation started, and liked what he saw. She looked very much as he'd earlier imagined. Her hair, loose and tousled, fell in wavy disarray. She wore a high-collared, prim cotton nightdress, a pale blue color, worn and a bit too large, but it looked nice on her nonetheless.

Even as he noted how weary she looked, he selfishly decided he couldn't let her go off to bed again just yet. "Look, I think I could use another bite of that peach cobbler before I settle back down for the night. It would be nice to have a little company, if you'd care to join me?"

She hesitated, then smiled. "Very well, maybe just for a minute."

Lucy disappeared into her room for a few minutes and Reed took the opportunity to return to the barn and fetch a shirt. By the time he returned to the house, Lucy, now wrapped in a robe, was in the kitchen, brewing a pot of tea.

Without a word he moved to the counter and spooned up a serving of cobbler for each of them and set the saucers on the table. Then he grabbed a couple of cups and joined her at the stove. Lucy filled the cups with tea and then they each took a seat at the table.

As soon as they sat, Lucy took a nice long sip and then met his gaze gratefully. "How did I ever get along without you?"

Her eyes widened and her cheeks pinkened. "Oh my goodness, I'm so sorry. I must be more tired than I thought."

Reed smiled. "No need to apologize." Her slip had been a pleasant surprise, but he decided to ease her embarrassment by changing the subject. "Does Toby get like that often?"

Lucy took another sip of tea and by the time she responded she appeared to have regained her composure. "Not very. It's been about six months since he's had an attack this bad. He'll be okay in the morning, though, just tired."

"Why don't you let him sleep late? I can handle his morning chores."

"That's kind of you. And thank you again for your help. Not just with Toby's cramps, but the way you handled his feelings. He gets very down and embarrassed when this happens."

Reed shrugged. "He shouldn't be made to feel guilty for something that's not his fault."

"I wish the good people of Far Enough saw things that way."

Something in her voice made him think she was referring to more than Toby's leg cramps.

She sat up straighter. "Not that it matters very much," she added quickly. "Isolated the way we are here, we don't come into contact with the townsfolk very often."

Was she isolated by choice? Or was something else going on here?

He chose his next words carefully, wanting to keep her talking. "You said that you lived in New Orleans for a while. Did you like it there?"

She eyed him warily, but answered his question. "Uh-huh. It's a wonderful place." She smiled then, as if recalling fond memories. "Crowded and noisy perhaps, but there's so much energy there, so many things to see and do. And I learned so much from Madame Robicheaux."

"What did you like best?"

She waved a hand. "Mostly the people. I met some wonderful folks, made some very special friends."

Special friends? Like his brother? Reed decided it was contempt and not jealousy that stirred him.

But Lucy wasn't finished talking. "Before my time in New Orleans, I'd never dreamed there was so much out there, outside Far Enough I mean. The docks, the marketplace, the grand houses, the theaters, it was all new and magical and so much bigger and grander than I'd imagined."

"So why did you come back?"

"As I told you, my mother needed me." She glanced up at him from beneath her lashes. "There's more to it than that bald statement, of course. About a year after I left, my parents were involved in a train accident. My father was killed outright and Mother's legs were crushed. The funeral and medical bills took every bit of their savings, and then some. Without father's income, we had no way to pay our bills. Mother could no longer get around without help. Eventually we had to sell our nice house in the middle of town. Mr. Crowder, who owns this place, had a soft spot for Mother and let us live here. He also helped me learn to handle the livestock." She reached down and picked up her fork. "And that's how we ended up out here. Which is more of an explanation than what you asked for."

She smiled but he saw the moisture in her eyes, saw the slight tremble in her hands.

Almost without thinking, Reed reached across the table and took her hand and gave it a comforting squeeze. "I'm so sorry. That must have been a difficult time for you."

She stiffened and drew her hand away. Without looking up, she traced the rim of her cup with one finger. "It was harder on Mother." She shrugged. "I'd been on my own for a while, so I'd learned how to make do for myself." She flashed him a smile that he didn't quite believe. "At any rate, we made it. And Toby and I are still making it."

Reed could sense she was tying to shake off his sympathy, to pretend she was all right with the way things were. But he saw the pain beneath the façade. And that struck a chord with him, touched him in a way he couldn't quite explain.

Impulsively, he stood and moved around to her side of the table, taking hold of her hands. He pulled her to her feet, and studied her face. When he saw emotion there, the vulnerability and sweet courage, he felt an overwhelming urge to comfort her. Watching her face, he lowered his own, slowly to give her every opportunity to protest. When he saw her eyes widen and then her face lift in tacit permission, he pressed his lips to hers. It took all of his control not to deepen the kiss, to remind himself he was offering comfort, nothing more.

When he broke it off, he wrapped his arms around her in a gentle hug.

"I'm sorry you had to face all of that alone," he said softly.

She relaxed and leaned her head against his chest with a sigh.

Reed rubbed her back with gentle, circular motions, enjoying the feel of having her lean against him so trustingly. Perhaps he'd been wrong about her after all.

That thought brought him up short. What was he doing? He had to maintain his objectivity if he was going to take care of what he'd come to Texas to do.

Reed dropped his hand as if scalded and stepped back. He gave her a short bow, ignoring the confused look on her face. "Forgive me. It's been a long day. I think it best if I retire now." And with a curt nod, he turned and walked away.

$\sim$

*B*ewildered by the abrupt change from tender concern to cold rejection, Lucy felt as if her face had been slapped. With a hand to her throat, she stood there, staring at the doorway he'd just exited through. She hadn't asked for either the kiss or the hug, in fact had been startled by them. Not that she hadn't enjoyed it. It had been so very long since someone had showed her such tenderness and she'd wanted to simply soak it in.

Still, he was the one who'd initiated it. So why had he seemed so angry just now?

A hot flush crept up her cheeks as realization hit her. She had shamelessly allowed him to kiss her and then hold her with Toby sleeping right down the hall. Not only allowed him to, but had practically melted against him. Had he thought her actions too forward, wanton even?

No wonder he'd turned away.

She'd wanted that embrace, more than she'd wanted anything in a very long time. For just a little while she'd felt cherished and protected and worthy. Did wanting that make her wicked?

Lucy plopped back down in her chair, unable to stand any longer. She'd taken some measure of comfort these past six years, cold as that comfort had been, in knowing that her sordid reputation was unearned. Truth to tell, that knowledge made her feel righteous, like a noble martyr. But now...

Now, she'd not only compromised her vision of herself, but she'd no doubt lost Reed's respect in the process, a thought that turned her insides sour, and made her eyes sting.

Blinded by unshed tears, she reached again for the locket that wasn't there.

Oh Momma, what have I done? How do I fix it?

By the time she'd cleared the table, Lucy had herself back under control. Her best recourse was to carry on as if nothing had happened, and to make sure nothing like that happened again. After all, he'd only be here a few more days. And after tonight, it might be a shorter stay than expected.

⁓

*R*eed threw himself on his makeshift bed and flung an arm over his eyes. Still seeing the stricken, wounded look in Lucy's eyes as he'd turned and fled, he reviled himself for a fool. Whether that look was real or feigned didn't matter. The fact that she wasn't a maiden was also beside the point. There was just no excuse for his conduct. He, who prided himself on his pragmatic outlook and rational behavior, had taken advantage of the woman in her own kitchen, not more than a stone's throw from where her six-year-old son lay sleeping.

What was the matter with him? How could he be so attracted to anyone, much less the kind of woman he believed Lucy Ames to be, that it shot his judgment and control all to pieces?

Reed groaned and rolled over again. He could understand now why Jonathan had found her so hard to resist. But that was no excuse. He pounded a fist against the bedding.

Thunderation Jon, what did you do it for? You left the family, left me to pick up the pieces, then you cheated on Iris with this woman. This woman I could let myself feel —

He stopped that thought before it could go any further, turning his mind firmly in another direction.

Had Lucy loved Jon, or was it more a matter of passion and lust? How did she feel now? Did she regret her fall from grace? If Jon had lived would she still be with him? It was becoming increasingly important to him that he learn exactly what her and Jon's relationship had been based on.

And the fact that it *had* become so important was just one more intolerable aspect to this whole intolerable situation.

∾

*D*espite his intentions to the contrary, Reed found Lucy already up and about ahead of him the next morning.

And she'd been up for a while. Breakfast waited on the stove, cooked and ready to serve. She sat at the table, rhythmically shaking a large covered jar filled with some sort of white substance. It took him a minute to realize that she was churning fresh cream into butter.

Lucy glanced up but didn't quite meet his eyes before looking down again. "Good morning. Breakfast is on the stove if you don't mind serving yourself. I took your advice and let Toby sleep late this morning, so I'm running a little behind with the chores."

Her voice sounded pleasant enough but Reed noted the shadows around her eyes. "About last night—"

She cut him off before he could finish. "Yes, thank you again for your help with Toby and tactful kindness. You were wonderful."

"You're welcome. But I wanted to talk to you about—"

Again she interrupted. Her movements lacked their normal grace as she set the jar down, rose, and moved toward the hall. "Excuse me, Mr. Wilder, but I think Toby's slept long enough. You just go on with your breakfast while I see about getting him up."

And Lucy left before he could say more. It seemed she didn't plan to let him discuss the moment of intimacy they'd shared. It also seemed they were back to "Mr. Wilder."

With a frustrated sigh, Reed raked his fingers through his hair. For someone who prided himself on his control, he'd shown precious little of it these past few days.

Lucy managed to keep her distance the rest of the morning. Oh, she remained as polite as ever, but she maneuvered her activities so that she was never alone with him for more than a few seconds at a time.

Reed finally gave up the effort and headed for the barn, Toby at his heels. He'd noticed an old wagon stored there that looked like it needed some work.

He and Toby were still working on it when Lucy called them in to lunch.

"Mr. Wilder and I are fixing the wagon, Ma. When we get through, you won't have to walk into town anymore."

She looked from Toby to Reed in surprise. "Why, I thought that old thing was beyond any hope of repair. Do you really think you can make it serviceable again?"

Reed nodded as he helped Toby set the table. "The frame and body are basically sound, they just need a bit of securing and patching. A few new boards will make the seat good as new. The harness needs mending too, but I think I can handle it with the tools and materials I found in the barn. The wheel is your real problem. It'll require the attention of a wheelwright or a blacksmith. I noticed the barn roof needs some new shingles, too. Maybe I should plan a trip into town."

"That won't be necessary. You've done enough for us already."

From the stiffness of her tone, Reed could tell he'd said something wrong, but he wasn't quite sure what. "It's no trouble, I—"

Her chin jutted up a notch. "I don't have the funds for either a wheelwright's services or roofing materials."

He started to speak but she forestalled him with a raised hand. "Don't say it, please. I won't let you spend any money for repairs to this place. That responsibility is mine and the landlord's. If you need something that's not available around here, make me a list and I'll see what I can do next time I go to town. I've done without a buggy these past four months, I can do without one a good bit longer if I need to."

What was going on here? She hadn't been so particular about such things when his brother paid for her quarters in New Orleans. Still, she seemed so sincere, the very picture of a proud woman, determined to make her own way. Had she really changed so much? "Of course. I'm sure I can find something else to keep me busy." He'd find a way to fix that busted buggy, in spite of her objections. It wasn't only inconvenient but it was outright dangerous for her to be way out here without any sound means of transportation.

Lucy bit her lip and forced a smile. "I'm sorry. It was good of you to offer. But I feel guilty enough allowing you to do all this work, I just couldn't allow you to spend any money on us. I hope you understand."

Reed gave her a reassuring smile. "Don't worry, I have a rather thick skin. It takes a lot to insult me."

As they sat down to the meal, Reed found himself thinking of how Lucy Ames continued to contradict every preconceived notion he'd held of her. Far from the grasping, coarse woman he'd expected, she behaved like a lady. She never complained or bemoaned her fate. Her life centered on the boy, and she worked hard to give him all that she could. Had motherhood softened her perhaps?

The prayers she offered at mealtimes, and the ones she oversaw as she put Toby to bed, were filled with thanks for what they had, not petitions for material relief or rescue from her conditions. He couldn't imagine his sisters, or any other woman of his acquaintance for that matter, reacting in such a manner.

If this was all an act, it was a very convincing one. Maybe, for the boy's sake, she'd reformed, faced up to her weaknesses, and mended her ways.

Not quite ready to ordain her a saint, Reed nevertheless began to wonder if mitigating circumstances had forced Lucy's hand in the matter of the stolen ring and her illicit relationship with Jon.

Again he wondered what her and Jon's relationship had been. Maybe passion, for a brief moment in time, overcame both her and Jon's moral defenses. Had Jon, out of guilt or love, promised her the ring when he learned she carried his child? Or had she seen it as Toby's birthright, or even a means of survival once she realized her situation?

He was beginning to feel that Jon might bear more of the blame for all this than Lucy. She'd been nineteen and alone. Jon had been older, more experienced, married. Not that she was entirely innocent. She'd been found lacking when temptation came her way, become "soiled goods" to be blunt. That should have been enough to put him off. So why hadn't it?

One thing was apparent, no matter what her sins in the past, Toby meant everything to her these days. Would he really be able to take the boy away from her when the time came?

Reed squared his shoulders. Of course he could, he'd made tough decisions before where family was concerned, and Toby was family.

But he wished there were some other way.

～

*A*s Lucy worked on one of the dresses for Lowell that afternoon, she wrestled again with thoughts of how to escape the stifling confines of her life. It was hard to come up with fresh ideas, though, when she kept picturing her mother looking at her with that you-already-know-what-to-do look.

It was the sound of a carriage approaching that brought an end to her musings and to her needlework. She groaned aloud as she realized who'd come calling. When she and her mother first moved to the Jeeter place, Joseph Crowder agreed to visit once a month to identify and take care of any major repairs that might be needed. Lowell took over that duty about two years ago with the result that very few repairs had occurred since. He was more inclined to use these visits to press Lucy for a commitment than for anything else.

Lucy took a deep breath, then hurried to the door, sending up a quick prayer of thanks that Reed had taken Toby fishing. She wasn't ready for the two men to meet, though she refused to examine her reasons too closely.

She greeted Lowell at the front gate, keeping her tone polite but cool. "Good afternoon, Lowell, have you come to take care of the leak in the barn roof?"

Lowell doffed his hat as he stepped down from his buggy. "Now there's no need to get right down to business. Why don't you invite me in for a glass of cider? I even brought flowers for you. Picked 'em myself." He wore a pleased-with-himself smile that only served to irritate her.

Lucy took the flowers with a reluctant "Thank you," but stood firm. "I'm out of cider. The flowers are nice, but if you're not going to take care of the needed repairs, I'd appreciate it if you'd just go on and let me get back to my chores."

"Peace, Luce, please. I'm not just here as your landlord, but as your friend. If there's no cider, I'll settle for some water. Why don't we go inside and find a vase for these? I thought we might sit a while and talk. I've brought the rest of the fabric with me so you can get on with your sewing." He patted the brown paper wrapped package he carried.

Then he smiled persuasively. "Of course, I'd rather talk about our wedding. Don't you think it's time to stop acting the martyr and admit you need me? You've been resourceful and brave, and you've proved you can make it on your own. Now, be strong enough to accept some help, and help Toby at the same time. Say we can set the date and you'll make me a very happy man."

Lucy still didn't want to marry Lowell, didn't feel it was the right move for either her or him. But his mention of Toby reminded her of what she'd felt as she watched Toby respond to the attention Reed gave him. Toby needed a man in his life, a father figure. Was this the change she needed? Stay and marry Lowell rather than start over somewhere else?

Then she bit her lip as her one piece of luck ran out. There was Jasper, and that meant Toby and Reed wouldn't be far behind.

~

*T*oby and Reed headed toward the house, a string of four fair-sized fish in hand. Reed spotted the carriage before Toby. "Looks like you have visitors."

The boy's gaze followed Reed's, and he sobered at once. "That's Mr. Crowder's buggy. He comes by to visit sometimes."

Reed recognized the name and frowned. This was the man mentioned in Dobbs' report as the other contender for Toby's father. He'd also been involved in some local scandal with Lucy just before she left for New Orleans, though Dobbs' report had been lamentably lacking in details on that point. Reed fought to control the wave of jealousy that surged through him at the thought of Lucy with another man.

Judging from the flatness of Toby's tone, this visitor wasn't a favorite of his. "Don't you like Mr. Crowder?"

The boy frowned and kicked a pebble, avoiding Reed's gaze. "I wish he'd stay away. He makes Ma do things she doesn't like."

Reed checked in mid-stride, all his protective instincts surging forward. "What kind of things?"

Toby, fortunately, was too preoccupied to hear the menace in Reed's tone. "Can't tell. I promised Ma not to."

By this time, they were close enough for Reed to get his first glimpse of Lowell Crowder. Toby's words had prepared him to dislike the man on sight, and he wasn't disappointed.

Reed tried to picture Crowder as Toby's father. There were physical similarities. His hair blazed as red as any Wilder's, and he stood almost as tall as Jon had.

After a closer look, though, Reed decided the resemblance was only superficial. Crowder's features were less angular, his face rounder, his frame lighter than those of either the Wilder clan in general or Toby himself.

Jasper, sidetracked by a game of chase-the-squirrel, caught sight of the visitor and began yapping furiously. Crowder turned with an annoyed expression. Spotting Reed, his expression changed to angry surprise.

"And just who is this?" Crowder's question was almost a growl.

Lucy, with obvious reluctance, performed the introductions as Reed neared. "Lowell Crowder, this is Reed Wilder. Lowell, Mr. Wilder is my guest. He's staying here while he recuperates from injuries he received a few days ago.

"Mr. Wilder, Lowell is my landlord."

Both men nodded stiffly at the introduction, neither bothering to extend a hand to the other.

Crowder seemed to return Reed's antagonism in spades. His voice carried a territorial challenge as he amended Lucy's introduction. "More than a landlord, Luce. Why, you and I are old friends, used to play together as kids and all that."

The pompous oaf laid a hand familiarly on Lucy's arm and Reed saw her stiffen. He also saw the flowers she was holding. What was going on here?

Then Crowder looked pointedly at Reed. "Recuperating, huh? I'd say, except for those cuts and bruises, you seem pretty healthy right now, Mr. Wilder."

Lucy stepped away from her visitor's hold, and turned to Toby. "Take Jasper around back and see if you can calm him down. Then, after you set those fish in the kitchen, I'd appreciate it if you'd put these flowers in some water for me."

The two men, glaring at each other, ignored her for the time being. Reed shrugged, but the glint in his eye looked anything but casual. "Oh, I'm much better now, thanks to Miss Ames' care. I plan to stick around for a few days, though, and show my thanks by helping out around the place. Things seem to have fallen into a state of some disrepair."

Reed watched in satisfaction as Crowder's face turned an angry shade of red.

"Now look here, Wilder," the landlord blustered, "are you saying I don't do my duty by this place? Why, I've yet to see a dime in rent in all the years Lucy and her mother lived here. They're lucky I'm kind-hearted enough to let them pay me off in other ways." The glance he sent Lucy's way was highly suggestive and she reddened. Reed noted the blush and his lips tightened.

Crowder puffed out his chest. "Anyway, Lucy and I thank you kindly for any repairs you've made, but I think it's time you move on. I'm sure you wouldn't want to be burdening her with your upkeep when she has so little to spare. You can rest assured that I'll take care of any other work that needs doing around here."

Lucy rounded on her landlord, poking a finger at his chest. "Lowell, Mr. Wilder is my guest, and you have no right to send him packing. He or I will decide when his visit is at an end, not you. Now, I think it best if you leave."

Lowell again reddened angrily. "So that's the way of it, is it? And just how else is Mr. Wilder showing his gratitude?"

That was too much for Reed. His brows drew down furiously as he stepped forward and landed a punch square to Lowell's jaw.

Lowell staggered back, nearly felled by the force of the blow. With an angry growl, he started forward, his own fists raised.

CHAPTER 13

*L*ucy grabbed Lowell's arm and stepped between him and
Reed, shocked by the display of violence from two men she
thought of as sensible and intelligent. "Stop this at once! I
will *not* have you brawling on my front lawn."

She held her ground as the men glared at each other. Then
Lowell turned to Lucy and his expression shifted, became
conciliatory.

"I'm sorry Luce, I spoke before I thought. It's just—"

"I know what you thought." Lucy interrupted him, fighting the
bitter taste in her mouth with stiff dignity. How could she have
contemplated marriage to him for even a few seconds! Without
trust and respect, married life would be more stifling, less fulfilling,
than even her current existence.

She fisted one hand on her hip and poked his chest with a finger
of the other. "But hear me well. Mr. Wilder is a gentleman and has
treated me with nothing but respect. Far from being an imposition,
he's more than paid his way with the amount of sweat he's poured
into this place the past few days. Whether you choose to believe
that or not is of absolutely no concern to me. My obligation to you

ends with the rent, and who I invite onto this property is no business of yours. Now please leave."

Lowell looked uncomfortably caught between contrition and suspicion, but Lucy refused to feel sympathetic. Finally he shoved the package he held toward her "I guess maybe I had that coming. Forgive me, Luce. I was out of line, but let's not argue in front of strangers. Here's a special something I think you'll like. It's the prettiest piece of fabric I've seen in a while, and it'll make a beautiful dress. There's gold thread worked into it that matches your eyes perfectly."

$\sim$

*R*eed watched the by-play between the two, taking pleasure in Lucy's dressing down of Crowder. But his eyes narrowed as Lucy accepted the gift. He'd expected her to fling it back at the man. Instead, she clutched it to her, staring at a point midway between the two men.

"You're forgiven." Her voice sounded gruff, as if it hurt to speak the words. "Now I think you should go."

"What about him?" Lowell tossed his head in Reed's direction. "I can't leave you here alone with him. It just wouldn't be right, or even safe."

"Oh, for goodness sake." Lucy's eyes drilled into him. "I told you, Mr. Wilder's been perfectly civil. Besides, he's been here for over a week now. I don't think a few more days will make any difference, one way or the other."

Lowell's jaw clenched even tighter, and Reed thought he might protest again. But then, with a stiff bow to Lucy, he turned and stalked to his carriage. Reed ignored Lowell's exit and watched Lucy.

"That man is a pig," he said stiffly.

"Please don't condemn him." She lifted a hand and then let it drop. "He's not a bad person, you just caught him by surprise. Besides, he has reasons for feeling the way he does."

Now what did that mean? Was she admitting to some personal attachment between the two of them? Some intimate relationship? Reed latched onto her elbow. "Reasons?"

Lucy looked at his hand on her elbow and then slowly moved her gaze to his face. Reed guiltily released her arm, immediately regretting his blurted inquiry. He stood his ground, however, even though he knew she had every right to tell him it was none of his business.

When Lucy did speak, her voice was unemotional and unapologetic. "He wants me to marry him." Then, without another word, she turned back to the house, presumably to put away her gift.

Reed watched her go and felt like a complete idiot. Once again she'd surprised him, and he didn't like the feeling. Never had his cool head and logical approach to problem solving failed him so miserably as it did where it involved this woman.

Feeling the need for some vigorous activity to work off his temper, Reed went around to the back of the house, grabbed the ax, and headed into the woods. Miss Ames would be getting more firewood whether she needed it or not.

∼

*T*hat night, as Reed strolled out to the barn, he tried to analyze the situation with Crowder.

If the oaf really wanted to marry her, why did she hesitate? Considered dispassionately, it seemed the answer to her problems. She might not be thrilled with the match, but she seemed at least able to tolerate the man. Why wouldn't a person in her situation jump at the chance to have someone make a "respectable woman" out of her? It didn't make sense. Didn't she want to make a better life for herself and Toby?

And if she wasn't inclined to accept Crowder's offer, why in the world had she accepted his gift? It would have been more in character for her to spurn such an offering. True, she didn't have many nice things in her life, but to subjugate her pride for some flowers and a piece of fabric?

He remembered Toby's cryptic comment about Crowder making Lucy do things she didn't want to, and his hands fisted. She'd introduced him as her landlord. If he learned that the lout tried to force her into something sordid under threat of eviction, Reed would personally see that she wasn't put in that position again. The very idea of Crowder laying so much as a hand on her set Reed's blood boiling again.

Then his lips twisted in a self-mocking smile. When in the world had he taken on the role of Lucy Ames' protector? Not that she didn't need taking care of, despite her hardheaded insistence to the contrary. Never before had he met a woman who needed so much protecting and yet seemed so able to take care of herself at the same time. Yes, she'd definitely gotten under his skin, and not just because of what he owed her. In spite of everything, he was coming to realize just how difficult it would be to leave her when the time came.

Then again, why should he? He'd thought to offer her a generous stipend to help ease the loss of her son when he claimed Toby as a Wilder. But now he suspected that while she would want what was best for the boy, she'd never take money from him as part of the deal.

Why not take her with him? He could set her up in a nice little cottage in the general vicinity of the Wilder Estate, no strings attached, so she and Toby could maintain close contact. Reed smiled to himself, pleased with the magnanimity of that thought. After all, he *did* owe her for saving his life. It would get her away from the hard, lonely life she lived here. And having her nearby wouldn't be such an unpleasant happenstance.

Reed felt much more cheerful now than he had earlier.

One thing he was sure of, regardless of what may or may not be going on between Lucy and her landlord, she wasn't in love with the man. She'd said Crowder wanted to marry her, not vice-versa. And far from encouraging her would-be suitor, Lucy had stood up to him and challenged his authority over her actions. There would be no emotional tangles of that sort to keep her here.

His thoughts strayed to how she'd looked last night, how right she'd felt in his arms. If he closed his eyes he could still smell the faint scent of roses, hear her soft sigh.

Too restless to settle down, Reed didn't climb up to the loft right away. He gave Ranger an extra grooming, and then found himself puttering around, cleaning and organizing the garden and carpentry tools stored in the barn.

An hour later he climbed the ladder, ready to turn in for the night. Glancing through the loft door toward the house, he saw the soft light that indicated Lucy was still awake. No wonder she seemed so tired lately. Didn't she ever sleep? Maybe she was afraid of the dark and slept with her light on. Or maybe she was just admiring her gift from Crowder.

On that sour thought, Reed plopped down, determined to get some sleep himself, even if she stayed up all night.

～

"*L*ook, Ma, did you see? It skipped eight times!"

Lucy oohed and aahed over Toby's feat, and then drifted back to the shady haven of the picnic quilt where the remains of their lunch were still spread out.

Reed felt very pleased with himself. It had been his idea to have their Sunday lunch picnic-style out here by the pond, and it had turned out quite well. The day was beautiful, the sky sported only fluffy white clouds, and the temperature was warm but not oppressive.

He watched Lucy sit down, arrange her skirts modestly, and then pick up a peach from the basket. A moment later he joined her, flopping down a few feet away with his back against the trunk of a large cottonwood tree and his feet stretched out in front of him. "I suppose you realize that's the last peach?" he asked severely.

"Uh-huh." She flashed him a dazzling smile as she took a large bite.

"The very last peach, from that basket I so painstakingly filled this morning."

"Uh-huh."

A bit of juice dribbled from the corner of her mouth, and Reed watched its progress, mesmerized by the sight. "It looks mighty tasty," he said, his voice only a tad husky.

Lucy, apparently missing the undertones of his remark, gave in to his unsubtle hints with a laugh. "All right, I'll share. Here you go." And she tossed the peach to him.

Reed caught the half-eaten fruit with a roguish, unrepentant smile. "Thanks."

He munched his prize, peripherally watching her watch him. After a few moments she broke the silence. "I notice you're not limping at all any more."

"Yep. Leg's good as new."

"I'm glad. I was afraid it was going to give you a lot more trouble."

Reed threw the peach pit toward the pond and Lucy's gaze followed its arc. "I'm glad you suggested a picnic. This reminds me of Sunday afternoons when I was a little girl. Daddy loved picnics."

"Tell me about them." He liked her this way, all soft and dreamy-eyed.

"Well, Mother would fix something yummy, usually ham or fried chicken, along with biscuits and potato salad and apple pie and lemonade. Then we'd head out for Simpson's meadow, over on the other side of town. While Mother set everything up, Daddy and I would fly kites, or make little rafts out of sticks and sail them in the creek. And then, after we ate, we'd all lie down and find cloud pictures."

Reed wrinkled his brow in question. "Cloud pictures?"

"Uh-huh." Then her eyes widened. "Haven't you ever looked for cloud pictures?"

"No." He could tell she enjoyed the feeling of having the upper hand. "How do you find pictures in the clouds?"

"Oh there's nothing to it. It just requires a bit of imagination. Watch, I'll show you. Lie down, flat on your back."

When he'd obliged, Lucy lay down as well. She positioned herself at a ninety-degree angle to him, with her head near his. He could almost touch her, could hear the soft sigh of her breath.

"Now look up at the clouds and see if you can find one with a shape that resembles anything at all."

Trying to concentrate on her words rather than her presence, Reed looked at the bits of fluff floating overhead. He pointed at an oval-shaped blob. "I suppose that one could be an egg."

"Oh, you're not really trying. You have to set your imagination free. An egg indeed. Why, anyone can see that's a turtle that's retreated into its shell. Here, let me try."

She stared up at the sky for a few minutes and then smiled and pointed. "There. You see that one just to the right of that willow tree. Doesn't it look like a train engine?"

Reed stared at it, trying to see it as she did.

"Tilt your head a bit to the left," she said, as if to a child. "See it now? See, the part sticking out of the top is the smokestack, and the part where it sort of tapers in front is the cowcatcher. It's sort of fat and squat, but it's a train engine all right."

Reed rolled his eyes, but admitted that maybe there was a vague resemblance to a train engine after all. Her exasperation at his obtuseness only brought a smile to his lips.

"All right," she said, "now you try again. Let's see if you can do any better this time."

Reed took his time, letting his gaze scan the sky. Finally, he pointed. "There. That one looks just like the head of a horse."

"Oh, I see it!" She squeezed his hand, congratulating him for his efforts. "There's hope for you yet. Now it's my turn again. Let's see..."

～

*O*pening her eyes with a start, Lucy realized she'd dozed off. Reed still lay nearby, but now he'd propped up on one elbow to face her, stretching his soft blue shirt taut across his broad shoulders. His gray eyes turned to smoke as he studied her with an unblinking intensity that set her pulse racing.

She could hear Toby and Jasper romping nearby, but caught by that look, Lucy felt as if there were no one else in the whole world but just the two of them. For one breathless moment, she thought, hoped, wished that he would kiss her again.

Instead, Reed gently stroked her jaw with the back of his hand, and she felt herself shiver in response. He drew his hand away, his expression turning pensive. "Do you mind if I ask you a personal question?"

Lucy stiffened, her mind wailing in protest. *Oh no, please, don't bring up Toby's father again. Not now.*

"If you don't want to answer, don't. I'll understand." He looked at her until she gave a cautious nod. "You told me yesterday that Crowder wants to marry you. I gather from the way things stand right now, that you've turned him down."

Lucy's first reaction was relief that she'd guessed wrong. Her second was concern over where this question would lead. She sat up and again she nodded.

"Why? I mean the man is an oaf, granted. But most women in your position would jump at the chance to have a man shoulder her burdens and offer her some kind of security."

Lucy turned to stare at the clouds, her fists clenched and pressed to the ground at her sides. She fiercely resented his question, resented the implication behind the phrase "women in your position," as if she had less right to her dreams than other women.

But a part of her accepted the resentment and pain as the price she must pay to keep Toby with her. And that part of her felt the need to really answer his question, to try to make him understand what her motives were. And maybe she needed to hear those

143

words out loud herself, to examine them under the bright light of his skepticism and see if they could survive.

She traced the stitching on the quilt with her index finger, keeping her face averted. "Despite what you think of him, Lowell is a fine, decent man, with good, even noble intentions. When we were children, we were each other's very best friend. We shared secrets, examined dreams, confessed fears to each other that we would never divulge to anyone else. When his dog Rusty died, I helped him bury it, and we cried together. When I embarrassed myself at the Fourth of July picnic at age thirteen by falling face first in a mud puddle, he threatened everyone within an inch of their lives if they so much as smiled crooked at me. He was my defender, my confidant, and the big brother I never had."

She paused, choosing her words. "But there was never anything romantic about our relationship. We loved each other, but were never *in love*. When he married Anne, I was happy for him, pleased he had someone to cherish and be cherished by. Anne, bless her heart, was a dear sweet girl. She loved Lowell fiercely, but she never did understand our relationship."

She watched the progress of a small black beetle lumbering across the edge of the quilt. "Anne died about four and a half years ago. Lowell began his campaign to marry me about six months later. Not because he's in love with me, but because he's still trying to protect me, and because he thinks he owes me something."

She cocked her head and glanced his way. "You and he have something in common, come to think of it. I saved his life once too."

He reacted with raised eyebrows. "Did the Jeffersons attack him too?"

She smiled. "Nothing so dramatic." She almost left it at that, almost switched the conversation to another topic. What could she gain by exposing more of her personal history to him? But something inside her wanted to unburden herself, to get it all out, come what may. Maybe this was another sign of her need for liberation. She took a deep breath and pressed on.

"One evening, about seven years ago, Lowell's horse came home without him. Just about every able bodied man in town turned out to help search. Late afternoon of the next day I suddenly realized where he had to be. I won't go into how I knew, I just put some things together that I knew about him and that he'd said. I intended to tell Daddy or someone on the search party, but everyone was out looking. So, rather than wait, I just left a note and rode out myself to check it out."

She plucked a blade of grass and twirled it in her fingers. "I found him, all right. He'd fallen into a gully and busted his leg. By that time, he was wet and feverish and delirious. I couldn't move him to my horse, and I couldn't leave him alone, not in his condition, so I stayed with him, trusting Daddy would find my note and rescue us both. Meantime, I tried to keep him dry and warm. Problem was, my note wasn't found until late that night. I wasn't missed because mother was helping at the café, cooking and serving meals for the searchers.

"They found us early the next morning. I was..." she paused and swallowed. "I was holding Lowell, trying stop his thrashing and to share my body heat with him. Doc Lawton said that was the right thing to have done, that it may have saved his life." Lucy felt her cheeks grow warm. "But it generated some gossip, and made Anne uncomfortable. That was when my parents finally agreed with my plan to travel to New Orleans and spend time working under Madame Robicheaux."

She hugged her knees tighter. "When I came back with Toby, scandalizing the whole community, Lowell again tried to be that big brother-protector. But things were different, *we* were different. He had a wife. I had Toby. Anne didn't want him to have anything to do with a "woman in my position" as you so tactfully put it. And he had trouble reconciling his own moral conscience to my status. He did what he could for me anyway, helping behind the scenes, so that his marriage and his business interests were protected. Thanks to Lowell, I am able to make a life for my family."

Lucy paused, wondering if he'd really wanted this much of an explanation. But she couldn't seem to stop herself; the words had a life of their own now. "I've seen the guilt edging the concern in his eyes when he looks at me. Lowell blames himself for my leaving Far Enough, and for the... the problems that resulted. After Anne died, he decided he should make an honest woman of me. He even tries to convince himself he's in love with me. But he's not. And I'm not in love with him."

She picked up a pebble and flung it toward the pond. "Someday he's going to find a woman who loves him deeply, and wants nothing more than to cherish him and share in building his home and his family and his life. But I'm not that woman, and I don't plan to be the reason he's not free when he finds her. He deserves more than someone who'll settle for him out of need rather than love."

Then Lucy looked at Reed and grimaced. "That sounds so noble and selfless, doesn't it? Actually, there's another, much more selfish reason. I want more than that for myself."

She looked away again, and her hand reached down to smooth the wrinkles from the picnic quilt. "My parents were very much in love. You could see it in so many little ways, in the way they looked at each other, touched each other. You could hear it in the way they spoke to each other, and in the way they laughed together. You could feel it in the implicit trust they had in each other."

Her hand closed around the locket which had worked its way outside her dress. "I made myself a vow a long time ago that I would never marry until I found a man who would share that kind of love and trust and oneness of soul with me. I know it's idealistic and more than a little selfish, what with everything Lowell could do to make Toby's life easier, but I haven't been able to convince myself to settle for something less, even given my current prospects."

Lucy didn't dare look at him, afraid he would see the truth she had discovered as she spoke. She could no longer deny with her mind what her heart had known for some time.

I could love you like that, Reed Wilder.

I'm afraid I already do.

CHAPTER 14

oby and Jasper raced away from the pond, bounding exuberantly through grass that reached the boy's knees. Reed, basket in hand, set a more sedate pace for himself and Lucy.

Once her confidences ended, Lucy had jumped up and begun packing the picnic things. Reed, unsure how to respond to the need he sensed in her, had been grateful for the reprieve.

Their discussion since then had moved on to more mundane, less personal topics. He noted now, though, as they strolled down the path to the house, that her hand kept reaching up to touch the locket she wore as if she sought strength from it. It was an expensive looking piece and he wondered if it had been a gift from his brother or from Crowder.

Reed mulled over her words. Not the story she'd told him, but the between-the-lines image they'd given him of what she'd been like before New Orleans. Her words painted the picture of an innocent, impulsive, caring girl. One who was loved and protected by her family. One who gave no thought to herself when others needed her. And one who'd been wounded by the unbending moral code of her neighbors and friends.

Is that what led to her eventual downfall? Had that shattered idealism, that hurt, made her vulnerable enough to compromise herself? His handsome, charismatic brother had turned many a girl's head in his youth. Reed could well imagine that Jon's charm, along with his protective nature, would make him quite attractive to a lonely young woman exiled from her home.

Jasper's excited yipping interrupted Reed's thoughts. He and Lucy had caught up to Toby near the peach trees. Jasper, bouncing noisily about, had treed another squirrel. As they moved past, Toby joined the adults, leaving the dog to follow at will.

The trio hadn't quite reached the back porch when a visitor stepped around the corner. Reed, taking Lucy's arm, eyed the stranger suspiciously.

But Lucy's lips had already curved into a welcoming smile. "Sheriff Morton!"

The Sheriff removed his hat and returned her smile with an apologetic one. "Hello Lucy. Hope you don't mind me poking around back here, but I heard voices and thought I'd make my presence known."

"Of course I don't mind." Lucy moved forward to greet her guest as Reed released her arm. "You're welcome anytime, but whatever brings you out this way on a Sunday afternoon?"

"Just thought I'd stop by and see how things are going for you. I haven't been out this way in a while and I'm past due."

Reed almost snorted. Likely story. He didn't believe for a minute it was mere coincidence that this visit came the day after Crowder discovered Lucy had a stranger for a houseguest. Had the oaf tried to press assault charges against him?

"As you can see, we're fine." Then Lucy's glance darted between the Sheriff and Reed. "Oh, excuse me. This is Reed Wilder. Reed, this is Sheriff Leland Morton."

The men exchanged greetings and handshakes. Reed relaxed slightly. He could tell the Sheriff was taking his measure, but at least the formidable looking lawman didn't seem on the brink of arresting him.

"I was just about to brew a fresh pot of coffee," Lucy continued. "Would you care to join us for a cup?"

The Sheriff turned, moving with them into the house. "Thanks, don't mind if I do."

Reed escorted the visitor to the parlor while Lucy paused in the kitchen. He didn't wait for the Sheriff to speak; instead he took the offensive himself. "I'm glad you came by Sheriff. I'd planned to pay you a visit as soon as I made it into town."

Sheriff Morton raised an eyebrow. "Were you now? Anything in particular I can help you with?"

"I want to register a complaint against two local boys. I think Lucy called them the Jefferson brothers."

The Sheriff sat up straighter, frowning. "Roy and Vern? I thought they were long gone. What've they been up to now?"

"Ambushed me a little over a week ago. Pounded me almost senseless and tried to steal my wallet and my horse. Until Miss Ames persuaded them otherwise, that is."

This time the Sheriff's expression was eloquent with unvoiced skepticism, and Reed grinned. "Don't let her size fool you. She can stand her ground with the meanest of 'em, and she can shoot better than a lot of men I know."

Sheriff Morton's expression softened. "That's her father's doing. I never knew a man who could shoot like he could. He was one of the finest men I ever knew."

"Thank you." Lucy had walked in as he spoke. "You know he felt the same way about you."

Both men stood and waited for her to be seated. Then the Sheriff turned back to Reed. "So tell me more about this ambush. Caught you flat-footed, did they?"

Reed's expression turned rueful. "Afraid so. I'd stopped at the creek crossing to get a drink and water my horse when they came up on me from behind."

Lucy spoke up, as if feeling the need to defend Reed. "He seemed to be giving as good as he got when I arrived. Until Vern hit him from behind with a rock, anyway."

Sheriff Morton looked at her curiously. "How'd you come to get involved, Lucy?"

She gave him a self-deprecating smile. "Toby and I were out to pick blackberries. We heard the fight, and I slipped closer to get a peek. When I saw what was going on, I couldn't just walk away. I wouldn't even leave a dog with those two."

Reed winced at this casual dismissal of his importance.

"So, I pulled daddy's pistol out of my pocket and—"

"You carry a gun with you to go blackberry picking?" The Sheriff looked startled by her admission.

Lucy waved it off. "Of course, ever since Joey Conners was attacked by that rabid dog. I don't take chances with Toby's safety.

"Anyway," she continued, "I pointed the gun at those two and told 'em to ride out. That was all there was to it."

Reed wasn't about to let her get away with such a watered down version. "Actually, there was quite a bit more to it. She faced them down, threatened to have them arrested if she ever saw their faces again. After they turned tail, she managed to get my barely conscious, uncooperative carcass up on my horse and here to her house where she tended my injuries."

"I see." Sheriff Morton gazed at Lucy with new respect.

Reddening, Lucy popped up from her seat. "Excuse me, please. The coffee ought to be ready by now."

Taking his seat again after Lucy made her exit, Sheriff Morton resumed his questioning. "So, what are your plans now?"

"Well, for the next few days I plan to stay right here and do some handyman work for Miss Ames. Seems the least I could do." Then he shrugged. "After that, well, I'll probably just go on as I'd intended before the Jeffersons interrupted me."

"And that is?"

"Just some investigative field work."

"Care to elaborate on that a bit, son?"

Reed gave the Sheriff his most authoritative look. "No, sir, I'm afraid I'm not at liberty to go into any of the details of my current assignment."

"I see." The Sheriff gave him a searching look and then let the matter drop. "And right now you only have Lucy's best interests at heart?"

Reed resisted the urge to shift his gaze under that steely stare. It felt as if he were facing the protective father of a sheltered maiden. "I assure you sir, I have the utmost respect for Miss Ames, and am very aware of how indebted I am to her."

"I'm glad to hear it. Lucy may not have family in these parts, but she's the daughter of a very good friend of mine. I'd hate to see anyone hurt her."

"So would I." Reed, who knew he'd been put on notice, never let his gaze waver. "And, not that it's any of your business, Sheriff, but I spend my nights in the loft of that leaky barn."

The Sheriff nodded his understanding of what Reed implied. Then he rubbed his chin thoughtfully. "Lowell's sporting a bruised jaw. You know anything about that?"

Reed's face hardened. "He insulted Miss Ames. To my way of thinking, he got off easy."

The two men stared at each other long and hard, neither of them giving ground. At last Sheriff Morton nodded, as if satisfied with what he saw.

The lawman reached into his pocket. "By the way, Mike Slater from the telegraph office asked me to deliver this. Came for you two days ago, but nobody knew who you were or that you were here."

"Thanks." Reed took the paper and stuck it in his pocket without reading it. He'd wait for a bit more privacy.

Once Lucy's visitor finally took his leave, Reed headed to the barn. Though he'd managed to sidestep most of the Sheriff's questions with vague answers and carefully crafted half-truths, it hadn't been easy or pleasant. He suspected he'd revealed more than he'd intended.

Sheriff Morton seemed an intelligent, tenacious man. It wouldn't take such a man long to start digging into Reed's story. Reed took comfort in knowing he would have his business in Far

Enough settled long before the Sheriff had the answers to his questions. At least he hoped so.

Leaning against the creaky barnyard gate, Reed pulled the telegram from his pocket. As expected, it was from his father, demanding a status on the investigation. Patience had never been one of Captain Wilder's virtues. At least he'd had the sense not to mention Lucy Ames or the ring directly. Reed read the last line, frowned and read it again.

Blast! That cutthroat Jake Morgan was trying to move up the closing on the Claymore deal. His father was volunteering to take care of that 'little matter' if Reed didn't make it back in time.

Reed loved his father and admired his skills as a ship's captain. But when it came to this kind of negotiation, the old salt had about as much skill as a six-year-old. Morgan had the face of a choirboy and the instincts of a shark. The contract, one Reed had labored over personally, was so complex, so sensitive, that one seemingly innocent change could toss away all the benefits to Wilder Enterprises, leaving them with a burden rather than a sound business venture.

The deal Reed had poured months of effort into could go sour in a hurry if he didn't do something to head this off. But he couldn't shortcut his obligation here—he'd already given his word.

Too bad he couldn't be in two places at one time.

～

*L*ucy had trouble concentrating on her sewing that evening. And it wasn't just the flickering candlelight or even the building weariness from the night after night of eye-straining work in the privacy of her bedroom. Her mind kept returning to the unsettling revelation she'd had earlier. Heaven help her, she *was* in love with Reed. Not just grateful or infatuated, but honest to goodness, from this day forward, impossibly in love. Just the thought of never seeing him again was enough to make her want to sit back and wail.

She anchored her needle in the fabric and stood for a moment, trying to ease some of the strain from her cramped muscles.

Reed would move on in a few days and would probably never again give this interlude more than a passing thought. Because, much as it hurt to admit it, she knew he didn't return her feelings. How could he? Oh, he had some feelings for her, but they were a mixture of gratitude and perhaps friendly affection, with a bit of physical attraction thrown in. There was nothing deep and lasting in that.

Already he'd made a quick trip into town this evening. Said he needed to send a telegraph. She worried about what he'd hear, how he'd look at her when he returned. But from the short while he'd been gone, it didn't seem he'd had time for idle chitchat with the locals. And his opinion of her didn't seem to have altered on his return. Still, it was just a matter of time.

She sat down and bent over her work again. Why this man? Why couldn't she feel this way about Lowell, good-hearted, dependable Lowell, who'd all but begged her to marry him?

It wasn't Reed's looks or his temperament. He wasn't conventionally handsome, though she rather liked his looks. And he wasn't particularly even-tempered or agreeable. In fact, he was touchy about his ability to be in control, and he had been a decidedly grumpy patient. But he was good with Toby, and he treated her as an equal, even given what he knew and deduced about her position in the community. He had a strong sense of honor, sometimes overbearingly so. And he had a way of smiling, or just looking at her really, that set her insides fluttering. But did all of that add up to reasons enough to love a man?

She remembered the embrace they'd shared, the delicious way she'd felt, the sound of his heart beating against her ear, the gentle stroke of his hand at her back, the warmth of his breath on her hair. It had been wonderful and absolutely unlike anything she'd experienced before.

Watching her parents, she'd learned how love brought joy and comfort and that special spark to your life. But she'd had no idea before now what it would actually feel like. To think that she'd never feel that again...

Lucy pushed those thoughts aside. So, what did she do now? It was critical to her peace of mind that Reed not find out the true depths of her emotions. As for the physical aspect, much as she'd like to be held and caressed again, to perhaps experience another kiss, the memory of that one embrace would have to do. It was one thing for him to ignore her reputation while they were here on the farm, but it would be another matter entirely when they were around others. She was determined not to give him any further reasons to believe the worst of her. She wasn't sure she'd be able to stand it if he even once looked at her with disdain or pity in his eyes.

No, she'd have to keep up the pretense of feeling nothing more than friendship for him until he was gone. Her heart lurched at the thought of him leaving not only her house but Far Enough itself, and returning to his home in Delaware. Her future loomed before her, lonelier than ever.

Ripping out a wrongly sewn seam, Lucy finally gave up and put the richly patterned fabric and her sewing basket away. Maybe she'd be better able to concentrate tomorrow.

Lucy pulled the pins from her hair and shook the heavy tresses free. She unclasped the locket from around her neck, then paused in the act of setting it on her vanity. Rubbing her thumb over the rubies and pearls on the surface, she recalled a long ago talk with her mother on how to find her own true love.

"Lucy Jane," her mother had said, "true love is not something that comes from your seeking of it. It can neither be forced nor denied. A person has no real say who their heart chooses, and once it does choose, it will be forever."

Her mother's gaze turned toward the parlor, where Lucy's father sat reading a book, and her expression softened. "There's no reasoning with a heart, and sometimes no understanding its choices either. Because the heart recognizes what the eyes can't— the certain someone who is your other half, who complements your life and makes you whole. A person can decide to ignore the heart's choice, but never change it or overrule it."

Remembering those words now, and the soft tenderness in her mother's voice and gaze, Lucy tilted her chin at her reflection in the vanity mirror. "Now I understand what you were trying to say, Momma. And for good or ill, my heart has chosen."

She set the comb down. "And I think it may just be the death of me."

~

The next morning Reed sat under the oak tree, sharpening the ax blade. It was still early, but breakfast was over and Lucy was in the backyard doing laundry. She seemed even more tired than she had last night. He wondered what time she'd turned out her lamp and gone to bed. The woman's nocturnal habits were a puzzle to him.

He still couldn't get the story she'd told him yesterday out of his mind. The town had condemned her simply because, in following her own noble, generous impulses, she'd inadvertently broken some rule of propriety. What self-righteous hypocrites—would they rather she had let Crowder die?

But, remembering the attitude he'd arrived with, Reed guiltily wondered how he would have reacted to her situation just a few short weeks ago. Would he have been any less ready to look down his nose?

A lot had changed in one week. His movements slowed for a minute. One week. Today was the end of the first of the two weeks he'd set himself to work for her. His time was nearly half over. What then?

Uncomfortable pursuing that line of thought, he tried focusing instead on his trip to town yesterday. He'd sent a telegram to his father, informing him that he'd encountered a slight delay, but not to worry, things were still on track. More important, he'd instructed him to stall Morgan till his return. Surely his father would heed him, would rein in his tendency to barge in, full steam ahead, for a change. To see a year's worth of plans turn to dust at this late date would be a bitter pill to swallow. He needed to get back to Baker's Cove. Maybe he should just halt this charade, confront Lucy and settle matters now. They'd no doubt all be better off if he ended this now anyway.

So absorbed was he in his thoughts, that the visitor's buggy almost reached the front gate before Reed became aware of it.

The black clad occupant was an older man, in his early fifties Reed guessed, with a full head of white hair, bushy eyebrows to match, and a stern, intelligent look about him. Reed stood as the man dismounted from his buggy and entered the yard.

"Good day to you, young man," the visitor said. "I'm Reverend Joseph Cummings, the minister for Far Enough's one and only church."

Reed extended his hand in greeting. "Glad to meet you, sir. I'm Reed Wilder. I assume you're here to see Miss Ames. She's out back right now, but if you'd like to go on inside and have a seat in the parlor, I'll let her know you're here."

But Reverend Cummings forestalled him. "Actually, I wonder if you and I could have a few words before you announce me."

He'd guessed right then, this wasn't a casual visit. Assuming the air of authority and cool dignity that made him such a formidable businessman, Reed raised an eyebrow and signaled for the visitor to have a seat on the log. He himself propped a foot on the log and regarded the reverend without a word. He might have to hear this out, but he was disinclined to smooth the way for what would no doubt be an uncomfortable interview.

Reverend Cummings began their talk innocuously enough. "I understand you ran into a bit of trouble a few days ago."

Reed wasn't fooled by the oblique approach. "Yes sir, a couple of brutes ambushed me not far from here."

"I can see by the bruises and cuts you're sporting that it must have been a rough fight. I hope they didn't inflict any permanent damage."

"Fortunately, no. But that's because Miss Ames came to my rescue. Quite a courageous, generous woman, wouldn't you say?"

Reverend Cummings shifted in his seat a bit. "Uhm, yes, quite. That was a terrible ordeal you faced. But you seem to have come through it remarkably well."

"Yes, thanks in large part to the care Miss Ames afforded me." Reed was determined to keep hammering this point home.

"Yes, well, I'm glad that you've had such fine care." The reverend sat up straighter. "And that brings me to the reason I'm here. I won't mince words, Mr. Wilder. It may have been unavoidable for you to remain here while you recuperated, but surely you see how improper it is now that you are recovered."

Reed stiffened. "Are you suggesting that there is something immoral or illicit going on here?"

The reverend either didn't hear or wasn't intimidated by the soft warning in Reed's tone. "As to that, I will not speculate. I understand from Sheriff Morton that you sleep in the barn, and that demonstrates you understand the need to adhere to the proprieties. But that's not enough. It is not my place to judge my neighbors. The perception of guilt or innocence, however, makes just as strong a witness as the reality of it."

The Reverend leaned forward earnestly. "The thing is, the townsfolk have heard that you are staying here, and are concerned for Lucy's well being, both physical and moral. I won't presume to question your moral strengths, but Miss Ames has already demonstrated an unfortunate susceptibility in this area."

He paused a moment, drawing himself up authoritatively. "The congregation has asked me to look into the situation and provide whatever counseling might seem appropriate."

Reed straightened. "No offense, but I owe my life to Miss Ames. That's a debt I don't take lightly. I'm trying to show my gratitude by investing a couple of weeks of manual labor on her behalf. Much needed labor, I might add, since it's obvious from the state of things here she hasn't had help from her so very concerned neighbors, and has had to make do entirely on her own."

He fought to keep his tone polite. "I won't just forget my debt and walk away. Miss Ames is a good, decent woman, who hasn't done anything to make me think otherwise since she took me in. But it's my understanding that she is already shunned by the townsfolk. Can you assure me the good people of Far Enough will accept her back into their fold, lend her a hand when needed, if I leave?"

Reverend Cummings held up a hand. "Mr. Wilder, please, I understand why you feel the way you do, but it's my duty to see to the spiritual welfare of my congregation. And though she is no longer an active member, I consider Lucy part of that number."

Reed eyed the clergyman steadily. "Perhaps I'm the one who's misunderstood the situation. So, you've prayerfully ministered to her and her family since she moved back with Toby. You've looked past the gossip and seen for yourself what an intelligent, giving, truly good person she is. Encouraged her to put her past behind her and try to rejoin the community. Counseled the townsfolk on the value of compassion and the evils of gossip and judgmental attitudes."

Reverend Cummings' Adam's apple bobbed as he adjusted his collar. "Well, I—" A screech coming from the back yard rescued him from completing his stammering reply.

Both men rushed to find the source of the cries. Reed arrived on the scene first. There he found Lucy, a wet shirt clutched in a stranglehold to her bosom, her eyes a bit wild, her body tense. She stared at Toby who swatted energetically at something on her clothesline pole.

Reed relaxed and caught Toby's eye. "A spider?"

Toby gave him a man-to-man look. "Yep. All taken care of." Then he turned to Lucy "It's gone, Ma. You can relax."

With a last shudder, the tension left Lucy and she turned with a sheepish smile. But the smile died as she caught sight of her visitor, and she sent a reproachful look Reed's way.

"Reverend Cummings! Mr. Wilder, you should have let me know that I had company."

"Sorry," Reed said, feeling anything but. "The reverend only arrived a few minutes ago and we were getting acquainted."

Lucy shot him a suspicious look, then turned to her guest.

"I apologize if my cries alarmed you, Reverend. I'm afraid I'm squeamish when it comes to spiders."

Reverend Cummings gave her a fatherly smile. "No need to apologize, I understand completely. My Dorie feels the same way. I hope I haven't called at an inconvenient time."

She set the shirt back down in the laundry basket and wiped her hands on her apron. "Of course not. Please, come in and have a seat in the parlor. I'm afraid the only refreshments I can offer you at this hour are a cup of coffee and some biscuits."

Reed noted that her tone was polite but reserved, and that she had an air of wariness about her. No doubt she'd already deduced the reason for this visit.

The reverend spread his hands. "Coffee would be fine, but I don't want you going to any trouble."

"It won't be a bit of trouble." Then she turned to Reed. "Would you check the peach trees for me this morning? See if you can find a few ripe ones that we can have with lunch."

Reed stared at her speculatively. She seemed bent on hearing Reverend Cummings out alone. Under the circumstances, he wasn't sure he should abandon her to that fate. But he wasn't proof against the unvoiced plea in her eyes. "Of course. If you'll excuse me."

~

*I*t took only a few minutes for Lucy to settle her guest in the parlor, a cup of coffee in hand.

"Now, Reverend, perhaps we should get down to the purpose of your visit. I assume this is not a social call?"

"Regretfully, no. I'm here to help you recognize and rectify an untenable situation."

"Untenable?" Lucy was pleased to find her voice remained even, betraying none of her emotions.

Her guest wore a look of determined fatherliness. "Please don't make this more difficult than it has to be. You no doubt know why I'm here. Despite past indiscretions on your part, you have shown commendable decorum and filial dutifulness since your return from New Orleans. You were raised by decent, God-fearing parents. So you must know how improper it is to have a man living here, however innocent it may actually be. I know the circumstances were unusual, but it is time to bring this to a close. It has already caused quite a bit of talk."

Lucy clenched her hands in her lap. "Reverend Cummings, it may have escaped your notice, but there was already quite a bit of talk concerning my reputation before Mr. Wilder ever arrived."

He brushed her comment aside, pressing his point with single-minded purpose. "Be that as it may, it just will not do for Mr. Wilder to continue to reside here without a chaperone. You cannot flaunt such unseemly behavior in the face of your neighbors without grave damage to your reputation."

Lucy bit off a bitter laugh. "My reputation! Surely you don't believe that sending Mr. Wilder packing will make me more acceptable to the good citizens of this community."

"At least give some thought to the example you are setting for your son."

Lucy tried to match the reverend's composure. "I appreciate your concern for Toby. But, until now, he has had no man in his life to set an example. Mr. Wilder is a good, hard working, honest man, and has had a positive influence on Toby. I think in this case, the good far outweighs the bad."

She leaned forward. "The issue is there is a man staying at my place. The town gossips have something to speculate over, and the more self-righteous folks feel outraged."

Lucy raised a hand to her locket and lifted her chin. "Well, I don't care. Those are the same people who condemned me for what I did in rescuing Lowell. They are the same people who refused to believe the truth about Toby when I tried to explain. And they are the same people who abandoned my mother to this life of isolation. My mother, who was always there for whoever needed her, who was church organist and head of the Women's Charity League, who taught school here for sixteen years and who hosted the quilting circle in her home, was forced to live her last days in relative exile."

She paused long enough to draw a breath and shook her head. "No Reverend Cummings, I will *not* turn out this good, decent man who treats me with politeness and even respect, simply to satisfy the moral conscience of the good people of Far Enough."

To her horror, Lucy found her hands shaking when she finished speaking. The anger that had been bottled up inside her for so long had finally begun to surface. Only through an extreme effort of will did she keep the tears from flowing. She would *not* break down, not here, in front of the reverend.

Reverend Cummings reached over and patted her hand in a gesture of comfort, and it took all Lucy's control not to snatch it away. "Lucy, child, I'm sorry to have distressed you this way. I know life has not been easy for you. And perhaps I haven't been a proper minister to your family, and for that I sincerely apologize. I know Mr. Wilder has been kind to you, and that must be like a rain shower after a long drought for someone in your position. But if you look into your heart and conscience, you will know that this situation cannot continue. It seems you have no concern for your own reputation, but would you repay Mr. Wilder's kindness by besmirching his reputation this way?"

Lucy sat back, stricken. "Oh no, I never thought—"

"My reputation is my concern, not Miss Ames'." Both Lucy and Reverend Cummings looked up, startled by Reed's sudden entrance.

~

*R*eed had stood in the hall, unabashedly eavesdropping. He was angry at the way the reverend seemed to be manipulating Lucy, making her feel guilty. The self-recriminating note in her voice just then had yanked him out of the shadows, ready to come to her defense.

Reverend Cummings seemed to recognize Reed's mood and he spread his hands with a conciliatory smile. "Mr. Wilder, do come in and join us. I was just trying to explain to Miss Ames here that she must view this situation from all sides. Your being here is just not proper."

"He's right, I'm afraid." Reed had had time to cool down and think things over during his quick trip to the orchard. Though his eavesdropping had riled him all over again, he knew the reverend was right. He wasn't doing Lucy any favors by asking her to disregard the rules of civilized behavior. He wouldn't give the self-righteous fools like Crowder and this preacher further reason to treat Lucy as a sinner.

The reverend recovered first. "Well, I'm happy to hear you say that, son. That will make matters much easier to settle. I'm sure Venable's Hotel in town has an empty room."

Seeing Lucy's stricken expression, Reed knew she'd misinterpreted his motives. He wanted to explain things, make her understand, bring her smile back. But first, it was time for Reverend Cummings to leave. "That sounds acceptable. I'll gather my things and check in at the hotel later this evening."

"Excellent. I'll let Mrs. Venable know to have a room ready. And perhaps while you're in town I can arrange for you to meet some of the other citizens of Far Enough. I'd hate for your run-in with the Jeffersons to color your view of us."

"That's kind of you, sir, but Miss Ames has done an excellent job of convincing me that there is more than enough good to offset the bad in this part of the country."

Reed's words had the desired effect. "Of course. Well, I must be going. Thank you for the coffee, Lucy. Mr. Wilder, I look forward to seeing more of you in the days to come."

Reed and Lucy followed Reverend Cummings out of the house and as far as the front porch. As the clergyman rode away, Lucy turned to Reed, her voice and expression flat. "I left a half-filled basket of laundry out back. I'd best go tend to it."

She started to leave the porch but Reed stopped her with a touch. "Lucy, much as I hated to agree with the good reverend, some of what he said made sense. My staying here is no longer appropriate. Nothing will change for now, though, except where I sleep."

She raised a hand to finger her locket, but her expression never wavered. "The idyll is over, Mr. Wilder, the world has intruded. Perhaps it's time you resumed your life, and Toby and I resumed ours."

He wanted to shake her, force her to see his sincerity. "I promised you two weeks, and I aim to keep that promise. I'll be back in the morning."

Lucy only shrugged. "As you will. Now if you'll excuse me, I have chores to finish. I also need to let Toby know that you're moving into town. He might have a few questions about the sudden change."

～

*T*oby did indeed have questions, quite a few of them. "But *why* does he need to move to some old hotel? Doesn't he like it here any more?"

Lucy stooped so that her eyes were on a level with Toby's and rested her hands on his shoulders. "It has nothing to do with whether or not he likes us, Toby. There are certain rules adults must follow if they want to be considered civilized and moral. One of these is that a man and woman don't live in the same house unless they are closely related, married, or there is another respectable adult present to act as chaperone."

"Chaperone?"

Lucy sighed. How did one explain such concepts to a six-year-old? "A chaperone is someone, usually a relative of the woman, who is present to see that the man and woman conduct themselves properly."

"But I could do that."

"No, darling, a proper chaperone must be another adult, preferably older."

Toby looked confused. "But y'all haven't been misbehaven', have you Ma?"

Lucy recalled that one memorable embrace and felt her face warm. "No darling, not really. But even the appearance that we might be is not proper. It's like minding your manners and using proper grammar. We do it because it's the way civilized people behave, not because it's easy, or because someone's watching."

She stood. "Besides, I told you Mr. Wilder wouldn't be staying very long. Consider this his first step back toward his regular life."

She turned to her laundry, not wanting Toby to see her expression. Because regardless of what Reed said or believed, Lucy knew this signaled the beginning of the end of his stay. What they'd had the past few days would never survive under the town's scrutiny.

He would hear all about her now, learn just what an undesirable sort she was. After that, it would be easy to let his business matters reclaim his attention. In no time at all he'd be ready to leave the area, return to his own home. His stay here would no doubt be quickly forgotten, or remembered only as anecdotes to be shared with friends and family.

$\sim$

*D*uring lunch, Reed carried most of the conversation. Lucy had retreated into reserved politeness, and Toby's natural exuberance was affected by her mood and knowledge of Reed's impending departure.

Afterwards, Reed and Toby moved to the parlor for a math lesson, while Lucy cleared the table. When she'd finished, a restlessness overtook her. She should get back to work on the dresses.

There was a lot left to do if she wanted to finish on time. But she didn't think she could face the task just now.

Feeling like a truant child, Lucy impulsively headed out the back door, grabbing a pail as she went. She needed time away from the house and away from reminders of what she was about to lose. Maybe thirty minutes of berry picking would give her that respite. Toby had been hinting just this morning that a cobbler would be a welcome treat. It seemed as good an excuse to get away as any. She'd be back before anyone missed her.

Trudging through the quiet, shady wood, Lucy indulged herself in a bout of self-pity.

How in the world had she let things come to this pass? Two weeks ago she hadn't even known Reed existed. Today, she was devastated by the thought that she might never see him again.

She thought she'd prepared herself for his leaving, had accepted it both mentally and emotionally. But she was wrong. Knowing that he would walk out of her and Toby's life as easily as he'd walked into it had in no way prepared her to deal with the event itself. It hurt, in a wrenching, heartbreaking way that she'd never experienced before.

Lucy reached her destination, the spot where she'd first laid eyes on Reed. She began to collect the berries, plucking them and dropping them into the pail with automatic movements as she continued to struggle with her thoughts.

What a pitiful fool she was. So much for her prideful stand of independence, of not needing anyone to survive. Problem was, surviving just didn't seem to be enough anymore.

Apparently she was so starved for attention and adult companionship that she fell head over heels for the first person to extend her a bit of kindness.

No! She shook her head, refusing to accept such a cowardly explanation. What she felt for Reed encompassed more than that. If companionship and affection were all she craved, she would have accepted Lowell's offer a long time ago. What she felt for Reed went much deeper. Something in him made her feel complete, made her more than she was without him.

It seemed only minutes later that she became aware of the weight of the pail and realized with a start that she'd filled it to near over-flowing.

So much for restoring her inner peace and confidence. It was time to head back and she was as miserable as when she'd left the house. Starting down the familiar path for home, Lucy felt the tears begin to trickle down her cheeks, and fought to stem them. Trying to regain her composure before she reached sight of the house, she bowed her head and sent up a silent prayer.

Dear Lord, I'm indeed grateful for the gift You sent me when You put this man in my care, no matter how temporary our time together. You've allowed me to feel the joy and keenness of spirit that comes from meeting that one who speaks to your heart, something I feared would be missing from my life forever. This experience, this feeling of connecting to a part of me I didn't know was missing, is something I will cherish forever and count well worth the pain. But I'm not strong enough to deal with his leaving on my own. Please, help me.

Suddenly, Lucy pitched forward. Berries flew in all directions as she reached out with both hands to break her fall. A sharp pain in her left arm wrested a cry from her just before the blackness blotted it all away.

CHAPTER 15

*R*eed was worried. After he and Toby finished their lesson he'd gone in search of Lucy.

He didn't like the way she'd withdrawn since the reverend's visit this morning. They needed to talk, to clear the air a bit. He would continue his work here; she'd learn that soon enough when he came back in the morning. But there was something else bothering her. He suspected it might have something to do with the things the reverend had said to her. If that was an example of what she'd been subjected to over the past several years it was a wonder she had any self-confidence and spirit left.

It wasn't her emotional well-being that worried him now, though. He'd checked in the house, looked in the barn, the garden, even out by the pond, and she was nowhere to be seen. Lucy was missing and he was at a loss as to where to look next.

He didn't believe she'd go to town without saying something. Wherever she'd gone, she no doubt planned to be back before she was missed. No, something was wrong, he could feel it. A sudden image of the Jefferson brothers flashed through his mind, and his gut clenched with anxiety.

After stepping into the front yard, Reed strode quickly over to where Toby and Jasper held imaginary outlaws at bay.

"Hey, Toby, I can't find your ma. Any idea where she might have gone off to?" Reed kept his tone casual and hoped his expression matched. He didn't want to worry the boy.

Toby frowned. "No sir." Then he brightened. "Unless she went after some blackberries. I asked her if we could have cobbler tonight. Let me see if the berry pail is missing." And he took off at a trot to the back of the house.

By the time Reed joined him, he was all smiles. "Yep, that's where she's gone all right. Just wait until you taste it. Ma's blackberry cobbler is even better than her peach."

"Sounds great." Reed's fears were only slightly mollified. She'd been gone way too long. "I tell you what, why don't I just go along and see if she needs any help. Think you could keep an eye on the place while I'm gone?"

Toby's chest puffed out. "Of course. Me and Jasper will take care of things all right and tight. You can count on us."

Reed smiled at the boy's confidence. "I know I can. Now, where would I be likely to find her?"

Toby pointed toward the woods behind the barn. "See that path up yonder by that big pecan tree? Just head straight down there. It takes you back to Cutter's Crossing, where we found you the other day. It's the best place around for berries."

Again the image of the Jefferson brothers crossed Reed's mind, and his whole body tensed with the need for action. He considered fetching his pistol, but decided it would only worry Toby, and besides would waste precious time. So, with a caution to Toby to take care and stay put, he headed out, keeping to a fast walk until out of sight of the boy. Then he picked up speed, keeping alert for any signs of trouble.

When Reed finally spied her it was almost anti-climatic. Rather than injured or in danger, she merely sat beside the path, resting against the trunk of a tree, the picture of someone without a care in the world.

His relief was quickly replaced by anger. How dare she put him through so much worry! Didn't she realize how long she'd been gone? Didn't she worry about how Toby might be feeling? The least she could have done was let them know where she'd be.

"Enjoying the solitude?" The cutting sarcasm in his tone was deliberate.

But Lucy seemed not to notice. Her face lit up with relief and something else he couldn't quite put a name to. "Oh Reed, I'm so glad you're here."

He only had a moment to puzzle over her tone before he took in all the details he'd missed earlier. The tumbled pail and scattered berries, her disarray, the way she held her left wrist protectively, the knot on her forehead showing starkly in her white face. He was at her side in a flash, kneeling beside her. "You're hurt. What happened?"

Her laugh was shaky at best. "It was the silliest thing. Like a henwit, I wasn't watching where I was going and tripped over a root. The fall knocked me out for a bit and I seem to have hurt my wrist."

Gently he took her arm. "Here, let me have a look at you."

She let him take her arm, but couldn't seem to stop talking. "I tried to get up after I came to my senses again, but I got dizzy and had to sit back down. I... I wasn't sure what to do. I thought, if I just rested a while, the dizziness would go away and then I could make it home on my own."

Her teeth had begun to chatter and Reed could tell she was much more shaken by the experience than she let on. "It's all right now," he soothed. "I'm here to help and I'll get you home in just a few minutes."

She nodded, and then sniffed as one lone tear trickled from the corner of her eye. "I'm sorry." She wiped it away with her good wrist. "I don't know why I should feel like crying now that I've been rescued."

He sat down beside her and put an arm around her shoulder.

"Don't apologize. You've been through a lot today. Go on and cry if you want to. You can even use my shoulder if you like."

She pushed ineffectively at his arm. "Don't be silly. I need to get home before Toby starts to worry." But even as she spoke, the tears came, slowly at first, and then more quickly.

Reed gathered her into his arms, careful of her injured wrist, and let her cry. He wished he could do something to ease her pain, a pain that he knew was much more than physical.

Oh but it felt so good to hold her. He'd looked for an excuse to take her in his arms again ever since that night in her kitchen. But now was not the time to think about what he wanted. So, contenting himself with trying to comfort her, Reed stroked her hair, and rocked her gently in his arms.

By the time she'd quieted, Lucy was limp, her face and his shirt equally damp. She kept her head down, buried in his chest.

"Feeling better?" he asked when she'd sniffed her last.

A nod answered him. Reed felt an aching tenderness for her as he tilted her head up with a finger. "Well then, as nice as it feels to have you in my arms, it's probably best that we get you back to the house." He smiled teasingly as her face reddened, and he received a shy smile in return.

"Do you think you can stand?"

Again she nodded.

"Good." Reed disengaged his arms from around her, and stood in a quick, fluid motion. Then he reached down to help her up. As soon as she stood upright, he scooped her into his arms.

Lucy, being Lucy, protested. "This really isn't necessary. I can walk now, if you'll just let me hold on to your arm. For goodness sake, Reed, your own injuries aren't fully healed. You'll—"

He gave her a light squeeze. "Will you be quiet and stop squirming? I'm going to carry you home regardless of what you say, so you might as well just settle down and enjoy the ride."

Lucy's mouth snapped shut and she glared into his eyes. Then her expression changed, softened. She nodded and snuggled more comfortably into his arms, her head against his chest.

Reed smiled in satisfaction, liking the feel of her arm around his neck. "There now, much better."

~

*T*he rest of the trip back was accomplished in a comfortable silence. *Very* comfortable, Lucy thought, rather liking the idea of being carried so protectively through the woods.

When they emerged from the shady peace of the wood, however, the sound of Reed biting back a growl had her looking around in alarm.

She groaned when she saw Lowell heading toward them, face red, expression belligerent. Dealing with a jealous suitor was the last thing she needed right now.

Lowell, of course, seemed ready to interpret things in the least favorable light. "What's going on? Put her down at once."

Reed settled Lucy more snugly in his arms. "Calm down, Crowder. There's been an accident and Lucy's hurt."

Lowell checked a moment. "Hurt! Lucy, what's wrong? How bad is it?"

Toby, too, clamored for reassurance. "What's the matter, Ma? Did you hurt your leg like Grandma Bea? Is that why Mr. Wilder's carrying you?"

Lucy answered Toby first. "It's all right Toby. I just tripped on a tree root. I felt a little dizzy so Mr. Wilder decided to carry me, but I'm better now. In fact, if he'll put me down, I can walk the rest of the way myself."

But Reed didn't loosen his hold. "I'm sure your ma is going to be just fine, Toby, but I think it best she stay off her feet for now. Why don't you go on and get her bed ready?"

"Yes, sir." And with one last, troubled look Lucy's way, the boy sped off toward the house.

Lucy scowled up at her captor, incensed at his I-know-best behavior. "That was uncalled for. You could see how worried he was. Why didn't you just put me down and let me walk?"

Reed seemed unmoved. "Time enough for reassurances later. First we need to let the doctor have a look at you."

She fumed silently as he turned back to Lowell. "Lucky thing you happened by, Crowder. You can run fetch the doctor, while I see that Lucy gets settled in and rests like she ought to."

From the look on Lowell's face, he didn't appreciate Reed's high-handedness either. "Oh no, I'll take care of Lucy while you fetch the doctor. You can take my buggy."

Reed's smile was less than friendly. "Sorry, I don't know where the doctor is or even how to get around in that town of yours. Better use of time all the way around if you do the fetching. Now hurry along. The quicker the doctor has a look at these injuries, the better we'll all feel."

Lowell's face turned a deep red and he took a belligerent step forward. "Now see here!"

Lucy felt her exasperation rise. Really, these two were acting more like spoiled little boys than Toby ever had. "Oh for goodness sake, Lowell, what he says makes sense. I'll be perfectly fine with Mr. Wilder. Just find Doc Lawton and fetch him here so we can get this whole thing over with."

Lowell frowned, but apparently realized he had little choice. With a curt nod, he left, threatening more than promising to be back in short order.

Lucy turned from Lowell's retreating back and gave Reed a fierce look designed to tell him just what she thought of his smug grin. When his expression turned suitably abashed, she directed him to either put her down and let her walk, or get moving and carry her inside like he'd promised.

By the time Reed got Lucy to her room, Toby had the bed turned down and ready for her. Reed set her down gingerly, and she reluctantly unwrapped her arm from his neck.

Toby hovered around the bed, his worry palpable. "Are you sure you're going to be all right? Does it hurt bad, like my leg cramps do? Can I do something to make it better?"

Lucy reached out and pulled him closer. "I promise, Toby, I'm going to be just fine. It's only my wrist and it hardly even hurts anymore."

Reed intervened, placing a hand on Toby's shoulder and drawing him away from Lucy. "Mr. Crowder's gone to fetch the doctor. Now, if I know anything about doctors, he's going to want lots of hot water when he gets here. Not sure why, but doctors always want hot water. Do you think you could take care of stoking the stove and putting some water on to boil?"

"Yes, sir! I'll get to it right away."

When he'd gone, Reed turned to Lucy. "Now, let's see what we can do to make you comfortable until the doctor arrives. First thing we need to do is take off those shoes so you can put your feet up." He sat down on the bed beside her and patted his knee. "Come on let's have them."

Lucy shook her head, appalled at the very idea. "Really, that's not necessary."

"You can't take them off one-handed, and I'm not about to let you use that left hand of yours till the doctor has a look at your wrist. So come on, up we go." And he lifted her left leg and placed her ankle on his knee.

Lucy felt the heat rise in her face as he moved the hem of her dress up to mid-calf. Truth to tell, she was even more embarrassed by having him take such a close look at the state of her footwear. Her shoes, worn and mottled with age, were designed to be serviceable and sturdy rather than feminine and ornamental. And her stockings had been patched and mended countless times. She knew Reed was aware of her lack of finances, but she hated having him see such tawdry proof.

He kept his head down, sparing her the need to meet his gaze. The feel of his hands on her ankles sent little shivers of awareness coursing through her. Did he feel it too?

~

*R*eed spared little thought for the state of her footwear. Rather, he found himself admiring her slender ankles, and her tiny, very feminine feet. He could barely fight the temptation to caress them. That was the reason he kept his head down, his face averted. If she could read his thoughts, which must surely be mirrored in his face, she'd take back those words she'd thrown at Lowell about being safe in his care.

Reed tossed the second shoe on the floor beside the first and stood quickly. "There now, is there anything else I can do to make you more comfortable?"

"I told you, I'm fine."

His lips twitched as he looked down at her. "It seems the roles have reversed on us."

She grinned back at him. "Perhaps, but you'll find I'm a better patient."

He raised a brow at that. "I've yet to see any evidence to support that claim."

He was almost disappointed to hear footsteps in the hall signaling Toby's return. He'd been enjoying the teasing give and take of the past few moments.

Reed turned as the boy entered the room. "Glad you're back, Toby. Why don't you help your ma finish settling down while I fetch the medicine box? There's a few cuts and scrapes I can take care of while we're waiting for the doctor."

And with quick instructions from Lucy on where to find said medicine box, Reed made his exit. As he headed down the hallway, he tried to examine his own admittedly confused feelings for Lucy.

He could no longer let himself believe he felt contempt or anger toward her. For good or ill, he found himself attracted to her. But could he get past the fact that she'd had his brother's baby out of wedlock, when Jon had already been married to another woman, a woman who'd also been her friend?

He was supposed to be the strong one, the one who could withstand the types of emotional blackmail and appeals to his sentimental side that his family had thrown at him over the years. It just didn't seem logical that her vulnerability should have affected him this way.

But deep inside he knew that, no matter what she'd been in the past, Lucy was a good woman now, a caring, brave, responsible woman. Of course he hadn't yet confronted her about the ring, but he believed now that it was quite possible she'd taken it out of need rather than from more mercenary motives.

When he opened the kitchen door he was no more certain of his feelings than he'd been earlier.

He opened the cabinet Lucy had directed him to and then let out a low whistle. The medicine box sat right where she'd said it would, but next to it stood an almost full bottle of very fine, very potent whiskey.

Reed carried both items, along with a glass, back to Lucy's room. He arrived to find her semi-reclined on the bed, propped up by pillows at her back. Toby sat beside her, feet dangling off the edge. Reed smiled at the boy and then sent him out to check on Ranger.

Lucy frowned when she saw what he carried. "What are you doing with Mother's pain tonic?"

"It was in the cabinet next to the medicine box. It was your mother's?"

"Uh-huh. Doc Lawton prescribed it for her. Said to give her a half-cup mixed with warm honey whenever the pain in her leg got too bad for her to sleep."

Lucy watched him pour up a generous portion, then he carried the glass to the bedside. "Now sit up straight and drink this."

She shook her head. "It always had a strange effect on Mother, almost as if it made her tipsy."

He smiled crookedly. "I understand but it'll help you relax and may numb the pain a bit."

Lucy shook her head, holding him off with a raised hand. "No. I don't think...I mean... I'd rather not..."

Reed interrupted her stuttering protests. "Look, I can tell that your wrist aches more than you're letting on, and goodness knows what else might be wrong. Now will you please just do as you're told and drink this up."

Lucy stared at him a long moment, but he kept his expression implacable. Finally, she gave in with a reluctant nod.

Not giving her a chance to change her mind, he put a hand behind her back and held the glass to her lips. She tried to take small sips but he was having none of that. Her first swallow was a large gulp that set her to coughing and sputtering. He gave her a minute to recover, and then had her drink the rest of it in a few quick gulps.

By the time she finished, Lucy felt a warmth beginning to spread through her mid-section. She also felt alarmingly light-headed.

"Now then," Reed said as he set the glass down, "let's have a look at your hands shall we? Lean back and give me your right hand."

Responding to the authority in his voice, Lucy did as he asked.

Reed took her hand and set to work. There were three scratches on her palm and two on her arm, all superficial. He cleaned them and then decided they would do just fine without further doctoring.

He didn't want to bother her injured arm. Instead Reed focused on her face.

He took a fresh washcloth, wet it and wrung it out. When he sat back down beside her he noticed she had taken hold of her locket and was stroking its surface with her thumb.

"That's a fine looking piece of jewelry you have there. Is it an heirloom?"

She started guiltily, then smiled as she held it out for him to get a better look. "Yes. It was my mother's. Daddy gave it to her on their wedding day. It had belonged to his grandmother before that."

He studied the ruby and pearl studded surface. "It's quite beautiful." Then he lifted his hand and began to wipe the dirt from her face. "Let me know if I hurt you."

She nodded and closed her hand around the locket again. "I suppose you think it's rather strange of me to wear it with my old work clothes."

He shrugged. "I'm sure you have your reasons."

"Mother gave it to me two days before she died. It was almost as if she knew..." Lucy paused and then flashed him an over-bright smile. "Anyway, she wore it all the time, said it made her feel closer to Daddy. And she told me I should do the same thing. That it wasn't meant to be hidden away, it was meant to be worn and enjoyed."

Reed turned to rinse the rag out. "Sounds like your mother was a very wise woman."

"Uh-huh." Then, as he resumed his ministrations, "That feels nice."

Hearing the slur in her voice, Reed hid a grin. A moment later she gave a great, heartfelt sigh, and he sat back, capturing her gaze. "What's wrong? Am I hurting you?"

"No. You have a wonderfully gentle touch. I just wish you weren't leaving here thinking that I'm a loose woman."

He frowned. "Whoa there. I *do not* think you're a loose woman." At least not any more. "Whatever put that nonsense into your head?"

She squinted at him. "You don't?" The she waved a hand. "Oh, you're just being nice again. It's all right. Everyone thinks it of me. I was just hoping you'd be different."

Reed set the cloth down and took her hand. "Look, I don't lie, not even to protect someone's feelings. Perhaps you *were* indiscreet in the past, but that doesn't make you wanton now. You've conducted yourself like a lady since I arrived here, and that's how I think of you."

Lucy shook her head. "That may have been true at first. But when you embraced me the other night, the way you left so abruptly? You were disgusted by my unladylike behavior, I could tell. And I... well I've let you take other liberties since. Like that embrace earlier today. A real lady wouldn't allow that."

Mentally berating his lack of control, Reed tried to make her understand. "I was disgusted with myself the other night, not you. Your response was unexpectedly compliant, true, but it wasn't wicked. As for the other, well you were hurting and you're a woman with honest emotions and needs. You have a loving nature, Miss Ames, but that does *not* mean you are wanton. I let my own feelings cloud my brain. I left the room the other night so I wouldn't further take advantage of you." Among other reasons.

"You did?" Her gaze searched his face again.

"Yes, ma'am. That's the kind of effect you have on me."

"Oh." Then she looked at him shyly. "You have that kind of effect on me too."

Reed grinned. That glass of tonic seemed to be having a very interesting side effect. "Glad to hear it."

She returned his smile and then her expression changed, grew wistful. Plucking at an invisible bit of lint on the bedspread, and not quite meeting his gaze, she asked, "Do you think, maybe, some-time, you could kiss me again?"

CHAPTER 16

*R*eed stilled. She looked so fragile, so beautiful sitting there, looking at him with desire and vulnerability in her sun-kissed eyes. To refuse her was unthinkable, no matter what it did to his carefully laid out plans or peace of mind. Slowly, tenderly, he gathered her to him and pressed his lips to hers.

He thought himself prepared and intended to make it nothing more than a gentle, cursory response to her sweet request. And that's how it started. But then she reached up to touch his cheek and she gave a little breathy sigh and the kiss turned into something warmer, deeper.

Her hand moved from his cheek to the back of his neck and he no longer had any thoughts of ending the kiss.

Finally, breathless, he broke it off, but gently. He hugged her to him, fighting to control his breathing.

She snuggled her head into his chest. "That was quite wonderful." Her voice had a dreamy, content softness to it. And he remembered that glass of tonic. He pulled back to look into her face, and was greeted with a yawn.

Reed grimaced. "You certainly have a knack for puncturing a gentleman's ego, Miss Ames."

She reddened in embarrassment. "Oh, I'm so sorry."

"Don't be." He kissed the top of her head and stood. "You just lie down. If I'm not mistaken, Jasper's announcing the doctor's arrival now."

A few minutes later, Toby escorted Doc Lawton and Lowell into the room. The cozy bedroom suddenly seemed very crowded.

"Hello, Lucy. Lowell tells me you've been hurt." The doctor brushed Reed aside and took his place beside the bed. Lowell already hovered on the other side, so Reed moved to the foot.

Lucy's answer was lost in a hiccup, and she brought a hand to her mouth with a lopsided grin. "Excuse me." She lowered her voice conspiratorially. "It must be the tonic"

The doctor cocked a sternly questioning eyebrow Reed's way, but Lowell wasn't so reticent as he rounded with a belligerent glare. "What did you give her? So help me, if—"

Lucy's shocked gasp cut him off. "Lowell Crowder! I'll thank you to watch how you speak to guests in my house."

Reed ignored Lowell and offered a sardonic smile to the doctor. "For medicinal purposes only, I assure you. I thought it might help her relax and dull the pain a bit."

The doctor's expression remained disapproving. "I see. Toby, why don't you fetch some clean cloths and a pitcher of water. You two *gentlemen*, just clear out so I can have some room to work. I'll call if I need anything."

Assuming the role of host, Reed stood at the door and let Lowell precede him, a gesture that seemed to infuriate Lucy's landlord. They exited the house together, Lowell glowering all the while.

In deference to Lucy's desire for peace, Reed decided to put some distance between himself and Crowder. "The gate on the barnyard fence needs work. I think I'll get Toby to help me with it. Might take his mind off his worries. Just make yourself at home here on the porch while you wait for the doctor."

Lowell's jaw clenched. "Don't push me, Wilder. I don't know what your game is, but you're not the man of the house. In fact you're more of a guest here than I am."

Reed pitched his voice in the silky tone that had intimidated many a business opponent. "I don't play games. You might want to remember that. Now, as I said, I've work to do."

As promised, Reed kept Toby busy until he saw the doctor step outside. He was on the porch in a matter of seconds, Toby at his heels. "So, what's the verdict? How bad is it?"

Doc Lawton addressed his remarks to Lowell. "She's got a nasty bump on her head, but there's no sign of a concussion. She'll likely have trouble with headaches for the next day or so, but nothing more serious."

Then he rubbed his chin. "Her wrist is another matter. It's not broken, but it *is* sprained. I've wrapped it, and she should use a sling when she's up and about. She shouldn't use her left hand for any lifting or grasping for the next week or so."

An amused *humph* escaped from Reed. The doctor didn't know Lucy very well if he thought a mere sprained wrist could keep her from her normal routine.

Doc Lawton shot a disapproving glance his way, then allowed a question from Toby to distract him.

"Is it all right if I go back in and see her now?"

The doctor nodded. "Just be careful of her left arm."

Toby slipped through the door, and the doctor turned back to the two men. "She's already told me she doesn't want any tonic for the pain, but if she should change her mind, send somebody by the clinic and I'll take care of it. I recommend that she come by in a few days in any case, and let me look at her again."

He moved away. "Now, if you'll excuse me, I have another patient to check on, and the town council meeting starts in about an hour, so I'm in a bit of a rush. Lowell, you coming?"

"You go ahead, Doc. I'll be there in time for the meeting, but I want to check in on Lucy before I go."

Reed lounged against a support post as Doc Lawton tipped his hat and left. Lowell turned to him and pasted on a conciliatory expression. "I heard you were checking into the hotel tonight. Maybe I can show you the way."

Reed flashed a smile. "That's mighty considerate of you, Crowder. But I plan to stay late and finish up a few things that need seeing to around here. I wouldn't want to keep you from any business you might have, like that meeting the doctor mentioned."

Lowell's scowl only served to increase the size of Reed's grin. With gritted teeth, the man spun on his heels and headed back into the house.

Reed followed at a more sedate pace. He wasn't surprised to find Lucy already up, seated on the edge of the bed. Toby sat on the floor, helping her get her shoes back on.

She flashed Reed a look of irritation. "You too! This is my bedroom, for goodness sake. Don't either of you *gentlemen* believe in a woman's right to a bit of privacy?"

Reed smiled sympathetically, guessing that her outburst had more to do with frustration over her situation than with his presence. The vulnerable air she'd worn earlier had now vanished.

Lowell, however, began a hasty apology. "Sorry Luce, but I just wanted to see how you were doing. You had me worried. Are you sure you should be up so soon?"

"Oh for goodness sake, Lowell, it's just a sprained wrist, not a mortal wound. I'm fine, and I don't intend to fritter away the rest of the afternoon in bed when there's work still to be done."

Lowell drew himself up with an air of injured dignity. "I see. Pardon me for being concerned. I should have known you wouldn't react the way a lady with normal sensibilities would."

Her head snapped around and she stared at him with narrowed eyes for a few seconds. "Yes, I would have thought that, after all this time, you *would* have."

Lowell flushed a dark red. "I see. Well, I'd stay to help, but as Doc Lawton reminded me, the town council meets this afternoon and I need to be there. So, if you'll excuse me."

Then he checked as he saw Reed standing by the door. "Then again, if you'd rather I stayed for a bit longer, until time for Mr. Wilder to leave, I can probably—"

"Lowell, will you stop being so melodramatic and just go on?

I've been fine here with Mr. Wilder so far, and that's not likely to change because of a little accident. Besides, he won't be far behind you."

With a curt nod, Lowell turned on his heel and left.

Reed fought hard to keep the grin from his face. Being on the receiving end of so much sympathy only seemed to magnify Lucy's prickly side.

He felt a little more sympathy for Lowell, however, when Lucy turned her glare his way. "Well? I don't find this amusing, Mr. Wilder, and I sure don't remember inviting you into my bedroom."

Reed pushed away from the wall, remembering the way she had most definitely invited his kiss earlier. The memory of how wonderful she'd tasted, of how good she'd felt in his arms, widened his smile. Did she feel anything close to what he did? Did she even remember or was it lost in the whiskey-induced haze she'd been under?

But she was still staring at him frostily, no hint of her earlier warmth. "Yes, ma'am, I mean no, ma'am. I mean... come on Toby, I think your ma wants a bit of privacy right now."

❧

*A*s soon as they closed the door behind them, Lucy plopped back on the bed with a groan. Not only did her wrist hurt like it'd been snake bit, but the dull ache inside her head made it difficult to think straight. Her mother had always considered any form of liquor the devil's brew, and now Lucy knew why.

But more than physical discomfort bothered her right now. Heaven help her, she'd actually asked Reed to kiss her! What had possessed her? And after her supposedly firm resolve to keep her distance. She wished she could blame it on the whiskey, but she couldn't. Getting tipsy had only emboldened her to act on something she'd wanted to do for quite some time. What must he think, especially after the earful he'd gotten from the reverend?

It seemed she *was* a wicked, immoral creature. It wasn't her strength of character that kept her virtuous all these years, just the fact that she hadn't faced true temptation. Recognizing her self-righteous smugness for what it was, Lucy raised a trembling hand to her mouth. He said he didn't think of her as a "loose woman," but could he still say that after the way she'd thrown herself at him so shamelessly?

But her shame eased as she remembered the embrace. Something so sweet, so right feeling, couldn't be truly wicked. Could it? If Reed had been courting her, such an embrace would have earned nothing more than mild censure along with an understanding wink from most folks. Of course, that wasn't the case here, so it was a serious breach of propriety. But surely it didn't make her despicable.

The kiss *had* been amazing, so sweet and so passionate at the same time. She feathered a fingertip across her lips, feeling again the tender, demanding touch of his there. Almost worth the turmoil she felt now.

Well, she couldn't hide in her room forever. Lucy rose, ignoring her treacherous stomach. She washed her face and picked up her hairbrush. Several hairpins had fallen out and her hair now was more down than up. Unable to repin the heavy tresses with only one hand, though, she finally gave up and pulled out the remaining pins, letting it hang loose.

Once she reached the front hall, the murmur of voices and the aroma of fresh brewed coffee led her to the kitchen. Relieved that she wouldn't be facing Reed alone, she squared her shoulders and strode into the room, hoping her face reflected more composure than she felt.

Toby spotted her first. "Ma! Look, we made you a sling."

Lucy paused, trying to hide her dismay. She didn't care for the idea of wearing a sling, despite what Doc Lawton had said. It just seemed too pitiful, too much a symbol of weakness.

But Toby beamed with pride, wearing the air of someone offering a wonderful gift. Lucy couldn't hurt his feelings by seeming ungrateful.

She stole a quick glance at Reed's face, and though she could detect nothing in his expression, she had the distinct impression that he'd known exactly what her reaction would be, and planned accordingly.

"Don't you like it?" The uncertainty in Toby's voice brought her focus back to him, and she moved toward the table, giving him her brightest, everything's-just-fine smile.

"Of course I do. How clever of you to come up with such a wonderful surprise."

Toby brightened. "It was Mr. Wilder's idea, but I helped."

His words confirmed her suspicions, and she shot Reed a frown. But Toby reclaimed her attention. "Well, aren't you going to try it out?"

"Yes, of course I am." She reached down to pick it up, but Reed moved quicker, whisking the cloth from under her hand.

"Here, you'd better let me help you with that."

When he stood, Lucy found herself toe to toe with him and involuntarily took a step back. Reed smiled and took a half step forward, keeping a more respectable distance this time.

"Now, let's try this on for size. Place your arm in here. Now pull it back against your chest. A little higher. That's it. Does that seem a comfortable height to you?"

At Lucy's nod, he raised his arms, bringing the ends behind her neck. She lowered her head, but not just to give him freer access. His nearness already played havoc with her ability to breathe normally. Now the touch of his fingers on the back of her neck, and the warmth of his breath on her hair were coming dangerously close to undoing her altogether.

To make matters worse, he appeared to be having trouble with the knot, because his hands fumbled and teased at her neck for what seemed to be a torturously long period of time.

When his hands fell away and he moved back, Lucy didn't know if she felt relieved or bereft. She kept her face lowered, not daring to let him see what must be mirrored there.

"Now, how does that feel?" Reed asked. "Too tight, too loose? Just say the word and I'll adjust it for you."

"It's perfect," Lucy rushed to assure him. There was no way she would let him do that to her control again, especially not here in front of Toby. She changed the subject. "I sure hope there's an extra cup of coffee left in the pot."

Reed moved toward the stove. "Yes, ma'am. Just have a seat and I'll fix it for you."

~

*R*eed was glad to have an excuse to turn his back for a few moments. It seemed just touching the nape of her neck could send his thoughts where they had no business going.

A few moments later he placed a full cup of the aromatic brew in front of her.

"Thanks," she said, with a quick upward glance that went no further than the tip of his nose.

Reed decided the best way to put her at ease would be to get her riled. "You may as well know, Toby and I have decided that we're not going to let you do any work around here the rest of the day. So you can just find an interesting book to read, and relax in the parlor or out on the porch swing."

She bristled, as he'd known she would. "You and Toby decided that, did you? Well, you can just un-decide right now. It's the middle of the afternoon. There's laundry to bring in, supper to prepare, livestock to water, and any number of other things that need seeing to. This bit of fuss has already put me several hours behind. If you think I'm going to fritter away the rest of the afternoon with a book, you can just jolly well think again."

Reed hid a smile. Now there was his Lucy—direct to the point of bluntness, refusing to admit to any chink in her armor, and suspicious of any offer of help.

He held up a hand. "I'm willing to acknowledge your superior skills in the kitchen, but just for tonight, why don't you humor us menfolk, and let us try our hands at a few of your chores? You can supervise just as close as you like."

Toby added his voice. "Please, Ma. Doc Lawton told you to take it easy. Don't you want to make sure you heal all right? Mr. Wilder and I can take care of supper and the rest, honest."

Reed hid a smile as he watched Lucy's pride lose the struggle with her maternal instincts. She just wasn't proof against Toby's anxious expression.

"Oh, all right," she grumbled. "But I'm not about to sit with a book while you do it. I'm not entirely helpless. There's plenty to do, and not all of it requires two hands."

Two hours later, with most of the chores complete, they were ready to sit down to supper. A supper that Lucy had directed but not lifted a finger, other than to wag it admonishingly toward her helpers, to prepare.

Reed removed the apron that Lucy had gleefully insisted he wear, and shooed her away from the stove. "Everything's under control here. Why don't you have a seat at the table? For tonight, you're to sit back and allow me and Toby to wait on you."

She tried to sidestep him and move back to the stove, but Reed pointed a cooking spoon in her direction. "You're forgetting the rules again. You are not to lift a hand tonight. Now, have a seat."

He turned and winked at Toby, who tried to stifle a giggle. "Looks like this stew is about ready to dish up. Why don't you set the table?"

They asked Lucy to take the first bite, and she made an elaborate production of it. First she scooped a generous serving onto her spoon and brought it delicately into her mouth. Then she slid the spoon back out through pursed lips. Closing her eyes, she began to chew, and her face took on an expression of dreamy concentration, as if she were savoring each and every ingredient.

Finally, Toby, tired of the wait, broke the spell. "So, how is it?"

Lucy swallowed and opened her eyes. "Absolutely delicious," she said with a generous smile. "My compliments to the cooks. I suggest you two dig in and try it yourself."

Later, Reed took care of the dishes while Toby ran out to feed Jasper the scraps. He hung the dishrag up on a nail over the sink, then he turned to find Lucy watching him with troubled eyes.

She looked down, tracing a pattern on the table with her finger. "It'll be dusk soon. You probably should be on your way. Toby and I can finish things up here. The road into town is in pretty good shape, but it'd be best if you have some light to see by since you're not used to it."

Her voice sounded level and matter-of-fact, but Reed wasn't fooled. He crossed the room, pausing to stand beside her. "I'm all done. But there's no rush, I've time left before dark."

She looked up and then back down again, continuing to sketch patterns with her finger. After a moment, she spoke again, her voice soft but resolute. "This makes us even, you know."

Reed sat down and put his hand on hers, stilling her restless movements. His sleeves were rolled up, and for a moment he was struck by the contrast between his muscular arm and her own strong but more delicately formed one. The sight touched him as much as the feel and scent of her. It seemed none of his senses were immune to the attraction he felt.

But he could explore those feelings later. Right now he needed her to talk to him.

When she looked up, as if in answer to his unspoken request, her smile was over-bright. "I mean, you no longer need to feel you owe me anything. I took care of your injuries and now you've taken care of mine. When you leave tonight you can resume your life, free from any obligation to us."

Reed drew his hand back and sat up straighter. "You're comparing this to what you did for me? If I didn't know better, Miss Ames, I'd think you were trying to get rid of me."

Lucy's eyes widened and she shook her head. "You know better than that. It's only, well, your debt has been paid. You don't owe me anything more, and I don't take charity."

"You just don't understand, do you?" Reed leaned forward, trying to add emphasis to his words. "I'm here because I want to be, not because I have to be. I told you I'd be back in the morning, and I will." He stared at her, trying to drill understanding into her with his eyes. But she just sat there, chin up. Her hand reached up and clutched the locket as if it were a talisman that she drew strength from.

Sighing, he leaned back. "I know you won't welcome it, but I want to give you a piece of advice."

Her expression turned wary, but she held on to her silence.

"To put it bluntly, you need to learn how to accept help. And not only accept it, but do so graciously. It's not a sign of weakness, you know. It's all right, and even occasionally noble, to allow someone else to reap satisfaction from knowing he helped a friend in need."

She glared at him. "That's a case of the pot calling the kettle black, don't you think?"

Reed didn't back down. "Maybe. But there's a difference in my approach and yours. I may not like having to receive or ask for help, but when it's necessary, I grit my teeth and do it. You, on the other hand, fight it tooth and nail all the way."

Her color rose and her lips compressed. "I'll not be pitied or be someone's charity case."

They'd reached the heart of the matter now, and Reed was ready. "There's a difference between pity and charity. Pity is rooted in feelings of self-righteousness and superiority. Charity is rooted in love, and in a true desire to help. It's what real friends and neighbors feel when they see someone who has fallen on hard times of one kind or another. Surely you see the difference."

Her lips maintained their uncompromising, mutinous line, so Reed tried an explanation closer to home. "When you spoke of your parents, didn't you say that they were known for helping those who needed it?"

Lucy nodded, obviously suspicious of where he was headed. "And do you think there was anything ulterior in their motives?"

"Of course not. They—"

"And do you think they thought any less of the people they helped, just because they'd been forced to accept that help?"

"No, but—"

"Think back, can you recall a time when someone needed help, but because of false pride, refused to accept it?" He could tell she remembered something, and pressed on. "Who did their actions hurt? What about your attempts to help me that first day? What did you think of my attempts to take care of myself, my insistence that I didn't need your help? Did you think I was being brave and strong, or merely foolish?"

He paused, but she kept silent, staring at him with troubled eyes. "Lucy, pride can be a good thing, it can provide strength and conviction to our character. But taken to the extreme, it can over-power and cripple."

Gently, he hammered in the final nail. "Think about what you're teaching Toby. Do you want him to learn, through your example, how to receive as well as to give, learn the lessons of humility as well as pride? Do you want him to be strong enough to accept help if he should need it? Or do you want him to lean on the crutch of misdirected pride, no matter the cost?"

Lucy was spared the need to respond by Toby's return.

Reed, who'd only wanted to give her something to think about, decided he'd accomplished enough for one night. He was pretty sure that, given he would be taking Toby back to Delaware with him when he left, she'd want to come too. But knowing Lucy's prickly pride, one could never tell. She might insist on coming on her own terms rather than accepting the comfortable set-up he wanted to provide for her. And that would never do.

He stood and rolled down his sleeves. "Now, I need to get packed up. But I *will* be back in the morning."

Twenty minutes later Reed gave a final yank to the leather thong securing his bags to Ranger's saddle. As he led the animal out of the barn, Toby trailed along, dragging his feet.

Reed studied the boy's bent head. "Well, I guess it's time for me to head into town. I expect you to look after your ma and see that she doesn't try to use that hand of hers."

Toby nodded, not looking up. "Yes, sir."

Reed looked from Toby's bent head to where Lucy stood on the porch. It frustrated him to know they both were so unsure of his intent to return tomorrow after he'd given his word to do so.

He searched his mind for a way to provide some reassurance, and came up with an idea just as he approached the front of the house. "By the way Lucy, I have a favor to ask of you?"

She eyed him suspiciously. "Yes?"

He pulled his hunting rifle from the back of his horse. "I'd like to leave this with you for now if it won't be in your way. I won't need it while I'm in town, and there's no point in carting it back and forth."

Toby's reaction was swift and gratifying. A wide grin brightened his face and he stood straighter, erasing the slump in his shoulders. Just as Reed had hoped, this visible sign of his intent to return finally convinced the boy.

Lucy looked from him to Toby and then back. Her lips curved in a grudging smile. "Of course."

"Thanks, I really appreciate that." Reed handed Toby the rifle, assuring Lucy it was unloaded, then touched the brim of his hat in salute. Mounting the horse, he gathered the reins and looked toward the porch again. "I'll be here bright and early. Make sure you save me a couple of biscuits."

CHAPTER 17

"Welcome to Far Enough, Mr. Wilder."

At the unexpected greeting, Reed looked up from the inn's register. He'd arrived in town just before dark. Venable's Hotel and Cafe, while small by big city standards, stood as one of the bigger buildings in this town and had been easy to find. Most of the bottom floor was dedicated to the cafe, with only a small area near the entrance allocated to the hotel check-in desk. The hotel rooms, all four of them according to a sign near the front door, were located on the second level.

A young girl stood beside him now, aiming an almost too bright smile his way. Despite her straw colored, little girl braid and freckle-spattered nose, she had a certain determination of purpose about her that warned Reed to take her seriously.

"Miss," he acknowledged with a cautious nod, and waited for her to state her business.

"I'm Connie Sue Morton, Sheriff Morton's daughter. I heard from Reverend Cummings that you would be checking in here this evening, and I wanted to greet you personally."

Now that she'd introduced herself, he could see something of her father in her, especially in her don't-underestimate-me eyes.

Taking the hand she extended, he bowed slightly and released it. "Thank you, Miss Morton, I'm honored to make your acquaintance. I hope you haven't gone out of your way on my account."

She shook her head. "Not at all. In fact, after speaking to Father and Reverend Cummings, I admit to being curious about you." The engaging smile that accompanied her words offset any negative connotation they carried.

Reed, impatient to put away his bags and get Ranger stabled, tried for a polite smile. "As you can see, there's nothing about me to warrant the attention of a young lady such as yourself. Please give the Sheriff my regards." He nodded again and turned back to the register, firmly ending the interview.

But the girl persisted, either missing or ignoring his disinterest. "I was wondering, sir, if after you put your things away, you might like to share some of Mrs. Venable's cinnamon apple pie with me here at the cafe. It's the best pie in these parts and I would be glad to answer any questions you have about the community."

Reed raised an eyebrow. Now why would a young lady, and the Sheriff's daughter to boot, invite a stranger to share a table with her? "Curiosity" she'd said. Looking for a juicy tidbit to gossip about, perhaps? "Thank you miss, but that's not necessary. I'm—"

"Please, I'd be glad for the company this evening."

Something in her tone and expression prompted Reed to pause. Perhaps there was more to the invitation than he first thought. Studying her, he revised his earlier estimation of her age. Not an adolescent, more likely a young woman of nineteen or twenty.

His interest piqued now, Reed decided to accept her invitation, just to see where it led. "Well, since you put it that way, I'd be honored."

She smiled in obvious relief. "Thank you. Now, you just take as much time as you need getting your things settled in upstairs. I'll be right down here whenever you get ready."

"No need for that. I wouldn't want to keep you waiting." Reed caught the eye of a strong looking boy leaning against the front desk. "You there. How would you like to earn two bits?"

Peter Venable, the owner's twelve-year-old son, stepped forward with alacrity. "Yes, sir!"

"Here then." Reed handed over his saddlebag. "Take this to my room. When you get that done, you'll find my horse tethered right outside. Lead him over to the stable and tell whoever's in charge there that I'll be over later to settle the arrangements."

He turned back to the Sheriff's daughter and offered his arm. "Now Miss Morton, let's have a taste of that pie, shall we?"

She indicated her preference for a table at the far end of the room. As they started through the maze of tables and chairs, Reed noted that the two of them were attracting quite a bit of attention.

Miss Morton paused to speak to a middle aged couple seated near the front. "Mrs. Hopkins, what a lovely dress you're wearing this evening. I don't think I've seen such a vibrant shade of green before." Then, as if only just remembering her companion, "Oh, pardon me. Mr. Wilder, I'd like you to meet Mayor and Mrs. Hopkins. Mayor, Mrs. Hopkins, this is Mr. Wilder. He's visiting here for a spell and will be staying at the hotel."

The self-important couple obviously didn't welcome the introduction, but were trapped into at least the appearance of civility. So, greetings were exchanged, with amused politeness on Reed's part, flustered embarrassment on the mayor's part, and a frosty terseness on Mrs. Hopkins's part.

They moved only a short distance when Miss Morton stopped again. "Mr. Griffith, I hope Dolly's feeling better. Please tell her we missed her smiling face at the quilting circle today. By the way, I'd like to introduce you to a visitor to our town."

And so it went. By the time they reached their table, Reed had been introduced to no less than ten of Far Enough's leading citizens. He wasn't sure whether to be amused or angered by her high-handedness.

"That was quite a little performance," he commented as he seated her.

His companion didn't pretend to misunderstand. "I hope you

don't mind. I find it's best to meet closed-mindedness head on rather than hide from it or get defensive."

Before Reed could respond, a matronly woman, her face alight with curiosity, bustled up to their table.

"Good evening, Connie Sue. What can I get for you and your friend here?"

"Good evening Mrs. Venable. I'd like you to meet Mr. Wilder. He's going to be a guest here at the hotel for a while. Mr. Wilder, this is Mrs. Venable, the best cook in all of northeast Texas."

Reed stood at the introduction. "Glad to make your acquaintance, ma'am."

"No need to stand on formalities here, young man. You just sit yourself right back down. We're pleased to have you as a guest and will sure do our best to see that you enjoy your stay. Now, what can I get for you folks?"

"I hear the cinnamon apple pie is a specialty of yours. How about two slices along with some tea for the lady and coffee for me."

She nodded. "Good choice. Now you just make yourselves comfortable-like and I'll be back with it in nothing flat."

As soon as Mrs. Venable departed, Reed returned to the original topic. "Is this a normal Monday night crowd for the cafe, or is this all for my benefit?"

She smiled an apology. "I'm afraid news of your arrival preceded you."

Reed raised an eyebrow. "And word of where I've been?"

"We don't get many visitors here, so any stranger would attract attention. But yes, your story has stirred up quite a bit of speculation and interest."

"Gossip, you mean."

Connie Sue didn't even blink. "Exactly. A lot of spiteful, nasty things are being whispered about since word of your existence and whereabouts got out. And, since you apparently like being direct, I'll add that I was quite prepared to lay the blame entirely on your shoulders."

He leaned back in his chair. "Were you now?"

She nodded decisively. "Yes. Not only did your arrival stir up all the scandal surrounding Lucy, just when she might have had a chance to put it behind her, but the bruise on Lowell's jaw indicates a certain tendency toward violence on your part."

Miss Morton definitely shared her father's directness. "Yet, based on your little performance a moment ago, you seem to be letting the town know I have your stamp of approval."

"Daddy seems to like you. Not trust you entirely, but like you nonetheless. And he isn't worried about Lucy's safety. Daddy's a pretty good judge of people, so I have to believe you're not the villain I thought. That being the case, I wanted to make sure you get a fair shake around here."

Reed raised an eyebrow at that, but let it go. "You mentioned that Lucy had a chance to put the scandal behind her before I showed up. Care to elaborate on that?"

The arrival of Mrs. Venable with their order spared Connie Sue from an immediate response. Once they were alone again, however, she faced Reed squarely. She leaned forward, mimicking his earlier movement. "A few weeks ago, I attended her mother's funeral, and took a good look at her. I was both intrigued and embarrassed. Intrigued by the strength and honest pride I sensed in her, and embarrassed by the way she'd been either ignored or shunned by most everyone in town, including myself. I've made a few overtures since, but haven't met with much success. I think she's afraid to trust anyone anymore. She's a hard person to get close to. That's where I need your help."

Reed crossed his arms. "And just why do you want to get close to her?" He didn't try to hide his mistrust. Crowder and Reverend Cummings had made him wary of any who claimed to have Lucy's best interests at heart. He planned to buffer her from any more of that kind of "caring" if he could.

Not that it was really any of his business, he reminded himself. It was just that he was a guest in her house, and as long as he

A MATTER OF TRUST

accepted her hospitality, he did have an obligation to look out for her welfare.

Connie Sue didn't seem to take offense. "It's not guilt or pity or even a 'save the sinner' zeal, if that's what you're thinking. Actually, I admire Lucy a great deal. She's managed to make a life for herself and her family, despite all the obstacles thrown her way. As far as I can tell, she's refused to whine. She keeps her head high, regardless of any snubs or insults she receives. That takes courage and self-assurance. I couldn't have managed even half so well in her place."

She took a deep breath before continuing. "In short, Mr. Wilder, she appears to be someone whose company I would enjoy, someone I could share secrets and dreams with, without fear of derision or betrayal. I dearly want that kind of friend. And I could offer her something of the same in return."

Reed's analytical mind was working furiously, leaping ahead to what Connie Sue was trying to explain, what she could do for Lucy. What she didn't know was his plan to take Lucy away from here, set her up somewhere near his home in Delaware. It was his intent that Lucy never have to face the kind of rebuff, the isolation, the disgrace that she'd felt in this town again. It would be the final payment in the debt he owed her. Besides, she'd been a good mother to Toby. She deserved to live the rest of her life with some semblance of dignity. This had absolutely nothing to do with his own personal feelings, he assured himself again.

Connie Sue raised her head a notch, continuing her explanation. "Believe it or not, I do have a bit of influence with the people of this town. If she'll let me stand by her, I think together we could face down the gossips, and give her and Toby a chance to become a real part of the community again. And I think you can help me."

Reed, on the point of turning her down, paused. Miss Morton seemed sincere. It might do Lucy good to find herself on the receiving end of a friendly overture from someone in this town. Accepting friendship was a small step away from accepting help. Perhaps this would help pave the way for other things.

Reed saluted Connie Sue with his cup. "Miss Morton, I believe you and I are going to be very good friends. Tell me more of what you have in mind."

～

"Mr. Wilder!" Toby stopped sweeping the front porch as soon as Reed rode up. Abandoning his broom, he bounded down the steps, a welcoming grin lighting up his entire face.

Reed smiled, unexpectedly touched to realize the boy had kept an eye out for his arrival. "Mornin' Toby. Think you could take care of Ranger for me while I go say hello to your ma?"

"Sure thing." Toby, already stroking the horse's nose in greeting, looked up at Reed. "Oh, we saved you some biscuits, just like you asked."

"Sounds good." Reed handed the reins to Toby and headed for the front door. Amazing how this felt almost like a homecoming. He'd missed listening to Lucy sing Toby to sleep last night. He'd missed sitting down to breakfast with the two of them and planning out the morning chores. He'd missed the sound of Lucy's humming as she cleared the breakfast table. And, he might as well admit it, he'd just plain missed Lucy.

Toby stopped him, though, before he'd gone three steps. "Ma's out in the garden."

Reed raised an eyebrow at that. "She hasn't been abusing that hand of hers, has she?"

Toby shrugged, with a what-do-*you*-think expression on his face. "She's trying to be good, but you know Ma."

Reed shook his head and changed direction. As soon as he reached the corner of the house, he spied Lucy. Filling a bucket from the barnyard pump, she worked determinedly but awkwardly, her injured wrist still bandaged and tucked inside the sling.

The exertion had brought a flush to her cheeks and a fine sheen of sweat to her face and neck. Stray tendrils of hair curled raggedly at her temples, and a smudge of dirt adorned one side of her nose. The dress she wore was patched and faded, her ever-present apron wet and soiled from her work at the pump. But Reed felt he'd never seen a woman who attracted him more.

He caught up to her in a few quick strides. "Here, let me take that for you."

"You're out early today." Did he see a flicker of relief in her eyes? It was gone before he could be sure.

"No point wasting a fine morning like this. I take it you're watering the garden?"

She gave him a sidelong look but accepted his change of subject. "Uh-huh. We haven't had any rain to speak of for a few days now and things are starting to dry out."

"Tell you what. This will go quicker if we work together. I see a couple of buckets up on the porch. How about you fill them from the pump and I water the rows?" They'd reached the garden by then, and Reed didn't wait for her answer. Whistling cheerfully, he headed down the first row, leaving her with no choice but to fetch the other buckets.

Thirty minutes later, they were done. Reed and Lucy carried the empty buckets to the porch and sat on the edge to rest a minute.

Reed watched as, eyes closed, she arched her neck in an effort to ease her strained muscles. It was an unconsciously graceful and sensual movement. "We make a pretty good team, don't you agree?"

She opened her eyes then, and held his gaze for a long, breathless minute. He saw an intense longing that turned her eyes to molten amber. Reed fisted his hands to keep from snatching her into his arms again.

Then Lucy looked away, appearing to focus her eyes on the rooster strutting around the barnyard. "I've been thinking about what you said last night."

"Oh?" Reed cleared his throat as he tried to focus on her words.

"Yes, and I guess maybe there was some merit in what you had to say. Not that I'm ready to concede that I've done so terrible a job all these years."

Reed straightened. "That wasn't what I was saying at all! You ought to know me better than that. You've done a remarkable job providing for your family and raising Toby the way you have, and I'd never even hint otherwise."

Then he relaxed, trying to soften his next words. "It's just that, occasionally, when someone does put his hand out to help, you ought to at least consider the motives before you try to lop it off." *Let me take care of you like I want to when the time comes.*

Her self-deprecating grimace conceded his point, his spoken point at any rate, and her hand touched the bodice of her dress in that telltale gesture. "I know. Mother always said I had enough pride and directness for three people. Said I'd have to choose a husband carefully because I'd bowl right over most men, and I'd only be happy with someone who could hold his own."

"I said I would have liked your mother." Reed felt his heart swell with tenderness and admiration. He knew what such an admission cost her.

Then he snapped his fingers. "That reminds me, I met Sheriff Morton's daughter Connie Sue last night. Quite an interesting young lady." He paused a moment, knowing the kind of reaction his next words would bring. "She asked me to mention that she'd be coming by later this morning to pay you a visit."

Lucy's head snapped up. "Connie Sue's coming here? Whatever for?"

Reed shrugged. "She didn't say. I got the impression it was just a social call."

Lucy stood, pinning him down with an irritated glare. "You should have said something sooner. There are lots of things to do if I'm going to receive a caller properly."

Reed hid a smile. "Just make sure you keep that arm in a sling. Call me or Toby if you need help with anything."

He watched her hurry inside and nodded once in satisfaction. She might not welcome the idea of visitors, but her pride wouldn't let her give less than her best. It would do her good to have these little things to fuss over, rather than major questions of survival.

～

*F*or the next hour, Lucy, with Toby's help, worked to get her house ready for a visitor. She cleaned, baked cookies, picked flowers for the parlor, and set out her mother's china tea service. And as she worked, she kept going over those few minutes with Reed on the porch. He'd looked at her so intensely, so tenderly, she'd thought for a moment he might just kiss her again. But he hadn't. In fact he hadn't even touched her. She wondered now if she'd imagined it all, that she'd seen in his eyes only what she so desperately *wanted* to see there.

By the time Connie Sue arrived, Lucy was ready. Not only had she finished with her preparations, but she needed a distraction from her less than comfortable thoughts.

As she stepped out onto the porch to greet her visitor, though, Lucy discovered Connie Sue wasn't alone. Lowell, driving his buckboard, was right behind her.

Lucy threw Reed an accusing frown, but he shrugged. From the look on his face, she could tell he hadn't expected Lowell either.

Reed raised a hand to assist Connie Sue down, a warm greeting on his lips.

Lucy noted the quick smile they exchanged, and felt a little stab of jealousy. How much time had they spent together yesterday? They seemed like best of friends this morning. Perhaps it wasn't coincidence that brought Connie Sue here the day after she met Reed.

Connie Sue turned to Lucy. "I ran into Lowell this morning, and when I told him where I was headed, he insisted on coming along. Seems he's been planning to make some repairs to your barn roof, and now seems to be a good time, since Mr. Wilder is here to help. See, he's brought all the materials they'll need. I hope you don't mind."

Reed spoke up before Lucy could respond. "Of course she doesn't mind," he said heartily, though he threw Lowell a less than welcoming look. "Crowder, why don't you pull your wagon over to the barn and I'll help you unload it."

Then he turned back to Connie Sue, handing her a basket he retrieved from the seat of her buggy. "Miss Morton, if you'll just go on inside with Lucy, I'll take care of your horse and buggy for you."

Once inside, Lucy took Connie Sue's bonnet and led her into the parlor. But rather than taking a seat, Connie Sue remained standing, a determined smile on her face. "Now, where's your kitchen?"

Lucy stiffened. "My kitchen?"

"Yes. I heard about the injury to your wrist, so I thought I'd help out where I could today. I've brought a ham as my contribution for lunch, and I can help you get started on the rest. Those menfolk are going to have a pretty hefty appetite by the time they come down from the barn roof."

The offer brought Lucy's chin up. "I know you mean well, but I'm perfectly capable of providing the ingredients for our lunch and cooking them up myself. You're a guest in my house, not a servant."

But Connie Sue didn't flinch or back down this time. "This is not some impersonal handout, Lucy," she said with soft dignity. "This is one neighbor offering to help another."

Lucy's face remained closed for several very long seconds. Then she recalled Reed's words from last night and their conversation this morning. She studied Connie Sue's face, looking for some telltale sign of either insincerity or duplicity.

Finally, Lucy nodded. She'd all but promised to try things Reed's way, and this seemed a good time to start. "You're right. I apologize for my rudeness. The kitchen's this way."

Once in the kitchen, Lucy stepped out on the back porch to check on Toby. Just as she'd expected, he stood near the buckboard helping the two men unload the supplies.

It looked as if Reed and Lowell had reached a compromise of sorts. They were no longer squared off against each other, and if there seemed an air of competitiveness to their efforts, at least they weren't overtly hostile.

Lucy called out to Toby and got the attention of not only the boy but the two men as well. "When you get through helping unload the wagon, you have some other chores to finish."

Toby nodded. "Yes, ma'am. Then can I help them with the roof?"

Lucy studied the height of the barn roof. "I don't know—"

"Let him," Reed interrupted. "We could use a good helper. And don't worry, I'll keep an eye on him."

"Sure," Lowell added, not to be outdone. "A boy like Toby needs to be among menfolk, doing a man's work. You just leave him in our care now. I'll make sure he keeps safe."

Catching Reed's eye, and the non-verbal reassurance he offered, Lucy allowed herself to be convinced. "Well, all right. But Toby, you make sure you listen to what Mr. Wilder and Mr. Crowder tell you. And no horseplay up there."

"Yes, ma'am!"

"It must make you feel special to have two such fine men competing for your notice."

Lucy started, and not just because she hadn't realized Connie Sue stood at her shoulder. "Nonsense," she said as she turned, "you couldn't be more wrong."

She led the way back into the kitchen. "Their actions have more to do with male pride and competitiveness than with any real interest they have in me personally. Mr. Wilder is grateful for my rescuing him the other day. So he feels a responsibility to look out for me while he's here."

She offered Connie Sue a cup of tea as they sat at the table. "As for Lowell, he *thinks* he wants to marry me, but he's only fooling himself. He wants to make an 'honest woman' out of me, and is convinced we'll do fine together. He doesn't understand what I'm truly like. If I took him up on his offer I'd make him absolutely miserable."

Connie Sue took a sip of her tea and nodded. "I agree."

Lucy, taken aback by her quick agreement, paused and stared at her guest.

With a composure that surprised Lucy, Connie Sue elaborated. "You're absolutely right, at least about Lowell. You aren't the right kind of woman for him. You're much too assertive and vocal. You like to challenge the assumptions most folks have on how things are, and look instead at how they can be. Not bad qualities, mind you. In fact, I admire you for them. But Lowell needs someone who needs him, defers to him. Someone who'll be content to care for him and their family and to take her place in the community as his wife. Someone willing to look to him for answers and decisions."

Lucy stared at Connie Sue, surprised by what she read in the girl's face. "You're in love with Lowell."

Connie Sue's face turned bright pink but she held Lucy's gaze. "Yes, I am. I have been for some time now. Does that surprise you?"

The admission and question caught Lucy by surprise. "Yes. I mean, no. I mean, I never thought..."

Exasperation tinged Connie Sue's smile. "What you mean is that you never considered that a child like me would be able to form such an attachment. How old do you think I am?"

Flustered at having insulted her guest, Lucy did some quick arithmetic. Connie Sue had been in her early teens when she moved to Far Enough seven years ago, which would mean, "Oh my goodness, you're nearly twenty, aren't you?"

Connie Sue nodded forlornly. "I turned twenty last month. It's these dratted freckles and my lack of anything remotely resembling a woman's figure. No one in this town can see me as anything other than the gawky child I was when I moved here."

Lucy studied her critically. "It's probably presumptuous of me to say so, but with just a bit of change in hairstyle and wardrobe, we could erase any doubts about your status as a woman."

Connie Sue's eyes widened. "Do you really think so?"

"Uh-huh." Lucy leaned forward. "You have some beautiful features to work with. True, your freckles seem to dominate your face right now. But we could compensate for that by emphasizing some of your other features. Your eyes are a lovely cornflower blue, and your profile, especially that long lovely neck, is very elegant. Your hands, with those long tapered fingers, are very delicate and feminine. You may be flat-chested, but you're tall and have a nice, well-defined waistline. You're just not doing anything to make the most of these good points. Take your hair for instance."

Lucy stopped talking, and her face lost some of its animation. "I'm sorry, that was unforgivably forward. I don't suppose you want to hear fashion ideas from me."

Connie Sue shook her head, placing her hand over Lucy's. "Don't be silly. I'd be grateful to have you give me advice. Goodness knows, I'm not very good at this sort of thing on my own. And, since mother passed on when I was little, I haven't had anyone to guide me in the things a girl ought to know."

But Lucy disengaged her hand and rose, carrying their teacups to the sink. "I'm not sure your father would appreciate my interference."

Connie Sue raised her chin. "Father is one of those very people who needs to be convinced I've grown up. Besides, why would he object to my exchanging beauty secrets with a friend?"

Lucy started to protest again, but Connie Sue forestalled her. "Please, Lucy. It would mean a lot to me. I know it's an imposition, and you don't have to do anything if you really don't want to. After all, I'm not the best subject to work with. Just give me an idea of how to go about the transformation myself. I'm beginning to feel a bit desperate."

This time Lucy smiled, taken in by the girl's cajoling in spite of herself. "Oh very well. Let's set the vegetables on the stove to simmer and then we'll see what we can do."

CHAPTER 18

"*S*top squirming, I'll let you see in just a minute."

Connie Sue sat on a stool in Lucy's room, her back to the vanity mirror. Lucy had spent the last twenty minutes alternately snipping and arranging Connie Sue's hair, but she wanted to make sure she got this just right.

Finally, she stood back and studied her handiwork with a critical eye. Then with a very pleased-with-herself grin, she spun Connie Sue around to face the mirror.

"There, see what I mean. Wearing your hair this way draws attention to your eyes and neck, and gives you a more womanly appearance."

Connie Sue stared at her reflection in open-mouthed astonishment. She normally wore her straw-colored hair in a simple, rather untidy braid. Lucy had cut a soft fringe of bangs across her forehead, and then arranged them so that they fluffed becomingly. The rest of her hair had been gathered loosely on the back of her head and, with Connie Sue's blind assistance, arranged in a simple, elegant twist. As a finishing touch, Lucy pulled several strands free and arranged them to softly frame her face. The end result was quite striking. Not only did the hairstyle lend her an air of sophistication, but it drew attention to her eyes, making them appear larger and more luminous. Her own excitement added a bit of appealing color to her cheeks.

When Connie Sue tore her gaze away from the mirror, she looked stunned. "I can't believe what a difference a hairstyle can make. Lucy, you're a miracle worker."

Lucy laughed. "There's no need to thank me. It's your hair and face, I just helped you bring out the best in them."

Then she placed a fist on her hip as she studied Connie Sue's dress. "Now, the next step would be to add some flair to your wardrobe. I've noticed that you seem to favor dark colors. They have their place, of course, but you shouldn't shun brighter colors. With your complexion and eyes, you would look lovely in cheery blues or rose tints. Wait, I'll show you."

Lucy moved to the large dresser next to the vanity and pulled out a shawl of a deep rose color. She felt in her element again after a very long absence. Fashion and color had always ignited her imagination, fired up her creative energies.

She held the shawl up to Connie Sue's face. "See what I mean. This shade compliments your coloring nicely. Why, your eyes almost sparkle, and the soft color in your cheeks upstages the freckles on your nose.

"As for style, let's see." With a finger to her lip, Lucy studied Connie Sue again. "High collars like this are wrong for you. Nothing too daring of course, but a demure rounded neckline would show off the graceful line of your neck best. And we could add a wide band at the waist tied in a saucy bow in the back. That would accentuate your narrow waistline and perhaps the curve of your hips."

"Lucy!" Connie Sue's cheeks turned a fiery red.

Lucy smiled at the younger girl's embarrassment. "Well, you want to be seen as a woman don't you? And you do have nice feminine hips and a narrow waistline. I didn't say we'd do anything brazen, we'll just make sure your finer points are emphasized in a very subtle, very ladylike manner.

"Come on, follow me." Lucy led her to the sewing room, and opened a cupboard located on the wall behind the worktable. Inside were several fashion and pattern books that she'd collected from her days in New Orleans and from her work for Lowell.

Moving the books to the table with Connie Sue's help, she began thumbing through them. "Let's see now." In her mind she was a young girl again, her mind brimming with ideas on style and color. "I know I have a picture here of just the sort of thing I was describing."

Finally, she found what she'd been looking for. "See, this is just what I mean. Of course, you'd want to fill in the neck just a bit, and maybe make the sleeves fuller. Oh, this would look lovely on you, especially in a robin's egg blue."

Connie Sue looked from the books to Lucy's enthusiastic expression. "I've heard you worked for a seamstress when you lived in New Orleans. You seem quite good at this sort of thing. Design and style I mean."

Lucy shrugged. "I enjoyed working for Madame Robicheaux and learned quite a lot from her. But I'm not the couturier she was."

Connie Sue seemed undeterred by this admission. "Oh, but you have a natural eye for fashion, I can tell. I know it's asking a lot, but would you work on this with me? I'd furnish all the materials and I'd assist. I'm afraid I'm not much of a seamstress. If I tried to do something like this on my own, it would turn out looking like all my other dresses, I just know it. With your help, though, it could be something really special."

Lucy's pulse quickened at the thought of taking on such a project. This wouldn't be like her work for Lowell, where her creativity was stifled by the need to fashion it general enough to satisfy most women. To create something openly, for an enthusiastic subject, would be—

Then reality intruded. "Oh, Connie Sue, I don't think that would be such a good idea."

Connie Sue's smile faded and she bit her lip. "I'm sorry, I shouldn't have asked. You've other demands on your time and your hand is hurt." She sighed and gave an unconvincing smile. "It just sounded like it would be fun to work on this together. It was a silly idea. As if a dress could make much of a difference anyway."

She looked so sadly wistful that Lucy did an about face. "Oh very well, it might be fun at that. Let's take your measurements so we can figure out how much fabric you'll need. Once you have all the materials, just come by and I'll help you get started."

Connie Sue, all smiles again, reached over and hugged her. "I knew you were going to be a friend I could count on. Thanks so much. I promise to follow your instructions to the letter. If I can get everything together, can we start tomorrow?"

Lucy blinked at this sudden show of affection, but laughed at Connie Sue's enthusiasm. "Whenever you like. Now come on, we'd better check on lunch before we take your measurements."

As they moved across the room toward the kitchen, Connie Sue glanced sideways at Lucy. "You know, Mr. Wilder seems like a very nice man."

"Yes, he does." Lucy had a sudden image of how nice Connie Sue and Reed looked together as he handed her down from the carriage, and tried to ignore the sudden stab of jealousy.

"He's not like Lowell," Connie Sue continued musingly. "He has enough self-assurance and open-mindedness not to feel threatened by intelligence and strength in a woman. He *needs* a woman who'll challenge and surprise him."

Lucy couldn't help herself. "Just how well do you know Mr. Wilder?"

"Not as well as you do, of course. After all, I only met him yesterday. But we shared a couple of slices of Mrs. Venable's pie and talked for a while. He's easy to talk to, don't you think?"

"Umm," Lucy replied non-committally. She reminded herself again that she held no claim to Reed's affections.

Connie Sue moved to the stove. "He speaks highly of you too."

Lucy remembered the moment of intimacy she'd shared with

Reed on the porch just this morning and felt her face warm. "As I said earlier, Mr. Wilder feels a sense of indebtedness to me."

Connie Sue gave her an arch look. "I got the impression there was more to it than that."

Lucy held up her hand. "Stop right there. You're letting your imagination run away with you. Mr. Wilder is feeling grateful, not romantic. If it wasn't for his strong sense of responsibility, he would've been long gone by now." She hoped Connie Sue didn't notice how much it hurt to say those words.

"Perhaps. Oh, it smells like the carrots are about done." It was Connie Sue's turn to be non-committal. She didn't sound convinced, but seemed willing to drop the subject.

∾

Shortly after noon, Reed, Lowell and Toby trooped into the kitchen. Reed, leading the way, paused when he caught sight of the two ladies. They stood at the sink, laughing like schoolgirls over some bit of nonsense.

He smiled. This is how it should be for Lucy. She deserved such carefree moments.

He'd told Connie Sue that the secret to getting past Lucy's defenses was to make her feel needed. But it had to be sincere; Lucy was too astute to try to fool with some trumped up need. Apparently Connie Sue took his suggestions to heart, and one glance told him how she'd done it.

"Well, well," he said with mock-seriousness. "We menfolk spend all morning slaving in the hot sun, and come inside to find you ladies frittering the day away."

Lucy and Connie Sue looked around with identical caught-in-the-act expressions. But Lucy recovered quickly.

She drew herself up with a haughty toss of her head. "I'll have you know, Mr. Wilder, that we ladies have put in a full morning of cooking and planning. We just happen to believe in having fun while we work."

Then she moved to the cupboard that held the dinnerware, her posture and demeanor regal. "Now, it looks like you hard working gentlemen have already cleaned up, so if you'll have a seat while I set the table, Connie Sue and I will be glad to share the fruits of our labors with you."

"Yes, ma'am," Reed said meekly. "But let me lend you a hand with the table."

It was obvious from Lowell's frown that he disapproved of Reed's familiarity with Lucy's kitchen. But when the interloper spotted Connie Sue, his face took on a dumb-founded expression.

Reed saw Lucy's lips turn upward in a smile of satisfaction. "I see you've noticed Connie Sue's new hairdo, Lowell."

Connie Sue's gaze flew to Lowell's, but before Lowell could comment, Reed interrupted. "I heartily approve, Miss Morton. It gives you a very elegant air."

Connie Sue reddened prettily. "Why thank you, sir. But I wish you'd call me Connie Sue. Everyone else does."

Reed cocked his head at her with a warm smile. "All right, but only if you agree to call me Reed."

Lowell watched the lightly flirtatious by-play between the two of them with a deepening frown.

After they said the blessing, Lowell picked up his fork and pointed it at Reed. "Tell me, Wilder, where are you from? And just what brings you to these parts anyway?" The antagonism he felt toward Reed could be heard in his voice.

"My home is in Delaware. I'm on assignment to do a bit of investigative work right now." Reed ignored Lowell's antagonism, keeping his voice and expression unruffled.

Lowell frowned. "Investigative work?"

"Yep." Reed smiled as he gave the unhelpful answer.

"You planning to work around here, or were you just passing through on your way to somewhere else?"

Reed spread some butter on his biscuit. "No, I was headed for this general area."

"I see." Lowell stared at Reed a little longer, obviously expecting him to elaborate. When Reed just continued eating, Lowell resumed his interrogation. "Are you working on behalf of someone local?"

Reed was enjoying himself, knowing Lowell was frustrated by the lack of information. "I'm afraid I'm not at liberty to discuss the particulars of this assignment."

Lowell flashed an insincere smile. "Sorry, didn't mean to pry. I just didn't realize you had something to hide."

Reed's brows drew down over that remark and the smirk that accompanied it. But this time Lucy interceded, turning the discussion to other topics.

Lowell remained quiet for a while, still glowering at Reed. Suddenly, he sat up a little straighter, a speculative expression on his face. "Wilder? From Delaware? Are you by any chance associated with the group that runs Wilder Enterprises?"

Reed shrugged. "There *is* a family relationship, of sorts."

Lowell, looking smug, explained to the ladies. "Wilder Enterprises is a big time business empire with fingers in lots of pies. They own a shipping company, a ship building company and have timber interests all across the country."

Then he turned back to Reed, his smile condescending. "What are you, a distant cousin or something?"

Reed gritted his teeth, not sure whether to be amused or angry with this oaf. "Something like that."

Lowell's good humor seemed restored by his having ferreted out Reed's secrets. "Thought so. Nice to have rich relations to latch on to, I guess. Don't worry, your secret is safe. If your bosses don't want anyone to know they're looking at land around here, then we won't speak of it outside this room."

Reed took his irritation out on his ham, slicing it with quick, firm strokes. His voice, however, he managed to keep silky smooth. "I appreciate your willingness to be discreet, Crowder. But of course, I never said that Wilder Enterprises had anything to do with my reason for being here."

"Of course, of course. And no one will hear it from me."

~

*A*fter lunch, Toby and the two men headed outside, while Lucy and Connie Sue cleaned the kitchen.

When they'd put away the last of the dishes, Connie Sue reached for the bonnet she'd discarded earlier. "Well, I've enjoyed the visit, but I don't want to overstay my welcome."

Lucy smiled, surprised to discover she'd actually enjoyed the time spent with Connie Sue. "I'm glad you came by. Thanks for the help getting lunch together, and the cleaning up after. Come back when you get ready to work on that dress and we'll have it all fixed up in no time."

Connie Sue grinned. "Don't worry. As soon as I get my materials together I'll be knocking on your door again."

The two women were moving toward the barn, where the horses were already hitched to Connie Sue's buggy and Lowell's buckboard, ready to go. Lowell and Reed were loading a wheel onto the bed of the buckboard. Lucy temporarily lost the thread of her conversation with Connie Sue as she watched Reed work. His shirt strained across his back as he bent down. Then, as he and Lowell hefted the wheel into the wagon, the muscles on his arm tensed and corded, providing an impressive display of masculine strength and grace. The same strength and grace that, when redirected, could embrace her with such warmth and leashed strength. To feel that embrace just one more time...

Stepping back from the buckboard, Reed caught her stare. The knowing smile that lit his face brought a flush to hers.

Tossing her head to show how unaffected she was, Lucy took the offensive. "Just what do you two think you're doing with my wagon wheel?"

Reed's smile let her know he was on to her. "When Crowder heard about your broken wheel, he volunteered to cart it to the smithy for you."

Lucy turned to Lowell. "That's generous of you, but—" She bit her tongue when she caught sight of Reed's quirked eyebrow. After a long pause, she forced a smile. "Oh very well, thank you gentle-men. It'll be nice to have the use of a buggy again."

Reed rewarded her with an approving smile. "You're quite welcome."

Then he turned to Lowell. "Thanks again, Crowder for your help today. You're a pretty handy fellow to have around when there's manual labor to be done."

Lowell eyed Reed as if unsure if he'd been complimented or insulted. "No problem. After all, I do have some responsibility for this place and the folks living here."

Lucy took that as the cue she'd been waiting for. It was time to take care of some unpleasant business. Gathering her courage, she turned to Lowell. "If you've got a few minutes before you go, there's something I need to talk to you about." She saw a tremor of some emotion flash across Connie Sue's face and then disappear. Surely the girl didn't think she was planning a flirtation with Lowell?

Mercy but this was all getting so complicated. .

Lowell, his chest swelling, threw a quick, smug smile Reed's way as he offered his arm to Lucy. "Certainly. Why don't we sit over there under the tree, where you can be more comfortable? If you'll excuse us Connie Sue, Wilder."

Lucy waited until Lowell seated her and sat down himself. Then she got right to the point. "Lowell, with this injury to my wrist, there's no way I'm going to be able to finish all three dresses for you this month."

He leaned back and gave her a long meaningful look. "There's always the other option I offered you."

She rubbed her elbow through the sling. "You don't really want a wife who's only marrying you because she was backed into a corner, do you?"

When Lowell just sat there with a stubborn expression, Lucy sighed and tried again. "You've been good to me Lowell, the one person who's tried to help me since I moved out here. And I'm truly grateful. But you and I are not suited for marriage." Unbidden, the memory of the kiss she'd shared with Reed came to mind, and she found herself unable to imagine sharing that same kind of intimacy with Lowell. "I wouldn't be good for you. I'd make your life miserable. Not that I'd want to, but it would happen just the same. If you'd stop and really look at who I am instead of who you want me to be, you'd see that."

He reached over and took her hand. "You're wrong. We'd be good together. If you'd just let go of that stiff-necked pride of yours."

She pulled her hand away. "See, that's what I mean. Stiff-necked is what I am. It's a part of me that I can't change and that you can't love."

"No! You and I have always gotten on well, there's no reason marriage would change that. It's this Wilder fellow, isn't it? He's seduced you into thinking he loves you. What kind of promises did he make? Do you honestly think he'll take you with him when he leaves? Wise up Luce, he's just passing time, taking advantage of what he thinks are easy pickings. No matter what his sweet talk, when he leaves, it'll be alone."

Lucy clenched her hand into a fist, trying to ignore the sting of his words. "Reed has nothing to do with this. He's made no promises and pretended no affection. He's just paying off a debt of honor, nothing more. And he doesn't make me feel like 'easy pickings,' not like the folks in this town do."

Lowell had the grace to look contrite. "Aw Luce, I didn't mean that the way it sounded. You know how I feel about you. It's just that the thought of that fellow spending so much time around here drives me a little crazy. I don't trust him, he's hiding something."

Lucy made no comment to his almost-apology. Instead, she returned to her original purpose. "Will you give me an extension on the rent?"

His expression became calculating. "I'm a businessman, and I'd be a fool not to press an advantage when I have one." He leaned forward and took her hand. "Why don't you just admit defeat and marry me? You know you'll do it someday. Why continue to draw this out?"

Lowell raked his hand through his hair. "I'll be good to you Luce, and I give you my word I'll treat Toby as if he were my own son. Half the people in this town already think he is anyway."

She flinched at that, pulling her hand away. "Please Lowell, don't do this." Lucy suspected a bit of desperation stole into her voice. When she saw Lowell's expression, she knew it.

Not above taking advantage of her weakness, Lowell pressed his case firmly. "We made a deal and I know you're not one to renege. So, are you ready to set a date?"

She raised her chin, refusing to admit defeat. Besides, now that she knew how Connie Sue felt, she couldn't give in, no matter what. "I have almost two weeks until the first of the month. We'll set no dates till then."

The musical sound of laughter drifted over to them just then. Both Lowell and Lucy glanced over to seek the source. Reed and Connie Sue stood near the buggy, looking relaxed and friendly, and seeming to enjoy each other's company a great deal. Lucy stifled the urge to jump up from her seat. She wanted to march over to where they stood and insert herself physically between them.

Lowell stood and helped Lucy to her feet. "All right, we'll do it your way. I'll wait until the end of the month, but then we settle this once and for all."

Lucy moved past him. "It looks like Connie Sue is ready to go, and your buckboard is blocking her path. I'll let you be on your way."

A few minutes later, Lowell frowned down at Reed from the seat of his wagon. "Aren't you coming to town with us Wilder?"

"Not just yet," Reed answered cheerfully. "I've still got a few things I need to take care of around here. I'll head back to town later this afternoon."

Just as he had yesterday, Lowell looked prepared to argue, but

Connie Sue intervened. "Let's go Lowell. Your wagon is blocking my way. Besides, Lucy described a bolt of fabric she spied in your store that I'd like to have a look at."

After they'd gone, Reed turned to Toby. "I think we've got some arithmetic to work on this afternoon. Then there's something I want to show you in that astronomy book we came across yesterday."

Lucy trailed after the two of them, her feet dragging. Her enjoyment of the day gave way to a feeling of bone-deep exhaustion. She'd spent so many late nights working on those wretched dresses. She had one finished and a good start on another. It just wasn't fair! Regardless of her blustering to Lowell, there was no way she could finish the job with the use of only one hand. Unless a miracle happened and her wrist healed in the next day or two, she'd only delayed the inevitable.

Maybe marriage to Lowell wouldn't be so terrible. She'd refused all these years on principle, and because of her idealistic view of what a marriage could and should be. Why couldn't she be happy with this choice? What made her think she had a right to anything else? Lowell was a grown man and he knew her feelings. If he could live with such a choice, why couldn't she? And it would feel so good not to bear her burdens alone any more.

Besides, she'd found her Prince Charming, only to learn he was unattainable. Perhaps it was time to come down out of her ivory tower and do what was best for Toby. Forget all about what Reed had come to mean to her, that just the sight of him could bring a smile to her lips, that a casual touch from him set her pulse to racing. Ignore the ache in her heart when she thought of never seeing him again, the emptiness of a future without him.

Then she remembered Connie Sue's feelings for Lowell and realized that marriage to Lowell was no longer a choice either. Her new-found friendship with the girl was much too precious for her to betray it that way.

Lucy hunched her shoulders, the weight of her dilemma pressing down on her again. Even if she could throw away her dreams, she had no right to ruin someone else's happiness in the process. There had to be another way.

There just had to be.

CHAPTER 19

*R*eed headed down the hall, intent on fixing the squeak in Toby's door. Connie Sue's visit had had a positive impact on Lucy, just as he'd hoped. But something about her tête-à-tête with Crowder had brought the worry lines back to her face.

What sort of power did the man hold over Lucy anyway?

A commotion from the next room caught his attention just as his fingers closed on the doorknob to Toby's room. It sounded like a yelp of pain, followed by a clattering noise. He reached her door in three quick strides. Raising his hand to knock, Reed heard a sob from the other side.

His heartbeat accelerating, he pounded on her door. "Are you all right in there? Lucy, answer me, is something wrong?"

Sudden silence, followed by a long pause. "I'm fine, just a silly little accident. Sorry if I disturbed you."

But she didn't sound fine. "I'm coming in, whether you want me to or not." When he opened the door, Reed was glad he'd followed his instincts. Lucy knelt on the floor, surrounded by folds of fabric, holding the hand attached to her injured wrist. It was the utter defeat reflected in her eyes that drew him to her side. His heart ached to see such hopelessness replace the prickly pride that was so much a part of her.

She attempted to pull herself together, sending him a glare that almost disguised her misery. "I don't remember giving you permission to enter."

Reed ignored her caustic comment and knelt beside her. He took her left hand in his own, noting the blood welling from her index finger. Seeing the scissors on the floor gave a clue to what had happened. But he didn't understand why it affected her this way. "What happened here?"

Lucy shrugged, pretending nonchalance, but he could tell she was under some sort of strain. "Just a little accident with the scissors. Nothing you need to worry about."

Reed didn't buy it. "Come on, let's wash your hand at the basin. I need to see how seriously you're hurt."

She went with him docilely enough, and Reed kept an arm around her shoulder as he led her to the basin. He sponged water over her hand and then examined the cut. "Let me know if I hurt you. I know this must be painful."

But she seemed to be paying very little attention to his actions. "Don't worry, it's just a small scratch under all that blood. Hardly hurts at all."

Once he got a good look at her finger, he agreed with her assessment. If her cut wasn't the problem, what had upset her? Something was wrong and he aimed to get to the bottom of it.

The days of her carrying the world on her shoulder were gone; she just didn't know it yet.

Perhaps she was concerned about the fabric? It looked like the fancy stuff Crowder gave her the other day. He decided to test that theory a bit. "Do you think the cloth is salvageable?"

Lucy took a deep, shuddering breath. "I don't know. There's a bit of blood spattered on it that I might be able to wash out, but it's that gash I made when the scissors slipped that has me worried. I thought I might be able to make the gown one handed, but I'm just so tired. How could I have been so careless?"

Her despair seemed out of proportion to the situation. Reed pressed a little more. "Well, maybe once your wrist heals you can try again. I'm sure you'll be able to salvage something from it. And that color will look lovely on you."

She looked at him as if he were monumentally obtuse. And then her eyes flashed as her control seemed to snap. "Look lovely on me! Give me strength, do you think I'd get worked up over a dress I was making for myself? Where in the world would I even wear such a gown? This is not just a dress! For Toby and me, it's the roof over our heads and the food on our table. How do you think I support us? Lowell expects—Oh!" She lifted a hand to her mouth, her expression stricken.

Comprehension dawned on Reed, and he wondered that it had taken him so long. A quick glance around her room provided additional proof if he'd only looked earlier. A gown, draped on a form in the far corner seemed almost complete. Two bolts of fabric were stacked on a chair. "This is how you pay your bills to Crowder. And this is why you stay up late at night—to work on these dresses." That settled one mystery at least. Reed felt a surge of relief that the answer was so simple, so innocent.

Lucy groaned as her shoulder slumped. "Now I've done it. I gave Lowell my word that I'd never say anything to anyone about our arrangement. I've broken my word, and to top it off I've ruined a piece of fabric that I have no way of paying for. I'm not only irresponsible but utterly and completely untrustworthy as well."

By the time she finished, her voice was almost a wail. Reed, feeling guilty for his earlier relief, pulled her to sit next to him on the bed. "Don't be absurd. You're one of the most responsible people I know. Why in the world would Crowder make you promise not to tell anyone he hires you to make dresses?"

Her color rose. "No one in town would buy these gowns if they knew I made them. And it wouldn't help Lowell's reputation any if folks knew he was doing commerce with me."

And the man called himself her friend. "Well, I promise to keep your secret, so it's not like there's any real harm done. And it looks like the bleeding's stopped finally."

"Thank you, I'll be fine, really."

The words were timorously spoken at best, and again he had the impression that she held herself together only with the greatest of effort. He wanted to hold her, to caress away all her hurts, all her worries. But he still needed to get to the heart of her current distress.

Frowning, he thought over what she'd said a moment ago. "Look, it's obvious you won't be able to do any more sewing until you get your arm out of that sling. So what happens if you don't finish this by whatever deadline Crowder set?"

Her face shuttered, and she brushed a lock of hair over her ear. As usual when she didn't want to discuss something, she responded by climbing up on her high horse. "I don't think that's any of your business. Now, if you'll kindly leave, I need to clean up this mess and see if I can salvage anything from it."

But Reed prevented her from rising by laying his hand on her arm. "Lucy, what threat is Crowder holding over you? If you don't tell me, I'll ask him myself when I get to town."

Her quick intake of breath sounded like a hiss, and she glared at him in angry defiance. But Reed remained firm and, finally, she dropped her eyes and her shoulders slumped in defeat. "If I don't finish the three dresses he set as rent payment, he can evict us from this place."

Reed suspected she still hadn't given him the whole story. He didn't like Crowder much, but he didn't think the oaf would be petty enough to throw her and Toby out of their home. Especially given what Lucy had told him about their relationship. There was something else going on here.

Watching her, Reed packed as much outrage as he could into his voice. "Do you mean to tell me that Crowder would put you and Toby out of your home? That even knowing the circumstances, he wouldn't be willing to extend you a little credit? The man's despicable, a black-hearted pig. He's lower than a snake. How could you even tolerate having him at your table today knowing he could be so uncharitable, so unfeeling?"

He could see the internal struggle play out on her face. He could even pinpoint the moment she realized she would have to give him the rest of the story.

Lucy took a deep breath and shook her head. "The situation isn't quite as black as all that, and neither is Lowell. He's given me an alternative if I can't meet the payment he set. I just don't happen to care much for the option."

"And that is?"

She narrowed her eyes defiantly, but he just sat and watched her, not saying a word. Finally she tossed her head, giving in with poor grace. "We can set a wedding date!"

A bolt of jealousy sliced into him. He'd suspected something of the sort, and from a logical standpoint it seemed to be in her best interest to marry. But he didn't feel particularly logical at the moment. The idea of her married to that lout was ludicrous, was infuriating, was absolutely unconscionable. Besides, if Crowder married Lucy it would complicate the Wilders' claim on Toby. "I'll give you the money."

"What! You can't seriously believe I would accept money from you."

"Consider it a loan. You can take however long you need paying it back."

She stood and glared at him. "Aren't you listening to me? I said I won't take money from you. Now, please leave my room and let me clean up this mess."

"For goodness sake, just take the money." Reed ran a hand through his hair in irritation. Why was she being so stubborn over this? After all, she'd let Jon help pay her rent in New Orleans. But then, she'd likely been in love with Jon.

Lucy's expression softened and she sat down again. Reed thought for a minute she'd decided to see reason. But her next words set him straight.

"That was a very generous offer, and don't think I'm not grateful. But please understand. This is not like letting you do a few jobs around here. Taking money from you, just to avoid living up to a commitment I made, would be wrong. No, I'll find a way to take care of this on my own, or I'll marry Lowell."

He started to say something, but she raised a hand. "Please, the subject is closed."

~

*B*efore Reed left that evening, she made him promise not to approach Lowell about the rent or the conditions tied to it. He wasn't sure how she managed it, because he'd intended to apply some not very gentle pressure in that quarter. But she'd effectively tied his hands.

So when he arrived at the hotel he was already in a foul mood. Finding two telegrams waiting for him didn't soften his disposition any.

The first was from Lisa. She and Steven had had a fight and called the wedding off. She wanted him to know that if he wanted to extend his "little vacation" he should feel free to do so, since he no longer needed to worry about attending their wedding. But if he had a mind to come home early, it would be nice to have a big brother to talk to.

Reed groaned. Lisa and Steven had had such rows dozens of times, usually over the most inconsequential of things. Since Steven was a friend of Reed's, Reed had in fact introduced them, he'd always been the one to step in and arbitrate, to smooth things over. Well, this time they'd just have to work it out themselves or wait until he'd finished his business with Lucy.

The second was from his father. The Wilder patriarch demanded particulars on what kind of delay Reed had encountered. He encouraged Reed to concentrate on getting the ring back, and to not worry about the Claymore deal—he had it "under control." Reed crumpled the telegram in his fist, fearing the worst. Blast his father, why couldn't he have delayed things like Reed asked? This deal was too important to Wilder Enterprises to mess things up at this stage. All he needed was a few more days, just till his obligation to Lucy ended.

Grimly, he drafted responses to Lisa and his father. Then he drafted a third telegram, one to his lawyer. He could count on Jacobs to stall things as long as possible. He only hoped it would be enough.

~

*A*fter clumsily putting up her hair the next morning, Lucy picked up the locket and studied it, tracing a finger over its familiar surface.

Yesterday's mishap with the scissors had forced her to admit she would never be able to meet Lowell's terms for the rent payment this month. But, after learning of Connie Sue's feelings, she was more determined than ever not to accept Lowell's marriage proposal. Which meant she had to find another way to make the rent payment. She'd tossed and turned most of the night, searching for a way out. The only things she owned that had significant monetary value were the piano and the locket. She'd tried to sell Lowell the piano once before when she was having trouble making the rent. But he'd turned her down, saying there was no market for it in Far Enough and he had nowhere to store it. Which left only one option.

At last, in the early morning hours, she'd accepted what she had to do.

Lucy stared at her reflection in the vanity mirror, hating the defeat she saw reflected in her eyes, in the slump of her shoulders. Slowly she drew herself up and thrust out her chin. There, that was better.

Her hand squeezed the locket and she almost welcomed the feel of her nails biting into her flesh. It wasn't *fair*! She hadn't done anything *wrong*! Lucy drew her fist to her mouth and took a deep shuddering breath.

Momma, Daddy, forgive me.

~

*R*eed arrived before Lucy had finished clearing the breakfast dishes. He poured himself a cup of the still warm coffee and grabbed a biscuit from the platter waiting on the stove. "I ran into Crowder last night. He agreed to bring your buggy wheel back this morning."

Lucy gave him a searching look, but didn't probe past the surface of his comment. "You shouldn't have asked him to do that. This isn't exactly on his way to anywhere else."

"Don't worry. When he found out Connie Sue was planning a return visit today, he offered to drive her here and come back later to pick her up. Apparently he feels the need to keep an eye on things around here."

Lucy paused in the act of wiping the counter and smiled. "Or on Connie Sue. This'll give them some time alone together."

Reed raised an eyebrow. "Trying to play matchmaker?"

"Yes, but not because of what we talked about yesterday. Connie Sue has feelings for Lowell, and she's just the kind of girl he needs." Then she turned back to the counter and asked a bit too casually, "You don't mind, do you?"

Reed wrinkled his forehead. "Mind? Why would I mind?"

"Oh, I don't know. You and Connie Sue seemed to be getting along rather well yesterday."

"And you thought I might be attracted to her?" Reed smiled, delighted that she might actually be jealous. "I do like her, of course. Connie Sue is a sweet kid. She reminds me of my sister Lisa. But that's as far as it goes."

Lucy murmured something non-committal, her eyes shifting to his and then away again. Reed, feeling cheerier by the minute, decided to move the conversation to more neutral ground.

"Connie Sue seems excited about the sewing project. I think the only thing that kept her from arriving here at the crack of dawn this morning was the fear that she'd be imposing on you."

Reed carried his cup to the sink and rinsed it out. "Look, why don't you plan on spending the day in here with Connie Sue? Toby and I can handle most of the chores."

"But—"

"Are you saying Toby and I are incapable of handling your work?" He drew his brows down, affecting an air of affront.

"No, of course not."

"Well then, enough arguing. Besides, you don't need to be using that hand of yours any more than necessary. It'll only take it that much longer to heal."

Lucy appeared ready to protest again, then she paused and her expression shifted, taking on an exaggeratedly thoughtful air as she tapped her chin with a forefinger. "In that case, thank you, maybe I will take it easy today." She poured herself a cup of coffee and moved toward the table. "I was planning to air the mattresses this morning, and the rug from the parlor could use an airing and beating as well." She smiled sweetly as she leaned back in her chair.

Reed shook his head at her theatrics. "It seems I've created a tyrant. I'd best get out of here before you decide it's time to muck out the barn."

"Well, now that you mention it... "

He groaned and hurried out the back door, pleased to hear her soft laughter following him.

❧

*A*s Reed and Toby tackled the morning chores, he gained a new appreciation for how hard Lucy worked. How had she managed to keep the place running all on her own for so long?

Around ten o'clock, Lowell delivered Connie Sue as promised. He also brought the now-repaired wagon wheel. Lowell helped Reed unload it and fit it to the buggy, then said his good-byes. He promised to be back for Connie Sue around two o'clock, refusing

Reed's offer to escort her himself with Lucy's soon-to-be operational buggy.

Before he could climb back into his buggy, though, Lucy requested a few minutes to discuss business.

"Of course. What can I do for you?" Lowell, apparently remembering their last such talk, wore a cautious expression.

Praying for the strength to maintain her composure, Lucy took a deep breath. "I tried to work on the dresses last night and really made a mess of things. I know now that I won't be able to finish the work in time to meet your demands for rent payment."

Lowell's expression moved from caution to surprise to victory. He placed his hands on her shoulders, looking as if he wanted to embrace her. "Lucy! I know this isn't what you—"

"Stop!" Lucy watched the pleasure drain from his face as he lowered his hands. "You're getting ahead of me. All this means is that I need to find another way to pay you. And I have." She held out her hand, uncurling her fingers to reveal her locket.

He backed up a step, as if she offered a poisonous viper. "I can't take that."

This was more difficult than she'd imagined it would be. She tilted her chin. "Yes you can. It'll bring more than the dresses would have, so you can take the cost of the fabric out too. Credit any leftover money to my account at the mercantile."

"Lucy, be reasonable." He ran a hand through his hair. "What good is this going to do? What happens when you can't make next month's payment? Are you going to sell off something else?"

"You let me worry about that. Now take this and let's be done with it."

Lowell's jaw worked and she saw a flash of sympathy in his eyes. Then his expression hardened, and he closed her fingers over the precious heirloom. "You have until the end of the month to make your decision. If this is still what you want, then I'll take it. We'll play out this charade to the bitter end. But we both know what that end will be." With that he turned on his heel, mounted his buggy, and left without a backward glance.

～

*L*ucy and Connie Sue worked throughout the morning. Lucy altered the pattern to fit her vision of the design, and Connie Sue cut the fabric under her watchful direction. Next they meticulously pinned and basted, draping it over Connie Sue's form numerous times to satisfy themselves that the fit was just right.

By the time Lowell returned for Connie Sue, they were ready to begin the stitching, and had plans to continue the next day.

It was while Connie Sue and Lowell were leaving that the accident happened.

Connie Sue, laughing at something Lowell said, missed her footing on the bottom porch step, and tumbled to the ground, face first. Lowell arrived at her side immediately.

"Connie Sue!" With surprising gentleness, he knelt next to the fallen girl and turned her over, putting his arm under her head. "Are you all right?"

Obviously shaken, Connie Sue attempted a smile. "I'm not sure. My pride hurts too much for me to feel anything else."

She attempted to rise but Lowell stopped her. "Hold on now. You take it easy 'til we check you out."

Lucy knelt on her other side. "You've scraped this elbow. How about the rest of you? Does it hurt anywhere?"

Connie Sue shook her head. "No, I don't think so. I'm fine really. If someone will just help me up."

Lucy gave the girl an encouraging smile and then looked to Lowell. "Why don't you help her to the porch swing so she can be more comfortable while we make sure she's really okay." Then she turned to Reed. "Would you fetch some water and a couple of cloths?"

By the time Reed returned, Connie Sue was blushingly seated in the swing, Lowell solicitously holding her hand.

Lucy smiled a thanks to Reed, wet both cloths and handed one to Lowell. "You help wipe her face while I tend to her elbow."

Connie Sue flinched when Lucy first touched the raw scrape on her arm. Lowell noticed and frowned fiercely. "Go easy Luce, you're hurting her."

Lucy looked up with a quick apology, and then went back to work. Lowell, meanwhile, wiped the smudges from Connie Sue's face, touching her as if she were fragile as a soap bubble. Lucy caught Connie Sue's eye and bit back a smile. The girl was shamelessly enjoying every minute of it.

"How's that?" Lowell asked as he finished.

"Much better, thank you. You have a gentle touch for a man with such strong hands."

Lucy stifled a grin as she saw Lowell's chest puff out. She shot a quick, things-are-moving-according-to-plan look Reed's way, then set her cloth back in the bucket. "Well, you've got a nasty scrape here, but it looks like that's the worst of it."

"Thank you, all of you, for your help." Connie Sue smiled ruefully. "I'm so sorry my clumsiness caused all this bother."

Lowell gave her shoulder a quick squeeze. "It wasn't a bother, we're just glad it wasn't more serious. Not that that scrape is such a minor thing. You're being mighty brave to hold up so well."

Connie Sue blushed with pretty modesty. "You're being too kind. I think I can stand now, if you'll just lend me a hand."

Lowell did as she asked, helping her up and then putting his arm around her shoulder for support. "If you're up to a buggy ride now, I'll take you back to town. And I think we'll pay a visit to Doc Lawton before I drop you off at your place. No point taking any chances."

"If you think that would be best," Connie Sue agreed demurely.

Once they left, Lucy gave Reed a sidelong look. "Still think it's hopeless?"

He shook his head. "That girl was absolutely shameless. I almost feel sorry for Crowder."

"Well don't. She's going to be the best thing that ever happened to him, mark my words."

Then Reed turned serious. "I overheard your conversation with

Lowell this morning. You can't give up your mother's locket like that."

Lucy stiffened. She didn't want to discuss this now, her feelings about it were still too raw. "Do you make a habit of eavesdropping, Mr. Wilder?"

"It wasn't intentional. And don't try to change the subject. I've seen your face when you touch that locket. It would be like giving up a part of yourself."

She moved past him toward the porch, afraid he'd read too much from her face. "Really, you're putting too fine a point on this. It was a nice memento from my parents, but when all is said and done, it's only a trinket."

"Don't try to make light of this, Lucy. I won't buy it."

She glared at him, but couldn't quite meet his eyes. "It's a simple matter of doing what has to be done. By the time my hand heals, it'll be too late to finish the dresses."

He took her arm and, by silent command, drew her gaze to his. She flinched as his eyes seemed to see through to her very soul, to the throbbing hurt hidden there.

"Let me loan you the money." There was a harsh rasp to his voice.

She wanted to weep; her throat ached with the sudden need for release. But she lifted her chin, held the tears at bay by sheer force of will, and prayed he would understand. "I can't. This is something I have to take care of on my own."

Reed's jaw tightened, and she saw a small tic appear briefly at his left eye, but he nodded and withdrew his hand.

Lucy turned and fled into the house.

CHAPTER 20

"We need to talk."

Reed, with a foot already on the stair that led up to his hotel room, took one look at Lowell's grim expression, and nodded curtly. "All right. Where?"

"How about here?" Lowell waved to a small sitting area in a corner of the lobby.

A short time later the two men sat across from each other, eyeing each other with suspicion.

"So let's have it, Crowder. What's on your mind?" Reed, still seeing that bloodied-but-not-beaten expression in Lucy's eyes, wasn't feeling particularly charitable toward his companion at the moment.

Lowell took a deep breath, and, for all their quietness, the words almost exploded from him. "Are you Toby's father?"

Reed's head snapped up, and then he gave Lowell a long, slow smile. So, Crowder laid no claim to being Toby's father. Suddenly he felt inclined to be more charitable to the oaf. Not that he was ready to let him off the hook for the way he'd treated Lucy.

The smile only goaded Lowell further. "Wilder, I asked you a question, now I want an answer."

"Not that it's any of your business, but no, I'm not Toby's father."

Lowell stared hard at Reed, as if not sure he could believe him. Then he slumped back in his chair. "It's just that, well it's obvious you and Lucy feel an attraction for each other, and seeing you and the boy together, it occurred to me that you—Oh never mind. I guess it was a bit far fetched at that."

Then he sat up straighter and went on the attack again. "So what *are* your intentions toward Lucy?"

Reed frowned. "Intentions?"

"Yes, blast you, intentions. Are you just trifling with her, or do you really have feelings for her? You working to build something permanent here or do you plan to ride out in a few days and never look back?"

Reed's eyes narrowed. "I don't have to explain myself to you. What I feel for Lucy, and what sort of intentions I have for the future, are nobody's business but mine."

But Lowell, far from intimidated, leaned forward, his face hard. "That's where you're wrong. Lucy's welfare *is* my concern, and has been for more years than I can remember. She's been through a lot, victimized by gossipmongers at home, and then seduced and abandoned by some smooth talker down in New Orleans. I won't let that happen to her again."

"She told you about what happened—that she was seduced and abandoned?" Reed felt his stomach twist, pain for Lucy knifing through him. Surely Jon wouldn't have—

But Lowell waved that off. "No, of course not. But, to anyone who really knows her, the truth is obvious. Don't try to change the subject. If you do anything to hurt Lucy, you'll have to answer to me. Because I'm planning to marry her."

Reed itched to wipe the smug smile off of his face. "By threatening her with eviction if she doesn't, you mean. That shows a whole lot of concern for her welfare."

Lowell looked as if he'd been sucker-punched. "Lucy told you I—"

"Not intentionally. I stumbled on the arrangement you'd

worked out with her by accident, and put her in the position of having to defend you. Don't worry about your secret getting out, I promised her I wouldn't discuss it with anyone."

Lowell clenched his fists on the table, and Reed watched him struggle with his emotions. "She can't keep on the way she is, isolated from everyone but Toby, taking sole responsibility for her family's survival. I've watched her spirit shrivel up a little more each year. I can't let it just go on until there's nothing left of her."

Reed nodded, feeling a twinge of sympathy. "But she doesn't really want to marry you."

"I know that!" Lowell nearly shouted.

Reed ignored the man's obvious frustration. "The fact that she's willing to part with a family heirloom to avoid marrying you should tell you just how serious she is."

Lowell groaned and slumped down in his seat. "Why does she have to be so stubborn?" The expression he turned on Reed contained a plea for understanding. "She'll get it back once we're married. If I could figure out a better way to extricate her from this mess, I'd step aside. But there isn't one. Having a respectable husband will make her more acceptable to the people here. And it'll give her someone to lean on, to help bear her burdens. It's the best option, all things considered."

Reed snorted. "She'll never be fully accepted by the folks in this town."

Lucy's would-be husband set his jaw. "I'll just have to do my best to see that she is."

"What if there were another way," Reed said slowly. "A way to give her a fresh start somewhere else, where she wouldn't have to carry the burden of her past with her?"

Lowell leaned forward. "What did you have in mind?"

Reed shrugged. "Not anything I'm prepared to talk about right now."

Lowell's brows drew down. "If I thought for one minute you were going to make her some kind of sordid, illicit offer—"

His first reaction was anger, but he knew the man was only

looking out for Lucy. "Calm down, Crowder. I respect Lucy too much for something like that. No, it would be completely above board, something that would give her dignity and a measure of independence."

"Like what?"

"I'm not ready to elaborate right now. Just give me your word you won't do anything to force her hand right now."

Slowly Lowell nodded and extended his hand to seal the promise.

~

*C*onnie Sue, none the worse for her fall, came by each day to work with Lucy on the dress, escorted by Lowell when he could get away from the mercantile. Lucy reflected wryly that, prior to Reed's arrival, she'd seldom entertained visitors. Now, it seemed an everyday occurrence.

On Saturday, Lucy declared she'd had enough of the sling. She did give in to Reed's insistence that she keep her wrist wrapped a few days longer, but only because Toby looked anxious. And that afternoon, she and Connie Sue finished the dress.

Connie Sue drove herself for a change, and as Lucy escorted her out to her buggy that afternoon, Connie Sue hooked her arm through Lucy's. "Thank you so much. The dress is gorgeous. I couldn't have managed half so well without all your help."

Lucy gave her arm a light squeeze. "You'll look wonderful in it at church tomorrow, the envy of every woman there. Just remember to put your hair up the way I showed you."

Connie Sue chewed on her lip. "Do you really think I should? I mean, the dress by itself is a big enough change."

Lucy wagged a finger. "Now, don't you back out on me. Just remember the way your reflection looked in the mirror. Hold your head up and look folks square in the eye. You'll be absolutely grand. I just wish I could see the look on everyone's faces when they view the new you."

"That's a splendid idea." Connie Sue squeezed Lucy's arm. "Why don't you join us for church? I could use the support."

Lucy sobered immediately. Her growing friendship with Connie Sue was one thing. Facing the scrutiny of the entire congregation was quite another. "Thank you, but I don't think that would be a good idea. Besides, Toby and I always have our own service right here on Sunday mornings."

Connie Sue cocked her head. "Now who's backing down?"

Reed, busy hitching the horse to the buggy, added his support for the idea. "She's right. I'll escort you and Toby myself. And afterwards the four of us could have a picnic."

"Perhaps we could invite Lowell to join us." Connie Sue's voice sounded nonchalant, but Lucy could tell the idea of a picnic with Lowell held a great deal of appeal for her.

Reed frowned, then shrugged and replied with a noted lack of enthusiasm, "If you insist."

"Oh, that sounds like such fun. Lucy, do say you'll come."

Lucy wavered. She didn't want to subject either herself or Toby to the stares and whispers of the congregation. But she knew if she refused there would be no picnic. And the outing would mean a lot to Connie Sue.

There had been indications over the last few days that Lowell was taking more than a casual interest in Connie Sue. Nothing dramatic, just lots of little things. His hands tended to linger as he handed her into and out of the buggy. Their conversations became more animated, and he hung onto her every word. He still professed to be courting Lucy, but now the attention he gave her seemed more automatic and perfunctory, less impassioned. With a little bit of maneuvering, an outing like this picnic might be just the thing to tilt the balance.

Perhaps she could endure this one service after all. Reed's two weeks would be over in a few days. He'd likely be long gone by the following Sunday, so there would be no pressure to repeat the performance. And maybe the newness of the service and surroundings would distract Toby from the negative attention they would surely receive.

Decision made, Lucy sighed and nodded. "All right, we'll go. But don't expect me to make this a habit."

~

*S*unday morning arrived and Reed stood at Lucy's front door, ready to escort her and Toby into town.

The sight of him, all spruced up in his Sunday best, sent a little flutter through Lucy's pulse. Regardless of how they felt about her past, when she arrived on Reed's arm, she'd be the envy of every unattached female at the service, and perhaps some of the married ones as well.

Reed gave her a long appreciative look as he crooked an elbow for her to take. "Well, well, you sure look mighty fine this morning, Miss Ames."

Lucy grimaced. She knew better. Last night she'd pulled her best dress out of the back of her closet. But even after she freshened it up, it looked only marginally better than her everyday work dresses. This morning she arranged her hair in a softer, more flattering style and then, exasperated at her own vanity, took it down and rearranged it in her customary bun.

"I know that was kindly meant, but I don't hold to insincere flattery."

Reed raised an eyebrow. "There was nothing insincere about that compliment. I meant every word of it."

She rolled her eyes, but didn't comment. Worry about what awaited her made arguing with him over something like this seem insignificant.

Whether by accident or design, Reed timed their arrival perfectly. The bell had just begun to peel, calling the congregation in to take their seats. Reed, Toby and Lucy were able to walk into the church with the last few stragglers. Reed kept a firm hand on

Lucy's elbow, refusing to allow her to slip into the back row. Rather, he led her and Toby up the aisle to a pew near the very front.

Lucy kept her eyes forward and her head up, but she remained very aware of the whispers and general stirring that their entrance caused. Just when she thought Reed would to take them to the very front pew, he paused. There on the third row sat Sheriff Morton, already sliding down to make room for them. She returned his welcoming smile with a strained one, and took her seat as he and Reed shook hands.

As she settled back, Lucy noticed Mrs. Hopkins seated in the pew to their right. The woman's pinched lips and sour expression made it clear what she thought of Lucy's presence in this house of worship. Driven by a streak of perversity, Lucy flashed the mayor's wife her most drippingly sweet smile. Satisfied with the startled reaction she elicited, Lucy turned to face the choir, already seated in their place at the front of the church.

She scanned the group for a glimpse of Connie Sue. Lucy spotted Lowell first, and he smiled a quick welcome before returning his attention to the woman seated one row forward and two seats to his left.

Connie Sue! The sight of her coaxed a proud smile from Lucy. She felt like the fairy godmother in the Cinderella story. No one would mistake that self-confident, lovely young woman for an awkward adolescent today. Amazing how a new hairstyle and stylishly tailored clothes could transform a woman's appearance. Not to mention the boost it gave her self-confidence. And Connie Sue was getting noticed. The whispers buzzing through the church weren't all due to Lucy's arrival.

Connie Sue caught Lucy's eye and flashed her an impish grin and a surreptitious wave.

A quick glance in Sheriff Morton's direction told Lucy he'd noticed the exchange. Was he pleased with the change in Connie Sue's appearance or upset by it? And what did he think about his daughter associating with the likes of her in the first place?

As if reading her thoughts, the Sheriff smiled. "Connie Sue looks mighty nice up there this morning, don't you think?"

Lucy returned his smile with a tentative one of her own. "Yes sir, very nice."

"She tells me she owes you a lot of the credit for that."

"She's being too modest. I just gave her some suggestions on how to wear her hair and helped her make that new dress. Connie Sue has always been a lovely young lady."

"Yes, but you're the one who made her believe it. Thanks."

Lucy felt a warm glow settle inside her at this unlooked for appreciation. Before she could respond, Reverend Cummings stepped up to the pulpit and began the service.

As they sang the opening hymn, Reed's voice, strong and deep and powerful, caused heads to turn their way.

Once the congregation was seated again, Reverend Cummings began to speak. "My sermon today will be based on the Book of John, chapter eight, verses three through eleven."

Lucy turned her Bible to the referenced passage, and stiffened. Almost at once, the reverend began to read.

"And the scribes and Pharisees brought unto him a woman taken in adultery; and when they had set her in their midst, They say unto Him, Master, this woman was taken in adultery, in the very act. Now Moses in the law commanded us, that such should be stoned: but what sayest thou?"

Lucy fought to keep her churning emotions under control as Reverend Cummings read the entire passage. Had he picked this particular passage for her benefit or was it mere coincidence?

Reverend Cummings closed his Bible and looked out across the congregation. "My friends, there are two clear lessons we must take from these scriptures. The first is that Jesus himself warned that only God is without sin, therefore only He has the right to pass moral judgment on another. The other is that God is willing to forgive any sin, no matter how great, if the sinner truly repents and resolves to try to avoid sin in the future."

Throughout the long sermon, Lucy kept her head high and her

expression neutral, but it wasn't easy. The reverend wasn't being deliberately cruel. In fact, he probably thought he was smoothing the way for her return to the congregation. But Lucy felt herself the target of every pair of eyes there, felt herself being compared to the adulteress of the passage. Only her pride and the quiet support she felt from Reed kept her from bolting altogether.

By the time the service ended, Lucy could feel the tension inside her reaching the point of detonation. She needed to get outside in the fresh air as quickly as possible. Otherwise, she might just give these people something new to talk about.

Reed, however, seemed to have other ideas. As she stood, he again kept a firm grip on her elbow, forcing her to a sedate pace. After a quick, resentful glance at her captor, Lucy gave herself a mental shake and took a deep steadying breath. She let herself think of his grip as protective and comforting rather than restrictive and punishing.

Mrs. Hopkins and Lucy entered the aisle together, and Lucy paused to let the other precede her. With an audible sniff, the mayor's wife deliberately turned her back and flounced down the aisle. To Lucy, it felt like a slap in the face.

Those close to her, however, stepped into the breach. Sheriff Morton paid her a compliment on her singing voice, suggesting she'd make a fine addition to the choir if she had a mind to join. Then he placed a hand casually on Toby's shoulder and engaged him in idle conversation about their plans for the afternoon picnic. Lowell joined them, and for once both he and Reed were on the same side, determined to shield Lucy from further snubs.

Anyone viewing their little group as they made their way to the exit would know that Lucy Ames and her son could count Sheriff Morton, Lowell and Reed as her friends.

Friends! Lucy fought the urge to cry as the realization hit her. She'd been so long without that sort of companionship that she'd all but given up hope of feeling its warmth again. She looked at Reed, the catalyst for all of this. Mercy, but she did love him.

He saw her look and gave her arm an encouraging squeeze.

Most of the congregation seemed unsure how to react. No one actually came up to greet them, but neither did they shun Lucy as blatantly as Mrs. Hopkins had.

Connie Sue, surrounded by friends eager to compliment her on her new appearance, didn't catch up to them until they were almost to the door. She usurped Reed's position and linked her arm through Lucy's. Excited about the upcoming outing, Connie Sue bubbled over with enthusiasm. "I'm so glad you came. I know it wasn't easy, but it'll go smoother next time, you'll see. And the picnic is going to be such fun. I know Reed promised to provide the meal, but I brought some lemonade and my homemade sweet pickles. It's perfect picnic weather and we're going to have a wonderful time."

By the time they reached the church doors, Lucy could even shake the preacher's hand with some semblance of equanimity. No sense in letting his misguided attempts to redeem her ruin an otherwise beautiful day. She turned her face up to the sky with a sense of freedom. The worst was behind her and the rest of the day would be devoted to nothing weightier than enjoying herself.

∼

*R*eed watched as Lucy turned her face up to the sun, and he decided he'd never seen her look more achingly lovely. She was so special. Beautiful and courageous and generous and stubborn and sweet. And he wanted her, wanted her as he'd never wanted another woman. Reed knew now that it wasn't just lust. Somewhere along the way he'd fallen in love. He wanted to share with Lucy Ames a real, passionate, heart searing, love everlasting. He could overlook her past. Only their future mattered.

Her past indiscretions might give his family pause, but he knew he could work through that. The fact that she'd taken such good care of Toby would mitigate a lot in his father's eyes. And once they got to know Lucy, Reed was confidant they would come to love her as he did.

He rubbed a hand across his face, trying to erase any lingering signs of his sleepless night. All week, Reed had returned to the hotel to find at least one, sometimes two or three telegrams waiting for him. Most were from his father, expressing higher and higher levels of anxiety at Reed's lack of reported progress. Not only that, but he also managed to convey feelings of hurt that Reed seemed to have so little faith in his "business sense."

There were also telegrams from Lisa, asking for advice, and even one from Steven himself. He responded to these as best he could, and sent up a prayer that everything could hold together for just another week.

Yesterday, in addition to the usual missives from his family, Reed found a telegram from Jacobs waiting for him. The lawyer stated in the strongest of terms that he feared he would not be able to hold things up much longer. He advised Reed to return to Bakers Cove with all due haste if he wanted to make sure the deal was executed as he'd planned.

It was time he settled matters with Lucy and Toby.

Sheriff Morton claimed his attention just then. "I did a bit of checking up on you," he said quietly.

Reed, realizing the Sheriff had managed to distance the two of them from the others, kept his expression carefully blank. "Did you now?"

"Yep. Seems folks back in Delaware consider you an astute businessman, honorable but capable of ruthless decisiveness."

The Sheriff said the words with a disapproving frown, and Reed smiled. "I'm flattered."

The Sheriff ignored his flippant response. "I also learned that, contrary to what you led Lowell to believe, you *are* Wilder Enterprises. You live in a fancy mansion, and have more money than any twenty men together in these parts will ever see in their lifetimes."

Reed raised an eyebrow. "You planning on sharing that information with anybody?"

"Don't see why I should. What puzzles me, though, is why a

man with all that going for him at home, would be biding his time in a place like Far Enough."

"No offense, Sheriff," Reed responded, adding a touch of steel to his voice, "but it's really none of your business."

Sheriff Morton's lips parted in a wolfish smile. "Well now, it's true that this is a free country, son, and as long as you obey the law you have a right to go wherever you please. But the thing is, I'm Sheriff around here, and a mystery, even a small one, gets my attention. It goes with the job, if you take my meaning. I make it my business to keep on top of situations that might affect the law aiding citizens of this community."

Reed looked his inquisitor straight in the eye. "If you're trying to say that you'll be keeping a close watch on me, go right ahead. I don't intend to cause you or anyone else around here any trouble."

"Why thanks, I intend to take you up on that." While his easy smile remained, the Sheriff's eyes narrowed slightly. "And it's been my experience that what folks intend to do, and what they end up doing, are sometimes two very different things."

CHAPTER 21

"*L*owell offered me an extension on the rent payment today."
Lucy, feeling wonderfully content, caught Reed's eye as he
glanced up quickly. It was late afternoon and they were in
the buggy, not far from her home.

"Is that a fact?" he responded in mock-surprise.

"Uh-huh. And the best part of it is, he didn't make this offer
because he felt sorry for me. I know Lowell. He's beginning to
rethink his offer of marriage, but his sense of honor won't let him
withdraw it outright. So he's delaying matters until he can figure
out how to get out of this and still save face. And the reason he's
rethinking his offer, is because he's starting to take a real interest in
Connie Sue."

Lucy felt justified in taking some credit for her matchmaking
efforts. She gave a small sigh of pleasure. "Did you see how quickly
he offered to take her home? And I'm sure they were holding hands
while we packed up."

Reed quirked an eyebrow. "You don't seem upset with the idea
of losing your long-time swain."

She shook her head, not quite meeting his eyes. It wasn't Lowell
she wanted courting her.

"So you won't have to give up the locket."

Lucy looked up. "That's not why I encouraged this."

"I know."

His warm smile reassured her, and she relaxed. Oh, but she did love him. He understood her, knew her flaws and foibles, and still he seemed to enjoy her company, to perhaps even approve of her on some level. She felt so content sitting here next to him. She couldn't imagine anything more wonderful than having him beside her always.

They'd arrived at the front gate now, and Lucy cleared her expression of any lingering wistfulness.

Reed set the brake on the buggy and jumped out. He helped Toby down and then turned to Lucy. Rather than giving her his hand, Reed grasped her around the waist and lifted her bodily. Setting her on the ground, he held her just a moment more than necessary, and Lucy felt herself respond to his touch again. The afternoon had been wonderful, and Reed was wonderful. When he looked at her as he did now, she could almost believe he cared for her in a special way.

Looking away before he could read her thoughts, she watched Toby as he exchanged greetings with an enthusiastic Jasper.

Reed climbed back into the buggy. "You put the picnic things away. Toby and I'll take care of Moses and the buggy."

Lucy watched as he headed for the barn. There was something different about him this evening, a sort of suppressed excitement. She wondered what caused it.

～

*R*eed entered the back door to find Lucy sitting at the table, sipping on a cup of tea. Another cup sat on the table, waiting for him.

She looked up him with a smile, then frowned. "You're wet!"

He waved it off with a shrug. "It started to rain just as I came in."

She quickly glanced out the open door then back. "You should get out of those wet things and into something dry."

Reed smiled. He liked having her fuss over him. "It was just a sprinkle and I'm hardly even damp. Toby's still out in the barn. Why don't you come out on the front porch and we'll sit on the swing while this Texas heat dries me off."

By the time they were seated in the swing the rain had all but stopped. "Oh, look!" Lucy popped up and moved to the porch rail. "A rainbow."

Reed joined her there, studying the child-like pleasure in her smile rather than the arch of colors in the sky. "It's beautiful."

She looked up quickly, meeting his gaze, and the pace of her breathing changed. He placed a hand over hers on the rail, and something tender and warm stole into her expression.

After a few seconds she shifted her gaze back to the sky. "Your visit here has been like that rainbow." Her voice was soft and musing. "An unexpected blessing, replacing the gloom, bringing color, joy, and hope for better things to come. I don't imagine I'll ever look at another rainbow without thinking of you."

Reed's throat constricted at her words. Her voice held a bitter-sweet edge, as if she was already thinking of the time when he'd no longer be here. Did he dare believe she returned his feelings?

He lifted her hand from the rail, and drew her back to the swing. "I have something to tell you."

$\mathcal{L}$ucy felt the tension in him. "Is something the matter?" Had her words upset him? Did he think she wanted a commitment of some sort?

But Reed hastily reassured her. "No, nothing's wrong. It's just that I have a confession to make. It's time I told you the real reason I came to Far Enough."

She stilled, caught between interest and wariness.

"Actually, I'm not a detective as you assumed, but I did hire detectives, specifically to find you. It's the reason I came to Far Enough in the first place."

So, the sheet from the detective report with the name Lucy on it had referred to her after all. Suddenly chilled by a nameless fear, she wanted to stop his words, to have him take her in his arms and make her feel cherished, and special, and needed. Most of all she wanted to not have to say good-bye to Reed Wilder.

He paused a moment, staring into the distance. "I told you that I had two older brothers," he began. "Their names were Jonathan and Alex. They were true Wilders—big, brawny men, full of life and a love for the sea. Jon especially. He was daring and bold and had a charisma about him that few could resist.

"They were older than me, and quite close. The year I turned eighteen they were twenty-two and twenty-three. Jonathan already captained his own ship and Alex served under him. That spring they were making a run to England. When they returned, Alex was to get his own ship."

His jaw tightened. "But on the return trip they were caught up in a storm, a vicious beast of near-hurricane proportions. By all accounts it was only Jonathan's skill that got the ship back into port at all. The ship was badly damaged, though, and they'd lost three crewmen. Alex was one of those three."

Lucy placed a hand on his arm in sympathy, and Reed reached down and gave it a squeeze. "Jonathan blamed himself, of course, but no one else did. He was hailed as a hero actually. How he managed to save so many and make it home in that severely crippled ship not even the surviving crewmen knew."

He paused a moment, raking a hand through his hair. "But Jonathan didn't see it that way. All he could see was that Alex and two others had been lost under his command. He turned to the bottle for a while. He stayed more drunk than sober for a solid month and then the second tragedy struck. While riding back home one evening, drunk of course, his horse trampled a young boy underfoot, nearly killing him."

Lucy bit back a cry, but Reed seemed not to hear. He stood and moved to the porch rail. "Something broke inside him after that. He couldn't face either the family or the community, so he ran away. Left a note behind explaining how we'd be better off with him out of the way. Said he'd change his name and hide his trail, and we were not to expend any efforts on searching for him. But of course we did.

"Father hired the best detectives in the business to scour the country for Jonathan. A tip led us to believe he'd headed for California, so that's where we focused our efforts."

He gave a bark of laughter then, one that held no mirth.

"Then, in the fashion of the lowliest of melodramas, we got another setback, one that forced us to call off the search. Father's business manager, a very capable and trusted employee who practically ran the business side of Wilder Shipping, failed to show up for work. At first we were only concerned that something had happened to him. But when it became obvious that the man had left the city without a trace, Father grew suspicious, and asked me to have a look at the books. Sure enough, Anderson had bled the company dry. We were on the brink of financial ruin. Not only could we no longer pay the detectives, but we were in danger of losing everything—the business, our home, our standing in the community. And the downfall of our company would also mean financial ruin for the large number of others who counted on it for their livelihood."

Lucy moved to stand beside him, and placed a comforting hand on his arm. Without his saying so, she knew that this was the time when everyone started turning to him, laying the burden of their troubles in his lap to solve. And Reed, noble, caring person that he was, would have shouldered that burden without complaint, without asking for relief.

He smiled crookedly. "I won't bore you with the details, but it was several years later before we were able to spend time on anything but rebuilding our business and financial stability. By the time we could turn our attention back to the search for Jonathan, the trail had grown cold. Then, about a year ago, we stumbled across evidence that led us away from California. A survivor from a Mississippi riverboat disaster of some years back described in considerable detail the heroic captain who risked his life to save her. It matched the description of my brother."

"Johnny." Lucy whispered the name, moving her hand from his arm to her throat, reaching for the locket that wasn't there. Merciful heavens, what did this mean?

~

*R*eed noted the movement, noted the shock in her eyes, and something else he couldn't quite identify. "Yes. Even the name, Johnny Carlson, made sense. My father's name is Carl, you see." He looked into her eyes. "Jon is Toby's father, isn't he?"

Her features unreadable, her tone guarded, she answered with a single word.

"Yes."

"That makes Toby my nephew."

"Yes."

Reed frowned at her continued lack of responsiveness, her withdrawal from him. "What is it? I know this may be a bit of a shock, but I thought you'd be happy to find Toby has some family on his father's side."

"What do you plan to do now? Are you going to try to take Toby away from me?"

So that was what troubled her. "Of course not!" Then he smiled crookedly. "I'll admit that might have been my intention initially. But that was before I'd met you and got to know you. I'd never try to separate the two of you now, especially with all I owe you. You're his mother after all, and the two of you belong together."

Lucy didn't seem reassured by his words. If anything she'd withdrawn farther. "So, again I'll ask, what will you do now?"

"I'd like to take you and Toby to Delaware with me. He has a grandfather and aunts and cousins there who would like to meet him."

"Even if they believe him illegitimate?"

Reed winced at the harshness of her words and tone. He took her hand and squeezed it reassuringly. "They won't hold that against him, any more than I do. He's Jon's son, that's all that matters."

"And what about me? How will Toby's unwed mother be received? Are women of questionable virtue allowed in your home, to associate with your sisters?"

He felt a small tic at the corner of his eye, but kept the smile on his face. "What went on between you and Jonathan is in the past. I assume you loved him, and that counts for a great deal. My family will accept you. As for the rest, I'll see that you get the respect you deserve."

She gave him a humorless smile. "That's a nice sentiment, but you can't force people to respect someone."

Her pallor and continued withdrawal worried Reed. He'd expected her to be surprised, yes, but happily so. Something was wrong here, and he didn't understand what it could be. "No one will dare turn you away or treat you with disrespect, especially if I bring you home as my wife."

This time he did get a reaction from her. Her eyes widened, and her hand fluttered between them. "Your wife!"

This wasn't the way Reed had planned to propose to her. He'd wanted to take it slower and woo her with sweet words, not blurt it out. To let her know how much he cared about her, how he wanted to cherish her and be with her for the rest of his life.

But it was out now, and perhaps it was for the best. He would be foolish to try to compete with what she'd felt for Jon, but he *could* convince her of the practicality of the arrangement. Logic, after all, was his strong point. Determinedly, he pressed on. "Yes. That is, if you'll have me. It's the perfect answer, don't you see? You and Toby will have instant legitimacy. There will be no doubts as to Toby's place in the family, and he'll be afforded all the advantages the Wilder name can bring him."

He reached up and tenderly tucked a lock of hair behind her

ear. "That's something else I need to explain. I told Crowder that I
had some connection to the family who owned Wilder Enterprises.
Thing is, I'm not some poor relation, some hanger on. My father
and I *are* Wilder Enterprises. And as Jonathan's son, Toby is entitled
to a share of it as well. That means security and a proper education
and social advantages for him. You won't have to worry about his
future anymore."

He gave her hand another light squeeze. "As I said, it's the
perfect solution. The three of us get along well. Toby already feels
like a son to me, and I feel a closeness to you that I can only hope is
reciprocated. Together, we'd make a good family."

Reed leaned back, pleased with his arguments. He'd also
managed to let her know that he cared for her without making a
fool of himself with flowery speeches.

~

ell him! her brain screamed. *He deserves to know Toby's not
illegitimate. And maybe,* a small selfish part of her added,
he'll see you differently.

But Lucy couldn't say the words. All she wanted to do was
weep. Much as she wanted to believe otherwise, he didn't love her.
He'd never even said the word. He was just trying to neatly wrap
up all the loose ends and repay his debt to her at the same time.
She'd given herself away with her earlier words, and so he felt he'd
found the perfect way to make it right for everyone. His offer
wasn't very different from Lowell's. So why did it hurt so
much more?

She looked into his face. His expression was expectant and curiously vulnerable, as if her answer really mattered. And of course it
did. He felt he still owed her for saving his life. And Reed was such
a stickler for paying his debts.

"Lucy, I'm asking you to marry me."

"Why did you pick this particular time to tell me all of this?
Why not yesterday or tomorrow?" *Why don't you love me?*

"I had a telegram waiting for me when I returned to town yesterday. There are some things going on back home that require my attention. I'll need to leave soon, and I want to take you and Toby with me."

Lucy felt sorely tempted to accept, despite knowing he didn't love her. She would be a loving wife to him, do everything in her power to make him happy. And maybe, in time, he could grow to love her. If she let him go, it would never have a chance.

She had to tell him the truth. But she needed time to marshal her thoughts, to prepare herself for his reaction. Would he believe her? And even if he did, would he regret his offer, or would it deepen his sense of obligation? Please, please, don't let him feel pity.

She pushed a lock of hair back over her ear with a hand that trembled slightly. "Please, don't think me coy, but I need a little time before I can give you my answer. Whatever I decide, though, don't worry about me trying to keep Toby from his family. I would never stand in the way of his claiming his heritage."

Reed seemed disappointed by her answer but recovered quickly. "Of course. I shouldn't have sprung it on you so suddenly. Take whatever time you need."

"Just let me sleep on it tonight. I'll be ready to give you an answer by morning."

"As you wish."

"Now," she said, forcing a smile, "let's go find Toby and tell him about all of his new-found relatives."

~

*L*ucy turned the lamp up in her room and then opened the lid of her cedar chest. Reed had left about an hour ago and Toby had finally calmed down enough to fall asleep. He'd been so excited to learn Reed was his uncle. And the news that he could lay claim to three aunts, a grandfather and several cousins back in Delaware had all but overwhelmed him.

She retrieved a bandbox from the chest and carried it to her bed. Slowly, she untied the faded satin ribbon securing it and removed the lid. And came face to face with a picture of Johnny.

Dear, sweet Johnny. She picked up the photograph, tracing his face with the tip of her finger before setting it aside. Next came several documents, including Toby's birth certificate. She laid those aside too as she spotted the miniature of Iris and Johnny together. Lucy smiled, remembering the happy times they'd shared. Heavens, but she still missed them, even after all this time. There were other items—a heavy heirloom-like ring, a pocketknife that had belonged to Johnny, and Iris' wedding band. And a half dozen or so other mementos she'd saved for Toby.

She picked up the papers again. She'd already decided that tomorrow she would tell Reed the whole truth about Toby. It was only fair to Toby that she do so. Would Reed believe her? With the exception of her mother, no one else ever had. Even when she showed these supporting documents to Mrs. Hopkins, her mother's best friend, she'd been met with disbelief.

"Come now Lucy, I'm no gullible simpleton," had been the cold response. "Those papers don't prove a thing. It's easy to give a false name or to forge records, especially when you're dealing with officials who don't know you."

Lucy hadn't tried to plead her case since. She decided folks would either believe her word or not. Unfortunately, none had. Resolutely, she closed the box. If Reed loved her, he'd believe her, without her having to produce any proof. If he didn't, well no amount of proof would matter. Even if she did eventually convince him, she could never give herself to him without the existence of that level of trust.

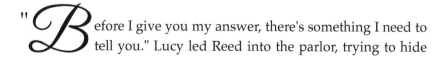

"*B*efore I give you my answer, there's something I need to tell you." Lucy led Reed into the parlor, trying to hide her nervousness. She hadn't slept well last night, knowing what she had to do this morning.

After taking their seats, she looked at him and attempted a smile. "I guess you could say that it's my turn to confess. I want to tell you how I came to have Toby."

Reed made an involuntary movement, as if to halt her words, then stilled, holding himself stiffly. "You don't need to explain anything to me. I told you, what happened between you and Jonathan is in the past. I promise it will never come between us."

"Nor should it," she said firmly. "Please, just listen to what I have to say. This is important."

Reed shifted in his chair, but he nodded for her to proceed, and she smiled gratefully.

"I met Iris soon after I arrived in New Orleans. She tatted beautifully and sold her lace creations to Madame Robicheaux, the seamstress I worked for. We struck up a friendship and it was soon as if I'd known her all my life. She was sweet and kind and had a unique perspective on life. She invited me to her rooms for supper on a few occasions, usually when Johnny was away, but once or twice when he was there. I liked Johnny right away. As you said, he had a great deal of charm."

Lucy paused, surprised by Reed's quick frown. Watching the way he steeled himself, as if waiting for unpleasant news, she wondered hopefully if he was perhaps just a tiny bit jealous.

"Except for Lowell, Iris and Johnny were the best friends I've ever had," she continued. "And they were the closest thing to family I had in New Orleans. When they learned Iris was pregnant they were overjoyed, and I was almost as pleased as they were. I felt as if I was about to become an aunt. They even asked me to stand as the baby's godmother."

She paused again, choosing her words more carefully now. "But Johnny worried about Iris. She had a delicate constitution, you see, and he worried about leaving her alone so much. He approached me and asked if I would agree to move into the boarding house where he and Iris lived so that I could keep an eye on her whenever he was away. They lived in a much finer place than the one where I boarded, and I shared my room with two of the girls I worked with. Johnny offered to pay the difference in the rent."

She lifted a hand from her lap, and gestured as if to help him see the uncertainty she'd felt. "I had some doubts about the propriety of the arrangement, but he told me if I turned him down he'd just have to hire someone else. Both he and Iris assured me it would make them feel better to have me close by, and to tell the truth, the idea of having a room to myself was too much temptation to pass up."

She looked up then, determined to make him understand. "But I did not become Johnny's mistress. Even if I had been madly in love with him, I couldn't have betrayed Iris' friendship that way. But I didn't love Johnny, at least not that way. And for his part, Johnny only had eyes for Iris. It was obvious to anyone who saw them together that they were head over heels in love with each other. Your brother did not betray his wife."

Reed frowned. "Do you mean that Johnny isn't Toby's father?"

She shook her head, raising a hand to stop his questions. "Please, let me finish. This is rather complicated."

Compressing his lips, Reed nodded and waited for her to continue. She smiled her gratitude, knowing how difficult it must be for him to withhold his questions.

"Word of Johnny's death came four weeks before Iris was due to deliver. As you can imagine, she took it hard. Collapsed on the spot. Iris went out of her mind with grief, and the doctor was concerned for both her and the baby she carried. He advised me to keep her quiet and in bed as much as I could, at least until she was better able to cope with her loss."

Lucy shuddered and looked down at her hands. "It was a terrible time. For three days she refused to eat or talk or even respond when I spoke to her. She didn't even cry, she just looked empty, as if all the life had been drained from her. I tried cajoling and fussing and preaching. I told her what Johnny would have wanted, and I told her she had to take care of herself for the baby's sake, but she just lay there."

Lucy took a deep breath, remembering how helpless she'd felt. "Then she went into labor prematurely. She had a difficult time. Her labor lasted nearly two days. But she finally snapped out of her despondency. She fought with all of her being to give her baby life.

"In the end she delivered her baby, a boy she named Tobias Alexander. It was the name Johnny had chosen for a boy. But she was dying, and we both knew it. She made me promise to find a good home for Toby. She grew up in an orphanage, you see, and didn't want that for her son. She died six hours later. And I had a newborn baby on my hands with no idea what to do with him."

Grateful for Reed's continued silence, Lucy told the most damaging piece of her story. "Finally I sent a cowardly telegram to my parents telling them I'd gotten myself into a bind and asking for help. I hoped daddy might have connections who could help us locate a good family to take Toby in. I also had some vague idea of asking them to raise Toby themselves. Daddy had always wanted a son."

"Just as I'd known they would, they boarded the next train for New Orleans. But they never made it. The train derailed. Daddy died and Mother suffered terrible injuries. All because I panicked and asked them to come help me with my problems." Her chin lifted a notch, though she still didn't look his way. Just a little more and she would be done.

"I had no choice. I bundled Toby up, and left to tend to mother. There was a lot of speculation when I showed up with a baby. At first I was too worried about Mother to pay attention to it. A few months later, when it looked like she would truly live, I looked around and found I'd been branded a fallen woman, and no amount of explanations would change people's minds.

"I've never regretted taking Toby in. I love him as if he were my own son. But I've always regretted that I didn't have a better life to offer him."

Lucy finished her story and sat there a minute, almost afraid to look up. How was he taking it? Now that he knew she wasn't Toby's mother, would his feelings change? Did he even believe her story? Why didn't he say something, anything? Finally, unable to bear the silence any longer, Lucy took a deep breath and sought his eyes with her own.

What she saw brought her hand to her mouth. The pity and disappointment reflected there spoke louder than any words.

CHAPTER 22

The disappointment hit Reed like a fist to his gut. How could she have so little faith in him? Did she think he couldn't look beyond her past indiscretions and love her for who she was today, that he needed pretty lies to make her acceptable? Did she have so little faith in his character?

"I told you I understood your moment of weakness with my brother." He could hear the coldness in his voice, and watched her flinch, as had so many of his past business opponents. "I was willing to accept that and go on. Couldn't you do the same? Couldn't you trust me to keep to my word?"

"I don't understand. I just—"

He wanted to grab her by the shoulders and shake her. "Lucy, stop this. I know your story is a lie. You're just digging yourself a deeper hole."

Lucy shook her head, reaching out a hand to him. "Reed! Please, I don't understand. Why would you believe—"

He ignored the hand as well as the pain and confusion in her voice. "Because when we went looking for Jon this last time, we found his widow instead."

Her eyes widened, and she moved the hand to her chest.

"That's right, I know for a fact that Iris is very much alive. As we speak, she's living at the Wilder estate with my father and sisters. And she told us all about her and Jon's child. A girl named Amelia who died just before her first birthday."

Lucy stood and clasped her hands with white-knuckled intensity in front of her. "That's impossible. Iris died six years ago, just as I said. I was there. Toby *is* her son."

Why couldn't she drop this pretense? "Look, I'm neither naive nor a fool. I had the detectives verify her identity before I ever told my family of her existence. The soft-spoken, blond haired woman now living with my family *is* Iris Carlson. The facts speak for themselves. Any number of people vouched for her. The riverboat company certainly believed her. They've been sending her his widow's pension for the past six years. She even had a number of Jon's personal effects, including a wedding certificate."

Crossing his arms over his chest, Reed channeled his bitterness into his voice. "Are you asking me to just ignore all of this evidence? Do you expect me to turn my back on my brother's widow? Send her back to eke a living from that small boarding house she was running in New Orleans when we found her?"

The blood drained from Lucy's face as she dropped back into her chair. She looked so lost and forlorn that Reed's anger drained away. He knelt beside her and gently forced her chin up with his hand, though she still refused to meet his eyes. "I know this is hard for you. You didn't know about Iris, so you couldn't know your story would hurt anyone. If the stain of illegitimacy on Toby worries you, I promise it will never stand in his way. But you must trust me enough to tell me the truth, no matter what. There's no need to sugarcoat your past for me. It's what we do from today that matters. I will never lie to you, and I must feel that you will afford me the same respect. Tell me you'll do so, and we'll forget this happened."

Lucy sat with eyes averted and hands clenched for a moment before finally meeting his gaze. "I will never lie to you."

"Thank you." Reed saw the sadness in her eyes and wanted to

gather her to him and kiss away the pain and hurt. He didn't hold her story against her any longer. She'd faced rejection and contempt for so long she apparently didn't believe he could really put her past behind him. It might take time, but she would learn to trust him.

Lucy stood and Reed followed suit. "Excuse me, I need to check on something I left on the stove. I'll be right back."

"Of course. Take your time."

～

They both knew it was just a ploy to give her time to regain her composure, but Lucy didn't care. She badly needed a few minutes to herself.

Reed believed Iris was alive and living with his family. He was so adamant that, for a moment, she'd doubted her own memory, but only for a moment. She'd held Iris' hand as her friend drew her last breath. She'd made the arrangements for the funeral. She'd stood at the graveside as they buried her. Iris *was* dead.

Should she give Reed the kind of proof he'd understand? Give him the documents and pictures that supported her story? It would provide her with a measure of satisfaction to fling it at him and watch him swallow his words, try to apologize for the hurtful things he'd said. Even if he suspected she'd faked the documents, as others had, he'd be forced to look into the matter. As thorough as Reed was, he'd learn the truth soon enough.

But that wouldn't really do anything to ease her hurt. What mattered now was that she accept once and for all that Reed didn't love her. He didn't believe the story she'd just told him, which meant he believed her capable of telling such a monumental lie merely out of her sense of pride. All he felt for her was a deep sense of obligation, and perhaps some physical attraction. He was also too honorable to either separate a mother from her son or to deprive his brother's son of his birthright.

Of course, if she married him, he would soon learn the truth of her innocence. But by then it would be too late, he would be legally bound to her. Would he feel trapped, or even that she'd somehow tricked him, played him for a fool? She couldn't stand to have him feel disgusted or burdened by her.

Heart breaking, she knew what she had to do. It was up to her to find Reed a way out. She'd give him his proof, of course. His family harbored an impostor in their home, and she had to make sure he was fully prepared to handle the situation when he returned. But she would do it for that reason only, and she'd do it her way.

～

*R*eed stood as Lucy returned to the parlor. She looked calmer, more resigned, than when she left a few moments ago. Had she finally come to terms with his acceptance of her as she was?

"I've made my decision Reed. I can't marry you."

"What?" She'd said it so softly, with such finality, that he wasn't sure he'd understood her. "What do you mean? Do you need more time?"

"No. As I said last night, I won't stand in the way of what you can do for Toby. But the deal does not include me."

"Just like that, no explanations." Reed's hands fisted at his sides, the only way he could keep himself from reaching for her.

She remained maddeningly unemotional. "I told you when we discussed Lowell's offer that I wouldn't marry where there wasn't the same kind of love and trust I saw my parents share. That goes for your suit as well. I hesitated last night because I thought perhaps I could compromise, for Toby's sake. But when it comes right down to it, I find I can't. I'm sorry."

Well, that seemed clear enough. She didn't love him and wasn't willing to settle for second best. Reed's jaw tightened. "I see. Well then, I believe I owe you one more day's service, and then I won't have to bother you with my presence any longer."

She could have been carved from stone for all the emotion she displayed. "I think it's best if we dispense with this last day. No point in dragging this thing out."

Reed wanted to protest, but his pride wouldn't let him. She obviously wanted to be rid of him. "As you wish."

"When will you be returning to Delaware?"

He picked up his hat, eager to get away and lick his wounds in private. "As soon as I can make arrangements."

"I'll have Toby packed and ready to go whenever you say."

Reed stilled. Despite the fact that he smarted over her refusal to marry him, he knew what a sacrifice she'd just committed to. "You're giving him up, just like that?"

She raised her hand in a sharp gesture that belied her composure and then stilled again. "Not for forever. But he needs time to get acquainted with his father's family. And I plan to keep in touch."

He nodded, accepting her sacrifice. "Very well. I'll be back tomorrow morning to pick him up."

❧

*S*o soon! Lucy clenched her jaw to keep from telling him she'd changed her mind, that it was all a misunderstanding. Her hand went out, but Reed had already turned away. She watched him walk out the door, out of her life, and then slumped down on the sofa. She had to explain things to Toby, but it would have to wait.

Her thoughts skittered around, trying to find something other than the looming loneliness to focus on. Wringing her hands, she rose, looked around the room, then moved to the piano. Playing always calmed her when her nerves were rattled.

As soon as her hands touched the keys, her thoughts settled, turned to the Iris-impostor, Reed's proof positive that she was a liar. Of course he'd believe such evidence above her word—only someone foolishly, hopelessly in love would do otherwise.

She'd figured out who the pretender was by now. From the clues Reed had provided, scant though they were, it couldn't be anyone other than Danielle Hebert.

Her fingers picked out the familiar tune as she called up memories of Danielle, the daughter of her New Orleans landlady. The physical description fit, and the name given to Iris' and Johnny's supposed daughter was an unusual one, one Danielle had talked about naming her soon-to-be-born baby, should it be a girl. Even the mention of her running a boarding house fit.

Lucy remembered Danielle as a sweet, tenderhearted young woman who'd led a hard life. A virtual slave to her tyrannical mother, she'd shown a rare streak of defiance when she became engaged to a young man her mother disapproved of. But her fiancé died three days before the wedding, leaving Danielle unwed, pregnant and more securely under her mother's thumb than ever.

Much as it shamed Lucy to admit it, she'd been so overwhelmed by her own circumstances when she left New Orleans, that she'd never given Danielle's situation further thought.

Reed had said this impostor had Iris and Johnny's wedding certificate. That's what had allowed Lucy to put all the other clues together.

Before leaving New Orleans, she'd hurriedly sorted through Iris and Johnny's things, filling two boxes with articles she thought would mean something to Toby when he got older. The rest she asked Mrs. Hebert to donate to charity.

But months later, when she could concentrate on something other than her mother's condition, Lucy found only one box had made it to Far Enough. At the time, she figured it had been lost or included in the lot donated to charity. Now she knew better. That missing box had contained, among other things, the wedding certificate and several of Iris' journals.

Poor Danielle, she'd been pregnant, unmarried and scared. And her closest friends, Iris, Johnny, and Lucy herself, had all abandoned her one way or another. The chance to start over, with dignity, must have seemed a heaven-sent opportunity. It wouldn't be hard to imagine her assuming Iris' identity, especially when she believed no one would be hurt by it.

CHAPTER 23

*L*ucy knelt down and smiled encouragingly to a sad faced Toby. "Remember what we talked about. This is not for forever. I promise to write and maybe even visit when I can."

Toby threw his arms around her and squeezed tight, not uttering a word. At last he let go, his eyes damp. "I'm ready now, Uncle Reed."

Reed nodded, his own smile not reaching his eyes. "You go ahead and climb up into the buggy while I load your trunks."

The boy nodded and shuffled out the door. Lucy wondered for the hundredth time if she was doing the right thing. Then she squared her shoulders. Toby belonged with the Wilders, was one of them. And Reed would take good care of him. Iris and Johnny's son would have a much better life there than he could ever hope for with her. Taking a steadying breath, she followed Reed into the hallway where Toby's bags waited.

He picked up the trunk and walked past her without a word. He returned for the few items of his own that remained here, and Lucy placed a hand on his arm, forcing him to look at her.

"Reed, I..." His expression remained icily unmoved as she

faltered. Gathering her shaky control about her once more, she continued in a firmer tone. "I promised Toby I'd write to him. I just realized I don't know where to post the letters to."

"Send them to Wilder Enterprises, Bakers Cove, Delaware."

He stood there, physically close but emotionally remote, and at last Lucy dropped her hand and stood back to let him pass. "Thank you. For everything. I won't bother asking you to take good care of Toby because I know you will."

Reed merely inclined his head and shifted the baggage to his shoulder. Then he walked out the door.

Lucy stood at the front gate, watching as they rode away, until at last they disappeared around a bend in the road. Her last sight was of Toby's despondent waving and Reed's stiff back.

Come back. Please, don't leave me. Lucy brought a fist to her mouth, fighting the urge to shout the words. Instead, she turned back to the house.

The tomb-silent, winter-nest-empty house.

Refusing to give in to self-pity, Lucy cleaned house as if her life depended on its appearance. She scrubbed floors and polished woodwork. Washed windows and beat rugs. Dusted bric-a-brac and turned mattresses.

Only when she heard Jasper's bark heralding a visitor did she pause. Had Reed and Toby returned? A quick, heart-pounding glance out the window told her it was Connie Sue instead.

Schooling her features to portray a serenity she didn't feel, Lucy greeted her visitor at the door. "Hello, Connie Sue. It's nice to see you, but I hadn't expected you back so soon, now that the dress is finished."

Connie Sue's face reflected her hurt. "Oh Lucy, is that what you think of me? That I just came by to have you help me with that dress? I thought you'd come to know me better."

Lucy's expression softened, and she stepped aside to let Connie Sue enter. "I'm sorry, I do know better. I'm afraid I have a lot on my mind today."

Connie Sue touched her arm. "I know. Reed stopped by to see me early this morning."

Lucy tried to keep her tone neutral, but Connie Sue's warm sympathy made it difficult. "Well then, I guess you know he's gone back to Delaware."

"Yes, and taken Toby with him."

"Did he explain his reasons to you?"

Connie Sue shrugged. "Not in detail. Just that it turns out he's really Toby's uncle, and that he's taking the boy with him to get acquainted with the rest of the family." They'd reached the parlor, and Connie Sue untied the ribbons of her bonnet. She placed it on the sofa, but remained standing.

Determined not to show an ounce of either emotion or need, Lucy stood ramrod straight, keeping her face expressionless.

Then Connie Sue handed her an envelope. "Reed asked me to give you this."

Lucy took the envelope and sat down on the sofa. Was it a good-bye message or another attempt to assuage his conscience? And when would she stop hurting, stop bleeding inside? Taking a deep breath, she unsealed the envelope and found two pieces of paper. The first was a letter from Reed and the second was a deed for the Jeeter place, made out in her own name.

She stared at the deed for several minutes, unsure what to think, before she finally turned to the letter.

*L*ucy,

    I knew you wouldn't accept this gift from my hands, so I asked Connie Sue to deliver it. I know how difficult it is for you to accept help of this magnitude, but please, humor me. I could not leave without doing this one last thing to repay the debt I owe you. I will rest easier knowing that you no longer have to make dresses for other people unless you want to, that you no longer have to worry about having a roof over your head in the coming months. The purchase has been made, the deed is legally filed, and the place is officially yours. If you don't care to live there any longer, sell it and use the money to start over somewhere else. Only please, let me know if you do, for Toby's sake. I'm sorry things didn't work out between us, but I will always remember you and the time we spent together with great affection.

Reed.

*L*ucy felt her hands tremble and fought to regain her control. She refused to let herself break down in front of Connie Sue.

"Please, let me be your friend," Connie Sue whispered, and she opened her arms.

Lucy resisted a moment longer. Then, her face crumpling, she slumped into Connie Sue's embrace, sobbing.

It took several minutes for Lucy to pull herself together enough to draw away. Connie Sue produced a lace handkerchief from somewhere, and she gave it to Lucy to dry her eyes.

"I'm sorry." Lucy's voice still quavered. "I didn't intend to break down like that."

"Don't apologize. We all need to give in to our feelings occasionally." Connie Sue paused and then said diffidently. "I don't want to pry, but I've been told I'm a good listener, if you'd like to talk about it."

Lucy held up a piece of paper. "This is a deed to the Jeeter place. I own it now, thanks to Reed."

"And that's what made you cry?"

Lucy sniffed. "Reed asked me to marry him."

"And you turned him down? But I thought... I mean... Oh goodness, Lucy, I thought you loved him."

Lucy forced a smile. "I do."

"Then what is it? Why didn't you go with him?"

"Because he doesn't love me."

Connie Sue wrinkled her forehead. "I don't understand. You said he asked you to marry him."

With a sigh, Lucy wiped her eyes. Then she said bluntly, "I'm not Toby's mother."

"What! But... oh dear, I'm more confused than ever now."

Lucy related the story of Toby's origins just as she had to Reed. Then she waved her hand listlessly. "When I returned to Far Enough, everyone drew their own conclusions as to what really happened, and nothing I said would convince them otherwise. I finally just gave up."

"And you told Reed all of this." When Lucy nodded, Connie Sue shook her head in disbelief. "Are you telling me that, once Reed found out you weren't really Toby's mother, he just took Toby from you? I can't believe I could be so wrong about someone. He seemed like such a fine, decent man."

"No, no." Lucy rushed to Reed's defense. "That's not how it happened. The problem was, he didn't believe my story. Thought I'd made the whole thing up to make him think better of me."

"But why would he think such a thing?"

"Because there's a woman living with his family who claims to be Iris Carlson, the woman I said I watched die."

Connie Sue shook her head. "Oh my goodness, this is just all so complicated."

"She's an impostor." Lucy steeled herself for the doubts.

"Of course. But how could you let Toby go with Reed knowing this woman is waiting there, up to who knows what?"

Lucy stared at Connie Sue, unable to credit what she'd just heard. "What did you say?"

"I said, how could you let—"

"No, no." Lucy gestured impatiently. "Before that. You mean you actually believe my story?"

Connie Sue cocked her head to one side, as if puzzled Lucy would ask such a question. "Well, of course. It makes perfect sense. I never could figure out how a person with as much self-assurance and strength of character as you, could get herself into such a fix in the first place, much less refuse to own up to it afterwards. And I understand why you refused to marry Reed until he realizes the same thing. But don't you think it might be uncomfortable for Toby, even dangerous, to live with the Wilders until you know what this woman is up to?"

Goosebumps rose on Lucy's arms. Connie Sue believed her! It felt so incredibly wonderful to have someone other than her mother accept her story at face value. She wanted to hug the girl and she wanted to cry again, but she did neither. "It's all right. I know who the woman is, and she'd never hurt Toby."

Connie Sue sat back with a frown. "You *know* this impostor?"

"Yes. She's the daughter of the woman who owned the boarding house where Toby's parents and I lived."

"How can you be so sure?"

"From some of the things Reed said when he told me Iris was still alive and in his father's home. The person he described could only be Danielle."

"But, why would she pretend to be someone else?"

"It's nothing sinister, of that I'm sure. Danielle has led a very difficult life, but she has a good heart. Yes, she's lied, but I am certain she would never do anything to bring physical harm to Toby, or any of the Wilders for that matter. And now that I've planted the seed in Reed's mind that she may not be who she seems, I'm certain he'll be on his guard. Otherwise, I'd never have let Reed take Toby with him."

Lucy sat up straighter. "Besides, by the time Reed arrives in Delaware, he'll be more suspicious of Danielle than ever. I have complete confidence that he'll look out for Toby."

Connie Sue's brow furrowed. "But, I thought you said he didn't believe your story? What makes you think he'll have second thoughts so soon?"

"Toby has a box that holds some of his parents' personal effects." Lucy leaned forward, eager now to explain her plan. "I told him to show it all to Reed on the train. There are papers and pictures and personal items, enough for Reed, with his reverence for the indisputability of facts and logic, to question the identity of his family's houseguest. By the time he gets home, Reed will be ready to dig deeper."

"But if you had all this proof, why didn't you show it to Reed yourself? That way you two could have worked out your differences." Connie Sue took her hand again. "Oh, Lucy, he does love you, I know he does. He just has the same streak of stubbornness that you do."

Lucy shook her head, her expression set. "I can't let myself believe that. This way, when he discovers I told the truth, we'll have already said our good-byes and he won't have to face me again unless he wants to. He'll go home and take care of the business with Danielle and be with his family and friends again. If, after all that, he comes back, we'll take it from there. On the other hand, if he's relieved to have escaped a close call, then I won't have to read it in his eyes. I just couldn't stand to have him reject me face to face."

～

*R*eed climbed the stairs to the third floor of the Mallow Hotel, the finest Silverton had to offer. As luck would have it, the train wasn't running today due to some problems with the track up the line. Nothing serious, but it had everything shut down for now. So he and Toby were stuck here until tomorrow.

He glanced at his pocket watch. Nearly two o'clock. He'd left Toby in the room, eating lunch, while he'd taken care of the buggy and horses. The owner of the Silverton livery promised, for a healthy fee of course, to see that the rented buggy and horse made it back to Far Enough by tomorrow afternoon.

Toby sat staring out the window, the remains of his meal on a nearby table. He didn't seem to be handling Lucy's absence any better than Reed himself.

"Hello. I see you left me some of the cherry cobbler."

Toby looked up, a smile easing his gloom. "It's pretty good, but not as good as Ma's." And his smile faded again.

Reed tried a change of subject. "You know, you look a lot like your father."

"I know."

"Do you now? I suppose your ma told you."

"She didn't have to. I have some pictures of him."

"You do?" Reed hadn't noticed anything of the sort displayed around Lucy's house.

"Sure, and lots of other stuff, too. You wanta' see?"

"You mean you have them with you?"

"Uh-huh."

"Well sure, let's have a look."

Toby jumped up and went to his trunk. "Uncle Reed, look! There's a package for you. Ma must have put it in here."

Reed knelt beside him on the floor and lifted out the brown-paper wrapped package. Sure enough, his name was neatly inked across the front.

"Well, aren't you going to open it?"

Reed looked up, realizing he'd been staring at the package for several seconds. He pasted on a hearty smile, trying to erase the puzzled frown from Toby's face "Well of course I'm going to open it. Come on, you can help me."

The two sat back down on the bed. Reed untied the bit of string and in one quick motion Toby ripped open the paper. Then he turned to Reed with a disappointed frown. "It's just the picnic quilt. Why would Ma give you this old thing?"

"Perhaps as a memento of my visit." Reed laid his hand on the worn quilt as a jumble of sharp images flashed through his mind— Lucy wrapping this around his shoulders that first day when she'd rescued him; Lucy bent over the quilt, mending it as she explained that quilts were made to endure use and bring comfort, that their beauty was just a side benefit; Lucy sitting on this quilt while she explained why she couldn't marry Lowell, revealing so much more than she'd intended.

Was she thinking of those things when she packed it for him?

Toby, unimpressed with Reed's gift, returned to the trunk and withdrew a bandbox. "Ma calls this my treasure box."

He settled the box between them on the bed and then opened it. Right on top lay a picture set in an oval rosewood frame. Toby dusted it off and handed it to Reed.

While Reed studied the picture of his brother, Toby turned to stare out the window.

Reed found a name and date penciled on the back of the frame. *Johnny August 3, 1885.* This picture had been taken just two months before Jon's death.

"Do you think it might rain tonight, Uncle Reed?"

Reed glanced out the window. There were a few clouds gathering, but so far it looked harmless enough. "Hard to tell. It may just cloud up and then blow over. Do you mind if I look through the rest of these things?"

"Help yourself. Mostly it's just papers and stuff. But there's a really great ring and a pocket knife."

A ring! Was this the heirloom his father had sent him to find? He'd almost forgotten about it. Yes, there it was, the familiar ruby ring, as impressive as he remembered. Reed found the pocketknife, and recognized it too. He'd given it to Jon himself on his eighteenth birthday.

Toby still stared out the window with a worried frown. "Ma doesn't care much for thunder storms. She doesn't mind the rain, but lots of thunder and lightening make her nervous. She used to let me crawl up in bed with her whenever we had a bad nighttime storm. Said it was to make me feel safe, but I knew she wanted to have somebody close by. She's all alone now."

Reed tried to respond to the worry and hurt he heard in the boy's voice. "This was her choice. It's what she wanted."

But Toby shook his head stubbornly. "No it wasn't. She cried last night, you know. She tried to hide it from me but I heard her."

Reed couldn't help but admire Lucy's courage and spirit. She really was going to miss Toby, but she'd put her son's needs above her own. Even though it meant she'd be alone now.

Toby's eyes slid away from Reed's. "I know you asked her to marry you and she said no. I heard some of your conversation. I didn't mean to eavesdrop, honest, it just sort of happened."

"That's all right Toby." Reed managed a smile. "I don't mind that you know."

Then Toby looked back at him, confusion in his eyes. "Why can't you two get married? Is it because of me?"

Gathering the boy up, Reed gave him a fierce hug. Sometimes he forgot that this precocious child was only six. He let the boy go, but said with conviction, "No Toby, none of this is your fault. You must never think that. It's just that your ma didn't have those kinds of feelings for me. I guess I just couldn't live up to the memory of your father."

"That's not what Ma says. When I asked her about it, she said she couldn't marry you because you didn't love her. That you were just asking her because you felt you had to."

Reed's heart skipped a beat, but then the cold reality of the situation hit him. Of course she'd say something like that to Toby. Not love her! What a laugh. He'd been ready to spend the rest of his life with her, to blazes with her past. It was she who lacked faith in him. Her convoluted, fabricated story provided proof enough of that.

The story was so easily proved false. Iris' credentials were rock solid, the facts thoroughly checked.

His skill at analyzing facts, using objective logic to solve problems and to plan his actions, was something he prided himself on. He excelled at it, drew satisfaction from it, and it formed the basis of any success he'd ever achieved. That talent allowed him to pull his family from the brink of financial ruin and go on to build a business empire. By contrast, the few times he'd let his emotions rule had resulted in unmitigated personal disasters. His spontaneous proposal to Lucy demonstrated that to perfection.

Yet, in spite of everything he knew, he *wanted* to believe Lucy spoke the truth.

Reed placed the ring and knife back in Toby's treasure box, and paced restlessly around the room.

The best way to overcome his purely emotional response was to analyze the facts, coldly and objectively. He would handle this as if it were a buy or pass decision on a new business venture.

On the one hand there was what he knew about Iris, or the woman claiming to be Iris, he corrected himself, determined to remain objective. In the category of hard evidence, Reed could list an impressive catalog of items. Her boarders and neighbors knew her as Iris Carlson. She produced the marriage certificate for Johnny and Iris Carlson. The riverboat company paid her Jon's pension. She had the birth and death certificates of her daughter, both naming John Carlson as the father. And she knew things, intimate things, that she couldn't possibly know unless she'd been closely associated with Jon. Pretty conclusive.

In the category of hearsay and gut feel, he thought over his eight-week acquaintance with Iris. She was sweet tempered, a bit timid, and almost embarrassingly grateful for the chance to join the Wilder household. He couldn't imagine her in the role of scheming deceiver.

What proof could be offered to support Lucy's claims? She'd given him absolutely nothing he could classify as hard evidence. There was no objective corroboration of her story. It was *all* hearsay. In fact, all he really had was her word.

Reed paused on that thought. This was the word of a woman who had, for six long years, stood up to a town who'd judged and shunned her, so that she could care for her ailing mother. A woman who refused to take the easy way out when a long time friend proposed to her, because it wouldn't be honest. She'd rescued a stranger at serious risk to herself. And she'd been kind and generous to that injured stranger, taking him into her home and nursing him back to health. She'd been honest with him, almost from the start, about her lack of a husband, past or present, when it would have been just as easy to lie.

So why would she lie now? Especially after he'd assured her he didn't hold her past against her. Then again, there was that kiss they'd shared, glorious and sweet, but leaving him with the impression that she was inexperienced in the sensual arts.

No, there were no hard facts, nothing but his knowledge of who she was. But he felt a growing conviction that he'd made a terrible mistake.

Just then, Toby picked up the picnic quilt and threw it over his shoulders, wrapping it around him as if it were his mother's arms. Then, as the boy shifted, something about the quilt caught Reed's eye.

He moved closer, examining the corner panel, noting the intricate stitch work that had not been there last time he saw it. Then recognition hit and he stiffened. The carefully placed stitches formed a rainbow design. And at the end of the rainbow, instead of the traditional pot of gold, was a tiny heart.

With a tightening of his throat, Reed heard again her soft words about his appearance in her life being like a rainbow. Lucy, who'd said she couldn't marry him, had sent him a very unique love letter.

Out of nowhere, Reed remembered the feeling of something missing when he reviewed Dobbs' and Iris' information about Lucy, and this time the answer came to him. Iris hadn't said one word about Lucy being pregnant or having a child. Yet Toby must have been born right about the time of Jon's death.

He pulled a chair out from the table and sat down, hard, as all the disconnected thoughts came together into one obvious picture. He was a blind, pompous fool.

He'd acted like a jackass, believing Lucy couldn't possibly be telling him the truth, because *he* knew better.

She'd said she would only marry where there was shared love and trust. Trust would include, of course, faith in your beloved, even when all facts pointed the other way. It wasn't she who had failed to love him enough, but he who had failed her. He'd been so busy being noble and forgiving, that he'd not even allowed for the possibility that she might be telling the truth.

She'd opened herself up, made herself vulnerable in a way that must have cost her dearly, and he'd taken that precious gift and trampled it. How often had that happened to her? She'd trusted him to be different, to see the truth in what she confided, and he'd let her down miserably. He looked at the quilt again, and it rebuked him with its silent message.

Reed wanted to howl with the remorse eating at him. He didn't deserve even the chance to beg for her forgiveness.

Then he clenched his jaw. But she absolutely deserved to see him do it. The Claymore deal would just have to wait. As for Lisa and Steve, they were adults, it was time they started acting like it.

"Pack up your things, Toby. We're going back to Far Enough."

CHAPTER 24

*L*ucy straightened as she heard the clock in the parlor chime out the hour. Six o'clock. Reed and Toby would be on the train now, headed east.

Connie Sue had tried to talk Lucy into spending a few days in town with her. Though touched by her concern, Lucy refused the offer. Connie Sue finally left with a promise to visit the next day. Lucy returned to her cleaning, working out her anxiety in a physical way. Anything to keep from thinking about what her stubbornness had cost her.

Walking into the kitchen, she frowned as she noticed how dark it was getting. There must be a storm brewing. Just what she needed. It would be good for the garden but not for her mood.

Alone.

She bit her lip in an effort to hold back the tears. She'd made her decision, and now she should just make the best of it and get on with her life.

It was time she made plans. With her mother dead and Toby gone, there was nothing to keep her here any longer. She could sell this place, as Reed suggested. Maybe it would earn her enough of a stake to buy her own dress shop somewhere else.

She *had* done the right thing. Toby would be with his true family, where he belonged. Reed would see the pictures and documents before reaching Delaware. The truth would come out, the stain of illegitimacy would be removed from Toby, and Reed would take care of Danielle and her masquerade. Reed would be relieved that he had been saved from unnecessarily sacrificing himself in marriage to her.

Enough!

She needed to find another chore to keep her busy. Looking at the darkening sky, Lucy decided to get the animals inside the barn right away. There were all the signs of a real toad strangler in the making.

Jasper sat on the back porch. Toby had insisted on leaving the dog behind to keep Lucy company. The sad-eyed pooch looked up at her, his tail thumping a desultory greeting. Lucy paused to scratch him behind the ears. "I know, you miss him too. You'll just have to make do with me from now on."

When she stepped off the porch, the dog trotted at her heels. Lucy led first Pansy and then Moses into their stalls. Then she shooed the chickens into the barn. They could roost in the loft tonight. If a big storm did roll in, the barn would afford better protection than the coop.

But Jasper, thinking it was time to play, began barking and running about excitedly, scattering the hens in every direction. Finally she took hold of his collar and tied him to an empty stall. "Sorry boy, but I need to get these birds settled down. I'll let you free when I'm done."

When the chickens were finally roosting in the loft, Lucy set out feed for Moses and Pansy and then stood absently scratching the mule's ears. Ruefully, she admitted to herself that she found even this innocuous bit of company preferable to going back into her echoingly empty house.

Lucy jumped as something brushed against her legs. Looking down she saw Mustard, stropping himself against her calves with every indication that he was looking for some company.

"Well, well, Musty, what's this sudden change in attitude? You feeling sorry for me, or is the weather making you nervous too?" Lucy bent down to pet him, but that proved too much for the cat. Giving her a reproachful look, Mustard pulled back and, tail high, stalked away to the nether regions of the barn.

"So much for a sympathetic ear," Lucy muttered wryly.

She had just put away the feed sack, when a sudden movement caught her eye. Lucy looked up to see a figure standing in the doorway. In the darkness it was hard to make out more than a distorted silhouette, but it was definitely masculine.

"Reed?" she whispered as her heart skipped a beat, and she took an eager step toward the still shadowy figure. But a low, threatening growl from Jasper froze her in her tracks.

"Well, well, eager to see me are you, Lucy gal? If I'd a'known how much you'd miss me, I'd a come fer you sooner."

The voice was ugly and unmistakable. Roy Jefferson was back. Behind him lurked a second figure that could only be Vern.

Lucy turned on her heel and sped toward the side door. She held no illusions as to why Roy and Vern were here. Her only chance was to reach the woods behind the barn before they did, and try to elude them in the thick underbrush. But the door was closed and she lost precious time fumbling with the latch.

She forced the door open in three achingly long seconds, but before she could slip through, a fist clamped around her wrist.

"Not so fast there girlie. Me and Vern are gonna feel like you ain't glad to see us if you run off like that."

"Let go of me." Lucy twisted and pulled, trying to break free, but succeeded only in getting her other wrist captured. Leering, Roy pulled her against him. Trying not to panic, Lucy stomped hard on his foot and yanked away at the same time. Roy bellowed in pain, but released only one of her wrists.

He cussed and slapped her viciously across the face. "I'm gonna enjoy making you pay for that."

Lucy's head snapped back and her vision blurred with the force of the blow. Helplessly, she stumbled as Roy pulled her inside and threw her on a pile of hay. She tried to scramble away but Roy dropped on top of her, pinning her with his weight and grabbing a fist full of her hair. "Don't worry, Vern," he called over his shoulder. "I promise there'll be enough life in her when I get through so you can have a bit of fun too."

Knowing what was coming, Lucy gave in to her panic with a full-throated scream.

Roy laughed brutally. "Scream all you like, missie. There's no one to hear you but me and Vern."

~

*R*eed rode hard that afternoon, eager to see Lucy and try to sort out the mess he'd made of things. The vision Toby had conjured up of Lucy alone and frightened by the oncoming storm only added to his sense of urgency. He'd made it back to Far Enough in record time and left Toby in Connie Sue's willing hands—he wanted to talk to Lucy alone first. The Jeeter place was in sight now, and only a few scattered raindrops had fallen. He'd beat the storm.

He took frowning notice of the strange horses tied up to the fence rail. A heartbeat later he heard Lucy's terrified scream and Jasper's frantic barking. He vaulted out of the saddle, pausing only to pull his pistol from the saddlebag, before he pounded toward the barn at a dead run.

Forcing himself to stop just outside the barn door, Reed quickly sized up the situation. The sight of Roy Jefferson manhandling Lucy, though, drove all thoughts of caution from his mind.

"Get away from her, you scum!" Reed bellowed, entering the barn, gun aimed and ready to fire.

Roy, startled, turned to face his attacker. The expression on his face warned Reed of the danger. Spinning around, he found Vern already swinging a sledgehammer. Reed avoided having his head split open by the barest of seconds, but lost his weapon when the makeshift club struck the gun from his hand instead.

The blow Reed countered with sent Vern reeling back. The younger man cracked his head on a support pole and went down. Not caring whether his attacker lay dead or merely unconscious, Reed retrieved his gun and turned back to his real quarry.

But by this time Roy had hauled Lucy to her feet and clutched her to him as a shield. "You're mighty brave with that gun, pretty boy. But I don't think you want to risk having either one of us hurt this little gal here, now do you?"

Lucy's face, bruised and swollen below her right eye, her lip cut and bleeding, presented a pitiful picture. Roy imprisoned one of her arms behind her back and had his other arm clamped around her neck so tightly she couldn't speak.

Reed's jaw tightened convulsively. Without a second's hesitation, he threw the gun away from both of them. "Let her go and let's you and me settle this. Unless, of course, you don't fight grown men without help from your little brother."

"Mister, you just got yourself a fight. I'm gonna enjoy messing up that pretty-boy face of yours." With a vicious shove that sent Lucy sprawling face down, he grabbed a nearby pitchfork and sprang at Reed.

~

*L*ucy pulled herself into a crouch in time to see Reed sidestep the deadly tines and grab hold of the shaft. Then the two men were struggling in earnest. Roy was bigger and brawnier, but Reed's wiry agility made him a difficult target. It was an ugly, no holds barred fight. Lucy pushed a fist to her mouth to keep from crying out as Reed took as many punishing blows as he landed.

She wanted to help, to do anything to give Reed an edge, but wouldn't intervene for fear of distracting him at a crucial moment. Then she remembered the gun. Searching frantically, she spotted it, and scrambled to where it lay. Picking it up, she aimed it at the combatants with trembling hands. Lucy didn't trust herself to fire as long as they were locked so closely together, but if they ever separated, or if it began to look as if Reed was in serious trouble, she'd force herself to shoot.

After what seemed a lifetime of anxiety, Lucy could tell Reed was starting to weaken. His injuries hadn't healed completely, and Roy seemed to instinctively know where to aim his blows.

Lucy cried out as Roy landed three blows in rapid succession. Reed went down on one knee, his one-handed grip on a nearby stall keeping him from crumbling all together. Roy grabbed the ax from a peg on the wall. With a barbaric yell of pure savagery, he lunged in for the kill.

Screaming Reed's name, Lucy fired, aiming straight for Roy's heart. Unfortunately, her tears and trembling threw her aim off. The shot went wild, and she missed Roy entirely. The only effect was to startle him into checking his stride for a split second. Then, growling, he surged forward again.

But Reed was ready now. He lunged to his feet and raised the pitchfork that lay in the straw nearby.

Roy's own momentum did the rest.

~

*R*eed straightened and, without sparing so much as a glance for the lifeless body at his feet, stumbled to Lucy. She had dropped the gun and was rocking back and forth, tears streaming down her face. Her arms were wrapped around her body as if to hold in some terrible hurt.

Kneeling beside her, Reed gathered her to him and pulled her head to his chest. "It's all right, darling," he soothed, his voice hoarse and ragged. "It's over. You're safe now."

"I missed," she said between sobs. "I tried to save you and I missed. Oh Reed, he could have killed you."

Reed smiled tenderly. With everything she'd just been through, she was worried about failing him. Gently, he lifted her face and brushed a tendril from her forehead. "But he didn't kill me. And I'm glad you missed."

Still sniffling, she looked at him questioningly.

"It would have been too hard on my pride if you'd had to save my life yet again."

She stared at him blankly and then gave a watery laugh.

"That's better." He'd succeeded in getting her to smile. But he was serious about being glad she'd missed. He was awed that she'd tried to defend his life by shooting his assailant, but not for anything in the world would he have her live with that on her conscience. Much better that he'd done it himself. Reed wouldn't lose a moment of sleep over what he'd had to do.

"Are you okay? Did that beast hurt you?"

"I fought him but he was so big. He was going to..."

She started trembling again and Reed tightened his hold, mentally berating himself for having arrived too late to spare her such violence.

After a while the trembling stopped and she wiped her eyes with her hand, giving him a brave smile. "I'm sorry. I'm fine, really. Only my mind keeps replaying the feel of his hands, the stench of his breath, the look in his eyes."

Reed kissed her forehead. "Don't apologize. You've just come through a brutal ordeal and you're handling it quite well."

A slurred string of invectives signaled Vern's return to consciousness.

"Excuse me just a minute, while I take care of some unfinished business." Reed rose and approached the groggily swearing Vern. He spoke to the lout, but too soft for Lucy to hear the words. The effect on Vern, however, was dramatic. Not only did he cease his cussing, but his whole demeanor took on a cringing, hunted look.

Grabbing a rope from a nearby stall, Reed bound him tightly. Then he freed Jasper before turning back to Lucy.

He held his hand out to help her up. "Let's move to the house, shall we? I don't care much for the company in here." He'd fetch the sheriff and the doctor shortly, but for now, nothing seemed more important than getting Lucy back to the house, making certain she was safe and tending to her injuries.

Nodding, she took his hand and stood on legs that wobbled. Reed swept her up in his arms and headed out the door.

"Oh, but you're hurt. I can walk, really."

Reed hefted her and gave her a squeeze. "We've had this conversation before, remember? Let me judge what I can handle. Now, settle down and stop squirming."

She nodded, tightening her hold on his neck and resting her head against his shoulder. As soon as they stepped outside, a light rain spattered them. The sound of distant thunder promised worse to come. But the inclement weather no longer bothered her. She was in Reed's arms and nothing could hurt her now.

Reed reached the back door and opened it without releasing his hold on Lucy. Then he went straight to her bedroom and set her down on the edge of the bed. "Change into something dry. I'll wait in the parlor."

Before he closed the door he added, "I'm not leaving you here alone again. You're going back into town with me tonight."

For once, she didn't look inclined to argue with his high-handedness.

Reed removed his wet shirt and pulled a towel out of the linen closet. He didn't have a change of clothes with him so that would have to do for now. He hung his shirt near the stove while he put the towel to good use. Then he donned the still damp shirt, and headed for the parlor to wait for Lucy as he'd promised. Too wound up to sit, he walked to the window and watched the lightening flash across the sky. Leaning his head against the pane, he said a prayer of thanks for whatever mishap canceled today's train out of Silverton. He knew the thought of what would have happened if he hadn't come back this afternoon would haunt him for quite some time to come.

Even though she made no sound, Reed knew the moment Lucy entered the room. It was as if he was attuned to her now, in some mysterious, never-to-be-severed manner. He turned to see her standing in the doorway, studying him uncertainly. She wore a fresh dress, primly buttoned all the way up to her throat. Her lip had stopped bleeding, and she'd wiped the blood and dirt from her face. She had a sweet, fresh-scrubbed look to her, despite the purplish bruise on her cheek.

As soon as his eyes met hers, she broached the subject he'd known she would.

"You came back."

"Yes." *But I was almost too late.*

Reed motioned for her to be seated on the sofa and then sat beside her.

"Why?"

"Because I realized what a pompous fool I'd been, and couldn't leave without begging your forgiveness. Can you ever forgive me for what I said and thought?"

"It's not your fault. You had evidence that seemed to prove me a liar. People who knew me my entire life judged and condemned me on much less."

Her matter-of-fact acceptance of such injustice cut him deeper than anger or recriminations would have.

With hands clasped tightly in her lap, Lucy regarded him with a steady gaze. "Are you sure? Isn't there some small doubt in your mind that I might have forged the papers or misrepresented myself to create the proof you saw?"

"Proof? What are you talking about?"

"The picture of Johnny and Iris together, Iris' death certificate, Toby's birth certificate, Iris' journal. Didn't Toby show you his treasure box?"

"Well yes, but I never got past the single picture of Johnny and the ring. I got distracted before I could dig any deeper."

"I don't understand." She pulled back, looking at him as if he were speaking a foreign language. "If that's true, then why do you suddenly believe me?"

Reed took her hand and smiled crookedly. "Lucy, Lucy, you're breaking my heart, making me feel more the fool than ever. You should be railing against me, asking why it took so long for me to believe in you, to take your words at face value, not why I do now. You wouldn't lie your way out of a dilemma, not you, not ever. I know that now—knew it all along really, if I'd just stopped long enough to listen to my heart."

He gave her hand a light squeeze. "I promise with all that I am that I will never again doubt anything you tell me. If you say the sky is brown and the seas are orange, I'll believe you. If you say that tomorrow the sun will rise in the west and set in the east, I'll stand at the west window with you to watch the sunrise. Only say you'll give me another chance to prove myself to you. Not because I deserve it, but because I love you."

Lucy ran a finger along his jaw and smiled wonderingly. "Such passion. One of the reasons I love you so much is that your feelings run so deep, are so intense."

She'd said she loved him! Reed was almost afraid to believe he'd heard right. But now wasn't the time to be cautious and practical. "You're the one who brings that side out in me. No one else has ever even taken the time to find it. You inspire me, Lucy Ames, and I love you more than I've ever loved anyone before in my life. I can't imagine living my life without you by my side. I want to protect you from brutes and self-righteous snobs and spiders. I want you to rescue me from my ledgers and boredom and emptiness. I want to laugh with you and argue with you and build a family with you. I know I've been every kind of fool and blind to boot, but say you'll marry me and I'll spend the rest of my life making it up to you."

Lucy, the answer singing from her expressive eyes, smiled teasingly. "That's a promise I will take great pleasure in reminding you of from time to time." Then, to be certain he understood, "If you're sure you still want me, I'd like nothing better than to marry you, Reed Wilder."

Reed crushed her to him, smiling despite the strong emotion overwhelming him. She did inspire him. She might be overly proud and frustrating at times. But she saw him as no one else did, not as heir to the Wilder empire, and not as an inadequate copy of his older brothers, but as a man in his own right. A man of spirit and action she'd called him. And when he was with her he saw himself differently as well. Above all else, when he was with her he was alive as he'd never been before.

Like the quilt she'd given him, Lucy was a homespun beauty, unpretentious yet full of warmth and comfort, made to be cherished.

~

*L*ucy felt the beat of his heart against her cheek. Sliding her hands around his back, she was surprised and thrilled by the play of his muscles as he reacted to her touch.

Reed said her name, his voice almost a groan.

Lucy stilled at once. "Am I hurting you?" Her voice sounded small and vulnerable.

He gave a shaky laugh. "Not in the way you mean." Reed leaned back and lifted her chin with a finger. He ran the back of his hand softly back and forth along the side of her face. "You are so very beautiful."

The look in his eyes warmed Lucy, sending delicious shivers all through her. He lowered his head to kiss her waiting lips, and her eyes fluttered closed as she lifted her face to him.

The kiss, which started out soft and tender, quickly turned to a passionate claiming, each of the other.

Reed finally pulled back just enough to see her face. Stroking one of her cheeks with not quite steady fingers, he smiled. "If I have to move heaven and earth myself, Reverend Cummings will have a wedding to perform tomorrow."

She smiled up at him but he saw the tears pooling in her eyes. Alarmed, Reed hastily tried to reassure her. "I'm sorry. If you're not ready—"

But Lucy put a finger to his lips. "I would very much like to be married to you tomorrow. You make me feel special and cherished and very, very happy."

"Then pack a bag, we're headed to town." But before he let her go, he gave her another tight embrace, doing all he could to let her know just how cherished she was.

Outside the storm broke in a burst of rain and thunder and lightning, pounding the house as if seeking to reach the two inside. But Lucy barely noticed. She was wrapped in the arms of the man she loved and she knew in her heart that he loved her in return.

Nothing could dampen her mood or dim the glow she felt.

EPILOGUE

"*I* should have known I'd find you in here. Don't you know what time it is?"

Reed looked up from the report on his desk as Lucy sailed into the room without so much as a knock on the door. Ever since he'd begun working from the study here at home rather than at the Wilder Enterprises office in town, Lucy took it as her prerogative to interrupt him at any hour. Often she pulled him from his desk for nothing more important than to insist he come admire a new bloom she was nurturing in the conservatory, or to join her for a walk because the day was just too glorious to spend indoors, or to help her decide which fabric to use on the curtains for the refurbished nursery. A nursery that would have a new occupant in about six months.

He'd never been happier.

Grinning, Reed leaned back in his chair. "Why, from the sounds of the clock chimes, I'd say it was two o'clock."

Lucy stepped around his desk, hands on her hips, the smile in her eyes belying her stern demeanor. "Exactly! Lowell and Connie Sue's train is due to arrive in an hour, and here you are, bent over your ledgers, your coat and hat nowhere in sight."

Reed reached out and drew her onto his lap, enjoying the feel of her beautifully ripening body in his arms. She was carrying their child! The idea still overwhelmed and humbled him. He feathered kisses across her forehead as his hands caressed the part of her that cradled their baby.

Lucy placed an answering kiss on his cheek, then pulled back slightly. "Really, Reed, we need to get ready to go." But she no longer sounded quite so adamant.

"The train station's only twenty minutes away. There's plenty of time." He bent his head to nibble on her ear, inhaling the subtle scent of roses that always clung to her.

Lucy gave a husky little sigh of pleasure and Reed ceased his nibbling, catching her gaze with a lifted eyebrow. "We could always just send the carriage."

She shook a finger at him. "We'll do no such thing. After they've come all this way to spend the holidays with us, whatever would they think of such a poor greeting?"

But the tell-tale hint of disappointment in her expression told Reed she was tempted. He captured her admonishing hand, turning it palm-upward to receive his kiss. "Darling, they've only been married two months. I'm sure they'll know exactly what to make of it, and understand completely."

Lucy's cheeks turned pink as she laughed and wrapped her arms around his neck. "You're impossible."

Unrepentant, Reed nuzzled her neck. "At any rate, we don't have to leave right now. Tell me how your day has been going."

She tilted her head, giving him freer access to the deliciously smooth column of her throat. "I received a letter from Danielle today." Lucy lightly traced his collarbone through his shirt. "She accepted my invitation to spend Christmas here with us."

With the help of a strong recommendation from Reed's father, Danielle had taken a position as manager of a boardinghouse in the next town. It had become increasingly obvious, though, that the elder Wilder had taken more than a passing interest in the repentant imposter.

Reed smiled knowingly. "Playing matchmaker again?" he inquired.

She nodded in satisfaction. "And why not? As I recall, my last effort in that direction was a resounding success."

"True," Reed conceded. "But I'll rather miss watching Father try to invent another excuse to visit Charlesburg this month."

He teased her ear with his lips and his breath, taking pleasure in her shivering reaction. "Tell me more about your day."

Her eyelids, which had closed, fluttered open again. "My day?" She seemed to have trouble gathering her thoughts. "Oh, well, Toby deserted me to accompany your father on an outing to the shipyard."

The blustery sea captain and the precocious boy had taken to each other immediately, sharing a bond that grew stronger every day.

With a playful push, Lucy stood. "Now, enough of this delicious distraction, you need to get ready."

He leaned back in his chair a studied her. "My dear, you get more beautiful every day."

Rather than looking pleased by his compliment, Lucy frowned. "How can you say that? My waist has thickened so that I won't even be able to button my gowns soon."

How could she think herself less than desirable? The fact that she carried their child made her all the more beautiful, more precious to him.

He stood and brushed a lock of hair from her temple. "We'll buy you a whole wardrobe of new gowns if you're uncomfortable. But I repeat, you are more beautiful, more desirable now than the day I met you. I won't allow anyone, even you, to say differently."

Lucy's features melted into an expression of aching tenderness. "Oh, Reed." Her hands lifted to stroke his chin. "You do say the sweetest things."

He captured her hand and brought it to his lips.

Then the clock struck the quarter hour and she stilled. "Reed."

Time to go. Reluctantly, he met her gaze. "Yes?"

But her tawny, lioness eyes were sparkling with feminine mischief and promise. "Perhaps we have time for just one more kiss."

With an exultant laugh, Reed reached for her and gave her the requested kiss and tender embrace. As he held her close and stroked her hair, he thanked God again for giving him this chance at happiness.

His Athena—patroness of warfare and wisdom. Her battle skills had rescued him physically, but it was her wisdom and courage that had rescued his heart and nurtured his spirit. At long last, Reed was at peace with who he was and what he had.

Because, as long as he had Lucy by his side, his life would always have what mattered most.

Did you enjoy this book? We hope so!

Would you take a quick minute to leave a review where you purchased the book?

It doesn't have to be long. Just a sentence or two telling what you liked about the story!

∾

Receive a FREE book and get updates when new Wild Heart books release: https://mailchi.mp/2b893646fb9c/freebook

Dear Reader,

Thank you so much for picking up Reed and Lucy's story and investing your time in following their journey to their personal Happily Ever After. This book, in a previous incarnation, was the first one of my stories to be published and so it holds a very special place in my heart. I loved having the opportunity to visit with the characters again as I read through it and made some necessary revisions. They speak to me now every bit as much as they did all those years ago when I first wrote it. I hope they'll touch your heart and your spirit too.

For more information on this and other books I've written, please visit my website at www.winniegriggs.com or follow me on facebook at www.facebook.com/WinnieGriggs.Author.

And as always, I love to hear from readers. Feel free to contact me at winnie@winniegriggs.com with your thoughts on this or any of my books.

Wishing you a life abounding with love and grace,

Winnie Griggs

THE ROAD HOME SAMPLE

If you enjoyed *A Matter of Trust,* check out *The Road Home* by Winnie Griggs.

From award-winning author Winnie Griggs comes an endearing Americana romance!

Unable to operate since a devastating accident, surgeon Wyatt Murdoch is left wondering what to do with his life. He reluctantly agrees to escort two young orphans to their only remaining relative, a great-uncle who lives in Texas.

Adventurous Anisha Hayes dreams of belonging. When she comes across a man struggling to control his young charges, she offers her help. He refuses—he doesn't need any help!—but Anisha knows better. Just as she knows the pain of being foisted on unwilling family... How can she convince Wyatt that she has a better option—for all of them?

Here's a short sample...

Where had they gotten off to?

Wyatt Murdoch's irritation was turning into worry. This was the third time his two young charges had tried to slip away from him on their journey from Indiana to Texas, and they'd only made it as far as Arkansas. Thank goodness they'd reach their destination tomorrow. Of course, that assumed he found them before the train left. This was the longest they'd managed to keep out of his sight and the train would be resuming its journey in less than twenty minutes.

Why did they keep running away when they had no place to go? And how could a ten year old girl and eight year old boy have so completely disappeared when he'd only turned his back for a moment?

He bore a large part of the blame, of course. He should have paid closer attention when he saw them whispering together as they pulled into the station. He just figured they were shutting him out of their conversation, just as they'd done for most of the trip.

He supposed he couldn't really blame them for wanting to get outside and enjoy the fresh air and warm spring sunshine, especially when they'd been cooped up on the train for four very long days. But they could have just asked him.

They were nowhere in sight. He scanned the horizon and caught sight of the circus tents off in the distance. Of course. That would have drawn Hallie and Jonah like ants to a picnic.

He started off in that direction at a fast walk. If they missed the train because of this nonsense...

He was some distance from the circus tents when he caught sight of his charges. But they weren't alone. A woman, small in stature but big in presence, walked between them holding onto a hand of each. There was something faintly exotic-looking about her —it had something to do with the warm golden color of her skin and the shape of her eyes.

There was also the fact that she wore some kind of padded leather affair on her left shoulder, and regally perched upon that shoulder was what looked like a large gray parrot.

Someone associated with the circus, no doubt. Was she an actual performer or just an assistant?

More importantly, had she caught the children trying to sneak into the big top or one of the side shows? Or worse yet, had they gotten too close to her parrot and hurt it in some way?

He hoped she was looking for their caretaker—namely him— and not the sheriff. But from the frown on her face and stiff deter-mination of her posture, she was obviously unhappy about something.

He quickened his pace. "You two have a lot to answer for," he said as soon as he reached them.

But it was the woman who responded. "You are the person responsible for these children?"

He noticed that she had a faint accent of some sort, but he couldn't quite place it. "I am. And I apologize for whatever they—"

She cut through his apology. "It appears you are not doing a very good job of watching out for them."

Her accusation and tone got his back up. "Keeping up with them is not the easiest job in the world."

"So watching over them is your *job*? Are you their nanny?"

"Are you their nanny?" The parrot squawked. "Are you their nanny?"

There were muffled giggles from the children at the bird's echoed words, which Wyatt chose to ignore.

He tugged on his cuff, trying to maintain his dignity. "No, I am *not* their nanny," he said. "I am their escort. Now if you will just hand them over, we have a train to catch."

If anything, the woman clasped their hands tighter. "They tell me they ran away because you have not been treating them well."

Wyatt glanced from Hallie to Jonah, making his displeasure clear. Another loud squawk from the bird did nothing to smooth his temper. "What you should know about these two runaways is that they are not only slippery, but they also lie."

Her frown only deepened. "Those are harsh words to use about children, sir."

How in the world had he gotten into this ridiculous discussion with a circus performer? Before he could respond, she turned to the children.

Her expression was that of a schoolmarm handing a failing grade to a favorite student. "Have you been telling me untruths?"

Both children shook their heads vigorously.

"He doesn't let us do *anything* fun and he's *always* fussing," Hallie said.

"Anyone can tell he doesn't even *like* us," Jonah added.

The woman once again turned an accusing look his way.

But it was his turn to cut her off before she could speak. "That is neither here nor there, madam. It is my job to escort these children safely into the keeping of their great-uncle, and I intend to do just that. Now, I don't have time to stand here and argue with you. We need to be on that train when it pulls out from the station." He held out his left hand, keeping his right carefully down at his side. "Come along you two."

The children looked up to their circus-performer friend, obviously ready to ask for her support. Had they formed such a quick bond because of the exciting nature of her life? Or was it just that they thought anyone better than he?

To his surprise, the stranger gave them a shake of her head. "Go on with your escort as he asks. It's his job to keep you safe. And you should apologize for causing him worry, even if you don't think he likes you. He may not be the most pleasant of people, but he is trying to look out for you, and you should respect him for that, not make his task more difficult." She shot him a quick glance, then turned back to the children. "Besides, I'm sure he's not really a bad man at heart."

Was that condescension in her tone? His irritation changed to shock when the children came to him without further argument.

"We're sorry, Mr. Murdoch," Hallie said. "Aren't we, Jonah?"

Jonah nodded.

Wyatt was dumbfounded. How had she gotten these two mischief makers to obey her without argument?

"She has a parrot," Hallie informed him.

"So I see." His dry tone seemed lost on the children.

"And it talks." Jonah said this as if it were the most amazing of miracles.

Apparently this was their idea of being nice to him. The train whistle sounded a warning. It would be pulling out of the station in just a few minutes. "We'll discuss this more once we're back on board the train. For now we need to make certain it doesn't leave without us. Tell this nice lady good-bye."

"But—"

Was their new-found compliance slipping already? "Now, Jonah."

The children reluctantly obeyed, saying their farewells to both the woman and her pet. Then, careful to use his left hand, Wyatt took Jonah by the hand and Hallie took Jonah's other hand and they started back to the train at a fast walk. A moment later, he realized the woman from the circus was hurrying alongside them. He didn't know her name, and he didn't have time to ask. Without pausing, he turned to her. "There's no need for you to accompany us. I assure you, I have them under control now."

"I'm sure you do, but I don't want the train to leave without me either."

He almost missed a step at that. "But...I mean, aren't you part of the circus?"

Her grin told him she was enjoying his discomfiture. "No, I arrived here on the train, just as you did."

Then how had she ended up with Hallie and Jonah? Had she had a hand in their escape?

But there was no time to discuss that now.

The woman reached for Hallie's hand, smiling down as the girl released her brother's. "What do you think? Can we females beat the menfolk back to the train?"

With a delighted smile, Hallie nodded, and the two of them broke into a very hoydenish sprint.

For a moment Wyatt was caught off guard.

But not Jonah. He tugged impatiently at Wyatt's hand. "Come on. We can't let a couple of girls beat us."

Wyatt gave in and broke into a run. Not that he'd let the impertinent woman goad him into it, he told himself. It was just that he didn't want the train to leave without them.

Of course, he could only run as fast as Jonah, and the girls did have a head start, so the outcome of their so-called race was a foregone conclusion.

Wyatt didn't share his companions' amusement at the outcome. Really, this unorthodox woman seemed almost as much a child as his two charges.

Wyatt helped Jonah mount the steps of the car that contained their compartment. "Thank you again Miss—"

"Hayes. Annie Hayes. And you're quite welcome."

Annie Hayes? That seemed such a commonplace name for a very uncommon woman. "Miss Hayes. I hope you have an uneventful trip."

"Ah, but uneventful is so boring. I'd prefer instead that you wish me an interesting trip."

That sassy sparkle in her eyes and fetching grin on her lips almost had him smiling back. Instead, he gave a short bow. "As you like." He could see why the children had taken to her so quickly. Even without taking her foreign appearance into account, she was an intriguing individual.

"Where are you riding?" Hallie asked.

"Sundar and I are in the coach section."

Sundar? Did she have a companion of some sort. "Who is Sundar?"

She lifted her shoulder slightly. "He is." She turned back to the children. "Feel free to come and visit us once we are underway, if you like." She glanced up at him. "As long your escort allows it, of course."

Before he could so much as blink, both kids were clamoring for his attention.

"Can we, please?"

"Yes, puh-leeeze."

He started to refuse—after all, it was difficult enough to keep them out of mischief when they were confined to the compartment. But then he remembered the way she'd managed to gain the respect of his two charges and insert a bit of discipline into their lives as well.

"I have a better idea," he said impulsively. "Why don't you join us in our compartment for a few hours. I'm certain it will be much more comfortable than your current accommodations."

And having her around to entertain the children so he could finally let his guard down for a little while would definitely make *him* more comfortable.

If having her around also satisfied his own desire to learn more about her, well, that was just an added bonus.

BUY AT YOUR FAVORITE RETAILER

Want more?

If you love historical romance, check out the other Wild Heart books!

The Trail Boss's Bride by New York Times bestselling author Erica Vetsch

Steve Ketchum loves being a trail boss, almost as much as he hates river crossings. But it's part of the job. As is moving an abandoned wagon out of the ford. But when he goes to haul it away, he's stunned to see what's inside.

Kitty Fareholm's good-for-nothing husband picked a lousy time to die. How could he leave her stranded, birthing a baby in the middle of nowhere? She'd prayed for help to come, but did God honestly think a trail-worn cowboy was what she needed? What's more, Steve's trail crew is dead-set against having a woman join their camp. He promises the men he'll leave her at the nearest town...but Kitty just might have other plans.

~

The Gentleman's Quest by USA Today bestselling author Camille Elliot

Honoria Dunbar wouldn't mind being a spinster if she weren't left at the mercies of her mean-spirited uncle. The only way to escape his begrudging care? Marriage to a lecherous widower. Then Christopher Creager appears—and *everything* changes.

Christopher hasn't let himself go near his best friend's sister since Stephen's death. But when there's a murder on his property—and *he's* the prime suspect—he has no choice. She may hold the key to proving his innocence. But he never expects the feelings that hit him when he sees her again—any more than he expects her asking to join him on his quest!

But if he says yes to her, will he be putting another person he loves in danger?

CPSIA information can be obtained
at www.ICGtesting.com
Printed in the USA
LVHW080214290321
682798LV00014B/525

9 781942 265122